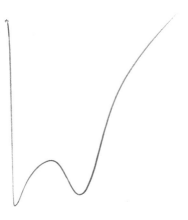

Tyrant's Blood

VALISAR: BOOK TWO

BOOKS BY FIONA McINTOSH

Tyrant's Blood

VALISAR: BOOK TWO

HARPER
Voyager

HarperCollins*Publishers*
77–85 Fulham Palace Road,
Hammersmith, London W6 8JB

www.voyager-books.com

Published by Harper*Voyager*
An imprint of HarperCollins*Publishers* 2009
1

A catalogue record for this book
is available from the British Library

ISBN-13: 978 0 00 727603 5

This novel is entirely a work of fiction.
The names, characters and incidents portrayed in it are
the work of the author's imagination. Any resemblance to
actual persons, living or dead, events or localities is
entirely coincidental.

Typeset in Goudy 11.5/15.5 by Letter Spaced

Printed and bound in Great Britain by
Clays Ltd, St Ives plc

Mixed Sources
Product group from well-managed
forests and other controlled sources
www.fsc.org Cert no. SW-COC-1806
© 1996 Forest Stewardship Council

FSC is a non-profit international organisation established
to promote the responsible management of the world's forests.
Products carrying the FSC label are independently certified
to assure consumers that they come from forests that are managed
to meet the social, economic and ecological needs
of present and future generations.

Find out more about HarperCollins and the environment at
www.harpercollins.co.uk/green

For Pip Klimentou, Sonya Caddy, Marianne D'Arrigo,
Margo Burns, Michelle King, Willa Michelmore.

———

ACKNOWLEDGMENTS

Knowing where to start this book was a tougher decision than for any previous novel. I was nervous about throwing readers into a contemporary world for the opening chapter but it felt right ... and I have learned to trust my instincts. I admit to being surprised by where the story has gone and as a victim of my own freefalling style of writing I couldn't foresee where two of the characters in particular would find themselves by the close of Tyrant, not to mention the shocking demise of one, and unplanned emergence of another. I do hope you enjoy it.

All the usual suspects have my thanks but especially the 'Latte Gang' who helped get me through a torrid period as I worked on this and other manuscripts whilst guiding and cajoling twins through their all-important Year 12. Our Friday mornings in Norwood at Caffe Buongiorno's and Remo's great coffees kept me sane through 2008.

I'm grateful to all the members of my bulletin board who visit regularly, and in particular, for their constant support, Trent Hayes in Australia and Phil Reed in the US who moderates with cheer and charm. In 2009, due to work and travel commitments, I had to withdraw from the monthly fantasy book club that has been running for the past seven years and my thanks to every one of its terrific members for their loyalty and friendship, especially Nigelle-Ann Blaser. Particular thanks also to Mandy Macky who permits us to take over Dymocks Rundle Mall each new moon, and to the bookshop's manager, Judy Downs, for her support.

I welcome Jason Lehmann into my life — thank you for the new portal website for fionamcintosh.com and for your constant enthusiasm and creativity in a world of technology I simply don't understand!

To all the fantasy booksellers around Australia who continue to handsell sff energetically — ongoing thanks for making my novels part of your day.

The team at Voyager continue to do a sterling job in helping to make my stories the best they can be and I'm especially grateful to editor, Stephanie Smith and to Natalie Costa Bir who runs the Voyager websites.

Having the time, space and peace to write requires a very understanding family and mine deserves a gold star. And well done, boys, we made it through Year 12. Here's to you, Will and Jack ... and also my ever-patient Ian.

PROLOGUE

'Hello, Reg,' she said as she approached. What an old-fashioned name Reginald was for someone his age; it didn't suit him at all.

'I thought you'd come,' he said, not looking up.

She loved his voice and his economy with words. Reg had always been able to comfort her even when he was silent, which was most of the time. 'Can I sit with you?'

She knew he smiled but he wouldn't face her. Her question did not require an answer, nor would he waste the breath to give her one. 'How are you?' she said, sighing as she lowered herself next to him.

'Same as yesterday.'

'Grouchy, then.'

'Not for you.'

'I'll take you in any mood, Reg, you know that.'

He looked around at her and after the unhappy morning she'd just had, which included watching a patient die, she felt instantly comforted and secure to see his sad, gentle face, buried beneath his straggly beard and the grime of his working day. She had long suspected that Reg liked to hide behind his longish, nutbrown hair, his hat, even that wretched beard, but try as he might, he could never hide his eyes. Intelligence — far more than he let on — lurked within those grey-green eyes that noticed everything and yet invited few people into his life, for he kept them mostly lowered when others were around. Now they looked at her; vaguely amused but above all knowledgeable. He had secrets, but then he was a secretive sort — everything about Reg was a mystery. The nurses cringed whenever she mentioned him, variously describing him as rude, deranged or creepy. He was none of those things. Not to her, anyway.

'A death?' he asked as she was staring at him.

How could he know her that well? It was infuriating sometimes. The tide of emotion she'd kept at bay rose but she wouldn't cry. Couldn't cry. If her training had taught her anything it had taught her to hold part of herself back from patients, or risk being swallowed by misery. But there was more to not showing her sorrow. In her quietest of moments she worried that she was a cold person; someone who let few past her guard. The truth was, she didn't particularly want to share her life with anyone. Reg didn't count, of course. He was a stranger she'd befriended so many years ago she couldn't remember her time in the hospital when he was not roaming the botanical gardens, ever near, always available to give her a few minutes, always able to say the right things … even when he wasn't actually speaking. Something was missing in her for sure — the lonely gene, perhaps … the one that triggered normal people to go in search of others and make friends. She obviously didn't possess that gene. It was as if she were a misfit, walking around a world of people she didn't feel she was a part of. She looked like everyone, talked like everyone, even to some degree acted like them. But there was a hole somewhere — a divide she couldn't bridge between herself and everyone else. Reg was her curious lifeline, for he too was a misfit and seemed to understand even though they never discussed such intimacies.

And so she went through the motions of life — always had … even with her parents. For many years she'd thought this was simply because she was adopted. It bothered her to the point where she'd even taken some therapy for it but she knew in her heart that this was not a learned response — something she had reacted to on discovering her adoption. No, this was deep. It was in the blueprint that had made her who she was. And its particular presence in her DNA or whatever it was, meant she didn't feel fully connected to anyone except Reg, the hospital groundsman.

'Yes,' she answered, finally able to accept that Jim Watkins was no longer of this life.

He said nothing.

'Mmm,' she confirmed but it came out as a soft groan, hugging herself as another pang of guilt reached through her body and twisted in her gut. She was answering a question he hadn't asked and yet they both knew the question existed, hanging between them.

She began to explain, even though he hadn't requested any further information. 'I try not to choose, Reg. I have to be careful.'

'Save all.'

'I can't. I'm different enough already; can you imagine what the media would do if it cottoned on to this?'

He shrugged.

She gave a mocking half-smile. 'Proper journalists are just the tip of the iceberg. The gutter press and popular magazines, the hacks and mischief makers and those awful revelation shows that masquerade as *current affairs*,' she said, mugging at him, 'they would just slurp this up.'

He shook his head now, slightly amused, mostly baffled.

'They'd never leave me alone, Reg.'

'You're looking thin.'

'That's a joke coming from you.'

'I could eat a horse and it wouldn't show.'

'You're lying. I know you so much better than you think. We're thin, Reg, because we're both hollow. Neither of us are filled with anything except a strange misery. I recognised it in you the moment I met you — the moment you walked into my life and tripped me.'

'I didn't trip you,' he growled gently.

'How else would you describe it?'

'*I* tripped, and stumbled *into* you.'

'And stopped me from going to see the clairvoyant at the Otherworlds festival.'

'Rubbish. We were strangers. How could I have any hold over you?'

'We weren't strangers. Even if we'd never met I've always had the curious feeling that we've known each other all my life.'

He made a scoffing sound, offered her half of the orange he'd laboriously peeled while they'd been talking. She took it, inhaling the fresh scent of citrus surrounding them.

'How old are you, Reg?'

'I'm not sure.'

She laughed.

He looked at the segment of orange in his hand. 'It's true. I've lived too long,' he said, looking down. 'So I've never really known.'

'Well, beneath all this fuzz,' she said, tugging at his beard, 'you look about mid thirties.'

'And you're just twenty and considered a genius, so you already know what it is to have that kind of attention levelled at you,' he replied, returning to their previous topic.

'Exactly!' she snapped. 'They didn't leave me alone for almost a year when they discovered I'd qualified for Medicine so young. It's all quietened down again. Now I'm just another intern at another big city hospital.'

'And uncannily, often inexplicably, saving lives.'

'Listen, I want everyone to just accept that I have talent and I developed really early. I can't help that. The fact that I have a sixth sense for patients can't be helped either but I don't want to turn it into a sideshow and that's what it would become if we continue down the pathway you suggest. The hospital will become suspicious, the community will start to request only me for all procedures and the media will start to hail me as some sort of messiah.'

'Perhaps you are.'

'Stop it!' she said, flicking him with the back of her hand.

She ate the orange, enjoying the tart explosion in her mouth and they sat in an easy silence for a few minutes and watched the world of the gardens go by — mothers pushing prams, dogs walking their owners, couples canoodling in the early autumn warmth.

'But how come we're so comfortable together, Reg? Do you think it's because we're both orphans?'

'Because we're friends.'

'Name another friend that you have.'

'I don't have any and don't say you don't either, because I've seen you with them.'

'Spying on me, eh?'

He gave her a disdainful sideways glance.

She tossed some pith of the orange she'd peeled off into the nook of the tree where they sat side by side. 'You've seen me with colleagues and acquaintances. You've not seen me with a friend. The only friend I have is you. Being with you is when I'm honest with myself and can be truly myself.'

'Then I'm privileged.'

'So explain why that is.'

'Because I'm such excellent company.'

She gasped. 'You're no company at all. You don't speak unless spoken to. You hold long, difficult silences,' she nodded when he was about to say something, 'not with me, I'll grant you, but even during the most normal small talk you manage to make whoever is with you feel incredibly awkward. I've watched you. No eye contact, no smiles, mainly shrugs and grunts. You terrify women.'

He shrugged as if to prove her point. 'It's my special skill.'

'I wish I understood you.'

He risked placing a hand on hers, then took it away quickly, as if burned. 'You do. And in doing so, you understand yourself.' Reg stood, helped her up. 'We're birds of a feather, us two. Just accept that we're the loners of the world and we're lucky to have each other.'

She nodded. Gave him a brief hug; knew it made him self-conscious but lingered anyway. 'Thanks, Reg.'

'People will talk,' he said, pulling away.

'Let them. I already feel like I'm being watched.'

Reg frowned; in his expression was a question.

'Can't explain it,' she sighed. 'But I have this frequent feeling that someone is watching me — you know — hiding and eavesdropping.'

He gave her a soft smile. 'He's probably in love with you but you're so unapproachable he doesn't know how to talk to you.'

'Oh really? And you'd know how that feels, would you?'

Reg grinned sadly and shook his head. 'Tomorrow? I'll bring more than an orange.'

'It's a date. Bring chocolate,' she said over her shoulder.

'Bye,' he replied softly and Corbel de Vis of Penraven lifted his hand in farewell to the gifted young intern who had no idea that she was royalty — a princess in exile — or that her healing skills were based on magic she brought with her from another plane, certainly another age ... or perhaps most importantly of all, that she was the woman he loved.

1

The man had been staring out of the window, watching the trees for movement but he turned at the knock. 'Come,' he called and waited while his private aide entered, balancing a tray. He frowned. 'You didn't have to —'

'I know, my lord,' the aide replied. 'But have a cup anyway.'

He sighed. 'There's still no sign of my raven,' he added in a grumpy tone.

'He'll return,' the aide replied evenly. 'He always does.' He set the tray down. 'He's obviously very familiar with the region now, and feels comfortable to be away that long. It's blossomtide, emperor. I imagine all birds are busy at their business.'

Loethar nodded gloomily. 'How is it down there, Freath?'

'Exactly as you'd imagine. Very lively — the leading families do enjoy this get-together and try hard to balance its political agenda with the equally important social binding. Even though this is the empire's third "Gathering" there's still that lingering tension. The Droste family is being snubbed as usual, but they're only marginally less happy than Cremond.'

Loethar lifted a brow in a wry expression. 'Well, at least they're all equal now. There are no royals, other than myself. Ah, there's that smile, Freath. What does it mean today?'

Freath bowed his head once in acknowledgement. 'Apologies, my lord. But nothing has truly changed for the Denovian people.

There may be no royal lines acknowledged as such but the new compasses, as you've denoted them, are still paying homage to Penraven.'

Loethar nodded. 'They've forgiven me, don't you think, Freath?'

'No, Emperor Loethar, I don't,' Freath said gently. 'Not even a decade can fully heal their perceptions of the wrongs. But I hasten to assure that you've certainly gone a long way towards leaving only scars, not open, festering wounds. You've been a generous benefactor to all the leading families, who still enjoy plenty of privilege and status — they can hardly complain.'

'Indeed. I've not interfered too much either in the running of their compasses.'

'And that's another reason why they appear so tolerant and will increasingly trust you, my lord. A new dynasty is about to begin and enough of them dread a second war so much that they will support your child with loyalty.'

Loethar smiled grimly. 'I can't wait for my son to be born.' Then he sighed. 'And how is the empress?'

'Grumbly, sir, for want of a better word.'

'Gown not right, hair not right, belly too big, drinks too sour, food too bitter?'

'Husband too distant,' Freath added.

Loethar's eyes flashed up to regard his aide's. It even baffled him at times how he permitted this dour man such familiarity. Even now he didn't fully trust the former aide to the previous royal family, but he believed Freath was the most intelligent of all the people that lurked around him on a daily basis. He appreciated the man's insight, dry wit, directness and agile mind. When he compared that to his brute of a half-brother, who was his Second, there was little wonder — for him anyway — as to why he not only permitted but quietly protected Freath's position. 'Should I be worried?' he asked, glibly, yet privately eager to hear the man's opinion.

'No, my lord. But if you want your household life to be less volatile it might pay to give the empress more attention. She is, after all, with child and feeling vulnerable.'

'How do you know, Freath?' Loethar sighed and took the goblet that his aide offered him.

'I spent years around a pregnant queen, my lord. Iselda lost quite a few babies but I know during her confinements she was generally irritable. She was no doubt anxious — and for good reason, having lost so many — but also worried that Brennus would stop finding her attractive.'

Loethar made a brief noise of scorn. 'I find that very hard to believe. Perhaps if you hadn't killed her, I could have married her!'

'I do hope the walls don't have ears, sir,' Freath said dryly and Loethar gave him a wry glance, knowing they were both well aware of Valya's unpredictable tantrums. 'Brennus was butter around her.'

'Is that so?'

'"Besotted" is probably the right word. Few couples achieve such devotion.'

Loethar grunted. Freath's counsel was no comfort at all. In fact, it served only to alienate him further. Marriage to Valya was a trial. Since the lavish wedding that he'd had to force himself to get through, she had become insatiable for power and wealth, especially the outward trappings of both. He understood why: she was proclaiming to the former Set people that while they had once gossipped and tittered behind her back at the reneging of the Valisar betrothal, now she was empress they were required to pay her homage. And once she delivered Loethar his heir at last, her position was truly sealed.

'Well, Valya's had a lot of unhappiness in her life. And not falling pregnant for so long has been a heavy burden for her. But that is changed now. Perhaps our son will bring her enough joy to leave her darkness behind.'

Freath straightened. 'You told me once that our empress had bravely defied man, beast and nature to find you on the plains but I cannot account for the significant gap of years between Brennus deserting their troth and my lady re-appearing in Penraven a decade ago.'

'It is of no harm for you to know, I suppose. Valya's father blamed her for Brennus's rejection, even though she hadn't seen her husband-to-be for more than a year. The king sent his only daughter and heir to a convent that nestled within Lo's Teeth, all but imprisoning her with the nuns. She admitted to me a long time ago that she was sure she turned mad for a while — several years probably. And while time scarred over her wounds, it never quelled her fury.' He stretched, reached for his glass on the weaven table nearby. 'She escaped.' He yawned. 'And then came looking for the Steppes people. She made it through those mountains alone. Impressive.'

Freath paused, considering this. Loethar waited, sipping his wine. 'So …' the aide began, frowning. 'Was the attack the empress's idea, my lord? This is old history now — it can't matter if you share it.'

'It was no one's idea in particular,' Loethar lied. 'I was a rebellious man, not satisfied with leading the Steppes people and wanting a whole lot more than the scrubby plains and the occasional visit from Set traders who felt they were superior to us. And then along came this striking woman out of nowhere, half-starved and with a rage to suit my own. She gave voice to what I was already thinking.'

'And history was made, my lord,' Freath said lightly.

Loethar sipped his wine again and turned away to regard the view out of the window. 'Seems hard to believe it was a decade ago that we stormed Brighthelm. I feel as if I belong here.'

Freath blinked. 'You do, my lord.'

'We've integrated well, don't you think, Freath?'

'Yes, my lord, surprisingly well.'

'So many mixed marriages,' Loethar continued. 'I'm very glad to see that the mingling of bloods has begun.'

'General Stracker might not agree,' Freath added, conversationally.

'He's short-sighted, Freath. Most of the Denovian people would be enriching the soil if it had been left to him. There'd be no one left to make an empire,' Loethar replied, yet again wishing his half-brother had even a fraction of his aide's insight. A knock at the door interrupted his thoughts and he nodded at Freath's enquiring look.

Freath opened the door and spoke briefly. Then closed it again, turning to Loethar. 'It's time to go, my lord.'

Loethar began buttoning his midcoat. Freath dutifully held out the jacket. 'I hate all this formal wear, Freath.'

'I know you do, my lord, but it's necessary. Can't have you looking like a barbarian.' They both smiled at the quip. 'What news from the north, sir?'

Loethar shrugged, allowing Freath to quickly do up his jacket while he struggled with his collar. 'All quiet for now. We've had patrols moving through the forest. The notorious highwayman and his daring minions elude me but we've silenced them for a while. There's been no activity in the region for several moons.'

Their conversation was interrupted by a bang at the door.

Freath frowned but Loethar inclined his head. The aide moved to the door and opened it.

'I need to speak with him,' a brusque voice demanded.

'It's General Stracker, my lord,' Freath announced, as the other man pushed past him into the room.

'Stracker. Speak of the devil!' Loethar said amiably. 'I was just telling Freath here that you were up north and all was quiet.'

Stracker grinned a sly smile. His green tatua slid in tandem, widening across his round, thickset face. 'Not so quiet any longer.'

Loethar stopped grimacing at himself in the mirror and turned his attention to his general. 'What's occurred?'

'We might have our elusive outlaw.'

Loethar's mouth opened in surprise and then he too smiled. 'Tell me.'

Freath quietly set about pouring the two men a cup of wine, unobtrusively serving it and then melting back into the room to stand silently. Though he wasn't intruding Loethar was aware the aide could hear everything. It didn't matter. He would discuss most of this with Freath anyway.

'I can't confirm what you want to hear — not yet anyway — but one of the men, and we are almost sure it's one of the outlaws, took an arrow wound.'

'Faris?'

'We think it could be.'

'So he's wounded and got away,' Loethar demanded.

'That's the sum of it,' Stracker confirmed, seemingly unfazed by the emperor's intensity.

'What makes you say you almost have him, then? Simply because you've wounded a man who *could* just belong to his cohort!' Loethar gave a sound of disgust and drained his cup.

'Not so fast, brother. Hear me out,' Stracker said, cunning lacing his tone. 'My men tell me that the wounded man took the arrow in the thigh. Now I'm sure even you would agree that in this situation it would be every man for himself.'

There was an awkward pause until Loethar grudgingly nodded. 'What of it?'

Stracker grinned. 'Not in this instance. Our soldiers confirmed that the renegades rallied around the wounded man, almost setting up a human shield. They half-carried, half-ran him away from our men. They're clever and fast, I'll give them that, and they know the ways and means of the forest better than our men ever could. They disappeared faster into the shadows of the great trees than our soldiers could scramble up the hill.'

'What's your point?' Loethar hated sounding so thick-headed and he knew it was disappointment making his comprehension sluggish.

Stracker clearly delighted in his slowness. 'Ask Freath, I'm sure he understands.' He casually took a long draught from his cup.

Loethar glanced at Freath, who obliged, tension in his voice. 'I suspect, my lord, that General Stracker is implying that the man was important enough for the others to risk their own capture or death.'

'Exactly,' Stracker followed up, sounding thoroughly pleased with himself.

Freath sounded awfully alarmed, Loethar thought, but he turned back to Stracker.

'But you let them get away,' he said, his voice quiet and suddenly threatening.

'No, I didn't, brother. I wasn't there. Had I been, I would have given chase until my heart gave out, but the captain in charge decided it was prudent not to venture deeper into the forest with only five men. He knew we would want this information and so I now have it and have brought it to you. But in the meantime I had Vulpan taken to the spot.'

This time Loethar had no struggle in understanding his brother's meaning. 'Inspired.'

'Thank you,' the huge man said, deigning to incline his head in a small bow.

'I'm impressed, Stracker. So what now?'

'We wait for news. We will find him, brother. Trust me.' Loethar did not resist his general's friendly tap on his face, for it was meant affectionately, but he despised it. Carefully, however, he kept his expression even as the general excused himself.

'Enjoy the nobles,' Stracker said, smiling ironically as he left.

Loethar stared at the open doorway absently until Freath closed the door. 'Freath, have I told you about Vulpan yet?'

'No, my lord. Perhaps you'll enlighten me now,' the aide said, returning to his previous task of brushing lint from the emperor's shoulder.

'He's one of our Vested. It's a strange talent but he only has to taste a person's blood to know that person again.'

Freath stood back from Loethar, his forehead creased in amused puzzlement.

Loethar held up a hand with helpless resignation as he swung around. 'I know, I know. But there's no accounting for these Vested. Some possess enchantments that defy imagination.'

'You mean his taste of blood works in the same way that a dog can trace a smell?'

Loethar grinned. 'I suppose. He never gets it wrong, Freath. We've tested him time and again … even tried to trick him.'

Freath frowned. 'So he has tasted the blood of the wounded outlaw.'

Loethar nodded. 'Why would they rally around the man unless it was Faris? There is no one else of any importance in that cohort.' He noticed Freath blink, but continued, 'And some day the outlaw will slip up and Vulpan will deliver him to me. I am a patient man.'

'Incredible,' Freath remarked, shaking his head as he stacked the cups on the tray. 'And this Vulpan is loyal, sir?'

Loethar shrugged. 'The magic is not in doubt.'

'Is Kilt Faris that important?' Freath asked, reaching to do up the emperor's top button.

Loethar raised his chin. 'Yes. He challenges me.'

'He did the same to Brennus before you, sir.'

'Is that supposed to reassure me, Freath?'

The aide straightened his lord's jacket, moving behind him. 'Forgive me, my lord. I meant only that Faris is a gnat — a vexing irritant — who thinks stealing the royal gold is somehow not the same crime as stealing from the good folk of Penraven.'

'Precisely, which is why I wish to hunt him down.'

Loethar's eyes narrowed as he heard the aide suck in a breath that sounded too much like exasperation.

'If you'll forgive me, my lord? May I offer a recommendation?'

'You usually do, Freath. Make it quick.'

Freath cleared his throat as he returned to face his superior. 'Let me escort you down, my lord, we can talk as we walk. We really must go.'

Loethar nodded and Freath moved to hold the door open. 'After you, sir.'

They moved through Brighthelm side by side. Loethar was sure the man was far too sharp to have ignored that the emperor permitted him equal status — if not in title, then certainly in access — to any of his closest supporters. Even Dara Negev, who was showing no signs that her god was preparing to claim her, still maintained the old ways of walking a few steps behind the man of her household. But it must be two anni now that Loethar had given up talking over his shoulder to Freath and insisted the man walk next to him when discussing state business. Though Loethar's mother, half-brother and even Valya had haughtily mentioned on many an occasion that Freath couldn't appreciate the honour, Loethar was convinced that Freath not only appreciated the shift but quietly enjoyed the privilege.

They approached the grand staircase, walking down a corridor of magnificent tapestries depicting the former kings of Valisar.

'Forgive me, sir,' Freath continued. 'Returning to our discussion, I was simply going to suggest that you should consider raising people's taxes in and around the northern area. Chasing through the Deloran Forest is time-consuming and a waste of your men's resources. It also makes a fool of the emperor.'

Loethar's head snapped to look at Freath. 'He is mocking me?'

'Tax those who protect and laugh at you, my lord. Tax the north. Any excuse will do. In fact, offer no excuse. Tell them the new tax is to cover the losses that Faris inflicts. Remind the north that it is their hard-earned, hard-paid taxes that are being stolen and if they won't help you find him, they will certainly help repair his damage.'

Loethar smiled. 'Very good, Freath. Very good indeed.'

He felt Freath shrug beside him. 'I would call off your men immediately, my lord. You should make it appear as if you don't care one way or the other, so long as you have the money due the empire. I would be happy to make that declaration for you, sire, should you need.'

'Not frightened of being unpopular?'

Freath gave a snort of disdain. 'They hated me a long time ago, Emperor Loethar. Nothing's changed.'

'I shall think on your idea.'

Freath bowed. 'I shall let the empress know, my lord, that you and her guests await her.'

As Loethar moved into the grand salon to the heralding of trumpets, Freath strode up the stairs, feeling an old familiar tension twisting in his belly. Once out of sight from the ground level he took a moment alone on the landing to lean against the balustrade, taking two deep breaths to calm himself. He hadn't felt like this in so many anni he'd nearly forgotten what it was to be poised on the precipice of death. Ten anni previous he'd been exposed to negotiating that very knife-edge daily. Though somehow he'd survived, his beautiful Genrie had not. The passing years had not made her loss any easier. He visited her unmarked grave frequently, and although it hurt his heart not to leave flowers — for he couldn't be seen to be mourning her — he left behind his silent grief. Her death had bought his life, and what a strange, evil life it had become: forever lying, masquerading and patiently plotting.

The only surprise had been his helpless admiration — although he fought it daily — for the man he knew he should despise. He found it easy to hate General Stracker, to inwardly sneer at Dara Negev and to truly abhor the empress. But Loethar was not as simple. The man was actually every inch the born leader that Brennus had been. And if he had been born a Valisar rather than a Steppes barbarian, Freath knew they'd all be admiring him. Loethar was taking an approach with the Denovians that could only be congratulated. There was no doubting that the new emperor was very tough — but which sovereign wasn't? None of the Valisars down the ages were known for being spineless. All were hard men, capable of making the most difficult of decisions. Any ruler who took a soft line with detractors would almost certainly perish. Freath often thought, hating himself as he did so, that if he had been in Loethar's boots, there was little he would or could have done any other way.

He'd tried to explain this once to Kirin, his constant companion, but Kirin would have none of it. Besides, Kirin always had him over a barrel whenever he resorted to the final demand, always impossible to answer. *Why, though, Freath?* he would challenge. *Why did he do it in the first place? It has to be in pursuit of power. And there is no honour in coveting what is not yours in the first place.*

Kirin was right — in principle — especially if you believed in fairies or the Legend of Algin, and that everyone wanted to live in peace and no one ever got jealous of anyone else. Freath grimaced. The Valisar Dynasty might be revered but it had been founded on bloodshed, acquiring land that had never belonged to the Valisars, not so very differently from the way that Loethar had taken the Set. The only difference was that Cormoron had seen the benefits of giving realms to families he could dominate, giving the false impression that he was a magnanimous conqueror — a benefactor to the region even. It was naive of Kirin to suggest that the Valisars — or any of the royal families — were blameless. All land, power and wealth were initially acquired through the spillage of blood. Loethar and his horde were no different — if anything, where Loethar was blunt, he was at least honest.

Despite Loethar's surprising explanation that his attack on the Denovian Set was purely a matter of opportunity, Freath still wasn't convinced fortuity alone had triggered the seemingly sudden invasion. The emperor's rationale was plausible, and probably true, but there was more to it, Freath was sure. The seven realms had peacefully lived alongside Droste to the north-east as well as further east over Lo's Teeth into the Steppes where the plains people lived. It was true that there had not been a great deal of interaction between Denovians and the Steppes folk but trade during the reign of Brennus had increased. Perhaps beginning to see more of the Denovians, their way of life, their excesses, had attracted Loethar's people?

Freath pulled out a kerchief and wiped his face, wishing that he could wipe away his fear. For ten anni patience had been all that shared his life. It was a companion that made him feel weak, disloyal, pathetic. He knew it was also his friend. Patience would win through for him, for them, for their cause. *Them.* He closed his eyes. He had bought them some more time in dissuading Loethar from hunting down Faris. Freath had presumed for many years now that the true king, Leo, had fled to Faris and his men. Now he must get word to Faris and learn at last whether the outlaw had raised a king in these intervening years. A decade of distance. A decade of hate. Would he even recognise Leo Valisar, King of Penraven? Would Leo ever forgive him?

He had to get to Kilt Faris before Loethar's men did. He had to pray that Faris was not the wounded man.

'Ah, there you are,' said a familiar voice. He looked up and saw Kirin approaching. 'Are you feeling all right, Freath?'

Freath nodded. 'Yes. A moment of reflection, that's all.'

Kirin smiled softly and there was so much sympathy in the gesture Freath had to look away. 'That's always dangerous,' his friend said.

'Very true. Were you looking for me?'

Kirin looked around, checking they were alone, and Freath

immediately felt his fear twist up another notch. 'A pigeon has arrived,' his friend murmured.

A combination of thrill and puzzlement skipped across Freath's heart. 'But it's been years.'

'It's an old pigeon,' Kirin said.

Freath erupted in an unexpected bellow of laughter at the comment. Few, if any, had ever heard such genuine laughter around the halls of Brighthelm, and Kirin's expression was delighted.

Freath continued chuckling. 'Lo, but that was a good feeling.' 'I wish I could do that more often,' his younger friend admitted. 'It gets better. The bird's from Clovis.'

Freath closed his eyes, shooting a silent prayer of thanks. They had both long given up hope of hearing from their old friend who had escaped Loethar's clutches in the madness of the original occupation. Freath had tried through every clandestine method he had available to find him, without success. 'Where is he?' he asked, breathless.

Kirin grinned. 'With Reuth. Medhaven.'

Relief passed through him before another, still more exciting notion struck Freath. He reached for Kirin's arm, squeezing it. 'Piven?' he whispered, daring against all his better judgement to hope.

Kirin's mouth creased into a wide smile and he nodded just once before he faltered. 'Later,' he said hurriedly. 'Someone comes.'

Freath let go of Kirin's arm, stood back, and within moments one of Valya's retinue of servants came scurrying up. She was a tribal woman. Freath liked her. She was quiet, diligent and good at her work — a lot like Genrie although she lacked spine against the empress. But that was understandable. Showing any sort of opposition to Valya, however minor it seemed, was met with punitive retaliation. Only Freath managed to rise above her dominion, and that was only because he had the protection of a higher authority.

'Bridie?' he enquired as the servant raced up.

'Master Freath, she is …' The girl stared at them both, lost for the right words.

'I know, Bridie. I'm coming now,' he assured.

The girl looked so relieved that Kirin shook his head. 'Don't let her bully you, Bridie,' he said.

'No,' Freath countered. 'Let her bully you. It will keep her claws out of you. Come on, we'll go together and tame her, shall we?' Bridie smiled tentatively and nodded. He looked over at Kirin. 'Later? Supper, perhaps?'

Kirin nodded. 'I'll be in the library if you need me.'

How very normal that sounded, Freath thought. Kirin, a man of learning, was off to the library, while he, an experienced steward, was off to see to his superior's needs. They had all settled down into a comfortable life, existing relatively easily with the barbarian horde — as though all the pain and despair never really mattered. And yet his heart was hammering and he knew Kirin was experiencing a similar rush of excitement that was a prelude to a new battle. This battle would not be fought in the fields with two armies. No. This one would be fought by subterfuge. Cunning alone had kept Freath and Kirin alive to fight this new day. And cunning would return the rightful king to the Valisar throne.

He strode alongside the scuttling Bridie, his heart suddenly full, his chest feeling broader than it had in the last ten anni, and his mind filled with wonder.

Piven was alive.

King and crown prince had possibly survived. He had never allowed himself to dream this much. But it seemed Lo had granted him his prayers.

If he achieved anything with his miserable double-life, he would see King Leonel crowned and the false ruler who called himself emperor humbled and brought before the Valisar sovereign.

Leo alone would decide Loethar's fate.

2

Two men were breaking their fast at an inn in Francham. The Amiable Dragon was a busy watering hole and resting spot almost at the base of the Dragonsback Mountains that separated Penraven from Barronel. It was in Francham that traders in particular, after a long trek through Hell's Gate — as the pass through the mountains was known — would stop for a day or so. Weary travellers would replenish their stocks, and those who were crossing in the opposite direction would make their final preparations for the trip. The traffic made for a lively town with a varied, transient population, which meant someone who wanted to remain relatively invisible could roam Francham without being noticed. It was an unspoken rule, in fact, that people were entitled to privacy in this town.

The weather was mild. Blossomtide meant Hell's Gate was well and truly open and thriving. The pair of diners was enjoying the morning sun, sitting at a corner table, facing the main street to the mountains beyond that loomed over Francham. One of the men, who had just finished eating and was washing down his early meal with a pot of steaming dinch, was explaining this to his companion. He leaned back with his mug and sighed his pleasure as he swallowed the mouthful of dinch. '... it used to be a great smuggling spot, you see, so the legacy of secrecy has been handed down through generations. I'm surprised I haven't told you this before.'

His listener grinned. 'You've only brought me here twice.'

The speaker gave a look of genuine surprise at this but the companion didn't look as if he was fooled, going by his wry expression.

He shrugged. 'Anyway, if you ever need to hide, this is the place to begin. The mountains are better but they don't offer a bed at night or an ale to quench a thirst.'

'Why are we here again?'

'I have to see someone.'

A huge man approached the table. 'It's true,' he confirmed.

The first man put down his mug and pointed to the pot. 'Help yourself,' he offered, but his thoughts were elsewhere, his gaze narrowed in thought.

'What does it mean, Kilt?' the big man said, sitting down and taking his friend's mug. 'I'll just have yours.'

'Jewd! Ah —' Faris said, with a sound of disgust. 'I'd just got that to the perfect temperature!'

The younger man sitting next to him laughed.

'I know,' Jewd replied, nonchalantly. 'Perfect for me, too.'

Kilt Faris signalled towards a table at the far end where a serving woman set down a plate in front of another guest. She saw his gesture and made her way to them, shifting her hips as she dodged around other people's chairs. 'Yes?' she said, looking distracted but not unfriendly as she gathered up their plates.

'Ah, pretty Ciara,' Faris said. 'Another pot of dinch, please, and we'll need a fresh mug. Liam, some for you?'

The younger man shook his head but looked appreciatively into the big brown eyes of the woman. 'Got anything sweet?' he wondered.

Faris broke into a surreptitious grin and looked over at Jewd, who winked in reply over the mug he was sipping from.

Ciara's lids lowered slightly as she regarded the youngster. 'We might have some syrupcakes left from yesterday,' she said. Then she blinked innocently. 'If that's what you mean?'

Leo cleared his throat. 'I hear they're always better the day after, anyway. Yes, I'll have a couple of those. Thank you.'

'I like good manners. Anything else?' she offered.

Leo blushed, hesitated, then smiled politely. 'I'll, er, I'll let you know once I've finished those, if that's all right?'

She returned his smile, seemingly enjoying the innuendo.

After she'd left, Faris looked over at Leo but spoke to Jewd in a murmur that only they could hear. 'It seems his majesty is in dire need of some female company.'

'I'll say!' Leo exclaimed.

Jewd spat some of his dinch with amusement. 'Now look what you've made me do,' he complained.

'Well, it's all right for Kilt, he's got Lily. And you, Jewd, I know you and the others can escape the forest whenever you want for some rumpy-pumpy.' This made both men roar with laughter. 'But you keep me on such a close leash. I'm twenty-two anni, I need some freedom and I desperately need a —'

'Here we are, then,' Ciara said, back with a pair of small, oval-shaped cakes dripping with syrup. 'Careful, they're moist. Don't get yourself all sticky.'

The men laughed louder and even Ciara threw them a backward glance of amusement. 'The dinch is on its way,' she said.

Leo looked indignant. 'Laugh it up, you sods. I really need —'

'I know what you need,' Kilt said, chuckling, 'and we'll fix that. I've been remiss.'

'You've been a gaoler more like,' Leo said.

Kilt grew serious. 'So, do we trust this man?' he asked Jewd.

His big friend nodded. 'Yes. He's genuine.'

'What's going on?' Leo asked, chewing on a cake.

Kilt fixed him with a grave look. 'The man you spoke of years ago. You know, the one who is now aide to the emperor?'

'Freath?' Leo said, looking between them. 'Tell me Loethar's slit his throat,' he added, putting his cake down and swallowing.

Then he glared. 'But then he'll have stolen more from me. I want to be the one to spill that traitor's —'

Both men shook their heads. 'He's not dead,' Kilt replied, cutting off Leo's words. 'He's made contact.'

Leo leaned forward. 'What?' he whispered, shocked.

'Well, not contact, exactly. But there's word out. We've just received it.'

'What do you mean?'

Faris left it to Jewd, who took up the thread of conversation. 'A few days ago Tern picked up snippets of information that money was greasing palms all over the north's "network".' Leo nodded with understanding. 'Word was moving in certain circles that an influential man was seeking an audience with the infamous highwayman of Penraven.'

Leo's expression darkened and he scratched softly at the close beard he was growing, his syrupcakes forgotten.

Jewd continued, 'We paid attention, of course, but we've had this happen before.' He shrugged. 'Lots of influential men want to speak with Kilt.'

'Usually to claim the bounty on my head,' Kilt grumbled.

Leo looked at him. 'You're safe, though, aren't you?'

'Not safe enough it seems. The barbarians came too close recently. We got sloppy.'

'You didn't,' Jewd admitted. 'That was my fault.'

Leo shook his head. 'Jewd, it was no one's fault.'

Kilt sighed. 'Attributing blame is pointless. The fact is, they nearly stumbled across you, Leo. We must never be off our guard. As for me, no one outside of our band even knows what I look like. Most people in this town, don't know who we are. And this town might keep its secrets quiet but it also knows everyone and everything passing through it.'

'Aren't you two rather easily identifiable?'

'Not when I wear women's clothing,' Kilt offered indignantly. Leo smiled.

'He's not jesting,' Jewd said, sounding slightly exasperated. 'He's done it many times. I've walked alongside him when he's been an old man, an old woman, a blind beggar, a noble.'

'Ah, but my leper was the best, wasn't it?' Kilt said.

'He was a triumph,' Jewd agreed.

'People gave me such a wide berth. It was wonderful. I shall have to find that old pair of clappers we've got somewhere and roll him out again.'

Leo frowned. 'I'm sure Lily would appreciate the humour.'

'No, well, that's right,' Kilt said, his theatrics dampened. 'It's why I haven't used him for a while. And anyway, it's not just me.' He lightly slapped his big friend's chest. 'Jewd loves all the get-ups too. He came into this very town not so long ago as a drunken friar.'

Leo looked over at Jewd and broke into laughter. 'And that definitely wasn't drawing attention to yourself, was it?'

'Aha,' Kilt said, waggling a finger. 'Sometimes you can deflect the scrutiny by giving people something else to focus on.'

'Is that why you're wearing that ridiculous twirled moustache, then?'

'Well, I'm glad you finally mentioned my ingenious disguise,' Kilt said, feigning offence.

'And I'm glad you're having fun,' Leo grumbled. 'My disguise is real.'

Both men glanced at the crutch balanced against the table. 'The arrow-wound is healing well. Give it time,' Jewd reassured. 'It will be as good as new as long as you trust Lily's herbals and the chirosurgeon's advice.'

'If only they knew,' Kilt mused. Then he smiled encouragingly at his young king. 'At least you'll have a warrior's wound to show for your time with us.'

'How long before I'm ready?' Leo griped.

'Not yet,' Jewd replied.

Leo glanced at Kilt, who shook his head. 'You're only just a man now, Leo. We have lots to plan before you can start plotting an overthrow. You can't ignore the fact that Loethar has been very subtle.'

Leo grimaced. 'He's a better ruler than I would have ever given him credit for.'

'I think the mere fact that you do credit him with this is a sign of your maturity. As few as three anni ago you wouldn't have been able to see that.'

The king became thoughtful. 'Perhaps he is all that the Set ever needed.'

Both men gave sounds of disgust. 'No, majesty,' Kilt murmured firmly. 'He stole your crown, he usurped your throne, he effectively murdered your parents and a lot of other good people. He wrote his imperial title in blood. And yet the true heir lives — he's a man now. One day soon he'll be ready to claim what is his. A Valisar has been on that throne for five centuries. It is your duty to return that regal line.'

Leo sighed. 'I know all the rhetoric, Kilt. I just keep thinking that there's peace now. It's been a decade. Everyone has settled down to living harmoniously. I can't forgive what he's done but I am only one person … with a grudge. I keep wondering whether it's better for the good of the Set, but especially for Penraven, that I suffer my family history and its sorrows in silence.'

Faris sat back, glad that they'd taken the precaution of seating themselves so well away from others. He could not have risked anyone hearing this conversation. He shrugged. 'Well, before we start any discourse with Freath, you'd better seriously consider your position. I gave your father my word about several things, and one of them was to do everything in my power to return the Valisar throne to you. But there's no point to that if you don't want it.'

Leo glared at him. 'Are you really going to meet with Freath? Is he mad, Jewd?' he asked, turning to their companion.

'I think so, is the answer to both those questions.'

'Kilt,' Leo spluttered. 'Freath is a snake. No, he's less. He's vermin. And he'll be up to something, mark my words. The man betrayed my parents. I watched him. I heard him. He laughed at both of their grisly deaths. He helped Loethar keep my brother on a leash, in a dirty shirt that carried the blood of my father. He would give you up to Loethar without a second's hesitation.'

'Which is why he won't get the chance,' Faris said jauntily.

'Kilt, don't. He's not someone to allow into your life. He cannot be trusted, I tell you. I'll kill him as soon as I see him.'

Faris looked pained by the younger man's bravado. 'Who said anything about trust? I want to know what his game is. If he's up to something — or if Loethar is, and I know the emperor wants my head staring sightlessly from a spike at Brighthelm — then it's in my interest to find out everything I can.'

'It's a trap, I tell you,' Leo said vehemently.

Ciara returned. 'Fresh dinch,' she said, laying down the pot and mug. 'You've got enough honey, I see,' she said, opening the pot on the table but looking at Leo.

Kilt grinned. 'Yes, I'm sweet enough, but this young man here needs something to wipe that scowl from his face. Can I offer you a silver piece to add some sugar in his life?'

Leo's elbow slipped off the table in shock.

Ciara gave Kilt a puzzled smile. 'Your young friend thinks you're staining my honour.'

'I apologise without reservation,' Kilt replied, lifting his pot of strong but milky dinch.

Ciara turned to Leo. 'What's your name?' she asked.

'Er, Liam,' he replied, sitting up straighter.

'Well, Liam, I shall see you this evening at the bordello.'

The king nodded.

'And you, Henk?' she said to Kilt.

'Ah, Ciara. I have a woman in my life now, and she would cut off my bordellos and feed them to me if she thought I was taking my pleasures with you.'

Jewd nodded. 'That she would. But I'm free, Ciara. Is that lovely buxom Jenny still working?'

'She is. I'll tell her you may stop by.' And with that she left them to it.

'*Henk?*' Leo repeated, reaching over and stealing the mug of dinch that his friend was about to pick up and savour.

'Hey! Oh, that's just not fair,' Kilt grumbled. 'Go and pay, Jewd. I'm heading off. I promised Lily some supplies.'

'She'll certainly have those "bordellos" off in a blink if you let her down,' Leo said between gulps.

They all stood.

'Get word through the right channels,' Faris said to his long-time friend. 'I'll see Freath. Let's find out exactly what he's up to, shall we?'

Leo scowled as Jewd nodded. The big man handed Leo the single crutch. 'Hope that wound won't slow you up tonight.'

The grimace left the younger man's face, replaced by a smile. 'Not a chance,' Leo said, limping to catch up with Faris. 'It will take more than a barbarian arrow-wound to keep me from Ciara.'

Faris had left Jewd and Leo to their pleasures, and was watching Lily pack up the stores they'd bought. He had never been happier and Jewd assured him frequently that this was due entirely to Lily's presence. Faris had dismissed the comment but now he wondered if there was something to it after all. Up until Lily, the only person he'd permitted intimacy with his thoughts was Jewd. No girl had ever come between them and Lily was secure enough emotionally to see that no girl should. She hadn't once created any bad feeling between the two great companions and, above and beyond that, she had been a blessing in terms of playing a big sister role to the young king over the years since his arrival into the camp.

Faris watched as Lily worked, seemingly oblivious of his scrutiny. He liked watching her move; loved the way she'd flick back her hair when it fell forward, how in that second he'd catch a glimpse of her lovely long neck. He wanted to kiss it now. In fact, he would. Getting up from his seat by the window of the inn, he walked over, put his arms around her waist from behind and kissed the exact spot on her neck he'd been watching. He snuggled into its warmth; could feel her pulse against his lips.

She laughed and squirmed. 'I'm busy, Kilt.'

'Never too busy for me, I hope?' he asked.

Lily turned in his arms. 'No, never.' She kissed him tenderly and it turned into a long, passionate embrace. When they parted, she looked breathless. 'What was that about?'

'Am I not allowed to show my love?'

'Your love?' She looked surprised by his use of the word, but quickly collected herself. She kissed him once again, softly and swiftly. 'Don't ever hesitate. It's just not like you to be so demonstrative.'

He sighed and let her go. He sat himself down on the bed. 'I'm very aware that you're one woman among a group of men. I don't want to rub it in that you're all mine.'

It was her turn to sigh. 'Well, I want you to rub it in. I'd quite enjoy the attention.'

'Oh?' It was Kilt's turn to look surprised. 'Do you feel ignored?'

She stared at him with a scornful expression. 'Kilt, how could I? You spend *so* much time with me, and you share your innermost thoughts with me to the point where I want to cover my ears and yell, "no more!".'

His gaze narrowed. 'Less of the sarcasm, please. We were enjoying a nice moment.'

'We could enjoy so many more if you'd only let me in.' Lily turned away and continued carefully packing goods into sacks and saddlebags. She inhaled a bunch of fleshy leaves. 'Ah, I love the smell of fresh borrega. We'll have some deliciously flavoured stews through Leaf-fall as this dries.'

Kilt wasn't ready to let their discussion go. 'Let you in? Where?'

Now she looked at him with exasperation, before moving across to where he sat. Tapping his head, she said, 'In here, you fool. That is the place I want to be permitted to glimpse.'

Ignoring her plea, he pulled her small, voluptuous body closer. 'Well, I know where I want to be in,' he said, his tone lascivious now.

She pushed away gently, slightly wearily. 'I'm busy and you're not taking me seriously.'

'I am,' he replied, his own exasperation matching hers. 'Now come here, one of your bodice's strings has loosened. I'll tighten it,' he offered, the tone in his voice and glint in his eye suggesting otherwise.

Lily deliberately moved further from him. 'Besides, it's not worth trying to be serious when you're in this mood.'

'What mood?'

'The one that is hoping for a tumble in the bed without talking.'

'Oh, Lily, isn't that what every man is hoping for?' he asked, frustration spilling over. 'You're ruining what could have been some precious time alone together.'

She didn't answer him; she gave him an arch glance instead as she packed away some threads and new needles, ticking them off her list.

'What do you want from me?' he asked, feeling injured.

'Is that a genuine question?' she commented, looking up from her list.

'Of course it is.'

'Because I'm not sure you want the honest answer.' Lily's hands were on her hips now, the list momentarily forgotten.

'Don't I?'

'No. Because honesty would require you to confront who you are, Kilt Faris. I've been with you for a decade now. I've healed your aches and stitched your wounds, I've washed your clothes and cooked for you. I've been your loyal companion and I've made love to you throughout that time and never tired of you. I've —'

'You're a perfect woman, Lily.' He cut across her words with a triumphant grin.

She looked sadly back at him. 'Everything's a jest to you, Kilt.' She turned away. 'Even us.'

'That's not true,' he said, scrambling forward across the bed. 'Don't be like this, Lily. I really don't know how to make you happy. Frankly, I didn't know you were unhappy.'

'I'm not,' she said, returning to her packing.

'You sound it.'

'No, I'm disappointed, that's all. I feel as though I'm always on the outside, Kilt. You only let me get so close and then you seem to draw curtains around yourself.'

'I don't understand.'

'You have secrets. They shut me out.'

'Me?' he asked, sounding astonished. 'No! How can you accuse me of that after so long together?'

'You're lying. There's something restless inside you that only you control, only you know about, only you glimpse. I can only get so far with you and it's because of that invisible line you've drawn around yourself that I know you can never fully love me the way I want to be loved. You take me and my affections for granted, Kilt. And the saddest part is, I'm a little trapped by how much you all need me. I'm not being a martyr, I'm simply stating a fact.'

He stared at her, genuinely hurt. 'How can you say that?'

She looked back at him, sad and resigned. 'When did you last tell me you loved me?'

'A moment ago, I think!'

'Did you? Did you actually come in here with the full intention of looking into my eyes and telling me you love me? No. You came in here to enjoy some lovemaking. I don't mean to complain, Kilt. But the fact is, you don't show you love me, and never, not once have you ever uttered the words, *I love you, Lily*.' She held up her hand. 'I know what you're going to say. The thing is you probably do love me in your own curious way. You are good to me and you keep me safe and you've been a strong figurehead for Leo. I've been a part of your life over these years, and that has been wonderful. But —' She shrugged. 'I don't know what else to do for you. I share every ounce of myself physically and emotionally. You don't or perhaps can't reciprocate in the same manner.'

Kilt looked pained. He sighed. 'But how do you know you love me? You've hardly lived, Lily. You could meet any handsome fellow tomorrow and fall head over heels.'

'Don't turn this on me. I'm not looking for anyone else and I'd love to know how you imagine someone handsome and available is going to stumble across me when I choose to spend my life in the forest with you. I only come into town twice an anni! Besides, we're talking about you and how you treat me. And by the way, your suggestion is ridiculous.'

'Don't be angry,' he said, reaching for her. 'I'm so sorry, Lily. Truly, I am.'

She allowed him to draw her into his arms, relaxing into them, and he could tell she didn't want to prolong this conversation. 'I'm not angry.' Her expression became more wistful. 'I suppose I am as happy as you permit, Kilt.' Her careful words were not lost on him.

'How can I make this better between us?'

'Let down your guard with me. I'm hardly a stranger and I would never do anything to hurt you or be disloyal to you.' She stroked his hair, touching the first silvering at his temple. 'Our relationship is a decade old, or do you forget?'

He shook his head and kissed her softly. 'No, you've saved me a fortune in brothel fees.'

Lily's eyes widened in horror and she mock-swiped at him. 'That is really going to cost you, Master Faris!'

He laughed, inwardly sighing with relief that she was keen to lighten the moment. He hugged her more tightly, knowing something profound needed to be said now to secure her faith in him. 'I'll have to marry you soon, Lily.'

That caught her attention. She didn't speak immediately, but stared at him silently, searching his eyes. 'Do you mean that?' she said, her eyes glistening, her voice soft, unsure.

'I've never meant anything more deeply. We're as good as husband and wife now. Let's make it official as soon as we can.'

Lily embraced him tightly. 'You don't have to do this.'

He laughed, twirled her around. 'This is going to make all the boys happy.'

'Are you sure? Jewd won't mind?'

He made a dismissive gesture.'He told me only last moon that if I didn't hurry up, he'd ask you and steal you from beneath my nose.'

She smiled. 'Well, it's tempting. I'm sure Jewd shares more with me than you ever could!' She didn't say it unkindly, though. Then she laughed. 'And Leo? You think he'll be happy?'

'Don't be vain. Leo got over you years ago.'

'Says the great father figure!'

'Well, in a way that's been my role.'

'You could have fooled me,' she said but her voice was light.

Kilt frowned. 'What makes you say that?'

She smiled, and again it was gentle. 'Kilt,' she began, her voice affectionate, 'you have left all the rearing to myself and Jewd. I've played the maternal role and Jewd has been at his side in everything. I'm sure I'm not being unkind when I say that if you do see yourself as a father figure, then you've been the most remote father I can imagine. Surely you can't deny that you keep him at arm's length?' She frowned. 'I don't mean that unkindly either, my love. I understand that being a kingmaker is hard enough without playing father to him. In fact, I've told Leo time and again that it's not that you don't like him, but that you have to keep a distance in order to keep what we're trying to achieve in perspective. He knows that you will likely have to make hard decisions and they can't be clouded by your affection for him.'

'He thinks I don't like him?'

'He used to. But he's older now.' She shrugged. 'He accepts that this is how you are with him.'

'And how am I with him?'

She regarded him quizzically now. 'Distant is how I'd describe it. I've watched you. You never sit near him. You certainly never touch him. You always cast off duties that might involve Leo to Jewd. You disappear for long periods when all of us are together. And it's got worse, rather than better. You spent more time with him as a youngster but you seem to have pulled back as he's grown and matured. Leo is perceptive, Kilt. Surely you can see how he might interpret this as a lack of love?'

Kilt felt sick, and angry with himself. 'I've just spent the last couple of hours with Leo,' he bleated. 'I can't believe —'

'Yes, I know you have. But this is how you behave. You go for weeks avoiding any sort of close contact and then, whoosh!' she said, making a sweep of her hand. 'You do something like this morning, as though you've come out of some stupor or you can bear to be near him for a short burst. Then you're gone again.'

'I wanted to see you,' he explained, sounding injured, but his mind was racing across all of Lily's observations. He hadn't realised it was so obvious.

'I know you did, and I'm glad you came to see me,' she said, kissing him gently. 'But once again you've left Leo with Jewd.'

'Not exactly. As we stand here I suspect he is getting a taste of all that he's been missing.'

She caught on immediately. 'Oh, Kilt, not The Velvet Curtain?'

'It's part of his education. We've been raising a sovereign, my love. He has to experience all that we can give him and The Velvet Curtain is integral to growing up. It's a rite of passage for all the young men in my band.'

'Led loudly by yourself and Jewd, no doubt.'

'Not anymore. I am a one-woman man. So let me prove it. I'll buy a ring next time we're in town, I promise, and I will talk to the preacher about a wedding in the next few moons.'

Lily gave a soft squeal of delight before adding: 'I can't believe the lengths I'll go to in order to get a new dress!'

Faris grinned, taking pleasure in Lily's obvious joy. Lily asked so little of him and yet had brought so much to the outlaws. It was true that he'd taken her support and constant presence for granted. 'You may have whatever you want, my love. But there is a favour I need.'

'Oh?'

He nodded. 'A man called Freath will be making contact soon. He's from the palace.'

'Freath? Why do I know that name?'

'He's the one Leo has declared his favourite enemy alongside you-know-who.'

Comprehension spread across Lily's face. 'Of course, the treacherous manservant.'

Faris nodded. 'The very one.'

'And he's contacted you?' she asked, incredulous.

Faris hesitated. 'Not directly. But in a roundabout way he has. It's certainly me he's after but he's being deliberately coy, as if protecting me. It doesn't add up. I want to know what he knows.'

'Isn't that dangerous?'

'Not if I take the right precautions — and you know me.'

'This isn't just a chance for you to wear one of my skirts, is it?'

'Lily, how unkind,' he said, feigning indignation. 'No,' he began again, turning more serious. 'There's more to this than meets the eye. Freath is coming to me and he's coming with stealth and care, it seems. He's found me in the same way that if I wanted to find me I would. Does that make sense?'

'You mean, he's not screaming your name from the rooftops.'

'Yes. Word has got through he is bringing only a small party. He plans to slip his soldier escort.'

'All right, so how does this involve me?'

'He has a companion. Just keep an eye on him for me, that's all.'

'One of the men can't?'

'You're far less obvious. I don't want you to do anything dangerous; I just want Freath alone and feeling vulnerable. I have no intention of talking to him in front of his companion.'

'How far do I take my spying duties?'

Faris shrugged. 'Well, don't sleep with him, my love,' he laughed, avoiding her determined slap, 'but stick close enough.'

'Don't let him out of my sight, you mean.'

'Exactly. We are going to separate them somehow and I want someone inconspicuous watching the friend to know if there is anything sinister about Freath's intentions.'

She sighed. 'Fine. When?'

'In the next couple of days. Now, forget that packing. Let me show you how much I care about you.' He arched an eyebrow.

Lily fell back into his arms and they toppled together onto the bed. Faris tried desperately to lose himself in their affections but at the back of his mind his demon, his ever-present companion, began to gnaw more urgently. He was shocked by Lily's observation; the fact that Leo had noticed as well meant that Jewd had long been aware of the deliberate distance Kilt had created between himself and the king. Jewd was too shrewd to make his queries as pointed as Lily; no, his friend would watch and make up his own mind. Kilt would have to be very, very careful from here on. He'd given his word to Brennus and would not break it, but in order to keep it he was going to have to exercise still more control while making a greater effort to close that gap between himself and Leo.

3

On the other side of the realm, in a sparsely populated hamlet not far from Minton Woodlet, a dark-eyed youth with hair the colour of damp soil broke his fast with a bowl of creamed oats. He sat quietly at a plain scrubbed table and stared out of a small window into the overcast, drizzly day that the south was experiencing. From time to time he'd trickle a small amount of thick milk into his bowl to cool and liquefy the steaming, delicious glug.

There were only three small rooms to the tiny cottage and a man bustled in from one of the others now. 'Nearly done?' he asked brightly. 'Did I get it right?'

The youngster turned and nodded. 'Delicious,' he said, wiping his mouth on his sleeve.

'Good. Hurry up and finish. I'd like us to get going early,' the man continued conversationally, leaning to look out of a window as he poured himself some dinch from the pot simmering at the fire. 'It's not too cold but the wet weather means you should be able to find us some saramac. I have to go out for a short while. Just to Minton Woodlet.'

The youth kept ladling the oats into his mouth, eating precisely, swallowing carefully.

'Oh, and excellent news, my boy. I don't know what you did but the hens are laying again and Bonny's leg is healed fully. She's going to be just fine. I'd like to think it was my herbals,' the man said, turning to stare affectionately as the boy scraped the last of the oats from his bowl, 'but I know it was you.'

The youth put his spoon into the bowl with a soft clang and looked up. 'Not all me.' He shrugged, self-consciously. 'I like to use it for good.'

'I know. Just remember, we must keep those skills between us. Never show them off. Never.'

The boy nodded. 'I know that. I'm finished,' he said, standing. He lifted the bowl and jug to take them outside to rinse.

'All right, then. You leave that. I can clear things up. Let's get you on your way. You know what to look for. I need as many of the fungi as you can find.'

'You won't be long, will you?'

'No, Piven.'

Piven nodded. 'Be safe, Greven,' he said, slinging a small sack around his body and reaching for his hat from the hook behind the door.

'You too, my boy.' Greven smoothed away the flopping dark waves of hair and kissed Piven's forehead, as he always did when they said goodbye.

Piven regarded him gravely. 'The sores have almost gone.'

Greven nodded. 'I can hardly believe it. All that's left to remind me I've had leprosy is this tremor,' he said, holding out a hand.

'I'm sure I can heal that too,' Piven said. 'If you'll let me,' he added.

Greven watched the orphaned adopted son of the Valisars leave the cottage quietly. He frowned. He'd never questioned that he'd done the right thing in stealing the boy away from the barbarian. That big black bird of omen had led him to Brighthelm and to the child in need — he was sure of it. He'd fought the inclination to follow the bird but he had especially fought getting so close to city folk, and particularly folk of the palace. But the raven had been persistent, staring at him for days, then when Greven finally agreed to follow, returning time and again, swooping and demanding that he continue on the pathway. And though Greven knew where the bird was leading him, he didn't know why and he feared what he might discover.

He found a helpless, invalid child. And the bird had somehow called to that child, for Piven had looked up and looked straight at them, even though they had been hidden in the tree line on the edge of the forest. The boy had risen and without any hesitation had moved towards them. Greven had felt the irresistible pull towards the young boy, and in spite of every screaming reservation, he had held out a hand and welcomed the child.

Their life had been quiet and uneventful, each of them deriving security from the other. And while Greven offered Piven a life, the boy — fast becoming a young man — had offered Greven hope.

He'd been running from the threat of his pursuer all of his life, so why now, when he was more free, more isolated than he'd been in a long time, did he feel so anxious?

People knew him as Jon Lark, the herbalist who lived with his son, Petor. Once again he was raising a child alone. He'd known about this adopted son of the Valisars who had been mute, indeed lost in his mind — everyone in Penraven knew of the beloved Piven. But within days of their first clasping hands Piven had shocked him by talking. At first it had been halting and of course childish. He had, after all, only been five. Now he was a gangly youth of fifteen anni.

Greven had hoped the boy would forget his past but Piven had forgotten nothing; his recall in fact was daunting. He could describe Brighthelm in detail, walking Greven mentally through the various chambers. He spoke lovingly of his parents especially his mother, whose face he remembered so well that he had drawn her for Greven, and he could see that Piven caught her likeness with uncanny skill. Most of all he talked about his brother, Leo, and had talked a great deal about reuniting with his sibling. He never spoke of Leo as his half-brother, nor did he speak of the years he had been trapped in his silence, his own world.

Greven had tried to discover why Piven had been unable to communicate and, more to the point, how he could suddenly speak so well and so easily for a person who had not used his voice. When he asked Piven the boy would shrug and become introverted and Greven had long ago decided that he was fortunate to have the child at all — and animated besides. The whys and wherefores of his life before they shared it were of no relevance — or so Greven told himself. He himself never spoke of the life he'd had before Piven, and when word had filtered down through the folk who lived amongst and around the forest that Lily had looked for him, he had resisted the deep urge to answer those enquiries.

But what did puzzle, and to some extent unnerve Greven, was the youngster's ability with magic. The extent of that skill remained untapped, and if Greven had his way, that was how it would remain. But Piven was still a very young man, with all the foibles of youth. There had been occasions on which Piven had shown off, hoping to impress Greven with what he could do. And there were other times, when he was angry, that Greven feared for what havoc the child might wreak. He mostly contented himself with healing magics but Greven was worried that Piven was simply biding his time with his skills. More recently he had begun to catch his adopted son deep in thought, a darkness haunting the youngster's face, giving it shadows that shouldn't be there at his age. But Piven refused to discuss those haunted moments.

To be fair, as he matured he also refused to take credit for all the brightness that his skills did bring. Curing the leprosy had been an astonishing feat that Greven still struggled to comprehend. How had Piven done that? He had simply passed his hands once over the afflicted areas and the eruptions that had once so plagued Greven's life had instantly begun to recede until only the lightest of scarring could attest to the fact that he had ever suffered the disease. And the scars continued to lighten. The tremor alone told the truth of what he had been … what he still was.

In the last few moons, though, the moments of shadow had increased. Not so noticeably that it had become an issue but sometimes he would catch Piven standing alone outside, as if caught in a trance. And when Greven would call out to Piven, and the boy would turn and look at him … there was something odd about it. It wasn't frightening so much as unnerving; he couldn't fathom what the boy was thinking. He sometimes wondered if Piven knew the truth when he looked at him like that.

The most recent of these events had occurred six days previous, when he had risen to give Piven the news that Bonny, their donkey, had gone lame. Piven always rose first, curiously enough, and had set the oats on to cook, stirring dutifully to release all their gluey starch. After Greven had told him about the donkey Piven had gone outside, saying he would milk Belle, their cow. Greven had let him go, thinking the boy was upset about Bonny, but not long after he'd walked up to the hearth and found Piven in one of his dark trances, his face pinched in a frown. Greven had said his name loudly but Piven had not reacted, or even given the impression he'd heard. But moments after that the boy had returned, beaming a smile that looked full of the warmth of a thousand suns. 'You don't have to destroy Bonny. I believe she will recover,' Piven had said.

Right enough, the swelling around the beast's leg had begun to dissipate when Greven went out to check. He'd shaken his head. He had thought he would be slitting the animal's throat. Instead, he was giving it a fresh nosebag of feed. Now the leg had healed.

Yes, life with Piven was good.

However, as if Lo himself had decided to intervene, word had arrived from Master Junes at Minton Woodlet that there was a nice couple looking to speak to him — *an older couple from Medhaven who seem to know you from your youth*, Junes had added and for some reason Greven's internal alarms had begun to sound. He didn't know why but he found it worrying that these people were interested in his child. In Piven. Did they know? He felt anxious and fearful.

'But it must not show!' he admonished himself. And it wouldn't. His grey-peppered hair was tied neatly back into a pigtail. He had clipped his beard this morning and he had on his best shirt. He looked tidy, clean, respectable ... not at all like the once-wandering leper who had crept through the forest with a five-anni-old boy and a strange black raven for company.

He left the cottage. It was time to face them. If worst came to worst, he and Piven could go on the run again, but he needed to know what they were up against. He needed to know if Emperor Loethar had discovered his secret.

Piven disappeared into the shadows of the forest but once he knew he was no longer visible he turned and watched the cottage. He may be young in summers, he thought, but no one realised, perhaps least of all Greven, how much older in his mind he truly was. In fact, Piven was keenly aware of his own curious maturity and he deliberately tried to keep it hidden as best he could. Initially he had been embarrassed by his own perceptive ability but now he realised it wasn't a gift. No, to him, the new knowledge, the increasing sense of purpose that was still tinged with confusion but nevertheless gnawed at him relentlessly, had a far darker feeling to it ... and was part of the magic he had discovered within himself. His maturity had become his curse and now he hated where his thoughts ran.

As his self-consciousness had increased, he had become cagey about his awareness, hiding it by acting far more naive than he was, hoping his contrived innocence might appear acceptable for a youth of his age. But while he and Greven did lead a closeted existence, well removed from others, naturally their paths crossed regularly with the villagers of Minton Woodlet. During these times he interacted with his peers, and in their company he felt like a stranger. Not because he didn't know them — some he knew well — but because the trivia that occupied their conversation or their play seemed so juvenile.

The raven arrived, swooping to land on a branch just above his head to interrupt his thoughts.

'Hello, Vyk,' he said softly. 'Your timing is perfect as always.'

The great black bird stared at him from above and Piven read query in the look even though his companion's expression never changed. He explained about Greven's urgency to get him out of the cottage. 'He says he's got an appointment but Greven doesn't have *appointments*.' He loaded the last word with irony. 'He's up to something. He was nervous this morning, very anxious to get me gone.' He glanced at the bird and continued as though it had spoken to him. 'No, I don't know why but I can sense that it's connected to me; something he's frightened about. But he can't have guessed.'

Piven sighed. 'It's hard to imagine that I spent the first five anni as a halfwit. Now I wish I wasn't so aware of life around me. Why can't I be like other boys my age and fret about whether a girl likes me, or why I can't kick the pigskin around as skilfully as John Daw, or jump a horse over the nine-mile gate as fearlessly as Doon Fowler? Instead, I'm having thoughts about the politics of our land, or I'm considering the undercurrent in a conversation between Greven and the widow, Evelyn; or I'm constantly ten steps ahead in every discussion I share with Greven, trying to prepare the way so he doesn't discover that I understand so much more than he thinks … and that I know so much more than he does.'

Piven broke a small twig from a branch in frustration. 'Why is this happening, Vyk? I'm fifteen, not fifty. I want to be like the boys I know. Instead, I'm terrified by my own dreams. I'm dreaming regularly about a woman. I don't recognise her but I know she's special. She's so real in my mind that I often try and reach out to touch her but she's just a vision, nothing more. And yet,' he glanced up at the bird, who appeared to be paying close attention, 'there are moments when I think she's aware of me.' He shook his head. 'I know that sounds ridiculous. She's a dream. But she's so different from my other dreams — the ones that scare me, the ones that are dark and filled with anger. They urge me to allow my true self to come through, but I'm too scared to find out who I am.'

Ravan flapped down and sat on the boy's shoulder. Piven smiled. 'You are a comfort to me, Vyk. You always have been. I know you go back to Loethar whenever you're not here. I like that you listen — I couldn't let anyone else hear these thoughts. Look,' he said, pointing. 'There goes Greven. Why would he be so dressed up? His meetings are usually with farmers and he only wears that jacket and shirt if he's attending a wedding or a funeral. And I know he's going to neither.'

Piven watched in silence as Greven disappeared down the incline. Then he continued. 'Whoever he's meeting, I know it's not good news for us. I know it's going to affect me and this is not a good time.' He banged the tree. 'Not a good time at all! Something's happening to me. Do you know I soured the milk yesterday? Greven made me cross because he didn't like my mending a squirrel with a broken leg, and my bad humour curdled the entire pail I'd just milked from Belle. I'm sure he knew it too because he hasn't said too much about Bonny's lameness that is now miraculously cured.

'I thought curing her would make me feel happy; I try to use my skills wisely but for all the good they can do, I'm paying a price. I'm sure of it. My heart is filling with hate, Vyk; I feel increasingly angry at my situation and yet just a few months ago I couldn't have been happier. And nothing's changed. I'm leading the same life, which I love, and yet I feel such rage. I can control it — my anger — but when I exercise that control, quelling the power inside, quietening my fury, something bad happens, like the soured milk. And it's going to get worse. I sense it. I'm frightened by it. I just want everything to remain the same but I think Greven's meeting today will change everything.' He knew he was rambling; words were tumbling out of his mouth furiously, crowding together and turning into a tirade.

The bird shifted on his shoulder, making a clacking sound near his ear. It sounded like a question.

'I don't know. That's just it, I don't know, but this darkness, this growing up so fast and this new awareness about myself is driving me towards something, or someone, and I'm not sure I can control my urge any longer. Besides, Greven thinks he's got me fooled. I admire his cunning and I especially admire his courage because this life of his must require a will of iron, but he underestimates me. And soon I won't be able to shield him from the truth any longer.'

He shrugged and the raven leapt to another branch. 'It's the magic, Vyk, it's not me. Promise me we'll always be friends, no matter what. I sense you understand me, even if you can't tell me as much. Don't desert me, even if I disappoint you — or frighten you. The magic controls me now and I need to understand it more. Someone somewhere must know what it wants.'

Piven turned sadly and trudged deeper into the forest in search of the fungi he knew they would never use.

4

Oblivious to Piven's pain, Greven strode into Minton Woodlet, a village with one inn but with a second being built, testimony to the growing importance of the village's hardy golasses vines. It seemed the barbarians enjoyed the dense, dark wines of the south that drew their flavours from the salty air of the sea nearby and the earthiness of the forest that they flanked. Greven was sure that even within a few anni, Minton Woodlet would be a flourishing southern town with a burgeoning population, swelled by the transient workers who streamed into the region at grape-picking time. His and Piven's days were numbered here.

'Hello, Jon,' an attractive woman said, slowing her walk as she approached him.

He liked Evelyn but not as much or in the same way that she liked him. He could almost regret the tumble they had taken together in his bed when Piven had once again been out hunting down the precious saramac fungus. That had been when the outward signs of his leprosy had begun to disappear and he had been feeling particularly joyous about Piven's astonishing healing skills. Piven could work miracles; the boy made him look like a charlatan with his silly herbals. But now those skills frightened him. Piven had been a lot sunnier then and Greven knew that the boy's present disposition was not simply the result of becoming a moody youth; it was more than that. It was a feeling of darkness.

'Jon, you old devil, you look more handsome with each passing moon,' Evelyn said. 'Your skin looks mighty good.'

Even from the early days with Piven the side of his face most affected by the lesions had dried up, looking more like a skin complaint than anything more serious. He'd stuck to that story, explaining it was a result of accidental poisoning from some of his less predictable plants, and people had accepted it, especially as the sores no longer looked like traditional leprosy.

'Yes, it seems the poison has finally worked its way out of my body,' he smiled.

'Indeed. You look very good, very smart.'

'Thank you. I'm seeing some people who knew me from my childhood at Medhaven,' he said, hoping to move on quickly.

But Evelyn clearly wanted to linger. 'Oh, that would be the couple staying at the Grape and Whistle?'

Greven felt a prick of fear sting him but he kept his voice even. 'Probably,' he replied absently and then in an effort to distance himself from the visitors added: 'I hope I recognise them. I haven't seen them in many anni.'

'I've just been speaking with them. Clovis and Reuth, right?'

Greven feigned a smile. 'That's right,' he said, as if he'd heard their names for the first time in a very long time.

'Nice people.' She frowned, and he could almost see her reaching for the opportunity to prolong this meeting. 'How do you kno—?'

'Forgive me, Evelyn, but I mustn't be late. And I've promised to call in on old Bern; his gout's playing up.' Greven began to move forward. 'I really must find a better remedy than the one we're using now.' He smiled in genuine apology. 'Sorry to rush off.'

She returned his smile, although hers was tinged with sadness, as if she knew he needed to escape her. He would have to confront this matter again, he realised. He needed to be forthright but gentle, rather than relying on this cowardly avoidance. But not today.

He lifted a hand in farewell and turned his back on Evelyn to complete his journey into Minton Woodlet. It was a busy morning. He'd forgotten it was market day but that suited him; more people around meant it would be easier to talk to the strangers without drawing attention.

The Grape and Whistle loomed. Greven felt a mad desire to turn and run, to run as far away from this place as possible. He had an ominous sense of doom closing in. It was getting harder to fight the illness he'd suffered since birth, of course. He thought of it as a disease and rather than fighting his urges he'd given in to them, little by little. By exposing himself to his desires, he had taught himself how to stay on top of the driving need. The forest helped, and the forced removal from society that the telltale leprosy had required was the best remedy of all, but still he tempted fate, deliberately remaining close to the eye of the storm, in the hope that as the years passed he would master full control.

And he had. By the time he found the courage to follow the raven to the fringe of the forest that day, he was confident of his immunity to his weakness. And had demonstrated it. But he wondered now if Piven's wild and powerful magic might somehow seek out the truth. He didn't understand it — it didn't make sense — but he found himself unable to spend great lengths of time around the boy. He particularly hated his testiness around his child but lately he was having to dig deeper and deeper to wrestle his urge to walk out of the forest that hid him so well. Perhaps he should tell the boy. Piven might be able to help him.

Greven shook his head. It was a glorious Blossomtide day, and this meeting had nothing to do with that old fear. Still, he needed to summon his courage to force himself across the threshold of the inn.

Minton Woodlet was not a direct route to anywhere in particular but it did serve as a logical stopping point for anyone heading to or from the island of Medhaven. As he cast a glance around the main front room of the inn, he saw only strangers — all travellers, he assumed — aside from the familiar faces of the people who worked at the inn.

'Ho, Jon,' someone said and Greven looked over to the counter where the innkeeper was drying and lining up cleaned mugs for the day's service.

'Hello, Derrin.'

'They're out the back, in the courtyard. Warming their bones, they said.' Derrin smiled. 'They said they haven't seen you for donkey's anni. Family?'

Greven shook his head. He wanted to say as little as possible about these people he feared. 'People I knew when I was very young.'

Innkeeper Derrin nodded. 'Plenty to chew the cud over then,' he said. 'Shall I send you out a pot of dinch? They're taking their time over a morning meal.'

Greven nodded. 'A strong one.' He moved to the back of the chamber and through a doorway into the back of the property where a picturesque walled courtyard opened up. A small, circular fountain in the middle was the focal point. Around it skipped two children, the boy older than the girl, who was presumably his sister. And sitting at the back wall, talking quietly, was a couple in their middle age. They both stood as Greven walked towards them, and Greven was taken aback to see that they appeared as nervous as he felt.

'I'm Lark.' He pasted an expression of puzzlement on his face. 'You asked to see me?'

'Clovis and Reuth Barrow,' the man replied. 'These are our children.' He held out his hand.

Greven prided himself on being a good judge of character. The face of the man standing before him struck him as sensitive. Despite his broad chest and height, Clovis Barrow didn't seem to be in any way threatening. In fact, it was the dark-eyed woman in whom Greven sensed real strength. He shook both of their hands.

'Welcome to Minton Woodlet, though what interest it could possibly hold for you I don't know.' He forced a gentle smile. 'This is a very sleepy hamlet.'

His amiable tone broke through the initial tension. 'Will you join us?' Reuth said. 'We've just finished breaking a late fast but —'

'Dinch is on the way,' Greven said reassuringly. Curiously, they sounded more unsure about him than he felt about them. Why would they be so hesitant?

'Please,' Clovis said, gesturing to a third chair at the small table.

'Forgive our mess,' Reuth added, trying to clear away the debris of four meals.

Greven sat, watching his hosts fuss. They were both roughly the same age — the woman slightly older, perhaps — and now that he looked at them more closely he would put them at approaching fifty anni, older than he'd first thought. The woman was silvering at the hairline while the man's hair and beard were streaked with grey throughout — and yet their children were young. Second marriage, Greven guessed. But what had this family to do with him? He waited, preferring to let them do the talking.

'I know you must be wondering why we asked to see you,' Clovis began.

'I am,' Greven replied.

'Please don't fear us, Mr Lark,' Reuth assured, looking at her husband and nodding encouragingly.

'I don't,' Greven lied.

'We're not here to cause trouble,' Clovis continued.

'Thank you,' Greven said, determined to give little of himself away.

Reuth looked up as the door into the courtyard banged. 'I think your dinch is here, Mr Lark.'

'Call me Jon,' Greven said, 'since apparently we're all old friends.'

The man and wife nodded, glancing nervously at each other. They were frightened, Greven realised. That made him feel more assured than he'd felt since the moment he'd first received word of being asked after. And Piven was safe in the woods, where no one would find him.

The pot of dinch was served. 'Can I get you anything else?' the girl asked his hosts.

They both shook their heads and she smiled sweetly and left. Greven poured from the pot, more for something to do than from a desire to drink. When the couple remained silent, he spoke up boldly.

'Master Clovis, Reuth, I don't know either of you but I've had to pretend I do in order not to confuse the folk I live alongside each day. Now whether you're from Medhaven or as far flung as Percheron I could not care, but I require an explanation for why you are here, masquerading as old friends.' He sighed. 'I don't care for secrets,' he lied.

Reuth nodded. 'Tell him everything, Clovis.'

Clovis cleared his throat and Greven gave the man his full attention, surprised to see the couple give a surreptitious glance around.

'We are alone,' he assured. 'Whatever you have to say will not be overheard.'

'I was at Brighthelm soon after the invasion of Penraven — so was my wife. We had been rounded up and taken with other Vested to learn our fate. Some of us they wanted, others they killed. There was no way of knowing which we'd be. It was a terrible time,' Clovis said and Reuth placed a hand on his arm. 'Anyway,' he continued. 'That's all history. We were saved by a man called Freath — one of the close aides to the Valisars. We never fully appreciated his perilous position and how he endangered his life daily to keep us safe and to protect the Valisar sons.'

'Forgive me. While tragic though it all was, I have to wonder at this point why I'm here ... what your story has to do with me,' Greven said, as politely but firmly as he could.

Reuth smiled. 'Clovis is always one to tell a story.'

Clovis cleared his throat. 'I shall finish it quickly then,' he said but without any offence in his voice. 'While Reuth was fortunate to be given an escape route by Freath, I was kept behind and became privy to some of Freath's plans. I know not only did the heir, Leonel, escape the palace but I also know that the other adopted son who was simple of mind, also somehow got away. He was lost, in fact, for want of a better word. Freath was inconsolable and as I did not have the stomach for his intrigues and what they required, I agreed to leave the relative safety of the palace to find Piven. I found Reuth first but I have never stopped looking for the boy.'

'This is all fascinating, I'll admit,' Greven said, eyeing the couple, masking his despair with an ingenuous smile and a soft shake of the head. It seemed his fears had finally come home to roost this bright Blossomtide day. 'But I fail to see how —'

'The boy you live with is the son of the Valisar royals, isn't he?' Reuth pressed, leaning forward.

Greven didn't know how to answer. He froze, searching for the right response that did not incriminate him or Piven.

Clovis sighed. 'Master Lark, you should know that as a Master Diviner, my inherent skills have assisted in finding you. But, more importantly, my wife has visions. It was her magic that, after years of me searching, led me to you.'

Greven regarded them both, his face deliberately devoid of expression but his insides churning with anxiety.

'You have nothing to fear from us, Master Lark,' Clovis repeated. 'As I explained, it has been my mission for the last decade to find the boy.'

'Why?'

'Do you admit that the child you call Petor is Piven, the invalid adopted son of the Valisars?'

'Absolutely not,' Greven replied, his throat threatening to close on the lie. He filled his lungs with indignation and continued, 'This is an outrageous claim and I'll ask you not to levy such accusations publicly.'

Clovis shook his head. 'I only want to protect him. I would do nothing that might bring him harm. I know you wish only the same, which is why you are covering Piven's true identity.'

'Master Barrow —'

'May we meet him?' Reuth asked, cutting across Greven's outrage.

'Pardon?'

'May we meet the boy? Although I only know of the child, Clovis has seen him at close range. He will know him.'

'I have no intention of permitting you to scrutinise my son,' Greven snapped. 'How dare you,' he muttered. 'How dare you walk into my life like this and make such claims.'

Clovis shook his head with sorrow. 'Master Lark, I witnessed many people lose their lives brutally on the order of the barbarian tyrant. Reuth watched her beloved former husband led away to be slaughtered in a dingy courtyard; she could hear his death cries alongside those of the others who posed as Vested. My first wife and my precious infant daughter were hacked to death by the barbarian warrior who calls himself general. Our magnanimous emperor who now masquerades as a just and good ruler stole his crown in a sea of blood, Master Lark. I'm sure you know that.'

Greven nodded unhappily, shocked and helplessly touched by the tale of this pair.

'We have reason to hold a grudge against the tyrant.'

'But what does my son have to do with your mission?' Greven asked carefully.

'If he is your son, then he has nothing to do with us,' Clovis said. 'If he is Piven, as we believe he is, then he is integral to the struggle.'

'The struggle? What are you talking about?'

Clovis lowered his voice still further. 'To reinstate the true king onto his throne.'

Greven looked back at the intense expressions on the couple's faces. They were earnest. 'Piven?'

'No, Leo,' Clovis said. 'We all believe he lives.'

'We?'

'The Vested,' Reuth answered. 'Those of us who survived took a marking.' She turned, pulling back her ear and Greven saw a crescent moon marked in ink on her skin. 'Master Lark, I should admit to you that my curious and contrary skill is to sense when something bad might occur. It is a strong power when it speaks to me but it speaks rarely. For instance, I knew they were coming for me, even though we had hidden my talent all my life. I also knew my husband would die, no matter what we did to protect him. I sensed that the royal family would suffer — I didn't see the deaths but I sensed there would be only misery for the Valisars who might survive. And, Master Lark, when you first walked into this courtyard I sensed a terrible foreboding. I don't know if it is for you, or your son, or whether it is the stars aligning to bring grief to your life but something very bad is going to happen. It is not far away. You should be warned.'

Greven stood. 'Stay away from me,' he demanded, pointing his finger at the two of them. 'Stay away from Petor.'

Clovis looked past Greven. 'You're alarming our children, Master Lark, and risking drawing attention to yourself.'

'You are strangers in this hamlet. I am not. My son and I have lived here for —'

'Ten anni,' Reuth finished for him, calmly. 'Yes, we know. And that's the exact amount of time that Clovis has been searching for the Valisar child. You forget that we were involved in the struggle for the Valisar survival at the outset. We have never given up our fight to return the rightful king to his throne.'

Greven leapt onto what he thought could be his final diversion. 'Except you are ignoring one very important fact.'

'And that is?' Reuth asked.

'You are very clear that the child known as Piven is an invalid.'

Clovis and Reuth nodded. 'He never spoke a word, and was very much lost in his mind,' Clovis said.

'Well, for your information, Petor is extremely able. He talks as any normal child of fifteen might talk,' Greven insisted, leaning forward on the table to impress his point. 'He is lively and animated.'

Reuth frowned, glancing at her husband.

'Check with the townsfolk if you don't believe me,' Greven baited. 'The child you seek is not my Petor. It's just an unfortunate coincidence that both boys are the same age.' He could almost see the disappointment emanating from them like a dark cloud.

Clovis sighed. 'Still, I would like to see him.'

'I forbid it. You will not frighten my child.'

'Master Lark, how can two people like us with our young family be in any way intimidating?' Reuth asked.

'Well, you've done your utmost to intimidate me and I refuse you access to my son, do you hear? Go away and leave us in peace.'

'I cannot,' Clovis said. His voice sounded grave enough to chill Greven. 'I gave my word to people who were risking their lives every hour of those terrible days of the overthrow to keep Piven alive. I promised I would find him. I think I have.'

'Go away,' Greven said helplessly. He turned his back on them, calling over his shoulder, 'And stay away.'

He threw two trents onto the counter before Innkeeper Derrian Junes and didn't pause to exchange pleasantries. He was gone in seconds, striding out of the Grape and Whistle and hurrying as fast as his long legs could carry him towards the forest, where the trees swallowed him up and, he hoped, could hide him.

5

Piven waited for Greven. He had filled the small sack near to brimming with fungi that would need to dry out on the hut's windowsill, and it was now duly laid out as Greven liked. Life with Greven had been tranquil, mostly serene. Each day was similar to the previous. And he liked it that way. He liked its order, its sameness … its predictability. He didn't call Greven 'Father'; couldn't call him by that name, much as he knew Greven would like him to, because he remembered King Brennus too clearly. He belonged to the royal family of Valisars — that could and would never change for him. He never wondered about his blood parents, refused to accept that somewhere in the Set a woman who had birthed him might still live or a man who had sired him might roam.

The raven had lingered, staying close as he busied himself finding the elusive fungi. He wondered if the bird — who he felt sure knew things — had sensed his change occurring. He knew Vyk could hear him; imagined the bird was capable of replying somehow, but that it had chosen not to communicate with him since he'd begun to talk. One day it would — of this he was sure. And so he talked, over his shoulder, never tiring of hearing his own voice, which had been silent for so long.

'… and should be back soon if you're wondering,' he said, laying out the fungi beneath the warmth of the sun. 'You'll be surprised when you see him. His face, body, arms are now all clear of the sores. The leprosy will have left him by the rise of the next full moon. It's my greatest achievement yet,' he murmured, not meaning to boast but needing to say it aloud, to affirm his new talent.

'I told you about the dreams,' he continued. 'Strange ones. People are hunting me. I don't know them but they want to use me and I don't know how or why.' Piven turned. 'Are you faithful to Loethar, or faithful to me? Until I know, I can't fully trust you with my secrets. One day you must choose, you know that, don't you?' He dragged back the flop of hair that had covered part of his face as he turned to look at the bird. 'You will need to choose,' he said softly.

'Who are you talking to?' Piven turned to see Greven approaching up the small incline that led to their hut. The man smiled. 'Ah, Vyk. Long life to you. Good to see you back.' Then he gave a feigned sound of disgust. 'Piven, I'm as bad as you, talking to the bird. Well done, my boy, that's a very good haul,' he congratulated, spying the neat row of fungi lined up. 'Excellent, excellent. Now, child, I want to talk to you about something.'

'Oh?'

'We need to move on,' Greven continued conversationally. 'I'm bored with this place, aren't you? Perhaps we could look at Gormand, or Cremond, get lost in and around Lo's Teeth or the Dragonsback Mountains. That would be quite an exciting trip. What do you say?'

Piven's expression turned to one of puzzlement. 'Why?'

Greven looked surprised. 'Why not, I say? Don't you want to see more of the world?'

Piven shook his head. 'I want to stay here. It's peaceful.'

'True,' Greven replied, thoughtfully. 'But we can find other tranquil spots.'

'Who are we running from?'

'No one,' Greven replied firmly and too quickly, Piven thought. Then his long-time companion seemed to reconsider his suggestion. 'There's no reason to move permanently. How about some travel? I think it's high time I gave you an education about this fair land. It's safe now to roam through the realms and we can do so easily enough — thanks to you that Bonny's well. We can even use some savings to buy a mule ... or even a horse and cart.' He sounded excited but Piven heard panic driving Greven's enthusiasm. 'What do you say, eh? Are you ready for an adventure, boy?'

'When?'

'No time like the present. Come on, let's pack up a few things. We won't need very much. We can close up the hut and go.'

'What about Belle?'

'We can leave a message for Jenna. She can take Belle down to her parents' place when she picks up the next crate of herbals for her father's apothecary.'

'Who will tend the fungi?'

Greven looked up to the sky momentarily as if to calm his patience, then back at Piven. 'Come on, don't put up barriers. Let's just pack a few essentials and be gone this night.'

'You've always said never to travel at night unless you're on the run.'

He watched Greven wrestle his exasperation back under control. This man he loved smiled gently. 'I did, didn't I? All right, why don't we leave in the morning? How does that sound?'

Piven didn't think it sounded good at all but he had little choice, for Greven seemed filled with a fierce drive to be gone. Already he was beginning to tidy the few items that had been left outside around the front patch of garden. Switching topics, even though he knew that lack of protest would be taken as his agreement to leave, Piven asked, 'What happened in town today?'

'Oh, nothing much at all,' Greven said. He was packing planting pots into a crate.

'Who did you talk to?'

'I met Evelyn on the way, I spoke to Innkeeper Junes … no one in particular. All quite boring, really.'

Piven knew, without any doubt now, Greven was lying. And the lie prompted him to make his final decision.

That night Piven dreamed.

In his dream he saw a woman. He recognised her instantly; he had been dreaming about her for the last few moons. She was slim, dark-haired, and exceptionally pretty with fine features that were so angular and precise they looked as if they could have been drawn. In the dream he was hidden but he didn't know where or why. As was usual, she seemed to sense that she was being observed; kept looking around to find the voyeur. She looked strange. No, that wasn't right. Where she was looked strange. The setting was foreign to him and one he couldn't comprehend. She was busy at something but he could make no sense of it. She was in a room that was predominantly white and she was tending to someone who was lying down. There were lots of other people crowded around her, all watching what she was doing. She appeared to be talking constantly.

He called to her, surprised that he knew her name, holding his breath in the hope that the other people wouldn't hear him. The woman paused, as if a thought had struck her, and then she looked up, slightly startled, and stared straight at him.

Piven felt himself falling backwards, as if from a clifftop into a great void. He yelled his fear as winds began to buffet him, shake his bones as though he were a rag doll.

'Piven!'

He opened his eyes, shocked and alarmed. Greven was shaking him by the shoulders.

'What's happening?' Greven asked, looking suddenly old and dishevelled in his nightshirt. 'A nightmare, I think,' he said, answering his own question. 'Rest easy now, boy. No more yelling. You've probably already forgotten it.'

Piven swallowed, alarm still clanging like windchimes in his mind. He had not forgotten any of it ... or her.

'It's nearing dawn. We might as well call it morning and make a start,' Greven said, scratching his chest absently. 'I'll get some dinch on.'

He left Piven to surface fully, rub the sleep from his eyes and drag himself upright. Lethargy pulled at him like a heavy blanket and his mood felt bleak. Greven's bright whistling at the hearth irritated him and an uncharacteristic scowl darkened his expression.

'You yelled someone's name. Who were you dreaming about?' Greven called.

'I don't know,' Piven replied. 'What was the name?'

Greven returned. He was stirring something in a small pot. Eggs, Piven thought, he's readying them for scrambling. He was not hungry. 'Do you know, I heard you scream it but I can't remember now. Can you?'

Piven shook his head. Not only could he not recall the woman's name but her features were disappearing from his mind. Suddenly he could no longer see her pretty face.

Greven chuckled. 'Ah well, fret not, my boy. Soon you won't be having nightmares about women. You'll be dreaming happily about them morning, noon and night!'

Piven's sour mood deepened.

'Oh, would you look at that!' he heard Greven mutter in disgust. 'I think the wretched eggs are off.' Piven watched Greven lift the heavy earthen jug and sniff. 'Bah! Gone! They're yesterday's, aren't they?'

Piven nodded.

'How can that happen?' Greven asked, and although Piven decided his question did not require a response, he had a sickening feeling that he knew the answer.

Reuth sighed. 'Perhaps we sent word too fast,' she said, wiping their son's face with a wet flannel.

Clovis grimaced. 'Too fast? It's been a decade!'

She gave him a look of soft rebuke. 'You know what I mean.'

He finished tying the laces on their daughter's dress. 'There you go. Now you look pretty enough to eat.' He pretended to chew her neck and his little girl squealed with frightened delight. He loved to hear her voice. And far from being embittered by it, he felt blessed by Lo that his second daughter reminded him so starkly of Corin, his first beautiful — now dead — child. Whether it was fact or his imagination, they seemed to share the same tone and pitch in voice; Corin used to squeal in an identical manner when he teased her. He could not risk his precious children — or Reuth, come to that. 'We are not wrong. We can't both feel so strongly about this child and be wrong.'

Reuth looked over at him sorrowfully. 'I worry that we've been searching for so long that we just want this to be him so badly that we've convinced ourselves it is so. Eat your oats, you two, they should be cool enough now,' she said, pointing to the faintly steaming bowls in which porridge had begun to set. 'Your father will pour the milk in, the jug's too heavy for you.'

They'd had food for the children sent up. They would eat downstairs in the dining room. Clovis trickled the creamy milk into two small bowls and the children greedily tucked into their first meal of the day.

'Slowly,' Reuth cautioned their son. 'Or you'll spill it.' He'd obviously heard the same cautions so many times before that he neither looked up nor slowed down; the words had become a meaningless mantra, Clovis could see.

'Listen to me, Reuth,' he said, once the children were ignoring anything but their bellies. 'I could feel his fear. The boy is Piven.'

'Well, unless we've been dancing to a different tune all these anni, Clovis, I could swear that the child we seek is mute, lost in his mind, even mad, some say. You yourself have told me he couldn't speak, communicate, showed no emotion ... acted like a moving statue, you once told me.'

Clovis nodded, trying not to interrupt her but knowing his senses contradicted everything he knew to be true. 'I did. And that is how he was.'

'And now you accept that he talks, is able, is fully healthy and as normal as our own son?' she demanded.

Clovis shooshed her silently with a gesture of his hands. 'I know how it sounds. I know how incomprehensible it is. But do you deny me that you too felt something when you met Lark?'

She turned away. 'You know I can't.'

'Tell me again.'

Reuth turned back to him, and he watched her quell her exasperation. 'I had a vision. Fast, gone in a blink. Doom surrounds him.'

'Think, Reuth. Interpret that doom for me.'

She looked lost. 'I can't,' she said helplessly. 'It didn't just spell doom for him, though. I got the impression that it was foreboding for all of us. Where Jon Lark treads, he will bring darkness to the world.'

Clovis shook his head, and walked over to the tiny window that overlooked the main street of Minton Woodlet. A young woman was leading a cow past the inn. Beyond her, vineyards stretched into the distance. She stopped to talk to an older woman, stroking the patient beast and pointing back up the hill. She had a pretty smile even though she herself was quite plain. At last she nodded, gave a small wave as the pair of them parted and then continued along at the ponderous pace of the black and white cow. He watched her disappear from the limited view the small window afforded him.

'What are you thinking?' Reuth prompted from behind him.

'I want you and the children to return to Medhaven.'

'We're not splitting up, Clovis.'

'You saw foreboding. I divined that we were closer yesterday to what we seek than we have been in the last ten anni. I sensed Jon Lark was lying. Now I don't know who or what he is. Neither do I care. I believe that he loves his son. I think both of us could tell he was protecting the boy, not just being belligerent. But I do think the child he loves is the orphan Piven. I can't explain Lark's claim that the boy talks. I can't comprehend why Innkeeper Junes should confirm the fact that the boy known as Petor is a run-of-the-mill youth. But, Reuth, you and I accept magic as easily as we breathe. We should be able to accept that some sorcery has occurred, something of an enchanted nature has affected this child.'

'If he's Piven,' his wife reiterated.

'If he's Piven,' Clovis repeated with resignation.

'And we can't be sure he is.'

'Which is why I want you to return to our home with our children and wait for word.'

'Where are you going?'

'To find Kirin. He has a different sort of skill. Perhaps together ...' Clovis shrugged.

'You're walking back into the palace?' Reuth exclaimed. 'It's your own death warrant you're agreeing to.'

Clovis shook his head. 'I doubt it. I shall dye my hair, shave off my beard. You agree I am only half the man I was when we met and I'm ten anni older. Different clothes, different look, different attitude. I can be someone different. And I doubt the emperor gives a fig about a man who disappeared so long ago.'

'No, but his evil general might. Remember how he vowed to track down every Vested in the land?'

'He will not know I'm Vested. No one will know. I will take a different name.'

'What if they ask for papers?'

'I'll have some forged.'

Reuth looked pained, but remained silent.

Clovis guessed her concern. 'Our savings will be put to good use, I promise. Besides, Freath can probably —'

'I don't care about money, Clovis. You are risking your life.'

'Reuth,' he began firmly. 'I was a coward all those years ago. Kirin wasn't. I have existed with the shame of my fleeing from Brighthelm to your arms. I gave my promise I would find Piven for Freath, and now that I believe I have, I intend to deliver on that promise. The least I can do is tell Freath — our only ally alongside Kirin at the palace.'

'*If that's him!*' Reuth said, her voice almost in agony.

'It's him,' Clovis said.

'And then what will you do? Hunt him down yourself?'

'If I must.'

She shook her head with a combination of vexation and anxiety and turned away. He put his long arms around her, and kissed her head, knowing she needed his tenderness. Finding Piven had been the only contentious part of their marriage. She had never fully understood his private crusade, although she had helped him constantly in his mission.

'Please, my love,' he said, turning her now to face him. 'Please understand. I do this not for personal redemption but for all of us. Your vision frightens me. I have lost one child, one wife. I refuse to lose this family and if what you see should be allowed to occur all of us will be under threat — once again.'

Reuth's forehead crinkled. 'It's a different sort of threat this time, Clovis.'

'What do you mean?'

She shrugged. 'I don't really know what I mean. I haven't seen anything other than what I've told you but what I felt when I had that vision was cold. Loethar was ruthless and did take his crown with a bloodied hand, but he has not laid waste to our land. The initial slaughter aside, he has performed somewhat magnanimously as an emperor.'

'I can't believe you just said that,' Clovis said, shocked.

Reuth shook her head. 'Believe me, if what I sensed does come true, this new menace will make the memories of Loethar's overthrow pale. I hope I'm wrong but I believe what's coming at us lacks a soul. No ordinary man will be able to stop this.'

They stared at each other for several searching moments as both digested Reuth's dire counsel. It was she who broke the spell between them. 'I'll pack up our things. The children and I will return immediately south to the ferry. We'll wait for word from you from Medhaven.'

Clovis hugged her tight, closing his eyes and breathing in the scent of his wife's hair … as his belly clenched with fear.

6

Freath slowed the horse to a gentle walk. It had been a long time since he'd visited the north and even longer since he'd entered Francham. The last time had been prior to Leo's birth, when he'd accompanied King Brennus and his new bride, Iselda, on an around-the-realm meet and greet. Brennus had been keen to show off his exotic wife from Galinsea and to silence the mumbling detractors who had begun to spread word that no woman from the Set had been good enough for Brennus. Freath knew the king had hoped that by introducing his lovely young bride to his people in person, they would fall in love with her as easily as he had. His strategy had worked.

Penraven hadn't seen anything like it since the coronation of Brennus but, as eligible and handsome as the new young king had been at the time, his 'crowning tour' lacked the glamour that a beautiful young woman added. And Iselda understood immediately how to achieve her husband's aim. She had never complained once about the gruelling schedule, Freath recalled. She had chosen her wardrobe with care to ensure that everywhere she visited the people were left in awe of her glittering presence — and, Freath remembered with a soft smile, Iselda had never needed jewels to glitter. Her smile was full and genuine and she had managed to draw all she met into its comforting warmth. She had possessed an unwavering ability to remain cheerful despite her fatigue, and dig deep to find energy that often surpassed that of her stronger, older entourage. It was Iselda who had first climbed down from her horse to pause a while and talk to people, to kiss the foreheads of babies and allow the women to clasp at her gloved hands. At first even Freath had been alarmed but alongside Brennus he'd watched how instantly and excitedly the folk had reacted to this show of generosity that had no precedent. And then word had spread so quickly that Brennus had had no choice but to take the unusual step of insisting the royal couple greet their people on foot everywhere from there on. It had won hearts right around the realm and Iselda's foreign status had been instantly forgotten, as had Brennus's unusual step of not taking a wife from within the Set.

Nowhere had Iselda made greater impact than Francham. Here, hardened men, used to traversing the most inhospitable of regions, had melted in her presence, grinning like loons. Freath was sure Iselda's popularity in this region was due to the fact that she had grasped just how tough life was on the road through Hell's Gate, and that winning the hearts of these men would spread word even faster as they were always on the move around the realm.

She'd agreed to sampling the local liquor known rather dauntingly as 'Rough'. To the delight of all in Francham, the new queen had stepped into an inn known as The Lookout and there she had surprised everyone by tipping back her head and swallowing a man-sized shot of the deep amber liquid. If it had burned — as Freath knew it must have — she had not shown it, having had the audacity to suggest the innkeeper pour her another 'for good measure' .

The silence that had gripped the inn had erupted into cheers and whistles. And as Queen Iselda had clinked glasses with King Brennus prior to downing her second shot of Rough, a rousing chorus of the realm's royal anthem had been belted out noisily by the crowd.

As Brennus had commented to Freath later that night, 'The queen has won more than hearts this day. In a single swallow she has guaranteed a loyalty to the Crown that feels unparalleled.'

Prophetic words, Freath thought now as he entered the main street. From that day, patriotism and genuine pride in the Crown of Penraven had escalated noticeably and not waned throughout the reign of King Brennus the 8th.

Next to him, Kirin cleared his throat. 'Master Freath, we're staying at The Lookout.'

It was fortunate Kirin had noticed he had been daydreaming, Freath thought, jolted out of his memories, or he'd have strolled his horse right by the inn. 'Yes, of course, thank you.' He looked around and noticed that the three bodyguards that Loethar insisted be sent along with him were regarding him sullenly through their tatua. 'Master Felt and I are sharing a room. I have made arrangements for two other rooms. Work it out.'

The Green nodded on behalf of his companions. 'We'll take the horses for stabling. Do you need us?'

Freath shook his head. 'No, but your emperor seems to think I do.' He smiled but it won no warmth in their faces. 'The local liquor here is called Rough. Try some. You'll be pleasantly surprised. I hear the brothel here is lively too. I will be eating in the dining room at The Lookout tonight, so I require no supervision.' As the Green began to protest, Freath held up a hand. 'I insist. Take your men for some relaxation. I am going nowhere. Tomorrow morning I will meet with the mayor to discuss the emperor's new tax levy. By noon I imagine I will be hugely unpopular and will require your presence more keenly. Until then, I can survive the odd gob of spittle or harsh word.'

He thought the two younger guards grinned but then again it could have been a grimace. He knew they considered him a traitor to his own. And therefore the lowest of the low, and they hated that he had the ear of their warlord, besides. He was also sure that Stracker did his utmost to poison his men's attitude towards any person from the Set. Stracker was still living in the past, believing that every Denovian should perish, or at least be treated like vermin. Although most of the Set had come to realise that it needed Loethar, the emperor's charismatic hold over his horde — and his blood-hungry half-brother — was all that stood in the way of ongoing death and destruction.

As the men walked the horses off in search of the inn's stables, Freath muttered under his breath, 'I have to seriously wonder whether they'd even care if a blade was slipped into my gut.'

'You can be sure they wouldn't,' Kirin said.

Freath nodded. 'I think you're right. Come on.' He breathed deeply. 'It's good to smell this fresh mountain air.'

'Is it?' Kirin grumbled. 'I've been a city lover for a long time.'

'Wait until you've tried some Rough,' Freath quipped.

'When is this meeting going to happen?' Kirin asked, looking around to see that they weren't being overheard.

'Tonight, I hope. We have to slip our guard somehow although once they begin drinking I reckon that won't be as daring as it sounds. By tomorrow I'll be watching my back.'

Freath led the way into the front door and his belly responded immediately to the aroma of roasting meat. Ah, he remembered now — the local delicacy.

Kirin gave an appreciative sound. 'What a delicious smell,' he commented, pulling off his hat and travelling cloak.

'I'd forgotten how unique the north can be, especially this town that feels the full effect of the various cultures brought in by the merchants and the folk who travel regularly. That smell just gets better, by the way. It's called "Osh".'

'Osh?' Kirin repeated. 'Please don't tell me it's mountain bear or something.'

'And if it was?'

'I couldn't resist it, I don't think.'

Freath gave a half-smile. 'Nothing so exotic. It's goat, ox, sheep, chicken, pig, deer. Slabs of meat are pinned onto huge skewers and roasted upright over woodfires made of flaxwood, whose embers release a special spicy fragrance that permeates the meat. The meat, I might add, is rolled in spices that we hardly see in the city: toka, ferago, leem and peregum.'

'I've heard of leem.'

'I've even seen leem, but not the others. The rest are found only in the mountains. When the meat is cooked, it is sliced off onto trenchers of herbed honey bread, and drizzled with oil. It's magnificent.'

Kirin nodded. 'I'm already hungry for it from your description.'

Freath looked over Kirin's shoulder. 'Ah, you must be Innkeeper Woolton?' he said to the ruddy-faced man crossing the large reception area towards them.

'I am,' he replied. 'Are you the party from the … er … city?'

'Indeed,' Freath said, glad that the man had taken his early warning of discretion seriously.

'Three rooms?' Freath nodded. 'They're ready and waiting for you, sir. Tillie will show you up.' He pointed to a rosy-cheeked girl, no more than thirteen anni, who, going by the dimple in her chin, was his daughter.

Her smile echoed her father's. 'It's upstairs, sirs,' she lisped.

Their room was very large, with a big window, two beds, and a fabric screen that surrounded a small basin for privacy.

'Nice,' Kirin said as Tillie left.

'Glad you approve,' Freath said, setting down his small leather bag. 'So, down to business. A message will be delivered to us but I don't know —'

A tap at the door interrupted Freath. 'Yes?' he called but Kirin moved to open it.

'Sorry to disturb you, sirs,' Tillie said, the words accentuating her lisp as she curtsied. She was carrying a vase of mountain flowers.

Freath was irritated by her re-entry. 'Pollen makes me sneeze,' he said.

Kirin glared at him. 'Over here, Tillie. I'll keep it on my side.'

She smiled gratefully, closing the door behind her as she entered the room, which irritated Freath all the more.

'Was there something else?' he asked, frowning.

'Yes,' she said clearly, her lisp gone. 'You are Master Freath, are you not? From Brighthelm?'

Kirin glanced at Freath, shocked. Freath had no choice. If worst came to worst, he decided in that moment of alarm, they could overwhelm the girl. 'I am,' he replied, masking his fear.

She nodded, her composure surprising him. 'Thank you, sir. I was asked to give you a message.'

'I see,' he said, clearing his throat of the relief that was clogging it. 'What is it?'

'I'm to tell you to be ready for when the games begin.'

'Games? Ready? For what?'

She shrugged. 'I've given you the message I was told to deliver, sir. There was nothing else.'

'But what games?'

'I don't know, sir.'

He nodded, resigned. 'All right. Keep that information to yourself.'

'I have and I will continue to do so.'

'Do you know who we are?' Freath asked.

'No, sir. Nor do I wish to. I'm being paid to do this and the man who paid me frightened me. I do not want to be involved.'

Freath nodded and she quickly left the room. He looked at Kirin. 'What do you make of it?'

Kirin gave him a look of disdain. 'You know what I think. Freath, you're a household servant of the palace and I am a man of the Academy who has also spent his last decade as a curious sort of servant to the ruler. But we're acting like spies or assassins or something equally clandestine and, even worse, we're pretending we know what we're doing. What is in our heads?'

'Loyalty's in mine,' Freath replied with equal disdain. 'But I'm scared too, Kirin. There's no shame in it. If anything, it will keep us sharp.'

'For what? Our own deaths?'

Freath smiled humourlessly. 'A long time ago Clovis told me you were the one who convinced him that the throne of Penraven and the honour of our Crown was worth rallying for … worth dying for, in fact. I'm sure he said that.'

Kirin grimaced. 'I'm sure he did.'

'Dying is easy, Kirin, my friend. Staying alive — especially in our situation — is much harder, and far more honourable.'

'I'll carry that thought with me as a blade enters my belly,' Kirin said, scowling.

Freath sighed. 'I suppose chasing here after hopes and shadows means we could be missing out on word of Piven.'

'Clovis will get more word to us when he can.'

'Piven will be almost fifteen anni. Imagine that,' Freath commented, awed by the thought.

Kirin's voice dropped to a low murmur. 'And our king, if this idea of yours bears fruit, will be a man. I'm sure in your mind you see the boy.' Freath nodded sadly. 'Well, he's going to be twenty-two anni, more than old enough to fight for his crown. Have you considered that?'

'I have,' Freath admitted wearily.

Kirin gripped his arm. 'We've probably aged twice as fast in living our lie at the palace all these years. Leo is likely brimming with bitterness that is fuelling his anger and passion.'

Freath looked at his friend. 'He's kept it well under control or someone has helped him to. But,' he sighed again, 'the time is nigh. Valisar must rise again or be lost forever.'

'Have you also considered that this peace we enjoy might be a better alternative?'

'What?' Freath said, pulling away.

Kirin raised his hands. 'Hear me out.'

'No. I can't believe you're thinking like this.'

'I don't care for bloodshed, you know that. What we went through a decade ago — all those deaths. Just think about those boys we personally had to witness being killed to save one life. What about the queen giving hers so cheaply to ensure your safety?'

'Don't you dare —' Freath began but Kirin overrode his protest.

'And Genrie? How about her agonising death to —'

'Stop!'

Kirin held his tongue and had the grace to look abashed. He sighed. 'The point is, Freath, we have peace. You yourself admire Loethar … you've expressed that to me on many occasions.'

'I do — I even like him in a strange sort of way. But that doesn't mean I would ignore who rightfully owns the throne of Penraven. My loyalties have not changed.'

'But does it matter anymore? Does it really matter what you or I, or any loyalist, wants? We feel it more because we were right there, wading through the blood. But look around you, Freath. Everyone's getting on with life. Penraven continues to be as prosperous as ever, the Set thrives and the realms seem more in tune with each other than ever before — surely you would admit that?'

Freath felt his lips thin. He refused to reply, hating Kirin for not only stating the obvious but for reminding him just how well the new empire was functioning. He knew it. He did not need it rubbed in his face.

Kirin continued, his tone now peppered with bafflement. 'The thing is, Freath, what we're pursuing now is more bloodshed. Is this what we want? Loethar has achieved what felt like the impossible all those years ago: peace, cohesion, dare I say harmony between not only the realms, including Droste, but also the Steppes people. We are truly part of an empire and are considered as such by kingdoms as far away as Percheron and Galinsea. We've had an envoy from Pearlis in Morgravia on behalf of the Triumvirate to lavish good wishes on Emperor Loethar's rule and I'm sure its ally Tallinor would gladly support that if it could ever make such a massive journey. Seriously, Freath, our people are strong and protected and peaceful —'

'If not happy,' Freath interrupted sourly.

'Who says they aren't?' Kirin countered. '*You* are not happy perhaps. And *I* may not be happy, and a very small band of rebels that we think might include a Valisar king are likely not happy. But think of the greater folk of our lands. They are content. Do you really think after what they've survived they care anymore who is on the throne? The fact is they live in peaceful, prosperous times and Loethar seems to have defied us all and got it right. I know I'm risking your fury saying this, but he's a good ruler. He's been frightening in the past but he's fair and his touch is light and if not for the hideous empress, life could almost be considered sweet in the palace. Yes, he took his crown from a sea of blood but he's made it up to the people of the Set ever since.'

'Damn you, Kirin! Don't you think I know it?' Freath's anger bubbled over. 'I work alongside him every day. And every day I have to temper my admiration with memories of how he drove Queen Iselda to demand her own death, how he forced our king to suicide and let's not forget how he roasted and ate Brennus in front of the queen and Piven. You conveniently forget he butchered thousands of good people on his way to claiming this throne, and —'

'I haven't forgotten!' Kirin growled back at him. 'I just don't want to live through it again and that's what your plotting is consigning us to. War again, when this realm and this Set has finally settled into peace. We want peace, Freath. Not more bloodshed.'

Freath waved a hand angrily. 'Then go, Kirin. You are no use to me.'

'I'm not sure I ever have been.'

Freath's head snapped up. 'How long have you felt like this?' he asked, shocked.

Kirin shook his head, clearly angry with himself. 'Why can't we just accept life as it is? Why are we pursuing something that we know will provoke war?'

'Because there's a king out there,' Freath all but hissed, his finger pointing beyond the window. 'A rightful king whose throne has been usurped by an intruder. I gave my word to King Brennus that I would do everything in my power to work against Loethar and that somehow, someday I would help his son wrestle back his crown. I will not break that oath. I made it in blood.' He raised his palm to Kirin to show the scar.

Kirin looked back at his companion of a decade and his sorrow was evident. 'Look at us, Freath. Truly, what can we achieve? I have a talent but you've already seen what it does to me. I am near enough blind in one eye and a finger now twitches incessantly.'

Freath turned, indignant. 'I haven't asked you to use your magic once in the last —'

'You're missing the point. My powers, though strong, are limited by the weakness of my being just a man. It will destroy me faster than I'll be able to help you — that's what I fear. I know you've been sparing. But once this new fight begins, you will call upon me again and again,' Kirin said wearily. 'I would wreck my body gladly if I thought it could last.'

Freath waved a finger at his friend, hating this schism when he most needed Kirin's loyalty. 'Listen to me. You can leave now if you don't want to be a part of this. Don't go back to the palace, just disappear and be free. I'll think of something to tell anyone who asks. But don't expect me to do the same. I cannot — will not — relinquish my loyalty to the Valisars.'

Kirin nodded sadly. 'Where is the army to come from, Freath, that will go up against Loethar? Where is the aegis that you believe will protect Leo? No amount of our searching has proved fruitful. What is the future for your new king when you have set off a fight that will lay this realm and others to waste?'

'I don't have the answers you want. I don't have any answers! But I fear I cannot do this without you. I have no allies in the palace without you.'

'Freath, we are pathetic.'

'I know. But we have to try, don't we?'

Kirin spun away, looking angry but also torn. Freath looked at the grey silvering Kirin's hair. It was only a few strands but they had not been there a year ago. He'd watched the lines in the younger man's face deepen; he'd witnessed wisdom and maturity replacing youth and energy in this man who could no longer be considered young at thirty-three anni. He wondered who Kirin would be had he been allowed to grow into his role at the Academy in Cremond, instead of facing the fear and bloodshed he had. He could wonder that for all of them, though. They would all be very different if their lives had not been scarred by Loethar's marauding horde.

He couldn't lose Kirin. Even though he had just urged his friend to leave, he would be devastated if Kirin walked away now. He had to find the right words to make his friend remain. He knew what to do.

'I think you need some time. Don't disappear, my friend. Instead, go and find Clovis for me. Get away from all of this. Who knows, perhaps you'll find Piven.' As he said it, Freath realised this plan was wise, far more sound than what he'd originally had in mind. 'Meet the boy on safe territory somewhere. Get a feeling for who he is now. Work out a line of communication between us so that we can talk without revealing ourselves. And while you're doing this, think about your role, Kirin. Consider how much I need you, how much the Valisar boys need every loyal soul we can muster.'

Kirin nodded. 'I will take this time you're offering. Ever since word came through about Piven I've felt excited and I've needed that after years of feeling hollow. But I don't want to use Piven to win back a throne. I've realised my excitement is for the fact that he's alive, not that he offers potential.' Freath bit back the retort that threatened to fly from his mouth. 'You follow Leo,' Kirin continued. 'I'll find Clovis and we'll take it from there.'

Freath didn't know what to feel. He was glad that Kirin wasn't deserting him entirely, but the separation felt bitter nonetheless. 'When will you leave?'

Kirin shrugged. 'Immediately. The note said Clovis was heading to Minton Woodlet. I'll start there.'

'What if he should send more news?'

'He has no more pigeons. He would have used the one you gave Reuth all those years ago; he never had one of his own. I reckon with a horse and some money I can find him faster than he can try and re-open the lines of communication.'

Freath nodded reluctantly. 'Money's no problem. We'll buy you a horse, though, from here. I don't think you should take a palace beast, just in case.' There was suddenly nothing more to say. 'So you'll leave, just like that?'

'Freath,' Kirin began gently, then sighed. 'Yes. I promise I will get word to you somehow.'

'Won't you at least share a plate of Osh with me?'

Kirin gave a soft grin. 'Do you always have to win?'

7

Greven dug his staff into the ground and hauled himself up the incline.

'Are you all right?' Piven asked over his shoulder.

'Don't worry about me, lad. I'm as strong as an ox.'

'Well an ox, as strong as it is, would be stupid to climb this hill. I still don't understand why we must.'

Greven gave a brief bitter laugh. 'Because only fools would.'

'There's a perfectly good road below us.'

'Perfectly good, yes. Also perfectly open, perfectly positioned for ambush, perfectly —'

Piven stopped and turned. 'Ambush?' he interrupted, his voice leaden with sarcasm.

Greven waved a hand. 'Just pause a while. Let me catch my breath.' He looked up to see the sun low in the sky. It was nearly time to think about an evening meal. 'You must be famished. Let's stop properly and eat something light. We can build a fire later and cook the rabbits we've brought.'

Piven unslung the water skin and offered it to Greven, who took it gratefully and drank a few mouthfuls. 'Ah,' he sighed with relief. 'I suspect I owe you an explanation.'

'I would agree with that,' Piven replied, sitting down beside Greven. 'What are you frightened of? What happened yesterday?'

Greven knew the boy deserved to know. And he felt safer now that they had put some distance between themselves and the interfering couple. 'A man called Clovis and his wife, Reuth, came to see me. They are looking for you.' As he spoke he delved into a small sack of food, pulling out a tiny loaf of bread, a hunk of cheese and some nuts.

'Me?'

Despite the note of surprise in his tone, Greven sensed that Piven had already guessed as much. The boy's perceptiveness was unnerving for one so young. 'I suppose it was wishful thinking to imagine that anyone from the former royal family would be left entirely alone,' Greven grumbled, more to himself. He placed a knife on the stump of a nearby tree that had obviously been felled a long time ago, its surface smooth enough now to act as a makeshift table.

'They would do better to hunt Leo,' Piven replied carefully.

Greven frowned. The boy was right. So why was he so frightened for Piven and, more to the point, of Piven and his powers? 'They probably imagine that Leo is dead. And he could be, for all we know. But someone obviously suspects you're alive and while you may not be blood, you are still valuable as a figure of hope to any pockets of loyalism.'

Piven shook his head. 'It's been ten anni!'

'Some people have long memories, son.'

'Do they know?'

Greven shook his head, understanding. 'No one knows of your change but you and me. And no one should know, if we're sensible.'

'You want me to pretend to still be simple?'

'I don't know what I want. I just don't want anyone to know about your true identity.'

'But they still think I'm an imbecile.'

'Imbecile? That's a harsh word. From what I could tell, Piven, everyone thought of you simply as an invalid. But you're right — they believe you to be older but exactly as you were when you were last at the palace. That's our one advantage. I'm hoping we can lose ourselves among people, especially as we are now hard to pinpoint given your maturity and the fact that my leprosy has miraculously cleared.'

'Don't avoid the truth,' Piven said, somewhat harshly. 'It's not a miracle. It's magic.'

'I know you're one for honesty, Piven, but you're never to speak of magic so openly again, do you hear?'

Piven scowled. 'Why are you so scared of it?'

'You could be killed for admitting you possess it, and let me assure you that being killed would be the easy let-off. I told you a long time ago that the barbarians were hunting down all Vested. I heard they rounded up quite a horde but I have no idea what happened to them. I suspect many were killed.'

'And was Clovis one of those rounded up?'

Greven's head snapped around. 'You catch on quickly for someone who was an imbecile,' he said, pointedly.

'That's because I never was one.'

Greven hadn't expected an answer and he certainly hadn't anticipated a response that would shock him. 'Pardon?' Piven smiled. Normally, Piven's smiles were warm and bright but Greven glimpsed cunning in this one. It was gone quickly but he'd seen it and it felt unnerving. Once again he was reminded to strengthen his resolve against his urges. Were they being unwittingly whittled away by Piven's power? Did the boy even understand it? 'What do you mean, child?'

Piven shrugged. 'I wasn't mad. I was lost, just as you said. There's a difference.'

Greven's gaze narrowed. 'We've never really talked about what happened, have we?'

'We've never needed to,' Piven said, pulling himself up by a tree branch. 'We've always just been glad I turned out as I have.'

Greven didn't move. He checked all the mental barriers he'd taught himself to erect. His mind was tight; no thoughts, no clues were leaking. 'You're right. It was as though Lo himself smiled upon you.' Again he saw Piven's lip curl slightly in a half smile, bordering on a smirk. 'It was enough for me. Do you recall when I found you?'

'Greven, why are we doing this?'

'What?'

'Talking about old times while perched on a hill that we are using to run away from the life we enjoyed.'

'Do you know, you've said more in the last day than you've uttered in your lifetime?'

Piven shook his head. 'I hate exaggeration.'

'Perhaps you've forgotten how silent you were.'

'You're deliberately trying to upset me, I think.'

'I love you, Piven. I would never deliberately do anything to upset you.'

'Then stop probing me.'

'Why?'

Piven kicked at a small rock. 'Because I don't want to answer lots of questions.'

'Although it seems you have answers.'

'Not necessarily.'

'Look at me, boy,' Greven demanded.

Piven sulkily met Greven's eyes. 'What?'

Greven could remember Lily being much like this when she had been around the same age as Piven. Sullenness and taking the opposite view of adults seemed to be the disposition of all youth. But he was certain there was something else between himself and his boy. 'What's eating at you?' Greven asked, his tone as reasonable and as friendly as he could make it.

'I'm just angry.'

'Why?'

'I liked where we lived.' Piven shrugged. 'I liked our life. I don't see why strangers should send us on the run and I don't see why I don't have any say in it.'

Greven nodded. 'You're right. I'm sorry I didn't consult you.'

Piven said nothing but Greven could see the boy's jaw working furiously. He was angry, and had disguised it well until now. 'Shall we talk about it?' he tried.

'Will it make any difference? Will it make you turn back?'

'No.'

'Then there's no point in talking about it.'

'Nevertheless, I think we should talk about those olden times you refer to.'

Piven gave a long sigh as though bored. 'And if I don't want to?'

'Then let me talk.'

Piven nodded, although Greven sensed that the boy felt he didn't have much choice.

'I want to talk about your magic.' He saw Piven's jaw clench.

'Why?'

'Because I don't understand it. Apple?' Greven held out the fruit he'd dug from his sack. 'Help yourself.'

Piven picked up the small knife and cut off a chunk of the apple. He bit into the fruit as he replied, 'What do you want to know?'

'You told me a while back that you could wield this magic. But you've never said how long you've known you've had the skill.'

The boy shrugged. 'I don't know. Forever.'

'Forever being from when you were little ... or from when you began talking?'

'I'm not sure.'

Greven nodded, not entirely convinced he trusted that answer. 'All right. When did you first use it?'

'To heal a robin with a damaged wing.' Piven tested the sharpness of the knife on his thumb.

'When was that?'

'In the woods, outside our hut.'

'When, I said, not where.'

Piven gave a vexed sigh. 'I can't remember, probably three winters ago.'

'And you've been using magic ever since?'

'No. The next time was on you.'

'Why?'

'To give you back your face. I —'

'No, Piven. I meant why did you wait? Between the robin and me?'

Piven shook his head. 'I didn't trust it. I didn't really understand it.' He hacked off another chunk of the apple and began chewing on it.

'Didn't trust it? Why?'

'I'm Valisar.'

Greven frowned, reached for some bread. 'In name only.'

Piven looked away, seemingly embarrassed.

'Had you forgotten you were adopted?'

'What I meant is, despite my seeming madness I've lived as Valisar and the royal family obviously made me nervous about magic. I didn't trust it.'

Greven felt a nervous energy ripple through him. He threw the morsel of bread left in his hand to some inquisitive birds nearby. 'So you could understand what they were saying around you?'

'I suppose.'

Greven tried not to lose his patience. 'Piven, help me. I'm trying to understand you.'

'There's nothing much to understand, Greven. I didn't use my magic because I wasn't sure about it. That's all.' Piven flicked the knife around in his hand, angrily.

'If you didn't use it, how did you know you possessed it?'

'I knew, that's all,' Piven said, and Greven could tell that his young companion would not be drawn on this.

'Do you know the extent of your powers?'

Piven shook his head, hacking at the grasses between his ankles with the knife, his head lowered.

'Forgive me all these questions, child, but you're all I have. I love you. I want to understand so I can always help, always protect you.'

'I know.'

'How do you explain that you have this magic?'

Piven shrugged. 'I'm Vested, I suppose.'

'In which case you can understand why I'm worried, why I feel the need to protect you from those who would want to make use of that magic.'

'If I have to use it, then I want to use it for the good of others.'

'Exactly!' Greven exclaimed. 'Exactly,' he repeated, relief flooding his body. 'My fears, child, are that people might want to use it for reasons that do not help others.'

'No one could make me do anything I don't want to.'

'You'd be surprised what people will do to avoid being hurt, or to prevent those they love from being hurt.'

Piven tossed away the apple core and wiped the knife blade clean on his trousers. 'So you would agree that there are occasions when we must hurt others to protect ourselves … or those we love?'

Greven baulked at the question but he could see Piven wanted a direct answer. 'I would do anything to protect you … or Lily. I would probably have killed or certainly harmed some soldiers once — if I'd been able — when your adopted brother, Leo, came into my life. That was a terrifying moment. Yes, I would have done anything to stop them hurting Lily — or him, come to that.'

Piven nodded as though an important admission had been made. 'What do you think the man Clovis is after?'

It was a straight question; Greven could hardly answer it indirectly. 'I believe he has been trying to hunt you down for many anni and was sure he had stumbled upon the right path at last. I think he wanted to see that it truly was you first and then I believe he would have tried to persuade you to join him.'

'Why?'

'That I can't answer. He is Vested. Perhaps he is in touch with other Vested and can sense you, or perhaps —'

'I think I can guess,' Piven said, sounding as if he had wearied of the conversation.

'Really?'

'Rebellion,' Piven stated, his tone bald and unimpressed.

Greven was shocked. He rocked back against the tree he was leaning against and regarded Piven. He'd underestimated his charge. For anni he'd just been delighted that something had unlocked the child from his prison of silence. But Greven was beginning to think he'd entirely misjudged Piven, accepting his quietness for lack of thought and his simple outlook for a lack of depth. 'Rebellion?' he repeated dimly.

'Do you really think the entire population of Penraven — let alone the masses of the Set proper — were going to just lay down arms entirely and accept a barbarian ruler?'

Greven looked at his child, astonished. 'But they have.'

Piven held a finger in the air. 'Most. Not all.'

Greven shook his head in bewilderment. 'How would you know?'

'I can sense it. But my skills aside, any rational person would have to allow that there would always be potential for rebellion, as long as a Valisar remained alive.'

'But you're *not* Valisar, Piven!'

Piven gave him such a look of disdain that Greven actually flinched. 'I was referring to Leo.'

'We have no idea if he's ali—'

'He is. I feel it,' Piven said casually, raising the water skin to his mouth. He swallowed. 'And as long as he is, there will be people who will rally for the Valisars. And I'm extremely useful, I'm sure, as a symbol for the Valisar Crown until he reveals himself.'

Greven cleared his throat. 'Piven, you sound so much older than you are.'

Piven turned and there was his beautiful uncomplicated smile again. 'Is that a bad thing?'

'No. No, not at all,' Greven said, gathering his wits. 'Refreshing, in fact … but unnerving all the same.'

Piven's smile widened. 'Sorry. But forcing me to leave my home has brought this all out of me. We've lived in a very protected, remote manner, haven't we, Greven? And now, suddenly, I'm being forced to confront the real world. Real dangers.'

'Indeed. I would save you from it if I could.'

'I know. You may have to yet.'

Again, there it was; knowledge of something … a cryptic comment in a response as though Greven had given some form of admission. He was baffled by it. The truth was, he realised, he was baffled by Piven this day. He could hardly recognise him as the same quietly spoken, generally remote youth he'd shared a home with only a day or so earlier. Now he felt as though he was talking with an equal — an outspoken, well-informed one at that. 'One more question, if I may?' he asked.

Piven looked up through his straggly dark hair. 'Yes?'

'When do you remember first making sense of what was being said around you?'

The boy nodded. 'I've asked myself that same question many times. I always return to the same answer.'

'Which is?'

'When my father, the king, died.'

Greven didn't have the heart to correct Piven. Besides, the boy would likely leap down his throat anyway. He didn't need any further reminding of his lineage. 'Can you describe that time? Not the horror of it but what was happening to you, I mean.'

'I can't, really. I just think I became more aware of everyone around me then. Real thoughts were impacting, people's comments made a little more sense, I could focus a little bit. But only a bit. My main anchor, I suppose you could call him, was Vyk. When he was around I could concentrate and all the noises and confusion that usually filled my head would lessen a lot.'

'Is the bird magical?' Greven asked.

Piven shrugged. 'He was to me.'

That was an evasive answer but Greven let it go. 'Where has he gone?'

'He'll find us.'

'Why are you so sure?'

'I just am. He hasn't finished with me.'

Greven knew he should leave it alone, but he couldn't. 'So you think it was the death of King Brennus that allowed you to … to …'

'To enter the world properly, yes,' Piven replied. 'But not immediately. It took time. You know how I was in the beginning.'

'I do. But now look at you. I feel as though you've changed since we sat down!'

Piven smiled, a true sunny smile. 'I think being on the run like this has made me accept that I can't keep hiding from who I am. Like you said, there will be people who would use my presence as a rally cry for those still loyal to the Valisars. And then there are those who would make use of my magics for their own gain. I'm not sure I would permit either.'

He sounded so grown up it was astonishing. Greven tried not to show his surprise. 'But we are loyal to the Valisars, surely?'

'Of course, but I won't be a pawn for someone else's rebellion, Greven. I think I must find Leo.'

'No, Piven. I had no intention of embarking on a crusade. I want us to escape attention, not go looking for it.'

'You were hoping we could blend into another invisible life — Jon Lark and his son Petor?'

Greven frowned. 'Yes.'

'Then you're being naive.' Greven felt a spike of fresh anxiety as Piven continued. 'If this man Clovis can find me now he can find me again. And if he can find me so can Loethar or anyone else who wants me dead, or alive, or as a symbol, or as a Vested, or as a —'

'Stop. Piven, what's happening to you?'

Greven watched the boy he loved take a long slow breath before he spoke. He watched as the dark eyes lifted to regard his. 'What's happening is that I'm being realistic. I am accepting that I cannot have the quiet life in the hut in the forest and that I can no longer be Piven in disguise as Petor Lark and I am discovering that my magic will *not* be still.'

Greven stared at him, awe and anxiety battling within.

'This magic I have,' Piven continued. 'Wild or divine or whatever in Lo's name this skill I possess is, it claws at me. It has for a long time. And I have resisted it for all that time. I'm beginning to think that those first five anni were protection granted by the heavens. Now I fear something dangerous is lurking.'

Greven didn't know what to say. He watched the youngster weigh the blade in his hand, and then, as if having made a decision, he handed it back to Greven. 'Put this back in your sack. We'd better clear up and be on our way again.'

Greven nodded dumbly, not understanding why he felt suddenly intensely frightened.

8

Freath looked expectantly at Kirin. 'Well?'

Kirin dragged his kerchief from a pocket and wiped his mouth. 'I'm not sure I'll ever eat anything again without comparing it to this evening's fare.'

Freath smiled. 'I knew you'd enjoy it.' He sipped at an ale he wasn't interested in. 'You were gone long enough. Did you make sure your horse is docile? They can be unscrupulous up in the north with unsuspecting travellers.'

'She's gentle enough. I'll be fine,' Kirin assured. 'In fact' — he bent to gaze out of the window — 'it's past dusk. I should go.'

'What a rotten time of the day to be setting out on a journey. You could be set upon by bandits.'

Kirin smiled. 'I've taken precautions. I met up with some merchants at the stables. A group of them are leaving at twilight and I'll accompany them. We'll likely travel through most of the night back towards the city. There's plenty of them and they have a couple of armed men besides. Don't worry.'

'But I do,' Freath said, scowling.

'Then the sooner I go, the easier on your troubled mind.'

'Kirin, I —'

'Don't. There's nothing more to say. We both know what we have to do and you know why I have to leave. I will make contact again and I won't leave it too long, either — that's a promise.'

'Find him for me, Kirin.'

'And you find his brother,' Kirin replied.

Freath nodded. 'An aegis would be helpful.'

Kirin grinned. 'I'll see what I can rustle up.'

'How will you take care of yourself? You know …' Freath didn't want to be obvious but he could see Kirin understood all the same.

'I've been lucky this past decade; you haven't asked much of me. We both know it will get worse if I practise. But that's my decision on when and how to use my skills and you're not to worry over my health.'

Freath sighed. 'Well, I'll just sit here and comfort myself with that thought,' he replied, unable to fully disguise his bitterness. 'Be safe. I shall miss you.'

Kirin stood, then surprised Freath by leaning down and hugging his old friend. 'I'll see you soon enough, I promise.'

All Freath could do was nod. He wasn't used to being touched in such an intimate way; in fact, the last person who had hugged him had been his lovely Genrie. And she was dead within hours. He felt the familiar bile rise but forced it back as he lifted a hand in farewell to Kirin, who had turned at the inn's doorway for one last sad smile in his direction. Freath watched a huge man step across the inn's threshold, pushing past Kirin, his size forcing one of the Vested's shoulders to swing backwards. Freath saw his friend shake his head at the poor manners and then he was gone. The big man moved deeper into the inn and although Freath's gaze absently followed him, he was more focused on how the inn had filled since he and Kirin had come downstairs. Suddenly he was aware of the noise of men drinking, the voices of serving girls laughing and teasing their patrons gently as they set down food. He heard the clatter and bustle from the kitchen and the clank of pitchers of ale and mugs of spiced dinch. He decided to free up his table, now that the debris of his meal was being cleared. He watched as the woman worked with quiet dexterity, piling up plates and mugs on a large tray.

'Thank you,' he said and she looked up at him with surprise. She must not be used to such politeness, Freath thought, removing himself from the dining area to a corner of the main part of the inn. A shelf was set at chest height right around the room's main chamber, accompanied by high stools for anyone who wanted to perch with a drink, though most men just leaned their elbows against the shelf. It was still relatively early so no one was rowdy. The patrons looked to be mainly travellers on their way through the town so none of these people would be looking for trouble. Instead, they seemed keen on swapping tales of the pass, or conditions in the mountains or news from the other cities and provinces.

Compasses! That's what Loethar called Barronel, Garamond, Cremond and all the other once proud realms of the Set. He scowled into his ale and as he settled back into the dark nook his eyes fell on the huge man who had entered as Kirin was leaving. What an enormous specimen he was. He had to be a bodyguard at that size and yet he seemed very relaxed, not at all unfamiliar with the surrounds. Freath watched how the man took in everyone with his loud remarks and equally loud jests. No one seemed to mind his brashness. Freath noticed how the man's brightly burning personality seemed to attract other men like moths to a flame. Soon enough a large group of them were clanking mugs of ale and laughing uproariously together.

The man sitting next to Freath, also alone, ordered an ale and as the girl arrived with his mug, she glanced at Freath enquiringly. 'Another, please,' Freath agreed. He didn't want more ale but he needed an excuse to remain a bit longer. He knew if he went upstairs he'd feel Kirin's absence too keenly and besides, it had been a very long time since he'd shared life among ordinary people. He was enjoying the anonymity and the relief of not having to watch his every move, every word, as he did in and around the palace. But, he reminded himself, he needed to stay alert. His reason for being here remained clandestine and with a very real purpose — he must not slip into the mindset that he was on some sort of holiday.

The girl arrived with a pitcher of ale and a mug. 'I thought yours looked a bit stale, sir.'

'That's very good of you,' Freath replied, accepting the fresh mug as the darkly golden liquid fizzed into its depths, releasing a musty smell.

'There you go,' she said, beaming, and moved on.

As Freath half-smiled back at her, he caught the gaze of the fellow next to him. 'Your health!' he said politely.

'And yours,' the man replied, grinning before he took a draught of his ale.

Freath noticed his barbarian escorts enter the inn. The Green looked around until they saw Freath. Freath nodded, subtly dismissing them, then returned his gaze to his new companion who had turned his back to the door. 'Are you local?' he asked. Without Kirin's company he would look every inch the dour city dweller if he didn't try and fit in. What's more, he could use some company, even if it was small talk with a complete stranger.

The man shook his head. 'But I like this town. I pass through it for work.'

'Oh yes, and what line of work are you in?'

'A merchant.'

'Ah, it seems everyone here but myself is a merchant of sorts,' Freath commented.

'And you, sir?'

'I am a scribe from the city,' he lied. 'On my way through the north offering my services to a number of the wealthy families.'

The man scratched at his beard. 'You have very clean fingertips for a man of ink.'

Freath forced a smile. 'Sand and vinegar, with a dash of almond oil, make a wonderful cleaner. I bleach my fingers in pure lemon juice each day. As you can see, it makes a difference.' Where he found the capacity to lie so convincingly or compile such credible-sounding nonsense was beyond him. His mother would turn in her grave. She would turn, anyway, to know the danger he had been living through these past anni, he thought sourly.

'Impressive,' the man said, staring at his own grubby hands. 'I mention it only because I work with a lot of linen dyes. These fingers were orange a few days ago. Now they're just fading to brown.'

Freath tapped his nose. 'Sand and vinegar.'

The man raised his cup again and grinned. 'I'll remember that. Look out, it seems we have a contest on our hands,' he said, nodding towards the main counter.

Freath looked over and right enough the huge man was taking bets; coins were exchanging hands rapidly. He glanced at his companion. 'What's funny?'

'I've seen this big fellow before. He never wins but still he plays.'

'Plays what?'

'Arrows.'

'Arrows?'

The man turned to stare at Freath as though he were simple. 'You don't know the game Arrows?'

He'd just made an error. Freath fumbled to correct himself. 'Er, well, I've spent the past few years working for the Drosteans. It hasn't reached that far east yet.'

His companion's nod suggested his excuse was plausible. 'It was begun here in the north. Watch. See over on the bar, that pot of arrowheads?'

'They're not full size.'

'No, that's right. Deliberately shortened with a sleeker point.'

Freath frowned. 'Why?'

'To throw them.'

'At what?' Freath asked, intrigued.

His new friend pointed again, this time at a man who was rolling out a wine barrel. He pushed it against the rough stone wall on its side so one end faced into the main room. 'The target is the bottom of the wine barrel.'

'He has to hit that circle painted on it, I see,' Freath said, fascinated.

His companion grinned. 'Except he never does. I've seen him now a couple of times. He loses badly. I hope he bets against himself.'

'It can't be that hard, surely?' Freath wondered. 'I'm sure even I could do it.'

'Really? Blindfolded?'

'What?' Freath exclaimed, nearly choking on his ale.

The man laughed easily. 'That's the point. Best you stay here and well behind him, Master Scribe, as those shortened arrows can be flung anywhere from that fellow's wild throw.'

'Lo, save me. Is this his invention?'

The man snorted. 'No. The proper game requires the throwers to get as close to the middle of that spot as possible. You bet against each other on three throws.' He finished his mug of ale. 'The game's developed, though, over the last decade. Quite a few people in the north play it and some have worked out a system of marking. You throw the arrows at rings painted on the barrel. The middle point is the highest and the further out you go from the middle the lower the score. It's more complicated than that but I myself have never played it so I don't fully understand the scoring. It's popular, though. Mark my words, Master Scribe, you lot will be playing this in the city and as far as Droste before you know it.'

'I dare say,' Freath said, watching with great interest as the huge man allowed himself to be blindfolded.

'Now the bets will be taken,' his bearded companion said.

As if on cue, pandemonium broke out among the patrons as the innkeeper gleefully watched money exchanging hands furiously.

'The innkeeper gets a cut of all the money laid down,' Freath's new friend explained.

Freath nodded, eyes riveted on the big man, who was being turned on his heels several times.

'Lo's breath! He could throw it our way,' he exclaimed.

'As I warned.'

Freath watched as the arrow-thrower, now appropriately giddy, was baited by his audience to choose his position. The big man roared his intention and then turned slowly, lurching once, before planting his feet solidly. The crowd stifled its laughter, and silence reigned as the big man took aim at the wooden counter, the innkeeper rolling his eyes and ducking below it for safety. The real target sat forlornly forgotten and as the arrow hit timber with a dull thud, the room erupted into hilarity, hats flung in the air, mugs clanked against each other, voices yelling and just about everyone on his feet.

In the midst of the noise, Freath's friend stood up and grabbed Freath's jacket-front. 'What the —?' Freath spluttered.

'Let's go, Freath. Time is of the essence.'

'But —?' Freath found himself being dragged out of the inn, unnoticed amidst all the cheering as men surged to their feet to watch the contest. The giant took his second shot as they exited, and Freath was convinced the second arrow landed in the door as it closed behind them. And before he could digest that, he found himself being hauled up onto a horse by a stranger.

'Hold on,' the stranger growled and within moments Freath was being galloped out of the town. Another horse, presumably with his companion from the inn, gave chase, but he dared not risk a look because his seating was already unsteady behind the rider. A fall at his age and from this height — and at this speed — would mean broken bones and a lot of explanation. No, he would not take the chance, so he closed his eyes and clung on as the horse he was sharing began to slow and climb. Presumably these were Faris's men. He would have to trust his instincts. The noise of all the hooves died away until he was sure there were just two beasts.

'Didn't mean to frighten you,' a familiar voice said, drawing alongside.

Freath opened his eyes, expecting to see his acquaintance from the inn. Although the clothes were identical, he would not have recognised the man. 'You can't be too careful,' his companion explained, seeing Freath's shock at his transformation.

'Your disguise is impressive,' Freath said, watching as the man pulled padding from around his girth and shoulders to reveal a much leaner frame. The gingery sideburns and reddish grey beard had already disappeared, along with the bright mop of auburn hair. 'You've forgotten your eyebrows,' he added.

'We're here,' the man said, glancing over Freath's shoulder as he dealt with the last of his disguise.

'Here?' Freath repeated, looking around. He saw nothing but a thickly wooded area, which was dark and foreboding now that the moonlight had been obliterated by clouds scudding over it. 'Where?' he asked.

His companion grinned. 'This is where we shall talk,' came the reply. 'You can get off your horse, for we go no further.'

Freath obediently slid off his mount, ignoring his fellow rider's hand of help.

'This is Tern,' his host introduced.

'Obliged I'm sure,' Freath said somewhat ungraciously to the man who had abducted him. 'And who are you? I had hoped to meet the outlaw Kilt F —'

'I'm Faris.'

Freath felt something coalesce inside into an excitement he had not permitted himself so far. 'How can I be sure of that?' he asked.

'Because I am a man of my word.'

Freath saw that the man called Tern was busying himself with some sort of shelter that was hidden in the trees.

Faris noted his gaze. 'It is a hideout. You will forgive us our low light. We are always careful this close to a town.'

'But we must be miles from Francham.'

'Nevertheless —'

'You can never be too careful,' Freath said at the same time as Faris.

The outlaw smiled. 'Join us, Master Freath. I can offer you something to warm old bones.'

Freath ducked into the small space created by a cunning canopy of slim branches woven together, their leaves creating a dense wall. Small stools were placed inside and tiny candles had been lit to offer a small measure of comfort. 'Must be tough in the cold months,' he commented.

'We are never this far down in the blow,' Faris replied. 'Make yourself comfortable,' he offered dryly.

Freath perched on one of the low stools. 'Was the inn not rough enough for you?'

Faris gave a low chuckle. 'Speaking of Rough, let me invite you to try some.'

'I'd rather not,' Freath replied.

'A small nip will not hurt you,' Faris said, taking tiny shot cups that Tern had miraculously produced. A small flask appeared as well from a saddle-bag. 'It is a custom in this part of the realm to take Rough together.'

'This is no realm, Master Faris. We live in a compass,' Freath said, his mouth twisting into a shape of disgust, 'or hadn't you realised?'

'I answer to a king, Master Freath, not an emperor.'

Freath's belly flipped. 'How can I know you are not an impostor? That this whole thing has not been a clever charade?'

'Why would anyone go to the trouble?'

Freath frowned.

Faris sighed. He removed a chain from around his neck. 'Do you recognise this?'

The low light made no difference. Freath could clearly see that the man was holding Queen Iselda's chain and locket. 'Where did you get that?' he demanded.

'From a king.'

'Which one?' Freath breathed.

'The first time or the second time?'

'Don't toy with me, man!'

Faris regarded him. Freath maintained his glower. He was furious but also tingling with anticipation. Leo was within his midst somewhere — the long-held dream of returning the Valisar throne to its rightful sovereign was within grasp.

The tallow candles guttered in tandem with his anticipation and Freath took his eyes off Faris to glance at them.

'Hog fat,' Faris said. 'We save our sheep-fat candles for polite guests.'

'Listen to me, Faris,' Freath threatened, 'lives are in the balance. Many have already been lost to protect King Leo. Many more have been pledged to save him. Don't make light of my suffering.'

'Yours?' Faris looked at him with disgust. 'Why shouldn't I just slit your throat here and now, Freath? Did you honestly imagine you'd leave this place alive? As it is, a word from me and your companion will be rotting in the earth somewhere between here and Brighthelm.'

'My companion?' Freath stuttered. 'Kirin? What do you mean?'

'Kirin? Is that his name? Well, my merchant friends will have no hesitation to end his life should that be necessary, let me assure you.'

Freath felt his skin turn clammy. The elation he'd experienced just moments earlier fled.

'It amazes me that you have not considered this outcome,' Faris baited.

Freath cleared his throat. 'It amazes me that you think I would invest my time and energy and no small amount of personal funds if I was anything but earnest.'

'So, despite all I've heard to the contrary, I'm to believe you are a loyalist?'

'To King Brennus? Yes!'

'But you work for the emperor. In fact, you're a close aide and indeed confidant of Loethar.'

'I am *seen* to play those roles.'

'Oh, is that so?' Faris replied. His tone was quietly mocking. 'And so why are you looking for me?'

'You know why.'

Faris knocked back his Rough in a single swallow. 'I want to hear you tell me why.'

'I am here,' Freath began, placing his shot glass, its fiery liquid unsipped, on the ground beneath his stool, 'to learn of King Leonel.'

'You call him king,' Faris replied.

'And you speak of him in the present tense.'

Faris nodded and smiled. Freath did not return it. He was not in the mood for games.

'What is your interest in the Valisars, Freath?' Faris pressed.

'The same as yours, I imagine.'

'Which is?'

'Revenge.'

'I have many enemies,' Faris said coolly. 'Yet I know none of them.'

'Then we are kindred spirits.'

'Ah, not so,' the outlaw replied, glancing over at Tern in what Freath sensed was some sort of silent signal. 'I know of at least two enemies of yours, Master Freath. And so do you.'

Freath shrugged, watching Faris's man leave the enclosure. 'I agree with you that I have many. It would not surprise me if you knew of them.'

'Is it true that you killed Queen Iselda?'

Freath hung his head. The old shame warmed his face and sent a fresh spike of self-loathing through his ageing body. 'I did.'

Faris drew a small but fearsome looking blade from his hip. 'I should gut you now for that admission alone and leave your entrails for the birds to peck at.'

Freath did not lift his head. 'Perhaps you should,' he sighed. 'I have walked a treacherous path, Faris. I suspect you would be doing me a kindness.'

'No,' said a new voice. 'He will not grant you such a swift end, Master Freath, not without my say so.'

Freath looked up in startlement. He could see only the bottom half of the man who had spoken. He frowned, crawling out of the enclosure, followed by Faris, to stand and face his accuser. It was dark and the weak illumination from the tallow candles threw up only a ghostly glow. Freath squinted through the shadows to see a young man: tall, lean, fair-haired and, although he bore little resemblance to either parent, his bearing was unmistakeably regal.

'Give me light!' Freath demanded. 'Now!'

Faris must have nodded because Tern lit a lantern from one of the tallow candles. 'It can only be lit for a few moments,' the leader of the outlaws growled.

Freath grabbed for it, swinging it perilously close to the young man's face. He knew precisely what he was looking for and there it was, the tiny scar above his right eyebrow that had been won when he fell from a pear tree, clipping his face on a branch. He sucked in a gasp of excitement. 'How did you get this scar?' he asked, pointing towards it.

He knew everyone was leaning in to scrutinise something they'd probably not even noticed before. It was tiny. Only just visible, a thin silvery blemish.

The younger man didn't hesitate. 'I fell out of a tree, hit my head on a knob of the branch. By the time the de Vis twins and I arrived at the infirmary, I looked as though I'd fought through a day's battle.'

Freath's lip began to tremble. 'What sort of tree was it?'

The younger man sneered. 'A pear tree. The fruit wasn't even ripe and to add insult to injury I got bellyache for my trouble and then the trots. My mother was not pleased with me. She worried I would be scarred badly but I can recall you scoffing at the suggestion, Freath. Besides, I always hoped it would add a warrior's mark to my soft appearance.'

'How old were you?' Freath persisted.

The man blinked. Freath held his breath.

'I was six. Mother had recently lost another baby so her mood made her overreact to my wound. She banished the de Vis brothers from my life for what felt like an age.'

Freath sank to his knees. 'It was four days, your majesty,' he said, his voice choked with relief. 'They were banished for four days.'

'They were only about eleven anni themselves,' Leo continued.

Freath nodded, his eyes glistening. 'King Leon —'

'No!' Leo yelled. 'You will not so much as speak my name, you treacherous, snivelling, arse-licking bastard!' He drew a sword with a chilling ring from its scabbard at his hip; even in this low light Freath recognised the sword.

He bent his head, accepting the rebuke. 'I am unworthy of being slain by Faeroe, your majesty.'

He sensed Leo's hesitation but it was Faris who stepped between them. 'Stop!'

'I warned you,' Leo bristled, his voice edged with emotion.

'Just wait, your majesty!' Faris demanded. 'Extinguish the lantern,' he growled at Tern. 'On your feet, Freath.'

Freath felt himself hauled upright. He still couldn't face his sovereign.

'Where's Jewd?' Faris asked.

'Just coming up the hill now with the others,' Tern answered. 'I can just see him. He's moving quickly which means his money pouch is a lot lighter.'

'Did anyone follow us?' Faris demanded.

'No,' came the reply.

Freath dared a look. Leo had not taken his gaze from the former aide to his parents, his face glowering with such open hatred that

Freath expected to feel Faeroe sliding into his belly at any moment. 'Hear me out, majesty,' he risked, for Leo's hearing only. 'I might surprise you.'

Leo said nothing, simply stared at him with a deepening sneer.

The man they called Jewd finally arrived, and Freath recognised him as none other than the arrow-throwing giant from the inn. Two other men accompanied him. 'It was a ruse?' Freath sputtered.

Faris nodded. 'I needed to create a disturbance so that we could get you out of there with no one remembering you leave.'

'For when we kill you and leave you for the wolves,' Leo finished.

Freath inwardly sighed. He could not blame the young man. 'Does he lose purposely, then?' he asked, simply for something to say that would throw Leo off his back.

'No, he does that without even trying,' Faris answered. 'He was born a shocking gambler,' he added, loud enough for the giant to hear.

Jewd ignored him. 'So this is our traitor, is it? Puny, isn't he? Shall I snap him in half, your majesty?'

Leo's lip curled. 'Not yet, Jewd. I want him for myself.' Freath watched the king's grip on Faeroe tighten.

Once again Faris calmed the tension. 'Right, you men, get yourselves something to eat. Thanks for tonight, you did well. No fire unfortunately this low in the woods, but tomorrow night I promise a meal of roasted meat.' The rest of the outlaws grumbled but meandered off leaving the four of them.

'Well, gentlemen,' Faris said, taking in the king and Freath with a roving gaze, 'it's time to talk. No swords needed, majesty.' He raised a hand as the king opened his mouth, no doubt to hurl more abuse, Freath guessed. 'Your highness, we are going to listen. If Master Freath is every inch the slippery snake you describe him as and as cunning as you suggest, then I have to query why he would willingly put himself into a den of Freath-haters unarmed, alone, and knowing full well that he carries a death wish by walking into our lives.' He paused before adding, 'We should consider the possibility that he's innocent.'

'Innocent?' Leo repeated. 'He threw the queen from the highest level of Brighthelm.' But he reluctantly sheathed Faeroe.

Freath swallowed. *How? Where had he been hiding in the palace to see so much!*

Leo continued, despite Faris's warning glare. 'He picked her up by her royal garments at her neck,' he said, pointing to his own, 'and at her tail, and without so much as a farewell, flung her through the window so she could smash on the flagstones below. And then he turned and smiled at the hag from the Steppes.' If winter had a voice, it would sound like Leo's.

'You saw,' Freath choked.

'Yes, I saw. I saw everything you did, Freath.'

'But you did not hear,' Freath defended.

Leo seemed unperturbed. 'I did not hear what you and my mother discussed before you murdered her, perhaps, but everythi—'

Freath interrupted, no longer caring about protocol. 'Because if you had been able to hear, you would have known that she instructed me to do that.'

Leo paused, astonished, and then leapt for Freath. Jewd hauled him back. 'Forgive me, *majesty*,' the big man growled into the young man's ear. 'We said we would listen.'

Freath rubbed self-consciously at his throat.

'Let's be seated, all of us,' Faris said, glaring at his young monarch.

Jewd threw one of the stools in Freath's direction. As Freath sat warily, Faris urged Leo to sit on the second stool. The outlaw adopted a crouch that he managed to make appear comfortable.

'Why don't you tell us everything you came here to share?' Faris suggested. 'Highness, during this time, why don't you ... er, respectfully, be quiet and still? Begin, Freath. If anything you say does not ring honestly to my ear, I will not wait for the king's command. Jewd will happily snap your neck for me as easily as he might a twig.'

Freath nodded. He gave his attention to Leo. 'It began with your father calling me into his salon on the day of your sister's birth, your highness …'

9

Kirin had fallen into conversation with a woman travelling with her brother. 'And what prompted you to go looking for such a long lost friend?' she asked, taking a sip from the water bladder that hung from her horse's neck.

Very few women travelled with merchants and most of those, for whatever reason, chose to be carried in the carts. He was impressed she was riding, and flattered that she had chosen to speak to him. 'It's been a decade. Friends should not fall out of contact,' he answered as vaguely as he could.

'He could be married by now,' she said.

'He probably is,' Kirin replied, shaking his head at her offer of a sip of water.

'Where will you begin?'

He looked at her quizzically. 'I have no idea. Why?'

She smiled. 'I think it's exciting. You're off on a journey of discovery. You could travel the entire realm … I mean compass … before you even get a clue as to his whereabouts.'

'That's true. And I may never get that clue.'

'That would be a shame. Think positive, Kirin Felt.'

'And so you're both travelling to Brighthelm?' Kirin asked. At her nod, he added, 'What are you, guards or something?'

'What makes you say that?' she asked, amused.

'Well, you're riding, for a start.'

'Very observant!' she replied archly. 'No, I'm just using the caravan for security. My brother and I need to get into the city to see some relatives but we didn't want to travel alone. So long as we pay our tithe and follow the rules, the merchants don't mind. They're good company as well.'

He nodded. He'd also paid a fee that allowed him the security of the merchant caravan and their mercenary guards. 'Where do your relatives live?'

'Er, in a village not far from Devden.'

He'd heard the hesitation in her voice. She was lying. Why? More to the point, what was her interest in him?

'How long will you stay?'

She grinned. 'All these questions, Master Felt!'

He shrugged. 'Just passing the time, Lily.'

'Somehow I feel your life is far more exotic and interesting than my boring existence in Francham.'

'Nothing boring about Francham, surely?'

'Well, I've been there all my life. How about you? Are you originally from the city?'

'No, Port Killen on Medhaven,' he lied, unsure why but driven by instinct now.

'Far away,' she sighed. 'You're lucky to see so much of our lands.'

'You'd like to travel?'

'Yes, of course. But it is unseemly for a woman to roam the compasses. I envy you. And I hope you find your friend.'

'Your brother is very silent.'

'He never says much. And he didn't really want to make this journey but we feel obliged.'

'And you live together?'

'Er, yes, we do.'

The hesitation each time he asked a personal question was telling. He was now convinced her easy conversation with him was contrived. She was also very pretty, which only served to make him even more self-conscious.

'How come you're not married, Lily?'

She shrugged, seemingly embarrassed. 'How come you aren't?'

'I didn't say that I wasn't.'

'You didn't say that you were either. I'm guessing not.'

'Why?'

She smiled softly. 'The way you look at me.'

Kirin bristled. 'My apologies, I didn't —'

'You misunderstand, Master Felt,' she reassured. 'Married men tend to have a hungry look in their eyes.'

He stared at her, only just able to see the amused expression through the murky light of the few lanterns they hung from the carts. 'And I don't look hungry?'

'Let's just say you aren't looking at all from what I can tell. Perhaps I should have said *the way you don't look at me*.'

Kirin swallowed. She was absolutely right. 'Should I start apologising again?'

'Not at all. I can't be offended by your lack of interest. I'm seeing a good man,' she said, her gaze as direct as her words.

'Will you marry him?'

'That's overly curious of you,' she admonished, looking for the first time as self-conscious as he was feeling.

It was Kirin's turn to shrug. 'Don't feel obliged to answer —' He stopped, looking ahead. 'People are coming. Quite a few.'

'What? How do you know?'

'Trust me.' As they both sat up straighter to peer ahead, the sound of hooves and the squeak and groan of approaching carts came out of the darkness.

The merchant caravan hauled to a stop.

'Emperor's soldiers,' Kirin breathed, feeling immediately nervous. He couldn't risk being recognised. He turned to Lily and noticed her pulling her shawl over her head, tying it under her chin. He frowned. 'What's wrong?'

'Just taking precautions,' she murmured. 'I'm a woman, Master Felt. It doesn't hurt to be wary.'

Kirin's puzzlement deepened. Lily was not travelling alone. Apart from the fourteen or so travellers alongside them both, she was with her brother, who was armed. Why would she feel so suddenly nervous? Kirin felt his earlier suspicions confirmed. Lily was not only hiding something, he could tell she wanted to hide herself along with it. 'Are you all right?'

'I'm fine. Let's not talk.'

'I'm sure you have nothing to fear from these men.' The soldiers, he could see, were escorting two carts holding people, none of whom bore tatua or looked at all like tribal folk. The man at the front waved a hand, asking the merchants to move to one side of the road. Kirin watched the leader of his caravan gladly acquiesce, obediently waving the group to shift as best they could.

'Who are these people?' Lily spoke softly for his hearing only, although the question was clearly rhetorical.

Kirin shook his head in reply but as he did so felt an assault on his mind. Though this had never happened to him before, he instinctively shepherded the probing magic, deflecting it he knew not where. It was gone no sooner than it had arrived and, startled, he wondered if he'd imagined it. His curiosity pricked, he risked a very small trickle of prying magic. He had been practising this over the last seven anni, teaching himself how to control the flow with precision, never allowing it to rush from him. It had taken much of his courage to risk the headaches, the nausea, fainting, and loss of his rationality that accompanied the use of his talent and he had learned that to let it flow from him too fast — no matter how small the trickle — was to invite pain and sickness. Using it still meant repercussions but he knew now how to control it with exquisite care so that he knew exactly how much it took from him to wield it.

He cast as gently as he knew how, stealing over time and distance, through flesh and bone, creeping invisibly into the mind of the man bearing the tatua of the Green who seemed to be leading this strange group. And in this man's jumbled, slightly angry, definitely alert thoughts, he thought he sensed what he sought. He pulled back with equal care and stealth and took a long slow breath to stem the inevitable rush of dizziness.

'Whoops, Master Kirin,' Lily warned, reaching for him. 'What's wrong?'

Kirin closed his eyes to steady the swaying sensation. 'Forgive me, I feel a bit unwell.'

'Nothing to forgive,' she said, sounding worried. 'Can I help?'

He pushed the heel of his palm against his forehead. 'No,' he replied tightly. 'This is probably the effects of the wine I drank in rather hefty quantity this afternoon.'

'Then I no longer feel quite so sympathetic,' she whispered, not unkindly.

He forced himself to focus. 'Lily, have you heard of the Vested?'

She shot him a glance as the soldiers' group began to advance again. 'Yes. Why?'

'I think the people ahead in the carts are Vested.'

'How could you possibly know that?'

He tried to shrug. 'I think I recognise one or two of the folk. I've —'

'You!' the lead soldier yelled, pointing.

Kirin looked over and noticed with a rush of fright that the man pointed at him. 'Me?'

He watched the man consult with another, who was not a soldier but wore distinctive scars, painted violet, that marked him as Wikken, a so-called seer of the Steppes. The Wikken whispered something to the soldier.

'Name?' the soldier demanded.

Truth was best, Kirin decided. 'I am Kirin Felt.'

'From?'

'Penraven.'

'Travelling from Francham?'

'Yes. I had business to conduct there.'

'What sort of business?'

'The emperor's business,' Kirin replied, hoping his cutting tone would dismiss further questions.

The man appeared unnerved but once again listened to his scarred companion. He nodded, then asked, 'Where are you going?'

'Heading back to Brighthelm.'

'Your business is done?'

'Yes.'

'And who are you to the emperor — what service is it that you perform?'

'Nothing of such importance,' Kirin began, trying to deflect attention that he had any relationship with Loethar. 'I am simply a man of letters,' he added, starting to craft a lie but realising instantly it was an error as the Wikken leaned across from his horse and whispered again.

'Good, we will ask you then to accompany us.'

'What?' Kirin exclaimed. 'No, I cannot, I'm afraid. I am expected at Brighthelm.'

'We will get you there.'

'But why must I come with you?'

'We could use your help as a man of letters.' Sarcasm had crept through into the soldier's tone.

Kirin shook his head. 'I'm sorry but I am supposed to go —'

The man laughed. 'These people we carry wield the magic of the Vested,' he said, untroubled by sharing this information with the whole caravan of traders. 'But my companion here is Wikken. He has "smelled you", Kirin Felt. You too are Vested.'

So it was the scarred man who had assaulted his mind, Kirin realised.

'Who is this woman you travel with?' the soldier demanded.

Before Kirin could respond, Lily spoke up. 'I am his wife.'

Kirin turned and stared at her, taking care not to betray his shock. What was she up to? Why would she take such a risk?

'Are you Vested?' the soldier asked her.

'Yes.'

Kirin could not tolerate this. 'This woman is —'

'Both of you will join us then,' the soldier said, waving a hand and urging his horse forward.

The merchant leader looked helplessly at Kirin and shrugged. He guided his horse to him. 'You'd better go, Master Felt. I'm sorry but I suspect they mean no harm.'

'Do you?' Kirin glared and then softened. It wasn't the trader's fault. He nodded sheepishly. 'My apologies, sir.'

'None needed. Go safely with Lo.'

There was nothing for it but for Kirin and Lily to turn their horses and join the group of soldiers, who coalesced around them without crowding them.

'What did you do that for?' Kirin demanded of Lily in an urgent whisper, staring ahead.

'I'm asking myself the same question,' she replied and he could hear in her voice that she was not lying.

'It was stupid, Lily. This feels dangerous. What about your brother?'

'Don't worry about him.'

Kirin stared at her. 'I'm not, I'm worried about you!'

'Well, don't,' she said, tartly. 'So, you're Vested?'

He nodded. 'You heard I work for the emperor,' and as he noticed her attractive face darken at his words, he added in the lowest of murmurs, 'but not in the way that you think.'

'What's that supposed to mean?'

'Not now,' he said, shaking his head. He was surprised to realise that in the last few minutes of alarm, the dizziness had passed and he was at least feeling well again, if not safe. 'I shall tell you more when we're alone.'

She seemed to accept this. 'Who's that man with the scars?'

'He's Wikken. Did you understand what the soldier was saying?'

'No.'

'A Wikken is a seer of sorts, from the tribes. Apparently this one can "smell" magic. I have little experience with them — he's only the second Wikken I've seen in my time. It was my impression they refuse to leave the Steppes.'

'Well, he smelled you.'

'Pointless, though, I have such little skill,' Kirin lied.

'Why's his face like that?'

Kirin didn't know the proper answer to that. He turned to the soldier riding nearby; now that the men knew Kirin wasn't planning on being any trouble, they had given the newcomers a wide berth. Kirin had to beckon the man, whom he guessed was around his own age, to guide his horse closer. 'Yes?' the soldier asked, his expression quizzical.

Kirin drew make-believe lines against his cheek. 'Can you tell us why he is scarred like that?'

The soldier smiled. 'When anyone from the tribes shows genuine promise as a seer, he is cut each year from manhood. The wounds are packed with the ashes of our ancient dead, which we have kept for as long as our people have lived on the plains.'

'Why?' Kirin asked, intrigued in spite of his anxiety.

'We believe that the Wikken will then carry the memories of our forefathers, so that he is enlightened by their knowledge and experiences.'

Kirin nodded, keeping his expression bland.

Lily was not so careful. 'You mean those scars are filled with the remains of cremated people?'

The soldier grinned. 'That's exactly what I'm saying. The wounds heal and push the packing of the ashes outwards and that creates those magnificent scars,' he said, awe in his voice. 'They're purple anyway but he stains them that deep violet.'

Kirin glanced Lily's way and she seemed to grasp his unspoken warning. 'How fascinating,' she replied. 'Thank you.'

'How many Wikken are in the Set?' Kirin asked, his voice casual.

'Shorgan is the only one now. There are only two living Wikken at present. The other is much older, far more powerful and remains on the plains.'

'So Shorgan likes it here, does he?' Kirin added, smiling, encouraging the man to spill as much information as possible.

'I believe he does. Our emperor sets little store by the Wikken today. He is keen that we do not dwell too much on the old ways of mystery and magic.'

'And yet he hunts down the Set's Vested,' Kirin commented.

The man shrugged. 'For different reasons. He wants control of the magic but he doesn't make a lot of use of it from what I've heard. It's too bad; I think I take an interest in sorcery.'

'How come?'

'Because my grandfather is the other Wikken.'

'I see. And you have no … ?' Kirin wasn't sure how to phrase his question but the youngster understood.

He shook his head. 'Nothing at all.' He smiled. 'I am all warrior,' he declared, banging a fist to his chest.

Kirin was pleased to hear Lily give a soft laugh on cue. He was relieved she had grasped that they needed to be as little problem as possible to these people.

'Why do they need my wife and myself?' Kirin asked, taking his chance and trying to make the words *my wife* sound natural even though they caught slightly in his throat.

The man shook his head, made a face to say he had no idea. 'Just interested, I imagine. These Vested are being transferred. I am guessing that Shorgan sensed you, and that our captain is simply taking precautions. He'll send a runner soon enough to enquire about you. It's likely you'll be escorted back to the city almost immediately.'

'And where are these people headed?'

'I haven't been told. I just follow the leader.'

'They're safe, though?'

The man frowned, slightly bemused. 'I wasn't here for the overthrow — I was just three moons too young as Loethar only allowed men who were two decades and older to march — but I hear it was a bloody one. I accept that those memories do not easily fade.' He gave a small bow that touched Kirin's heart. 'But our emperor does not want a massacre. We should not be feared as murderers.'

'He did a pretty good job of it ten anni ago.'

The man nodded and sighed. 'War is ugly. But now he wants everyone to be loyal to the empire and to get on.'

Kirin felt his own treachery quicken his pulse. This man riding next to him was either terribly naive or one of the most sincere people he was likely to meet. If only he knew that the companion he was talking so freely and openly with was part of a long-held plot to tear down the very empire he admired so much.

'If he wants that he should not treat these innocents as prisoners.'

The warrior frowned. 'Do they look like prisoners?'

Kirin looked over at the eight or so people he counted chatting amiably in the carts. One was telling a tall tale, it appeared, and even the soldiers riding alongside were joining in the laughter.

'No, but they're not free, are they?'

The man shrugged. 'What is freedom? Are you free?'

'What do you mean?'

'Well, do you answer to someone?'

'We all answer to someone.'

'Then none of us is free.'

Kirin's eyes narrowed. 'Let me say it another way. I didn't want to join this caravan but against my will I am being forced. To me that is not the choice of someone with freedom. These people would presumably not choose to be moved.'

'On the contrary,' his companion said, 'they all volunteered to move into another compass.'

Kirin blinked, surprised. 'Why?'

'I guess the emperor wants to put their skills to good use in another part of the Set.'

Kirin didn't think Loethar would relinquish control of anyone possessing magic but he let it pass. Whether or not these Vested had volunteered did not solve the dilemma of him and Lily being absorbed into this group, or him being dragged further from Clovis's trail.

'We do keep a record of the Vested, of course,' the soldier added.

'Oh?'

'It's a new method but very effective, transportable, and knowledgeable.'

'Knowledgeable?' Kirin queried. 'How can a list be discerning?' He watched the man's brow crease in puzzlement at this word. 'Er, how can a list think?'

'Ah, I see. It doesn't have to. It's not a list.'

It was Kirin's turn to be baffled. 'Not a list? What is it, then?'

The soldier laughed. 'It's a man. His name is Vulpan. He'll want to taste your blood, too,' he said, waggling a finger.

Kirin felt a thrill of fear spike through him. 'What?'

'You're both Vested, aren't you? He's based at the next town. That's where we're headed. Everyone in the group will be recorded then.'

No one had interrupted Freath as he'd told his terrible story. The tallow candles had long ago guttered their last and now the foursome was illuminated in soft moonlight, shaded by gossamer cloud. Grave, thoughtful expressions had claimed their faces and they were as still as the trees that encircled them.

It was Leo who broke the silence. 'My father asked you to do this,' he stated, as though needing to set straight in his mind all that he'd just heard.

'He could not know what would unfold but he certainly asked me to play the role of traitor if the Valisar throne was usurped. It was not a role I relished, your majesty, but I would deny my king and queen nothing, least of all my life. I loved both of them but I revered your mother. She was truly the most magnificent woman

I have known and I have never, your highness, ever come to terms with the manner of her death. But she demanded it of me.' He looked down.

Leo stood, his expression one of distress mingling with disgust. 'I've thought you treacherous for all of this time. I have hated you, dreamed of sticking my blade in your belly or dragging my dagger across your throat. I made a promise to myself that I would kill you at the first opportunity.'

'All perfectly understandable, your majesty. If I have managed to convince Loethar of my disloyalty to your family, what chance did you stand watching me from afar?' He gave a rueful smile. 'It seems I have fulfilled what was asked by my ruler.'

'How could my mother ask such a thing of you, Freath?'

'She never actually said the words,' Freath admitted, noticing the flare of fresh anger in the young man's face. 'But she conveyed just as well what she expected of me. She was so brave. I am glad you did not have to hear her shrieks, your majesty, for they were false and for the barbarians' benefit alone. She was not afraid to die, your highness. She was, however, afraid to live to see her precious children come to harm. If it is any consolation, majesty, she was aware that you had not been found. We couldn't be sure where you were but we knew you were safe — if I may dare use that term loosely.'

'And then you decided to find Leo for Loethar,' Faris finished, obviously impressed by Freath's incredible tale.

Freath nodded. 'It was either that or allow him to kill hundreds of boys, majesty,' Freath said sadly. 'I am yet to recover from the self-loathing of that incident but the awful plan kept the body count to nine, when it could so easily have become nine hundred or nine thousand.' He sighed. 'I see each one of those nine boys' faces in my nightmares. Tomas Dole — the one we used as you — even talks to me in them.' He gave a soft anguished cry that sounded like a choked sob. 'Says he forgives me.'

'What made you think Leo was with us?' Faris asked.

'Who else was there?' Freath challenged. 'I know the king came north not long before the wars began in the Set. At the time I remember thinking how odd it was that he came here without Regor de Vis. I travelled with him as far as Berch; he needed me alongside taking notes on what needed to be done before war arrived. You see, he was already making plans for the potential overthrow and I now realise he must have come and found you, Master Faris.' He looked at the outlaw. 'I didn't realise this at the time, of course. But the king was travelling extremely light — his horse, Faeroe, two soldiers, that's about all. And the day I left to return to Brighthelm, so did he, plainly clothed and this time with only one soldier. The other escorted me.'

Faris nodded. 'Yes, we saw him leave his man behind from miles away. He left Faeroe for his son and a locket that belonged to Iselda so that Leo would know it was no ruse.'

Freath looked amazed. 'The locket. I had the castle searched room by room for it. The queen was devastated by its loss. We believed it stolen and it has irked me ever since that a thief was among us.'

'My father wanted me to understand that he had been here, that Faris was not lying to me.'

Freath looked at the king. 'How clever of you, majesty, to work it out.'

Leo shrugged. 'I was raised on secrets, Freath. My father was a shrewd Valisar — it seemed he did not need magic to be a clever and cunning king.'

Freath understood. 'You do not require it either, highness, to claim back your throne. And you can be as cunning and ruthless as he was,' Freath replied. At Leo's glance of surprise, he raised his hands. 'Isn't that what this is all about? Are we not all trying to put the rightful king back onto the Penraven throne?'

'Leo's not sure whether anyone wants that anymore, Freath,' Faris sighed. 'He thinks Loethar is doing a good job.'

'He is. If I didn't know better I'd say he not only took up where your father left off, your highness, but he has continued in a way that would make your father and Regor de Vis proud.' He watched Leo bristle. 'Forgive me, but I speak only the truth. I despise him each day of my life but for every moment that I despise him, I also admire him. It is a war that rages within me constantly.'

Faris glanced above his head to Jewd. Freath wondered if that was the signal to snap his neck. 'You confuse me, Freath. What was your intention in coming here?'

'I came to warn you. I also ran out of patience with my own patience! I needed to know if we still had a Valisar king or whether my endeavours were in vain.'

'To warn us about what?' Faris demanded.

'Loethar seems to think one of your men took an arrow-wound recently. I was worried that it was you, Faris. They seem to be very hopeful it was you but I can see that you are well. And your giant friend behind me is also able, as is that man you called Tern. Presumably they were mistaken or it was —'

'What of it?' Leo snapped.

Freath hesitated, surprised. 'Er, well, only that whoever took that wound — if one of your band has — is now a marked man.' He watched Faris steal a glance at the king and heard Jewd move around to face him as Leo and Faris stood. Freath swallowed. Something was clearly wrong.

'You'd better explain that,' Faris said.

Freath looked at his captors. 'It's as I say. The wounded man is marked — or so I'm assured. They will hunt him down and I feared that if they can find this man, they might find you, Faris. And no disrespect to you and your men but my real concern was for Leonel. I didn't want his security threatened.'

'Loethar thinks he's dead.'

Freath nodded. 'Loethar has no reason to suspect otherwise. It hasn't entered his mind that there is anyone who threatens his imperial authority. Those loyal to you, highness, heard of your escape into the woods third-hand. We couldn't know for sure if it was you. We simply had to hope and pray that it was.'

'And how did you convince Loethar I was dead?' Leo asked.

'Magic, your majesty. The man that your protector here threatened to have killed not so long ago saved you from being hunted down all these years ... saved all of us from an early grave. His name is Kirin, sire. Kirin Felt. He is Vested but pays a hefty price for his skills.'

At their quizzical glances he explained quickly how Kirin had used his magic to make Lily and Father Briar identify Tomas Dole as Prince Leonel.

'And so Felt will die?' Leo asked.

Freath shrugged helplessly. 'I suppose so, eventually. He has already lost some sight in one eye. We have spared using him and he has been teaching himself how to control his magic but it will destroy him bit by bit as he uses it. Yes, your majesty, it will kill him. It is this uncanny Vested magic that has Loethar on your trail, Faris, and confident of hunting you and your men down.'

'I see. And why were you permitted to come north?'

'He wanted to send warriors into the woods and hills of the north but I suggested a more subtle way of finding you was to tax the north heavily. I assured him that the quickest way to capture you, without having to use brute force or bloodshed to compromise the magnanimous profile he is building, was to allow the northerners to yield you.'

'By taxing them?' Faris queried, incredulous.

'Yes. I said if he taxed them, blaming them for the money you steal, they would yield you.'

Faris pointed his finger. 'What makes you think —'

'I don't!' Freath snapped. 'It was all I could come up with on the spur of the moment. He was already sending men, including his brutish brother, who likes nothing better than the sport of bloodshed. It was the only way I could stop them sending enough warriors to saturate the north and find the wounded man. I was desperate, Faris. I needed to give you time to either bundle him off on a ship somewhere, or kill him. But whatever you decide, don't let him remain close, not even within a few miles of you or the king. If you ignore this warning you will be found and killed. He wants your head on a spike and he has the means to do so.'

Freath was surprised by the frigid silence that followed his comment.

'You're that certain?'

'I can only tell you what I know and what I know best these days is Loethar. This is a man not prone to emotional outbursts. For him to be so animated, so open about his potential success is unusual. I suspect this means he is awfully confident of hunting down the man who took the arrow. He would never reveal so much if he weren't utterly sure of his position.'

'How can he be that confident?' Jewd asked, the sudden rumble of his deep voice making Freath flinch.

'Because he's using magic!' Freath spat. 'Why aren't any of you taking this seriously? Loethar's in control of virtually all of the magic that once existed across our realm. He's clever,' Freath said, shaking his head. 'When he arrived he thought that he could literally consume the magic, endowing himself with it by eating people. I know now he was confusing this with a far more ancient and very specific practice available to only a handful of people. But I only discovered very recently that he no longer kills the Vested as he used to. Newly born Vested he protects. He rewards parents for owning up to their skilled children — provides housing, wages, all sorts of benefits. He looks after them. And in return, he knows where they are at all times.'

'And I suppose you're going to tell us that it's because of this Vested that we should feel uneasy?' Leo asked.

'Uneasy, your highness? No, you shouldn't feel uneasy. You should feel terrified. If what Loethar has said is true, then he has harnessed a skill with which any man or woman can be hunted.'

'But, Freath,' Faris interjected. 'This is foolish. No one knows what I look like; Loethar's people — magical or not — have no way of earmarking me.'

'Not you, perhaps — not at the moment, at least — but they have one of your men marked.'

'No one was seen,' Jewd qualified.

Freath shook his head sadly. 'But he bled.'

'So what?' Leo frowned.

'I can even tell you where he bled,' Jewd offered. 'He bled onto a tree. Not much either … unnoticeable to most.'

'One of the Vested,' Freath said seriously, 'according to Loethar, has the curious ability to recognise a person through their blood.' He watched his trio of companions frown.

'What?' Faris asked. 'How? Smell?'

Freath shook his head. 'Taste. He tasted the blood that was spilled from the arrow-wound and now Loethar is in a celebratory mood that it is only a matter of time before Vulpan marks the man. You have got to get that man away from our king.'

He watched Faris walk away to lean against a tree, thinking and then his big friend, Jewd, moved to stand near. Leo had not moved. 'Where did you hide, majesty?'

'That is a secret that I must pass on only to another Valisar, Freath.'

He nodded. 'In that case, you will be pleased to know the other news I have heard.' He flicked a brief glance at the two men talking urgently between themselves, then looked back to the king. 'We believe your adopted brother, Piven, though lost, has not perished.' He saw Leo straighten with interest and even in the dim light could see the monarch's eyes flash with a new intensity.

'You're sure?'

'No, sire, I cannot be sure but the person who sent the news is very reliable — a true friend and loyal to you. Kirin Felt has gone in search of him. We understand that Piven has been living in and around Minton Woodlet.'

He watched relief spread over the young monarch's features. 'I thought Loethar might kill him.'

Freath nodded. 'In his strange way, majesty, Loethar was fond of Piven. He once confided in me that he had two friends, neither of whom spoke. One was the bird that you know about, the one he called Vyk. The other was Piven.'

'My brother was always so affectionate and good to everyone,' Leo admitted. 'I hated watching him be so friendly to the barbarian.'

'The good thing is, your majesty, that he is considered long dead. Loethar has effectively dismissed both of you from his mind. If Piven is found, we can not only reunite you brothers but we finally have a reason to rally people.'

'Don't get ahead of yourself,' Faris counselled quietly to Leo, arriving back from his discussion. 'We have to take this Vested working for the barbarian seriously.'

Freath gave a sound of relief. 'Thank you. Just get your wounded man as far away from here as possible. Send him to Medhaven or better still, put him on a ship somewhere to …'

'You don't understand, Master Freath,' Leo interrupted. 'You see, the injured man is me.'

10

It was nearing morning and they'd begun travelling after midnight. Greven took Piven's hand and the boy hauled him up onto the ledge.

'If Leo was trying to find this Kilt Faris you speak of, what's our best direction, do you think? Heading more west towards Caralinga so we can hug the coast, or is it best to keep inland, perhaps veer slightly more east, making for Berch in the north via Tooley?'

Greven looked at Piven, baffled. 'Honestly, my boy, I can't answer that. Lily and Leo took off a decade ago. I've had no word. They may be south for all I know. They may be in another realm.'

'Compass,' Piven corrected.

'They could even be gone from our shores altogether.'

Piven considered this. 'I doubt it.'

'Why? Leo would be a man already, Lily might even be married, have children.'

'Because Leo is king, that's why. He belongs here in Penraven.'

'Despite what you sense, Leo might be dead. Have you considered that?'

'Yes.'

'And?'

'Well, then I would be king, I suppose,' Piven countered, pulling angrily at the leaves on a nearby bush. He scattered the tiny flecks to the wind.

Greven was disturbed. 'No, that's not right. The Valisar line ends with Leo.' He suddenly began to cough; his breath dragged in with short rasps.

'Greven?'

'Let me sit,' he managed to choke out.

Piven lowered him to the ground. 'What's happening to you?'

Greven clutched at his chest and winced. 'I'm getting old, I suppose.'

'Let me see.'

'Don't fuss, child.'

Piven pulled the older man's hands away. 'Look at me,' he demanded.

'Piv—'

'Please.'

Greven obliged, taking the opportunity to study the child in the moonlight. Piven's lovely face frowned and stared, his curious vision looking well beyond Greven's eyes, and then he felt a coldness, like a splinter of ice, passing through him. No, not passing through, but cutting through him. With his adopted son's hands holding him firmly by the shoulders, Greven let go of all resistance to Piven's magic and studied his healer. The man was emerging; in a few anni, probably only a couple, Piven's jaw would become more prominent, and those soft wispy dark hairs around it would toughen. Piven's hair was black, the colour of the raven he spoke about often, so his beard would likely be coarse. He'd have to trim it constantly to keep it under control. Those eyes of his, once so open and innocent, now looked so much more shrouded.

'There,' Piven said. He sat back gravely and studied Greven. 'How do you feel?'

Greven smiled. 'Better. My chest was feeling tight. It doesn't anymore.'

'Good. Your heart was sick.'

'Is it?'

'Not any longer,' Piven replied and Greven noticed how clouded the boy's expression appeared.

'Are you feeling as well as I do?'

Piven shook his head slightly. 'What's that expression that Mistress Bane from the village used to use?' Greven looked puzzled. 'Ah, that's right. I feel as though someone just danced over my grave.'

'Why?'

'I don't really know. That expression seems to sum it up.'

Greven didn't push. As he was about to change the subject a large grey wolf padded around the trees below them, sniffing the ground. Greven tapped Piven gently and then put a finger to his lips to ensure the boy remained silent. They'd seen wolves before but not this close. This one was a big wolf and young from what Greven could tell.

Just dispersed from the pack, he mouthed silently to Piven. *Looking for a mate.*

Piven nodded and smiled. As he did so the wolf seemed to sense a presence, sniffing the night air. Suddenly it spotted them. This had happened before in the forest and Greven anticipated that the wolf would watch them very carefully but also move on quickly. He knew a single wolf would not attack them, but nevertheless he reached for his blade, unsheathing it. Piven noticed and took the blade from him.

The wolf let out a low rumble of a growl.

'It's warning us,' Greven mentioned unnecessarily. 'We'll just let it go on its way,' he soothed.

The wolf showed its teeth, pulling back its lips.

'That doesn't look too much like a warning,' Piven replied.

'It won't attack us,' Greven assured him.

The wolf's growl changed, rumbling into a snarl. Its hackles were up and its eyes were beady and angry. Greven realised the animal was not looking at him. Its gaze was firmly fixed on Piven, watching his every movement. In fact, Greven felt certain he could get up right now and perform a small jig and the wolf wouldn't even cast a glance his way.

As if he could hear Greven's thoughts, Piven gave a soft snort. 'It's me he's directing that at.'

'So I notice.'

Piven stood. 'What are you doing?' Greven said, grabbing for him.

'He doesn't scare me.'

'Doesn't scare — What? Lo save me, boy, I'll —'

At first the wolf seemed poised to leap at them. It had taken a genuinely aggressive stance. But Greven was astonished to watch its ears flatten. He turned to Piven. The boy had not shifted, had made no move of threat, and yet Greven saw a ghostliness pass across Piven's face, a deep, chilling darkness. His body tensed with fright but his attention was distracted by the wolf once again when it lowered its belly and slunk away, whining softly.

Greven and Piven watched it in silence until they could see it no more in the darkness. 'What in all the stars was that all about?' Greven finally asked.

Piven shrugged. 'Strange, wasn't it?'

Greven wasn't convinced by Piven's innocent tone. 'Did you do that?'

Piven turned his head to regard Greven. 'What makes you think that?'

'The wolf was scared of you, boy, or didn't you notice?'

'Scared? I don't think so. Outnumbered, wise even, but no, not scared. It had no gripe with us.'

Greven felt vaguely manipulated but before he could push Piven further, the boy raised his head, sniffing the air. Greven smelled it, too, and his stomach tightened.

'Fire!' Piven breathed. 'Stay here,' he said and began scrambling up the hill. 'I'll take a look.'

Greven waited anxiously. 'What do you see?'

'An eerie glow in the distance and smoke. Too much. People must be in trouble but I haven't a clue where it is. It's south, though.'

'I'm not sure we can be much help,' Greven commented.

Piven scrambled back down. '*We* can't be but perhaps I can.'

The old man's head snapped up. 'What are you thinking now?'

'Greven, people could be hurt.'

'You said south, boy. That's back from where we've come.'

Piven frowned. 'Probably that hamlet we skirted. Green Herbery. I think I should help.'

Greven reached for his companion. 'Listen to me. It is unwise of you to declare your talent. Please heed me when I remind you that it was only ten anni previous that the barbarians slaughtered people simply because of suspicions that they might wield a weak magic.'

A look of soft irritation ghosted across Piven's face. 'No one's going to —'

But Greven gripped the boy's arm. 'Do not be naive, Piven. Do not declare yourself in this way.'

'I cannot walk away if people are in trouble. It's not in my nature to be that cruel.'

'Piven, please!'

'No. You don't understand. I have to do this! This magic must be put to good use or … or …'

'Or what?' Greven queried, alarmed by Piven's suddenly helpless expression.

'Stay here and rest,' the boy replied, his face clouding again. 'You should have no further trouble from your heart but you are weary from what I have done. Heed my warning. It's not such a long way back. I can be there and returned to you by morning. I promise.'

'What about the wolf? Perhaps he might decide to come back and attack me,' Greven suggested, desperately attempting to keep the boy near.

Piven's eyes narrowed. 'He won't be back, I promise you.'

Greven could see by the set of the boy's jaw that his mind would not be changed. He had not encountered such determined resistance before. *Do I even know this boy in front of me anymore?* he thought.

'Don't be ridiculous,' Piven said, pulling out some food from the sack.

'What?'

'You've known me longer than anyone. And you're the only person I've ever spoken to at length.'

Greven realised he must have uttered his fear aloud. Either that or Piven had read his mind. He was no longer sure. In fact, he was no longer sure about anything. And if Piven could read minds, then Piven already knew the deepest and darkest truth of all.

Freath had not spoken since the chilling revelation of Leo's wound.

'What do we know about this man?' Faris asked.

The emperor's aide shook his head in silent shock, mouth agape.

'Freath!'

Faris's raised voice snapped Freath from his sense of despair. 'Nothing, I know nothing,' he groaned. 'As soon as Loethar gleefully told me the news, I was on the first horse out of the palace, making every excuse under the sun to try and hunt you down,' he said to Leo, ignoring Faris, who walked away.

'Gavriel told me that one of his father's creeds was that we must never make judgements only on what we see. Looks are deceiving. I judged you, Freath.'

'I lay no blame. You had nothing else to go on, your majesty, except what your eyes told you.' He frowned. 'And now that you mention him, where is de Vis?'

Leo's expression clouded and he sighed. 'One of the great mysteries. I have no idea.'

'Weren't you travelling together?' Freath was aware of activity around him from the outlaws, who were clearly preparing to move. Jewd had joined an anxious Faris, talking between themselves out of earshot. 'He's not dead, surely?'

Leo shrugged. 'We don't know; that's the problem. He disappeared one evening and we've never seen him again. The last sighting we have is of him being pursued by three barbarian warriors. We know they captured him, beat him and were probably preparing to drag his battered body back to Penraven. We don't believe they knew who he was, only that he resisted them and that gave them cause for the attack. It seems they never got to take him back. The barbarians were all killed that same night, felled by arrows. I've kept one; it's distinctive, fletched by someone not of the Set. I keep hoping I'll find another arrow like it that might point me in the right direction. I never give up hope of finding him — or his grave. I don't suppose Corbel ever … ?' Leo didn't finish because Freath was already shaking his head.

'No, highness. I haven't seen Corbel de Vis since the day of the raid on Penraven by the barbarian horde.'

Leo nodded. 'Another name to add to the body count, no doubt. But I hold hope for Gavriel. His disappearance never made any sense.' He cleared his throat. 'Master Freath, I'm finding it hard switching you in my mind from villain to hero. Although Regor de Vis told us never to make judgements until we knew all the facts, it was my father who implanted a notion that has become my creed for life. He told me that if I make a solemn promise, whether it be to myself or another, to break it is to be damned by Lo himself.'

Freath gave the young man a look of understanding. 'King Brennus never broke a single promise in all the time I worked with him. He was a man of his word and you would be doing yourself no disservice to follow in his footsteps.'

'What I hadn't realised is just how ruthless my father was capable of being.'

Freath wasn't sure he understood what the young king was getting at but he nodded. 'The history books in the royal library attest to the ruthlessness of the Valisar sovereigns, your highness. Ruthlessness, though, has connotations of cruelty and although I could cite many an occasion when your forebears were capable of cruelty, I do prefer to think of their ruthlessness as a single-mindedness of purpose; a means to an end, you could say.'

'Indeed. So knowing my father as well as you did, I'm presuming you could never imagine he would go back on an oath?'

'Never,' Freath confirmed.

'What if he had learned new information?'

Freath's gaze narrowed. He wondered what the king was reaching for here. Giving a very small shake of his head, he replied, 'Your highness, your father was a confident, decisive man. He would not make a decision — or a promise — unless he felt secure in the information he had. All I can tell you is that, based on what I knew about King Brennus, if he had told someone he would do something, no matter what occurred to try and change his mind, he would not go back on his word.'

'Thank you, Freath,' Leo said, his voice sounding suddenly deeper.

No one could have anticipated it and when it occurred, it seemed to happen in its own space and time. Freath even had time to think that the sword seemed to take forever to lift from the scabbard and make its arc of death before it found its home.

11

They'd arrived at a town called Woodingdene. It was a pretty place, from what they could tell, nestling within a small fertile valley, with the mountains still a distant frame and its splendid cobblestoned market square cradled by pastel coloured buildings, almost all devoted to the government of the empire. It was here at Woodingdene that Loethar had established much of his administration — his mint, for instance, required a large workforce and the town was clearly thriving on the gold imperials and silver compasses in particular that were struck. The old copper trents from sovereign days had been retained, minted using dies.

Despite Kirin's escalating worry of being here rather than on the road to finding Clovis — and, more importantly, Piven, if the boy in question was indeed the adopted son of the Valisars — he was intrigued to learn more about the famous mint that had once struck coins for three of the other realms from the old Set. Now it was responsible for a simple trio of coins that served all compasses. The individuality that had made the Set realms so interesting was beginning to be lost through imperial rule, he realised.

Everyone was tired, having journeyed through the night and once the soldiers felt satisfied that Kirin and his companion were not planning to make any trouble for them, the pair had been largely left alone. They could speak freely enough.

'Now would be a very good time to tell me who you really are,' Kirin murmured. 'There is nothing to be gained from the secrecy.'

The woman at his side sighed. 'My name is Lilyan. I was sent to keep an eye on you.'

'I see. So Freath really doesn't trust me.'

'I don't know Freath — only of him — so I can't answer that.'

He glanced at her, seeking out guile, resisting the urge to use his magic. He couldn't face the sickness, not when he'd spent most of the journey recovering from the last bout. He couldn't see her clearly in the pre-dawn light. They were of similar age and over the course of the night he'd decided she was prettier than he'd originally thought. He stared at her, relying on his own instincts and what she reflected from those green eyes to tell him what he needed to know. 'Not Freath,' he echoed. 'So who? Who is your master, Lily?'

'I have none. No one makes me do anything I don't want to.'

He sighed inwardly. *Why were women so complicated?* Everything a man said could be taken wrongly. Little wonder he had not pursued a long-term relationship with anyone. 'Let me say it a different way. Who are your accomplices in this venture to keep an eye on me?'

She lowered her voice still further. 'Kilt Faris.'

'Fa—!'

She glared at him to stop him repeating the name too loudly, nodding once to confirm it. 'He didn't understand why you were splitting up from Freath. Asked me to find out.'

'You're a spy?'

'Of sorts. Now I'm a prisoner of sorts.'

Kirin sighed. 'Not if we're careful. I am attached loosely to the palace and they will find nothing to hold me for. But you, that was a stupid claim to make.'

'I had to think of a way to remain alongside you. How was I to know what they were going to spring on us?'

'Well, now you're a liability of sorts.'

She bristled. 'I'll tell them I just didn't want to be separated from my husband.'

'Oh yes? Inspired. And what do you think will occur when they discover that Kirin Felt is not married, has been living alone at Brighthelm for the past decade?' He could see Lily didn't have an answer to this. 'Why is your friend interested in me anyway?' he demanded. 'Surely his interest is with Master Freath, whom he was meeting last night.'

Lily looked surprised. 'My friend doesn't explain everything. I've told you what I know. I had anticipated travelling to Brighthelm, ensuring this journey was not connected with any guile on your part and then returning to the north.'

Kirin ground his jaw. 'Perhaps we still can.'

'Hardly,' Lily said, her mouth twisting with worry. 'You're not married and I'm not Vested.' Before he could reply, she added: 'Another thing, take a look at our companions. They don't seem so cheery now, do they?'

Kirin had ignored the other Vested during the journey. The last thing he wanted was to be lumped in with them. But Lily was right. 'They look morose,' Kirin said.'

Kirin glanced at her as she studied them. Her gaze had narrowed. 'You know, I could be wrong but even by lamplight and from this distance I think those people have been drugged.'

'What makes you say that?'

She gave a small shrug. 'Years of understanding how herbals and soporifics work. Look at that woman,' she said, jutting her chin slightly towards a middle-aged woman. 'Look at her pallor, those droopy lids. And they're all weary, we know that — they're tired from travelling but there's something else. Look at how restless they seem in spite of that fatigue.'

She was definitely right. Kirin could see it now. 'He lied to us?' he wondered quietly.

'I don't know why but yes, I think either our friendly barbarian soldier lied to us or he genuinely didn't know they were drugged.'

Kirin gave a sound of disgust. 'Now I want to know why.'

'Are you really Vested?' Her voice was grave.

He nodded. 'Unfortunately, I am.'

'How unfortunate?'

Could he trust her? He had to risk it. He trickled his magic, just for a moment or two, knowing the price for this alone would be enough. Lily was so open a flood of information crashed into his mind, overwhelming him.

'Kirin?'

Familiar nausea rose. 'I'm fine.'

'You don't look it. Suddenly you look like that woman we were just talking about.'

'You asked me a question.'

'Are you going to answer me?'

'Yes, I have the misfortune of being heavily Vested. But only two people, and now you, know it.'

They both realised the caravan of people, horses and carts had stopped. 'Looks as though we're here,' Lily commented, 'wherever here is.' She looked over at Kirin. 'So you trust me?'

'What makes you say that?'

'I know a thing or two about keeping secrets. I don't think that was easy for you to share ... but you did. So you must trust me. Kirin, you don't look fine at all.'

'No, but I'll survive.'

'This happened earlier. What is it?'

'I lied about indulging in too much Rough. I get headaches. I've had one all night. I thought I'd rid myself of it,' he lied. 'Now it's back,' he added truthfully.

'I can help with that.'

He looked at her as steadily as he could given his plunging stomach.

She gave a small, sheepish smile. 'When I'm not playing at spy, or prisoner ... or liability, I'm adept with herbs.' She dug into a pouch slung around her body. 'Try these.'

He stared at the tiny black seeds.

'Trust me,' she urged. 'Just suck on a few of them. Once the shell breaks, allow the juice to slide slowly down your throat. You'll be tempted to chew them but don't. Keep them in your mouth as long as you can. The longer you can suck them, the more potent their effect.'

'What are these?'

'Seeds,' she said evasively. 'Put them in your mouth, Kirin, and tell me you aren't feeling brighter in a very short while.'

He knew they couldn't help him. 'And if you're wrong?'

She gave a flick of her dark hair. 'You can have your wicked way with me. That's how confident I am!'

Kirin blushed and Lily looked away, suddenly embarrassed.

The soldier they had spoken to earlier in the journey approached slowly on his horse. 'As you can gather, we're stopping here.'

'Why are the Vested so ... depressed?' Lily asked. Kirin glared at her.

The soldier fortunately didn't notice the look between them. He shrugged. 'Tired, I imagine. They've travelled without stopping twice as far as you have. Anyway, we plan that you will both be seen first.'

Kirin returned the man's gaze, forcing an innocent, quizzical expression. 'Why the hurry?'

The man appeared equally innocent. 'I know you're here because we insisted you accompany us. It's only fair we deal with you quickly and get you on your way.'

'And my wife,' Kirin stressed.

'Yes, of course, both of you,' the soldier replied. 'It's tiring, I know, but I am happy to escort you immediately to the authorities.'

'Authorities?'

'A single person,' the soldier qualified. 'His name is Master Vulpan.'

Kirin had expected this but even so the mention of the man's name made his belly clench. Vulpan was the reason Freath and he had rushed north. He wondered if Freath had found Faris. He hadn't even asked Lily whether Leonel lived. He almost laughed at his own apathy. He'd been so furious at being entrapped by these men that he'd forgotten what this whole struggle was about.

'Fine,' he said, finding a tight smile. 'If he's up at this time of the morning, then lead the way. Come, my love. Let's get this all cleared up, shall we?'

Lily grasped his mood, it seemed. She returned the adoring glance and nodded to the two men who permitted her to move ahead of them.

'We're aiming for that pale building over on the right,' their companion said.

Kirin sucked on his seeds, hardly daring to believe the nausea might be disappearing, and feeling a fresh thrill of fear at what Vulpan was going to make of him and his Vested 'wife' of no magic.

Pandemonium raged in the village of Green Herbery. A barn filled with bales of hay and stores for the winter had gone up in flames, threatening various houses and Herbery's only inn. Even from this distance Piven could see it would be impossible to get the fire under control. People would have to watch their livelihoods go up in smoke and their homes burned to the ground. As he drew closer he could see it was not just buildings and provisions at stake.

Women were screaming. Piven began to run.

Dawn was waking to an unpleasantness; the orange of the flames and their dirty grey smoke were a blot on the otherwise picturesque setting. Now he could hear the ferocity of the fire as new flames erupted and a shower of sparks exploded from somewhere in the barn. Villagers stood by helplessly holding dripping buckets and vessels, contents long ago exhausted and useless against such a force. New flames began to lick around the sides of the barn, the older flames already arching further afield for fresh tinder.

'Help them!' screamed one of the women.

Piven ran headlong into the crowd, which was suddenly still, no doubt feeling the dread of the situation. He pushed his way forward to where a sobbing woman sat by an unconscious man. In the man's arms was a child, also unconscious it seemed, possibly even dead. It was a boy, Piven thought. People tried to loosen the man's grip on the child but to no avail and the woman, lost in her despair, screamed at them to leave him alone, while still beseeching someone for help.

Both man and boy were badly injured. Clothes were partly burned off, skin was scorched and the smell of cooked flesh permeated the otherwise crisp early morning air. People had begun to retch and the injured man, still holding the child, had begun trembling as the initial shock wore off and was replaced by pain. It was a tremble that would accompany him to his death, Piven believed; death was not so far away now.

'He ran in to save young Roddy,' a bystander said. 'Now they're both dying.'

'Don't say that!' the mother screeched, looking around wildly. 'Don't you dare!' she repeated before dissolving into helpless sobs as she bent over her son, her head resting on the child's small chest.

A friend stooped to hug her. A man, presumably the innkeeper, arrived with a cask of liquor.

'Get some of this down his throat — as much as you can,' he said. 'Let him die drunk, feeling nothing.'

'Let's all pray,' someone else said.

'I agree with Ralf. Numb both with the Rough,' another agreed.

'He can't swallow. His whole throat will be scorched,' yet another countered.

'Let's speed them on their way to Lo.'

'Is Roddy dead?' a child wondered.

The mother seemed to swoon and then a fresh cry went up from around the back of the barn as the structure began to collapse.

People began to run, leaving behind the dying pair, still clasped by the virtually unconscious woman, and the single woman who held her, plus the concerned innkeeper.

Piven took his chance. He turned to the innkeeper, who was still holding the flagon of Rough. 'Could you and this woman pick him up, please?'

Ralf looked at him dumbly.

'Now!' Piven urged.

Obediently, still in a shocked stupor, the man gently unwrapped the mother's grip from her child, lifting him off the man's chest. Piven turned to the female comforter, who eyed him suspiciously. 'Help Ralf carry him.'

'Who are you?' she snapped, distraught.

'A stranger, as you see, but I can help if you do as I say and you do it quickly.'

'She's unconscious!' the woman hissed, gesturing at the woman she was still uselessly comforting.

'Not anymore,' Piven said, reaching out to touch the prone woman, who roused immediately, moaning and whimpering. 'Stand her up and lead the way back to her house — quickly, before the mob returns.' He looked back at Ralf. 'Get him between you and her,' he said, pointing to the helper. 'This man's life is almost given to Lo. You have to hurry now.'

Piven didn't wait for any more questions. He bent and picked up the child. 'Hurry,' he growled, and suddenly everyone was moving.

The mother of the child could barely focus. She was disoriented and confused but her helpers urged her forward with encouraging words and soon enough Piven could see that they were all headed to a very small cottage on the rim of the village.

'Inside, quickly,' he ordered.

The dying man groaned softly.

'Let him die,' Ralf said.

Piven sensed he was concerned that they were simply adding to the injured man's agony. 'His pain is so intense, more is hardly felt,' Piven said reassuringly. 'Put him on that pallet, then go and tend to your inn. Help the others.'

'I want to —'

'Go!' Piven ordered, staring at him hard. The man finally turned without another word and left, glancing once over his shoulder.

Piven had already forgotten him. 'We need fresh linens, fresh water, and some animal fat. Fetch it quickly,' he ordered the woman. She moved without protest, not aware that he was giving empty orders simply to occupy her, and remove her from the room.

Now Piven looked at the mother, who had been unconscious just moments ago. 'How are you feeling?'

'You're not even a man yet, ordering us about. Who are you? Why are they following your orders?'

'I need you to get up and leave.'

'What?'

'You heard me. Please leave if you want your family to live.' And then Piven smiled. Its warmth reached across the room and stilled her shivering; it seemed to calm her ragged mind and ease her heart of the pain.

'This is not my fam … why must I leave?'

'It could be dangerous for you to be near,' he said reasonably.

'My son, I don't understand.'

'Neither do I,' Piven answered. He glanced at the pair on the bed. 'We have only moments. If you want your boy to live, go!'

The appeal in his voice must have got through to her because she hurried towards the door. 'Are you really going to help them?'

'No one else can,' he replied gravely. 'Shut the door behind you.'

When he heard the latch of the door dutifully drop closed, Piven moved swiftly. Laying a hand on each victim, he raised his head, closed his eyes, and reached for the light within. He found it easily and as soon as he touched its blinding brilliance he channelled it through him and from him, gathering it up into an invisible force that he shepherded towards his suffering companions.

'Let this work,' he muttered to himself.

He could just hear the man's rasping breath so he knew he clung to life. Looking within the child, he saw that the flame of life flickered unsteadily with none of the heat that now raged around the child's body. Something about this pair niggled on the edge of his mind but he ignored it. He needed to give this his all.

Cooling and calming and life-giving, Piven's magic moved with a sure touch, finding every inch of its recipients that needed healing. And as he felt the deftness of that healing touch working its miracle, Piven heard the roar of the flames outside intensifying, screaming their rage that he would dare defy their fury.

But there was also another reason for those flames talking to him. They knew and they were ready to fill him with their darkness.

Mercifully, no other villagers had been burned; the only other victims that were touched by the repercussion of the fire's wrath were a few hundred mice, several starlings and a sleeping cat trapped inside with the hay.

Outside, the people of Green Herbery watched with a horrified fascination as the barn finally collapsed in on itself and then — they would swear it must have been a rogue gust of wind — the fire appeared to surge with a new ferocity, burning with a queer 'blackness', as some of them would later agree. The flames arching, bending, reaching almost as one, straining to leap across several houses to scorch the trees surrounding the cottage of the Widow Layton.

Inside, Piven felt the invisible shadows creep deeper with sinister stealth within. He possessed no ability to control this new entity that seemed to be gathering around and within him. He found a smile, though, as the boy seemed to slough off his stupor.

'Who are you?' the little voice asked.

'I'm Petor,' Piven answered. 'And you're Roddy, aren't you?'

The boy nodded, eyes wide and wondering. 'I ran into the barn to get Plod.'

'Plod?'

'My cat.'

'Ah,' Piven said, fearing Plod was cooked, but he was saved a response by the door bursting open.

Roddy's mother's scream came out silently. Her hands were clasped to her mouth and her eyes were even wider than her son's, filled with disbelief.

'He's well,' Piven said as she swept Roddy into her arms. He cleared his throat. 'But I'm not sure about your husband, let's see if —'

'He's not my husband,' the woman stammered through tears and shock. She kept kissing Roddy's head. 'He's a stranger, like you. He told us his name but I've forgotten it.'

Piven blinked.

'Is he alive?' she asked, haltingly, none of the amazement from her voice gone.

'He hasn't moved. Perhaps we lost him.'

At these words, the man on the straw pallet flinched; his whole body jerked, in fact, and then he groaned.

Piven was at his side in a moment. 'Slowly, breathe slowly, deeply. No, don't move, not just yet.' He stared into the man's face, still blackened, though only from the smoke and dust. 'I'm Petor.'

'Help me up,' the man said, his voice raspy.

Piven pulled him to a sitting position. An awkward silence settled around the strange quartet in the room, broken by the arrival of the woman who'd gone to get supplies, balancing a jug of water, linens, the animal fat salve and various other items she'd obviously grabbed in her frantic rush to do as she had been told. 'I think I've got everything. I even brought some —' She stopped still, her mouth open, her expression filled with a dozen questions.

'Look, Aunty Fru, I'm not burned,' Roddy said, standing proudly to twirl around and prove that he was whole.

The jug smashed to the boards and as it broke spilling water everywhere, it broke the spell within the room. Suddenly everyone but Roddy was demanding an explanation from Piven.

Piven put his hands in the air, buying time. But he couldn't think of anything to say.

'How can you explain this?' Roddy's mother asked. 'How? I saw my son — he was roasted like a piece of meat.'

'Hush, Em,' the woman called Fru admonished, nodding at Roddy.

'The pain,' the man commented. 'I know I slipped into death. I'm … I'm certain of it.'

Piven looked around at them wildly. He had been stupid. He should have let Lo take his own as he saw fit. If their god wanted to claim their lives, who was he to deny him? *Another god?* his mind's voice queried. Why else would he be able to wield this magic? He was a good person. He knew it. He wanted to help others, he wanted to be loved as he'd been as an invalid youngster. He'd been trapped for so long; mute, his thoughts unable to be expressed, his ability limited to simple actions. Even though his mind could handle complex ideas, it was as though they could only last for so long before they fractured into thousands of pieces. And all he had been able to do for too long was smile. He craved affection and gave it in droves. He had loved everyone and he knew he had been loved in return. Why shouldn't he save people from death with this ability of his?

'You weren't dead,' he answered the man. 'Just close. A minute or two of life left, perhaps.'

'But they were burned!' Fru exclaimed. 'Now look at them,' she said, wiping away soot and grime from Roddy's face to reveal perfect skin beneath. 'Not so much as a light scorch!'

Piven looked at the women's expressions of accusation. It was as though he had done something wicked rather than good. He felt the now familiar fury rising.

'What are you?' Roddy's mother demanded, looking suddenly repulsed by him.

Her horror shocked him. The aunt's expression reflected the same sentiment. Pained by their fear and naked loathing, he surrendered to the darkness that had been tapping at his shoulder for too long.

His face contorted into an expression of hate. 'You will remember none of this,' he said, his hand making a slow, small sweeping motion.

Without looking back, Piven ran out of the Widow Layton's cottage, using the back door to escape being seen. He headed cross-country, following the tiny rivulet that would lead him back to Greven and safety.

He didn't see a man stagger slightly as he watched Piven's retreating figure, nor did he see a boy whose sharp eyesight watched Piven until he was no longer visible. And neither of the watchers was aware of each other, or their silent promise to follow the stranger.

Freath looked down at the sword in his belly, clearly baffled by what he saw. 'Majesty?' he groaned.

Faris's shock was overwhelming; he was down on his knees between king and servant, immediately cradling the wilting Freath. 'Leo,' he all but whispered in his disbelief. 'What have you done?'

Leo's lips were pulled back from his teeth in a primeval snarl. He withdrew Faeroe and flung the sword to the side, where it clanged against a boulder. The king looked somewhat confused, a mix of loathing and triumph on his face. 'I have fulfilled my oath. Freath himself gave me permission.'

Jewd was already signalling for help but Faris could see it was no use. 'He risked so much for you,' he accused, his own fury threatening to explode.

The dying man must have sensed it, despite his shock and pain. 'Stop,' Freath choked out. 'It is done. The king has acted.'

Leo stood over Freath. 'Just as I could never know what passed between you and my mother, you could never know what promise I made that was witnessed by Gavriel de Vis. But he will never forget, Freath, and wherever he is, I hope he feels this moment and knows it to be the moment of your death as I promised him a decade ago. You killed my mother. Whatever your reasons were, however honourable they might have been, you murdered the queen of Penraven and I have now avenged her death as a dutiful son and fulfilled my oath.'

Faris saw the deep sorrow in Freath's eyes, watched the man nod his acceptance of the accusation but murmur nothing in reply. Faris exerted all his willpower to refrain from speaking. He had never heard such a load of rot in his life. The Valisars were deranged if they'd put an angry childhood oath, fuelled by fear and an overload of emotion, ahead of a precious life — a life that had been given in the service of that same family.

Jewd recognised his building fury because Faris felt a reassuring and very firm hand squeeze at his shoulder. His friend bent down. 'It's not worth it. He's a dead man,' Jewd whispered.

Faris knew Jewd was right. And not even Lily was nearby to offer any relief with her clever medicines. 'Get the king away from here,' he replied, disgusted by the very sight of Leo but keeping his voice even.

'I'm already gone,' Leo said, turning to pick up Faeroe. 'But I'll not clean your blood from my sword, Master Freath. I recognise it has been, in the strangest of manners, loyal to the Valisars. I hope before you take your last breath that you will pay me the same due.'

Leo didn't wait for an answer. He followed a scowling Jewd down to where the mules had been tethered, away from the bloodied scene.

Freath didn't need a physic to tell him that his time was short. He could feel the life bleeding out of him with each hard breath he took. The pain was irrelevant. It hurt but he knew it wouldn't last long and until then there were important things to say. He knew now he could trust Faris. Was it his imagination, or had the night begun to lift? Perhaps he might be granted one final dawn before his pathetic life was taken.

As if he could hear him, Faris spoke. 'Dawn's almost upon us,' he said, his voice thick with regret.

'Come where I can see you,' Freath demanded, rallying for whatever little time was left.

Faris eased from beneath Freath's head and crouched at his side. 'Freath, I was slow to react; if only I'd —'

Freath gave a soft sound of dismissal. 'Don't waste the words or the time,' he said, his deep voice slower than usual as he worked hard to keep it steady. 'There are things to be said.'

'But I want to say on behalf of Leo that his betrayal of you is —'

'Forgiven,' Freath cut him off. 'Let me talk, Faris. Pay attention because I won't have the strength to repeat it.'

Faris nodded as Freath took his hand. Freath felt a firm squeeze and he found a smile for the outlaw. *Who'd have imagined this?* he thought. 'As much as the king wants Loethar's head, it is not the emperor who is his true enemy. Surrounding Loethar are creatures far worse in their intentions. Assure Leo that as long as Loethar is in control, the various compasses are safe. Should anything happen to the emperor, a person like Stracker would take charge and there's no accounting for the savagery that would follow. Stracker has no scruples — no soul, I fear. Do you hear me?'

'Yes,' Faris dutifully answered. 'I will warn him.'

'Use Loethar to keep that balance of power for the time being. In the meantime, it is Vulpan you should now fear. Leo must be kept from him. I trust Loethar when he says that Vulpan's talent is uncanny. Whatever he is, Loethar is not a liar, nor a sensationalist. He is amazed and impressed by Vulpan.'

'I'll take every care, I promise you.'

'Find Piven. He is alive. Blood or not, the people will rally to his name.'

'How do I find him?'

'A man called Clovis. Kirin will know.'

Faris nodded.

Freath continued, despite the struggle to talk. 'Corbel de Vis will not be dead. I have no idea where he is but I suspect he was sent away to protect that family. I can't think why else. But he must be found, as must Gavriel. Those two were privy to information I can't know or guess at. Their father was raised alongside the secretive ways of the Valisars and no one was closer to that family than De Vis.' He coughed and blood gushed through his fingers where he pressed the belly wound. He could feel its warmth against his chilled fingers and realised he could no longer feel his toes. Death was reaching for him. 'Lo! That hurts. Forgive me.' He breathed hard a few times to steady himself. 'The twins will re-ignite the flames you need to fire the Set's collective memory of what it once was. Their names, together with Valisar, are synonymous with what the Denovian Set was built upon. They know things, those boys. Mark my words, Faris.'

'I give you my word I will try to find them.'

'So many oaths flying around. Look at the trouble it got me into,' Freath said and chuckled. 'Is dawn here?'

Faris looked up, although he didn't need to. 'The sun will be risen shortly.'

'I hope I can hang on for a little longer, then. I would feel the warmth of a new dawn upon my face before I go to Lo.'

'I'm sorry, Freath,' Faris said, genuine sorrow in his tone.

'I know. It is not your fault and it is not his. He has suffered much and he is a true Valisar in his duty. I'd never have thought it of the lad I knew but I see the family blood runs strongly in his veins.'

'If only he had the magic. That would be helpful.'

'I don't believe it exists,' Freath admitted breathlessly. 'But

Loethar does. He got it into his mind somehow that you have to eat people of magic to absorb their power.'

Faris stared at him, dumbstruck.

Freath chuckled. 'Not many people know — and I don't make a habit of sharing this — but I fear Loethar tried to consume a small bit of each of the Vested he killed.'

'You jest.'

'No, my friend. But he has realised the magic was not transferred. And he was probably wise enough to also work out that many of whom he killed had falsely claimed to possess enchantments in a vain attempt to remain alive.'

'So he's stopped eating people?'

'Yes. I suspect he is confused with the legend of the aegis.' Freath's breathing had become shallow.

'Aegis?' Faris asked tightly.

'Kirin will explain. Essentially, you must consume some of your victim to trammel him, or bind him to you.'

Faris nodded. 'I seem to remember talk of this at the Academy.'

'You went to Cremond?'

'As odd as that sounds, I did, yes. Is there anything I can do for you? Someone I can contact?'

Freath shook his head with difficulty. 'I have no family. The problem will now be explaining away my death to Loethar. You will have to be clever for I fear my time has now run out and I can no longer use my cunning to …' Freath winced and another gush of fresh, bright blood overlapped the darker, older blood that had turned sticky.

'Freath!'

Freath felt his hand gripped hard. 'You're a good man,' he soothed. 'Brennus chose you well for his son. Counsel him against hurried decisions rather than admonish him over his actions. As much as I hate dying, Faris,' he said, somehow injecting irony into his voice, 'our young king made a decision which he felt was based on honour. We must admire it.'

'I can't admire stupidity, Freath. He is too brash.'

'And you never were?' Freath had a spasm of coughing during which he gave up all hope of holding his wound closed, exposing the glistening mess of his severed insides.

'Never,' Faris answered archly and both men's eyes met with a soft smile as the sun's fledgling rays sparkled down through the trees.

'Ah, there she is, my precious dawn. Death's come to collect me, Faris. I hope Lo continues to bless you with your uncanny good luck and I'll wish you farewell.'

'Freath?'

'Make sure the king knows I forgive him and that I was loyal.'

'He will know it.'

'Faris, there's a woman. You must find her. It's about the royal lineage. I know not ...'

He never finished what he was going to tell the outlaw, his body convulsing, before he lay still, his eyes staring towards dawn's light, the sharply golden beauty seeming wrong as it shone upon this ugly scene.

12

By mid-morning Piven had made it back to the sheltered ledge where he'd left Greven but the older man was nowhere to be seen. Alarmed by his absence and still churned up by the events at Green Herbery, Piven gave in to his emotional and physical weariness, flopping beneath the overhanging vegetation. He sank his head between his knees and tried to blank his mind.

He knew now he could not escape what appeared to be his destiny. He had been fighting it for too long now, believing that if he could just keep directing his magic to helping others he might be able to live as the sunny, loved and affectionate person he had been as a child. But the magic didn't work by those rules, it seemed. In fact, it didn't consider his needs or desires at all. It had released him from his void, which he now accepted had been a protection of madness, keeping the magic out. It had found a way to deliver him from the barbarian into the arms of a loving guardian, and to give him a level of maturity and awareness that was uncanny for someone of his age and sheltered upbringing. But it was now exacting its price.

He didn't know how long he remained staring blankly like that but he was gradually aware of his intense hunger. His throat was parched, even though he'd stopped frequently to drink from the rivulet during the journey back.

'Ah, Lo be praised. You're safe,' said the voice of the person he most needed to hear.

'Greven!' he said, leaping to his feet and hugging the older man. The affection was returned twice as hard. 'You look remarkably well for someone I left here ailing just hours ago.'

Greven grinned, held up a brace of rabbits. 'Never felt better, my boy. Look what I caught in the early hours.'

Piven nodded gratefully and was even more appreciative that Greven seemed to sense his inner turbulence and left him alone, quietly going about skinning and gutting the rabbits. Piven found the small axe they carried and dutifully set about chopping down some small branches to build a fire. The smell of the smoke turned his gut but he was too hungry and too eager to slip back into a familiar routine with Greven to dwell on that revulsion.

Finally the roasted rabbits seemed cooked sufficiently for Greven — who had been busily rooting around in the surrounding forest replenishing his stocks of herbs and plants — to lift the meat from the flames.

'Nothing to go with them, I'm afraid,' he commented.

'Nothing else needed,' Piven replied. 'My mouth is watering. I'm famished.'

Greven looked at him, a soft enquiring expression on his face. 'We'll just let them cool slightly.' He sat down opposite Piven, regarding him over the flames. 'How bad was it?'

Piven dropped his gaze. 'Bad enough.'

'Dead?'

'We managed to save two people although the village has lost all of its stores.'

'Did you help?'

He had never openly lied to Greven. 'I did what I could.'

'You're being evasive. Just the way you smell tells me you were involved.'

Piven couldn't look at Greven. 'Two lives should have been lost.'

'And you saved them,' Greven finished.

'I could not let them die. One was a child.'

'And how did you explain your actions to those watching?'

'There were only two witnesses.'

'I see. And you have secured a promise from two villagers whom you can absolutely trust never to mention that a stranger — a youth, no less — strolled into the village one day when it was on fire and conveniently possessed the most extraordinary power to heal and made two victims — almost certain to succumb to their injuries — live instead?' Greven's sarcasm cut. 'These people are so trustworthy that you can rely on them never to make mention of this phenomenon?'

'I did my best to secure their silence.'

'I see.'

'I don't think you do,' Piven said, feeling the sting of Greven's disappointment in him. As Greven impaled him with a stare, he wished he had not spoken so rashly.

'Why don't you explain it? There's a lot I don't understand about you recently, Piven.' He lifted his hand at Piven's leap to protest. 'No, hear me out. Something's happening. I sense it.'

'Sense it?'

Greven blinked, hesitated, and tried to shrug. 'Well, feel it, then.' He wasn't convincing. Piven knew they were both lying. 'However you wish to describe it,' Greven continued testily, 'you are not the same boy I lived with.'

Piven gave a rueful grimace. 'That's the curious bit. I am.'

'Then why do you strike me as secretive and manipulative and suddenly so careful around me?' Again he stopped Piven from replying. 'Before you answer that, I want to say something more. It's important.'

Piven looked down. 'All right.'

'I want you to know that alongside Lily — whom you've sadly never met — I love you. I have only truly loved three people in my life. I don't remember my parents. They died when I was very young. I was certainly fond of the relatives who raised me. But there's three of you who mean the world to me and I've lost two of that trio. My darling wife, my beloved Lily and, Piven, I fear with every inch of my bleeding heart that I am suddenly losing you.'

Piven's head shot up. 'You don't know how wrong you are.'

Greven shook his head. 'I hardly know you sometimes.'

'I'm sorry.'

'Listen to me,' Greven said, his voice instantly gentle — the voice that Piven loved — 'you're growing up, I understand that. It's probably time for me to let go. My work protecting you is done. You need freedom.' He held out the rabbit. 'Eat up,' he said. 'Use the knife or you'll burn yourself,' he added before continuing, 'I know you probably need more time away from me — in fact, I think you need to be around people. It was fine while you were a little lad and while you were coming out of your prison. But you're whole now. You're intelligent and curious, you're witty when you're prepared to let that humour out and, above all, you need company to feel like you belong. Growing up in a forest is all well and good but it makes one insular. I should know, I did the very same thing to my daughter. But she'd had the benefit of spending her early years in town. You haven't. I've had you isolated with only deer and rabbits for company, and a silly old man.' Piven held his tongue. 'I've decided that we should make for Cremond. It's a more gracious region and one that promotes learning and enquiry. We might be able to get you enrolled in the Academy there, where you can put that intelligence to good use, perhaps even learn about some of the powers you possess.'

'None of that is necessary,' Piven said, cutting off the meat with the blade Greven had given him. On chewing his food he realised it tasted like sawdust. He knew what Greven was doing — he'd take him to the Academy, enroll him, have him accommodated and then one night he would just disappear. He knew that as deeply and as nakedly as he knew that Greven was right; he was changing and it was pointless denying it. He hated capitulating to whatever this change was — he would fight it as best he could — but he also knew that he would fight in vain.

'What do you mean?'

'I mean, I don't need that sort of attention.'

'You don't think you do,' Greven said, tearing the cooked meat from the carcass of the rabbit. He waved the piece of meat as he spoke in his measured way. 'But you will benefit from having others around you.'

'I don't think so.'

'You're too young to appreciate it,' Greven replied, chewing.

'My age is irrelevant, Greven,' Piven said carefully. 'And you know it.'

They both eyed each other. Neither said anything.

'We both have secrets,' Piven finally said.

At this Greven laid down his meat, cleaned his fingers on his clothes and used his shirt to wipe away the juices from his lips. All of this was done silently, and in a methodical manner. Then he looked up and asked a single question. Piven knew what it would be before the words were out; he also wished Greven wouldn't ask it because it would irrevocably change both their lives.

Kirin and Lily had been kept waiting for so long, they were both drowsy with the sleep they'd had to hold off during the ride. They'd been left in the cool reception chamber, the clay-tiled floors and the plain stone walls not helping the temperature. Kirin was embarrassed at having to be shaken awake.

'It's time to go in,' the soldier said.

Kirin struggled to clear his head. He was relieved that the brief doze had helped with the pain and nausea, which had definitely eased. He hoped he would be able to hold down the little that he had in his belly. Lily looked lovely but wan. As they were ushered into the chamber, he realised that next to a surprising stirring of desire existed a cold clamp of fear on her behalf. They were about to wade into dangerous waters, he was sure of it.

This chamber was the opposite of the hollow, echoing reception. Softer furnishings, thick rugs, mellow honey-coloured furniture and a wall hanging depicting the artisans, striking new coins caught Kirin's eye.

'I see you're taken with the tapestry,' said a voice.

Kirin swung around to see a man entering behind them. 'I'm sorry to have kept you,' he added with a brief smile. 'I like that work too,' he continued conversationally. 'There's so much history encapsulated in that one piece, it's astonishing.'

He looked back at them, smiling benignly.

'It's lovely,' Lily agreed, when Kirin said nothing.

Smartly kitted out in a gentleman's attire of sombre charcoal-coloured fabric, the newcomer looked every bit the dour professional. If Kirin didn't know otherwise, he would have guessed the man to be a physician or lawyer, a counsellor of some sort even, perhaps to the nobility or even royalty. His beard was closely clipped; he was tall with a straight bearing. And he seemed to be well spoken; the man was clearly educated. Kirin was tempted to pry but he held his magic back, waiting to find out what this man had in store for them.

'Please sit,' he said, making himself comfortable behind a large desk. 'I understand that neither of you has had any sleep and that you've travelled through the night on horseback to be here. I am Master Vulpan and I am attached to the emperor's new School of Thaumaturgy; I'm its principal. Nearly one anni ago, when I was appointed, I suggested to the palace that we keep a record of Vested. Thank you for volunteering your information. Most Vested don't, for reasons I can't fully grasp—'

'Most likely for fear of persecution,' Kirin interjected. 'I have vivid memories of being persecuted by the emperor's men.' He felt Lily glance at him but refused to return her attention.

The man did not miss a beat. 'And now you work for that same emperor, I'm told?'

'I work for a man called Freath, who is personal aide to Emperor Loethar. I am based at the palace in Brighthelm.'

'And you were found travelling south from Francham in the far north, am I right?'

'Yes,' Kirin said, ensuring that his voice sounded even and patient. 'I was with a caravan of merchants, bound for the city.'

'And why were you in Francham?'

'Master Vulpan, with respect, sir, what business is it of yours what I was doing in the north?' He felt Lily stiffen at his side.

Their host did not react to the surly behaviour. 'It is my task to compile a record of Vested individuals, as I explained.'

'Is it also your task as a principal of a school to track those people's movements constantly?'

Vulpan regarded him, eyes narrowing. Finally Kirin understood what didn't add up in the smooth and slick presentation of the man seated before him. His eyes; they aimed to unnerve with their dark impaling stare. 'Track? No, Master Kirin,' the man said airily. 'We simply like to know about new Vested; have a rough idea of where they choose to live.'

'Why? And who is we?'

'The *we* is easy. It is the emperor's wish to compile a list of Vested. The why is his business and I am not privy to his plans.' The man was lying; Kirin was sure of it. 'I possess the skill to "know" people by the individual trait of their blood. It is a simple, clever way to keep a record of our citizens who possess special skills.'

'The fact that the emperor wants to keep a record of Vested but not his other citizens suggests to me that there is an ulterior motive to the list. That he intends to make use of it at some point.'

Vulpan's demeanour did not change. 'Master Kirin, it was my impression that you volunteered yourself. Am I now to understand that you are here under protest?'

'Put it this way: I didn't ask to be removed from the merchant caravan and sent in a completely different direction. I was on a work mission for the emperor, as it happens, and I'm not sure he will take too kindly to me being away from my post, so to speak.'

'I will certainly petition him on your behalf if that is —'

'No, that will not be necessary. I have never behaved in a manner that would concern the emperor,' Kirin lied, 'and he would assume I have good reason to be elsewhere right now.'

'Good,' Vulpan said, his voice polite but with a hint of dismissal. 'And this is your lovely wife?' he said, turning his cold stare on Lily. 'Lily Felt, yes?'

Lily smiled blandly.

'A marriage between two Vested. How fortunate for you both to have found one another. And such a handsome couple too,' he added with oily charm. 'Now, my dear, your husband has an ability to "divine" shall we say … he can see traits in people, which he believes to be a fairly useless skill, or so he told our men. Nevertheless, the emperor appreciates all level of magic and all types. What is it that you claim to possess an ability with?'

Lily flicked a nervous glance at Kirin and he sat forward to speak again but Vulpan held up a hand of warning. 'No, Master Kirin, let us allow your wife to explain in her own way. Go ahead, my dear.'

Lily cleared her throat. 'Er, thank you, sir. Um, well, as I also informed your soldiers, it is a low level skill. Simple healing.'

'I see. Healing with magic, rather than props?'

'Props, sir?'

Vulpan smiled indulgently. 'Oh, you know, plants and herbs and all that paraphernalia,' he said, giving a wave of his hand to suggest it was all a bit beyond his understanding.

'They are effective,' Lily began, but Vulpan stopped her.

'Nevertheless, you are here as Vested and that is what interests us today … you can heal through magic. Correct?'

Kirin held his breath. He desperately wanted Lily to come clean, tell Vulpan it was a mistake. But they were already in so deep, lying about being married, lying about her skills, Kirin himself lying about his role at Brighthelm. 'Tell Master Vulpan, darling, how you can cure small ailments through touch,' he encouraged.

Vulpan's gaze slid, slippery and with a wintry coldness, to warn Kirin, but his encouraging smile never left his mouth, and never reached his eyes.

'It's true,' Lily started again, haltingly. 'I'm sorry, I feel rather nervous. I don't like talking about my magic,' she admitted.

'Not many of us do, my dear. Ask your husband. I'll wager he kept his skills quiet all of his life. I myself never thought my odd ability could be seen as anything but a curiosity. It's quite odd, isn't it, to taste blood and then to simply recognise someone, even if you've never seen him or her before. Who'd have thought it could be put to good use?'

Good use, my arse, Kirin seethed. *I'll bet you've never even tried to put it to good use.*

'Let me ask, what sort of ailments could you heal through touch? A headache perhaps?'

She nodded. 'Usually.'

'How about a sore leg?'

'I will always try.'

'Well, let's test it, shall we? Rather than wasting everyone's time — because you don't seem terribly confident, if you'll permit my observation.'

Kirin felt the tendrils of fear flutter at his throat.

'Test it?' Lily repeated. Kirin had to admire that her voice didn't shake and her body didn't tremble. But all the same he could sense her fear. And likely so could Vulpan, who seemed to be enjoying this interview, watching them squirm.

Vulpan held up his hand. For the first time Kirin noticed the bandage on it. Until now their interviewer had kept his left hand either in a pocket or below the desk. 'Accidentally burned it last night. Lo, how it hurt,' he admitted with a rueful smile. 'I actually sickened, I think. I spent most of the night with my hand sitting in a bowl of water, which seemed to be the only relief I could achieve. The moment I tried to remove it, the pain descended.' He mimicked lifting his hand from the bowl. 'No wonder people who are burned by fire, or through accidents with cauldrons of boiling liquid, don't survive. It's not the wound, it's the pain. I'm sure the heart gives up. This hand gave me serious grief last night. It continues to throb now.'

Kirin could envisage what was coming. He couldn't bear having to listen to Vulpan build this scene any longer. 'Lily, my love,' he said sweetly, 'why don't you see what you can do to ease Master Vulpan's pain?' He gave her a smile of encouragement he didn't feel. Kirin's mind fled to how cunning and resourceful Freath always was in the face of impossible odds. He needed to show the same resilience. He nodded at Lily again.

'I can try, Master Vulpan,' Lily said, and Kirin felt his heart bleed to see how hard she was working to sound matter-of-fact. He watched Lily rise and give Vulpan a smile he knew she had to force.

Walking around the desk, she gestured to his hand. 'May I?' she said.

'Of course. Let me unwrap the bandage for you.'

'I can do that, Master Vulpan,' Lily said gently. Kirin watched her skilfully unravel the makeshift bandages to reveal the ugly burn. 'That must hurt, sir,' she commented.

'It does,' he said blandly, 'although I can manage some pain by shutting it elsewhere in my mind, using an odd skill I've had since I was a small boy. Do you understand what I mean?'

'No, Master Vulpan,' Lily admitted.

He glanced over at Kirin. 'Do you?'

'Not really,' Kirin lied. 'But it is an enviable skill, I'm sure. If you are not irked by the pain, though, do you need healing?'

Vulpan smiled and Kirin saw only malevolence behind it. 'Show me what you can do, Lily Felt. I'm very intrigued by healers.'

Lily frowned. 'It won't be immediate, Master Vulpan. You need to understand that healing — even by magic — is not an instant process.'

'Oh, is that so? I thought the wound would simply disappear after your ministrations.'

Kirin saw how she smiled coyly. He couldn't tell if she was genuine or just the best actress across the Set.

'But I'll feel something, won't I?' Vulpan asked. 'I mean, for the purposes of this trial, I will need to feel a change.'

The word trial was not lost on Kirin and he was sure it wasn't missed by Lily either. 'Oh yes, I'm sure you'll feel a difference,' she confirmed. 'I will need to hold your head. Will that be permitted?'

'Whatever works for you, my dear,' he said, his sarcastic tone evident.

'Lay your arm on the desk so I can see your wound,' Lily said, standing behind Vulpan. 'Now close your eyes, Master Vulpan. I need you to concentrate — just for a brief while — on the pain in your arm. I know you have banished it, but if you can bring it to the front of your mind you will help me reach the pain and deal with it. Does that make sense?'

Kirin stifled the thrill he felt at hearing Lily turn Vulpan's words on himself. It was a hollow triumph because their situation was so tenuous but he took pleasure in realising that whatever fear Lily felt, it wasn't going to get the better of her.

'Not a word of it,' Vulpan replied haughtily, 'but there's no accounting for our magical skills, is there, my dear?'

Lily smiled bleakly over the top of Vulpan's dark hair to Kirin and he saw her shake her head with an expression of resignation. She was playing for time. She glanced behind her deliberately, and he saw that she was directing his gaze towards a letter opener with a sharp point. Kirin carefully kept his face blank but his heart sank. Lily was going to do something so unwise he couldn't credit it. And somehow he had to stop it.

She was now uttering nonsensical words, massaging Vulpan's temples — first the right, then the left. After she'd massaged his right temple for the third time, she kept her left hand busy while reaching behind her for the blade.

Kirin knew he had to move *now*! 'Lily,' he interrupted, shocking her, doing his utmost to cover his anxiety. 'Surely that's enough, my beloved? Your skills work so fast normally.'

Vulpan's eyes, which had even conveniently closed as he enjoyed Lily's touch, snapped open. 'Shouldn't your wife be the judge of that, Master Kirin?' he demanded, vexation brimming in his tone.

Kirin matched the irritation in his own tone; it was the only way he could ensure the Vested's attention would be focused on him and not Lily. He stood and beckoned to Lily. 'Master Vulpan, forgive me, but I am now very tired. My wife clearly has more stamina than I, but if you're not ready to add us to your list, then perhaps you could summon us when you are. My dear, we should leave.'

As Lily hesitantly returned to his side, the blade left behind, he pried.

Vulpan stood. 'You will —'

Now! 'Sir, can you just tell us whether or not your arm feels any better,' Kirin demanded.

Incensed, Vulpan opened his mouth but the words seemed to catch in his throat and he frowned. Kirin held his breath, both from apprehension and against the rising tide of dizziness.

'Well, yes, as a matter of fact, it does,' Vulpan admitted, still frowning, shaking his head. 'It worked, Mrs Felt. I see the scar but I am healed of its pain.'

'Excellent,' Kirin managed to get out through gritted teeth just before he staggered forward. 'Forgive me, I feel unwell.'

He remembered reaching for the wall but found nothing of substance as he fell through darkness.

The roasted meat turned acid in Greven's mouth at Piven's words. *We all have secrets.* What did he mean?

He stared blankly for a moment or two at the half-eaten rabbit carcass, now carelessly tossed back amongst the embers. It had been a delicious meal up until this moment — he hated to waste it but he feared he would return everything in his belly if he so much as thought about the food again.

Greven found the courage to raise his eyes to Piven. He was comforted slightly to see that his beloved child looked daunted by his words. But it was too late for recriminations and definitely too late to take it back — not that Piven looked to be withdrawing from his statement; he simply looked shocked that he'd said it.

As soon as their gazes locked, Piven looked down into his lap, fiddling with the axe handle, his own food forgotten and laid aside.

The silence between them lengthened until Piven, it seemed, could no longer bear it.

'We could forget I just said that,' he offered, finally looking up at Greven.

'But it would always hang between us, and we have always been honest with each other.'

'Have we?'

'What have you not been honest about?' Greven asked, quickly turning the scrutiny on Piven.

'About what's happening to me.'

'Will you tell me the truth now?'

'I can try. I don't understand it but I have the feeling if I don't say something soon no one will ever understand or forgive.'

Forgive? Greven was already confused. 'Tell me what is happening to you, Piven, please.'

At first the boy didn't answer. 'I'm changing,' he finally said. 'Just like I found my voice and emerged from the imprisonment of the strange void I existed in during my early years. It seems whatever that change has been about hasn't finished.' His voice was filled with regret. 'I'm sorry that I can't explain it easily.'

Greven wasn't sure whether to be impressed or frightened. 'How are you changing? What do you feel?'

'Darkness. This is not a change for the better, I fear,' Piven replied, his tone turning harsh.

'Darkness? Do you mean —'

'I mean evil,' Piven snapped.

Greven rocked back. 'In what way?'

Piven shook his head and Greven wondered if he didn't see the lad's eyes watering. He had never seen Piven cry, other than for a scraped leg or that time he broke his arm. The arm was healed the next day, of course, but they had never spoken about that. Piven had been too young to interrogate and Greven had been too swelled with joy to have the boy emerging from the shadows of his mind.

'In the worst way.' Piven turned his head, raised his knees up and hugged them, the axe loose in his hand, forgotten.

'The worst way I can imagine is that you would want to hurt people.'

Piven's head whipped around. 'I don't want to hurt anyone. I want to help people, heal people. And the more I do to save animals or help others, the more I'm filled with hate.'

Greven didn't understand. 'Piven, there isn't a bad bone in your body,' he began.

'That's what you think. That's what you see, because I fight it every day. I ran into Green Herbery because I needed to do something for people, something that was positive and good. I wanted to find someone to heal and I found two. I made them whole, Greven. I ignored your warning and I turned two burned, dying bodies into whole beautiful people again. And you know what my reward is?' Piven jumped to his feet, his voice escalating in emotion as much as volume.

Greven was surprised to feel genuine fear. It was such a novel sensation that a sense of wonder surrounded it. *Piven!* The sweet, helpless, beaming child was causing fear in him. Ludicrous!

'I'll tell you what occurs,' the boy continued. 'I get accused of evil and further filled with darkness. Do you understand?'

Greven shook his head.

Piven mimicked scales, his hands balancing invisible weights. 'Like this!' He moved his right hand down. 'As I try to use my skills for the benefit of others, the … the …' — he reached angrily for the word — 'the *space* that the outflowing of my healing power leaves behind is replenished' — he rebalanced his hands — 'with a destructive desire. It wants to tear down all the good. It wants nourishment, Greven, and I cannot control it.'

Greven swallowed. 'How has this darkness manifested itself?' he said, hoping his voice sounded even.

'It hasn't yet but it's building within me. It wants something. And I know people will want to destroy me because of it.'

'Destroy you? Piven don't you think this is —'

'Don't, old man! Don't you belittle what I've just told you. You're involved in this, down to your very boots!'

'Me?' Greven said, astonished, his hands against his chest. 'Piven, I found you. I've sheltered and raised you. I love you!'

Piven had stood and begun to pace, tension contorting his normally sweet face. 'All of that is true. But why? Why did you find me, Greven? We are strangers. We are not related; our families never knew each other. You were living in the Great Deloran Forest, I was living in the palace. What on earth did we have in common?'

'Coincidence. I stumbled upon you.'

'No! You lie! Look over there behind me,' Piven taunted.

Greven, confused, squinted over the youth's shoulder. 'What am I looking for, boy?'

'Your guide. See him? In the nearest tree.'

Greven stared up into the tree Piven had pointed out. The raven stared back.

Greven shook his head, fearful. 'How long has Vyk been there?'

'He was here watching you the whole time. He has been waiting for me. He knows things. Don't you sense that?'

'I … I don't know.'

'Yes, you do. Does he talk to you?'

'No!' Greven felt horrified. 'Does he talk to you?'

Piven shook his head, but an expression of cunning crossed his face. 'But he communicates. And in the same way that he drew you to me, he beckoned me towards you that day.'

'Who is he? What is he?' Greven demanded.

Piven shook his head again. 'You tell me. All I can tell you is that he belonged to Loethar.'

'Loethar?' Greven's face twisted in fresh astonishment.

'I never mentioned it before because he didn't want me to. I don't know how I know that about him.' Piven shrugged. 'I just do.'

'This is the emperor's bird?' Greven squeaked, his tone filled with incredulity. 'What? From his aviaries?'

'No. It's his pet raven,' Piven declared. 'It was he who called the bird Vyk, not I. The raven came to Brighthelm with Loethar when he slew our people.'

'And you've known this from the beginning of our life together,' Greven commented.

'When you found me that day, sitting among the kellet, I can't tell you what my thoughts were. I'm not even sure I had thoughts. But certain things got through to me. The smell of kellet, for example, I now realise was my memory of the queen — she liked to chew it, you see?' He didn't wait for Greven to respond. 'And then Vyk. There was something about Vyk from the moment he entered the palace that reached through the mist of my mind and touched me. I can't really remember how or why but even when I was not really aware of other people, I knew him. I recognised him.'

Greven tried to shrug but he was too frightened to make it look convincing. 'So, the two of you have a connection.' Even that didn't sound as convincing as he hoped it would.

'As do we,' Piven replied.

'Well, that's perfectly understandable. We have lived together as father and son for the past decade.'

Piven's gaze narrowed. 'We have been connected long before that.'

Greven frowned, trying not to betray that his throat was closing with fear. He made a show of clambering to his feet, stretching and sounding offhand as he spoke. 'I'm not sure I know what you mean by that, son. But it sounds rather nice to —'

The fright he'd been trying to contain came out in a terrified yelp when Piven was suddenly upon him, leaping carelessly over the flames of the small fire, heedless of any danger, and grabbing Greven by his arm.

'What are you doing?' Greven cried, breathless.

'You should never have taken me if you didn't anticipate this might happen one day,' Piven growled.

'No, Piven, no! You're wrong. I'm not the one. Neither are you.'

'You belong to one of us,' the youth said, dragging Greven towards the trees. 'I don't know what kind of willpower it has taken for you to be alongside me all these years but I admire you. I admire your strength.' He yanked the older man closer. 'I admire your resilience,' he said, pulling him again, 'and I admire your control.' He grinned. 'But I am your equal, Greven, in all of those things.'

'Piven, please,' Greven begged, realising suddenly how tall and strong his boy had become. 'All my life I've run from this. I promise you, it's not going to work. Think about who you are. The blood is not right. Let me be, let me keep hiding from it.'

'I know why you have hidden so well. And I'm sorry. But I need you. You want me to need you, don't you? Isn't that why you've been a father to me?' Piven yelled, pulling Greven harder, uncaring that the older man was staggering.

'I had no choice. I had to help you. How could I ignore you — so small, so lost, so vulnerable?'

'I actually think Loethar liked me. He liked Vyk and me. We were both silent, you see. I think Vyk is not a bird — not in the real sense. He is different; one could say damaged. And I am certainly damaged. Perhaps Loethar is too. And maybe that's why he liked us. We're kindred spirits. I doubt he ever would have hurt me. Your concern was unfounded. You should have left me. But you were drawn to me, weren't you, Greven? In spite of all that careful control, years of training yourself to resist us.' On the final word he shoved Greven downwards and Greven could not resist the strength of his adopted son. He bent and fell to his knees without further physical protest.

They were both kneeling now, their two arms reaching across the wide stump, as though preparing to arm wrestle.

'Don't do this,' Greven pleaded.

'I need protection. That's a father's role.'

'It won't work!' Greven yelled. 'We will disappear. I promise you. We will find a ship and sail somewhere. No one will ever find us.'

'You don't understand. We could leave but the darkness won't. It will travel with us and I will wreak havoc wherever I go. People will want to kill me.'

'I won't let them. I won't let anyone harm you.'

'I know you won't, Greven,' Piven said, 'which is why this is so necessary.' He sounded almost kind as he raised the axe he'd carried with him and brought it down with blinding speed and ferocity to sever Greven's hand from his arm.

Greven screamed. But not from pain, though that would come later. He was screaming from the torment of his life and his birthright.

Overhead, on the branch of a nearby tree, the raven stared at the bloody scene, still, silent and unblinking.

13

Kirin woke in a strange room. He opened his eyes fully, trying to make sense of his surroundings. He expected nausea but it was not present. Instead, there was a new sensation: blindness. His left eye gave him no information. He instinctively reached to his face to check that he wasn't being fooled by a bandage but his hopes were dashed. His face was bare and he was blind in that eye.

Sorrow welled alongside anger.

'Kirin?' It was Lily's voice and he turned towards it. He hadn't seen her sitting there out of the range of his remaining good eye. How could he? He was blind after all, he thought bitterly. 'You frightened me, passing out as you did,' she said.

'Are we alone?' he asked, his voice scratchy.

'Yes.'

'I need water.'

She obliged, helping him to sit up and sip some from a small bowl.

'Strange,' he commented, 'normally I'd be retching by now.'

'I think those seeds helped but I've added some herbals to the water. Even though you haven't been aware of it, I've been giving you sips for the past few hours.'

'Then you must be a witch, because it's working.'

'What happened?' she asked.

'You tell me. What did he say?'

'He's confused and I haven't enlightened him on anything. He's somehow convinced that the pain of his burned arm has dissipated. You passed out and he had you carried away and I took that chance to suggest I put some of my herbals to work on his arm. Fortunately there was a half decent garden by the kitchens and I found most of what I needed. He's now got a paste on that burn being replenished each hour. That will be working in our favour; I know the pain will be greatly eased as a result.'

'So he believes us?' Kirin said, pushing himself further upright, surprised that he didn't feel overly dizzy.

'Well, he believes that I'm Vested.' She dropped her voice to a whisper. 'But I know I'm not.'

Kirin shrugged. 'Maybe your talent has shone through late,' he tried.

She gave him a hard look. 'I know I'm not. So that means you did something. What did you do?'

He sighed. 'I told you that I have some talent.'

'Some talent? You convinced a man he was feeling no pain when surely his arm was throbbing.'

'He'd done most of the hard work himself. He told us he could put pain aside, remember?'

'Yes, but I also remember how I asked him to bring it to the forefront of his mind so I could focus on it.' She gave a brief, rueful laugh. 'What was in my head?'

'Self-preservation, I imagine. Were you really going to stab him with that letter opener?'

She nodded gravely. 'Right here,' she replied, pointing to her neck and the jugular vein. 'He'd have bled out in moments.'

'And then?'

She shrugged. 'I couldn't think that far ahead.'

'No, I realised that.'

'So you saved me.'

'I did what I could.'

She took his hand. 'Well, it was impressive.'

He knew he should pull his hand away but he couldn't. It felt too good to be touched so affectionately, so gently. It had been a long time. His anger at his magic's price subsided. Since first meeting Freath, he'd always known his body was going to break down; it's not as if he'd had no warning. 'Tell me, is King Leonel alive?'

She regarded him carefully, fiddling with the cool compress at his head. He took her wrist. 'I am no enemy to him, Lily. Freath and I travelled north to find and warn Faris about Vulpan. If Leonel lives among you, he must be protected from this new threat.'

She looked shocked, stared at him, disbelieving. 'How do you know?'

'Loethar was bragging about it to Freath. We left the palace as soon as we heard and Freath set up the clandestine meeting with Faris. He will know all of this by now and hopefully already protective steps are being taken. Is Leonel alive? I've given my life to his protection; one day perhaps you'll learn the details but for now I think you know in your heart that I am no liar.'

She stared at him again, both of them suddenly aware that he was still holding her wrist. Kirin experienced a thrill of desire triggered by the flash of confusion he saw in her eyes. But just as swiftly her confusion turned to discomfort and he let go of her arm.

She hesitated, then finally nodded. 'The fact that you call him by his true title is an indication of your loyalty. Yes, Leo lives. He's a tall, strong, fine young man now.'

Kirin actually punched the air, promptly regretting the effort. 'Ouch, that isn't good for my head. But this is the best news of all,' he said, beaming, feeling instantly rejuvenated. Perhaps the fight had been worth it. He grabbed her hand again and kissed it. 'Thank you.'

Lily laughed at his courtly gesture. But as their gazes met, she hesitated. So did Kirin.

'Now, Lily,' he said, deliberately changing the subject and once again releasing her. 'Where the devil are we?'

She looked momentarily abashed and then gave a soft sigh. 'Not out of the woods, that's for sure. Vulpan was so taken by the help we provided that we're in some chamber adjoined near the kitchens.'

'So we're not free to go?'

'Actually we are … once we give blood.'

'Get them in here. Let them bleed us now and we'll be on our way.'

'It's not that simple, Kirin,' she said gently.

'What do you mean?'

The door opened before Lily could answer and Vulpan himself breezed in, saving Lily any further explanation. 'Master Kirin,' he said, all smiles. 'I'm glad to see you are recovered. Whatever happened?'

'Er, I'm not sure. I tried to warn you that I was tired. I've been having headaches,' Kirin offered, hating how unconvincing his pathetic hedging sounded.

'Well, you have the perfect nurse in your lovely young wife, here, Master Felt. She's certainly helped me.'

Kirin nodded, hoping he managed to achieve the smug expression he had reached for. 'Are we free to go, Master Vulpan?'

'Yes, of course … er, although I will want to have a sample,' Vulpan said. Kirin knew he was feigning awkwardness. This man, he sensed, thrived on awkward situations.

'So Lily was explaining,' Kirin admitted. 'How do we do this?'

Vulpan smiled. 'Perhaps I'll demonstrate on Mrs Felt. Come here, my dear.'

Lily approached him, her boots clicking across the flagstones. She instinctively held out a hand.

Vulpan's smile widened. 'I prefer here,' he said, pulling her hair away to expose her neck, touching her exactly where she had shown Kirin she'd have struck Vulpan if given the chance. The Vested unfolded a tiny blade that even from where Kirin sat, appeared viciously sharp. 'A tiny nick, nothing too deep, I promise.

It will leave a small scar, of course. But then that's my intention.' He glanced over at Kirin, the smile still present. 'I like to leave my mark … especially on a beautiful woman.'

Kirin bit the inside of his cheek. Vulpan was baiting him — they both knew it. Kirin just wanted to get himself and Lily as far away from this sinister man as he could. If it meant allowing Vulpan to touch Lily in this way, so be it. Clearly, the outlaw Faris reckoned she was made of stern enough stuff to risk putting her in danger. Kirin already hated Faris for sending Lily into peril and refused to ask himself whether that loathing was truly about gallantry, or a more helpless and basic masculine instinct.

'You're trembling, my dear,' Vulpan said, amusement in his voice. 'There is nothing untoward about this, although it is unusual, I'll grant you. Don't worry. Your husband is present.'

Lily said nothing but her gaze was fixed on Kirin, her eyes watering slightly. In that moment something passed between them. Kirin told himself it was simply a reflection of her fear, but he wished it was not. For now he permitted it to be a small measure of comfort in an otherwise desperately uncomfortable situation.

Vulpan laid a hand on her slim shoulder and then tilted her head. 'Like this,' he encouraged. 'Ah, perfect. Now, just a little pinprick of pain,' he said sweetly, before he drew the blade across what Kirin thought was the most perfect neck he'd seen in a long time. He watched blood bloom onto its flawless creamy skin and he tried not to dwell on Lily's wince. In his imagination he kissed the small wound better.

In reality, he instead watched Vulpan bend close to Lily's neck and ghoulishly inhale. 'Ah, the smell of fresh blood. Nothing so delicious — and nothing so intoxicating as blood from a woman's neck, especially one as pretty as you, my dear.'

Kirin was not a violent man but he understood now how people could be driven to violent acts. It took everything within to remain still, to appear unmoved. 'What now?' he asked in a tight voice, not taking his gaze from Lily's face, hoping his composure would help her to keep hers. He saw a tear roll out of one eye and down the cheek that was tilted towards him. He watched the tear splash on the flagstones and he hated himself for being so weak and vulnerable at this moment.

'Now comes this,' Vulpan replied and bent his head again, this time horribly close to Lily's neck, where several trickles of blood were traversing their manic pattern towards her collarbone. Slowly and lasciviously, Vulpan licked at Lily's blood. Kirin closed his eyes, hoping that Vulpan would be done by the time he opened them.

He was. Kirin found their captor lingering over the sensation, his tongue licking his lips clean, his eyes closed and an expression of rapture on his face.

Lily reached up and wiped her hand over the wound, pretending to pat at the blood, but Kirin knew she was wiping away the wet memory of Vulpan's tongue on her neck. For a moment Kirin felt a rise of nausea that had nothing to do with the potency of his magic.

'Delicious,' Vulpan admitted quietly. 'Your blood is sweet and fresh, Lily. Thank you. I will never forget you.' He looked across to Kirin. 'Your turn, Master Felt. Lily, you may go now.' She looked uncertain, glancing at Kirin, her anxiety plain. 'Hurry up now, Mrs Felt. Your husband will not be long and we can get you both on your way.' There was a firm tone of dismissal in his voice. Kirin nodded at her, his expression filled with encouragement and reassurance. It wasn't as though they had a choice.

When the door closed behind Lily he turned to Vulpan. 'Do you plan to lick my neck in the same manner, Master Vulpan?' he said conversationally.

Vulpan smiled. 'No, that manner is purely reserved for pretty women, Master Felt. I am not an attractive man; I have known that all my adult life. And, disconcerting as it is, I have also come to accept that women find me ... well, curious, shall we say.'

Disturbing, Kirin thought.

'And so I must take my opportunities to be close to women when I can,' Vulpan continued and gave a soft chuckle. 'My apologies, Master Felt, that I took my opportunity with your wife. Your thumb will do nicely.'

Kirin kept his expression blank as he stood, surprised at feeling so strong, and held out his hand. Even though Lily was not his wife, he still felt outrage on her behalf. 'I feel I should challenge you to a duel or something, Master Vulpan,' he said, as Vulpan unlocked the blade again, careful to ensure that a tone of amusement laced his words. 'I fear, however, that I am in no condition to make any challenge to anyone.'

'Indeed.' Vulpan sliced into Kirin's thumb. 'Do you know what I find most interesting about your wife, sir?' he asked as he squeezed the cut causing it to bleed freely.

Kirin shook his head, revolted by the thought of what was about to occur.

'She tastes different than all the Vested women I've experienced,' Vulpan explained before pulling Kirin's hand to his mouth and sucking the bright blood.

Kirin's stomach turned as the warmth of the man's mouth closed on his thumb. 'Am I supposed to be impressed by that?'

Vulpan closed his eyes, carefully tasting Kirin's blood and presumably storing the memory of that taste away. He returned his gaze to Kirin. 'Thank you. No, you shouldn't necessarily be impressed, but I should be intrigued … and I am. I shall take care to mention it.'

Kirin schooled his expression not to falter. 'Is it that interesting? How is she different?'

'In a unique way, actually.' Vulpan licked his lips as though remembering the taste. 'There is a common element to the Vested women. I can't explain exactly what that is but I can taste it. I taste it in you, too, but in a different way. That particular quality is, however, lacking in Lily.'

Kirin forced himself to shrug casually. 'I can't imagine why, though I rather like the idea that she is unique.' He frowned. 'Mention it to whom, by the way?'

Vulpan grinned and Kirin saw his own blood still staining the man's teeth. 'Why, the emperor, of course.'

Kirin found Lily in the kitchen, just finishing a bowl of creamed oats.

'I had to eat something,' she admitted, 'I was feeling so sick after that encounter.'

'Didn't do much for me either,' Kirin replied.

'You look so much better, though.'

'I feel it. Lily, we must go.'

'Yes, I realise but —'

'No, now.'

A man entered from the back door and smiled at seeing Kirin. 'Ah, you must be Master Felt. I am the cook here. Can I get you something to eat? Your wife has paid attention to my offer and helped herself.'

Kirin forced a smile. 'No, but thank you. We're in a hurry to be gone actually, but if I may, I would be grateful to grab some food to eat on my journey.'

Lily frowned at him in query but Kirin shook his head.

'Of course,' the cook replied. 'We have some delicious fresh goat's cheese and I'm sure you can smell that the bread's already baked for the day.'

'Thank you, that's what's making my belly grind, I'm sure. Come, my love, we must check on the horses and be away quickly.'

They waited only long enough for the cook to tie up some bread, cheese and figs into a square of linen. 'Here,' he said, 'drink this cup of milk as you go to the stables.'

'You're very kind, Jole,' Lily said and took the food. Kirin added his thanks with a smile and a nod before taking Lily's arm and all but dragging away.

'It seems you can charm any man you wish.' He ignored her look of surprise. 'How do we get out of here?' he growled.

'This way,' she said, pointing. 'What's going on?' When he scowled at her, she followed up with: 'I mean, other than the obvious.'

'I'll tell you once we're on the road. Hurry.'

Mercifully for Kirin, the horses were ready and they didn't see Vulpan again, although Kirin suspected he was watching them from one of the many windows. Kirin didn't look back, urging his horse forward, knowing Lily had no option but to match his pace. He had them galloping the moment they were out of sight of the town's entrance.

After a time of determined galloping, he veered off the main road, heading east. He allowed his horse to slow and Lily to draw alongside him. She said nothing as she caught her breath, waiting for him to break the difficult silence that suddenly hung between them. Buying time, Kirin slowed his horse further and reached to untie the food. He offered Lily some bread.

She shook her head. 'Are you going to tell me why we've left the road to Brighthelm?'

Kirin chewed slowly. 'Let me eat something quickly and then I'll explain everything.'

Lily waited while he took this chance to formulate how to tell her what needed to happen next. He wasn't hungry; his appetite was lost but he knew he had to eat and after swallowing all the bread and half the cheese, his belly felt full. He wrapped up the remains and put them away. 'We're on the road to Camlet,' he began.

'So I gathered.'

'I don't plan to go to Camlet, I'm just trying to find the next village or town that has a priest.'

She frowned. 'A priest?' Then she grinned. 'Oh, I see, to wash away the taint of Vulpan with holy water. Then I want him to bathe my neck with it because —'

Kirin cut her off. 'No, I need a priest so that he can marry us.'

At first Lily stared at him. He knew she was likely running his words through her mind to be sure she had heard right. Finally she pulled at her horse's reins, stopping it. 'Marry us? You and I?'

'I wasn't planning on wedding one of these horses,' he said, hoping sarcasm would cover his self-consciousness.

'I can't marry you,' she said, and he winced at the horror in her voice.

'Nevertheless, you must.'

'Kirin, I am to be married in the next moon or so,' she gabbled. 'I am to be the wife of Kilt Faris. This is ... this is ridiculous.'

'Is it?'

'Well, isn't it?' she demanded. Even angry she was attractive, Kirin decided, noticing the splash of colour at her cheeks, the way she flicked her hair and how her voice had deepened. 'I mean, we're strangers!'

'Indeed. But perhaps you should have thought of that before you made claim to be my wife or accepted the dangerous and frankly idiotic mission to play spy for your husband-to-be.'

'Kilt didn't expect all of this to occur,' she snarled. 'And I was in a bind.'

'And now you're in a bigger one. Vulpan knows you're not Vested. He doesn't understand how this can be, or why, but he senses a ruse. He plans to mention the discrepancy to his superior, who happens to be the emperor. Would you like to imagine how that conversation might go?' Kirin shook his head. 'Loethar knows I am not married. I left the palace barely days ago as a single man. So that combined with Vulpan's suspicions ... we cannot risk Freath and myself. We are the only allies to Valisar in the palace and now that we know Leonel lives, we have all the more reason to protect him.'

'When we were talking before you confessed you weren't sure the fight was worth it,' she accused.

He nodded. 'That's true. It's one of the reasons I left Freath alone to meet with your intended husband. I still believe that

Loethar is making a good fist of ruling the new empire and I needed some distance from our struggle to work out whether fighting him in this way is wise. But since meeting Vulpan, I realise Loethar is still overly concerned with manipulating power. He wants to control the magic Vested in our land through our people. One person alone should not have that sort of access or control. Freath is right; even though life is more than tolerable now, we should still attempt to return the Valisar line to the throne.'

'Vulpan scared you that much?'

'Vulpan is evil, Lily. You know it, you felt his touch. I looked within him; he craves power. He wants to be indispensable to the emperor. His talent is unique — I've never heard of such an uncanny ability — but because he strikes me as an individual with few scruples, he is also dangerous and frightening. If Loethar grants him too much power, who knows what the repercussions could be. He knows us now and he also knows one of your band, so you'd —'

'What do you mean?'

Kirin shrugged. 'I'm sorry, I should have mentioned this before. That's why Freath and I came north; to warn Faris that whichever man was recently wounded he is now known to Vulpan and thus to the emperor.'

'Lo save us!'

'What?' Kirin demanded, staring at Lily's greying face, her hand clasped over her mouth. Then it dawned on him. 'The king?'

She nodded, unable to speak.

'Vulpan has tasted King Leonel's blood?' Kirin clarified, hardly daring to believe his own words.

'It was an arrow wound, a chance encounter. Jewd got him away; though the wound was hardly a scratch, it was not life-threatening either.'

'Oh, but it is!' Kirin spat. 'Vulpan now knows him.' He looked away from her, dismayed and anxious. 'But Freath will know this by now so he will take measures.'

'What can be done?'

'I don't know. That's why Vulpan is so dangerous. He's in this area now because he's scouring the midlands, sweeping north until he recognises his man.'

'And he doesn't even have to know his face.'

'That's the true darkness of his skill. Once he has tasted you, he doesn't forget. He doesn't even have to taste you again. It's as if he can smell his victims.'

'What are we going to do?'

'I don't know. But right now we have a more pressing problem to solve. If your Faris is sensible, he'll remove the king to a safe place, perhaps beyond the empire.' He ignored Lily as she shook her head. 'But if you and I are going to survive long enough to see Leo on the throne, we must marry.'

'Kilt will never forgive me.'

'Faris will be lucky to attend your burial, Lily, if you don't marry me.'

She looked shocked and he was relieved — at least she was finally grasping the importance of what he was proposing.

'But what shall we say? No one's going to believe us. Least of all Kilt Faris.'

'This is not about Kilt Faris! You can tell him whatever you wish. What we have to worry about is what we tell the emperor.' He urged his horse forward. 'Come on, we can talk as we travel.' Reluctantly, Lily joined him. 'We shall have to say that I have known you since I was very young. Let's say we lived near each other on Medhaven — that's where I grew up.'

'But I've never been there.'

He shrugged. 'Can't be helped. Loethar already has on record that Medhaven was my home when I was a child.'

'And if they check up on me?'

'We'll cross that bridge if we reach it. So now let's get our stories right. We're about the same age, so it's feasible we played together as youngsters. My father was a fletcher. He's dead now. How about yours?'

'My father, when I last saw him, was a leper but also a talented herbalist. I have no idea whether he's dead or alive.' Kirin heard the emotion in her voice.

'I'm sorry to hear that.'

'Are you?'

'That you don't know whether he still lives? Of course I am. Why don't you know more about him?'

'It's a long story, Kirin,' she said, sounding suddenly weary.

'Well, we're going to be husband and wife. I need to know everything I can about you.'

'I don't know if I can do this.'

'We have no choice. When all is done and Leonel is king, you can divorce me. Until then, your decisions affect my life.'

'He'll never forgive me,' she repeated. Kirin made a dismissive gesture, but Lily persisted. 'No, you don't understand. Kilt is a man of his word. He's intense in a way I find hard to explain. He will see this as betrayal and forgiveness for a betrayal of this level is impossible.'

'If he can't forgive you, Lily, he can't love you enough.'

She stared at him, a mixture of indignation but also injury on her face. 'How dare you.'

Kirin shrugged, unyielding. 'If you were mine,' he said softly, 'and you told me about the life-threatening position you found yourself in, in which the only way to protect your life was to marry a stranger, I think I would find it within my heart to forgive you. No, I know I would. And I barely know you.'

Lily had no answer for his response. He could see the battle on her expressive face; offence was at war with how touched she was by his tender admission. Not another word passed between them until Kirin broke the awkward silence some time later.

'I see smoke. We must be approaching a village.'

'Possibly Hurtle, although I've lost my bearings,' she offered. Though her voice was tight he could tell she was making an effort.

'Lily, I know this is asking a lot of you but when we arrive we've got to look and act like lovers. You know, in the full bloom of love.'

She nodded, but said nothing.

He persisted. 'Whatever I do, I will do purely to protect our disguise. Once we're behind closed doors, I will not touch you, I promise.'

'How decent of you,' she said, her sarcasm biting.

'I'm sorry.'

She turned to him, apology on her face. 'It's not your fault, Kirin. It's mine. What's more, you've already saved my life once, and here you are doing it again. I'm being ungracious. My father would be ashamed of me. I'm ashamed of me. I'm the one who is sorry and I will try hard, I give you my word.'

'Well, that sounds like a good place to start,' Kirin said, trying to inject some brightness into his voice. 'Tell me about your parents. I'd like to know as much as I need to know.' He looked at her, meeting her eyes straight on.

She frowned as she regarded him. 'Why are you staring at me like that?'

'Yes, I suppose I should have mentioned it. I find myself blind in my left eye.'

'What?' she exclaimed.

'The price one pays,' Kirin said matter of factly.

'Blind, because of your magic, you mean?' Lily asked, aghast now.

'I'm afraid so. It's been threatening to go for years and now it finally has.' He gave her a rueful smile. 'It's a relief, really. Now I don't need to fight it anymore. Perhaps that explains to you, though, my reluctance to use my power.'

'I had no idea,' Lily said, her voice shaking.

'Why should you?'

'I'm sorry, Kirin.'

'Don't be.'

'But it's my fault,' she said, her distress intensifying. 'You gave your sight for my life.'

'I have another eye,' he dismissed. 'Now tell me about your father.' At her distraught expression, he added, 'Please, Lily, don't make this harder.'

'All right,' she agreed hesitantly, though it was obvious she was struggling to ignore his revelation. 'My father's name is Greven. I haven't spoken about him to anyone in many years. I'm not even sure whether to speak as though he is alive.'

Kirin listened as Lily sloughed away years of silence about her family, and sensed a melancholy settle around her like a shawl, until they were both enveloped within it.

14

Greven stared dully at the bloodied stump that his arm had become. He was quietly weeping. Piven had gone about the painful business of cauterising the wound by heating up the axe head and while Greven had still been in shock had placed the hot iron against the stump, sealing it.

Greven had shrieked and then fainted.

When he'd come to, Piven had regarded him with only love in his eyes. 'I won't heal this one, Greven,' he explained gently. 'My instincts tell me it has to remain this way. That's why I used the flames rather than magic to close the wound.' Greven had not responded, so Piven had continued, ripping up linen as a makeshift bandage. 'This will have to do until we can get to the next town. I've rubbed it all over with merkin-leaf, so no infection should penetrate immediately.'

They had not exchanged words for some time now.

Finally Greven stirred. 'Why did you do this?' he growled, his good hand pushing the tears off his cheeks, as though he hated himself for that sign of weakness.

'You know why,' Piven replied, not looking at him.

Between them in the fire lay Greven's hand. Greven struggled not to look at it, as each time he glanced at it he felt the bile rising.

'Why don't you tell me all the same?' he said.

Piven sighed. 'It's pointless. We both understand what this is about. I can't be sure but I think even Vyk does too. Perhaps you're the attraction rather than me.'

'He's here for you alone,' Greven said with no sense of doubt in his voice. 'But I want to hear it from you.'

Piven turned. 'How's the pain?'

'How do you think?'

The youth shrugged. 'I'm hoping it's bearable. On my way back from Green Herbery I followed a stream. Along its banks were some white willows and I grabbed some of the bark to boil with staren flowers that I found over there,' he said, nodding his head towards the forest.

'So you were very well prepared,' Greven said, unable to disguise his anger.

Piven ignored it. 'While you were skinning the rabbits, I prepared a liquor, much of which I poured down your throat when you passed out. That accounts for the stains on your shirt, if you're wondering.'

'Why don't you just take my pain away?' Greven sneered.

Piven checked his bandaging for any leakage but Greven snatched his arm away. Piven looked up at him. 'I told you, it has to be natural, or it won't work.'

'What won't work?'

Piven sat back. 'That should do it,' he said, concern in his voice.

'*What* won't work?' Greven repeated icily.

'The magic I need to draw from you.'

Greven gave a snort of disdain. 'You've mutilated me for nothing, Piven. You're delusional.'

Piven eyed him before shifting his gaze to the scorched hand that lay in the flames, bubbling and blackened. 'Let's see, shall we.' Using a stick, he flicked the ugly mass onto the grass. 'It doesn't take much.'

'Piven, don't,' Greven warned.

'But you're not a believer. I want to prove it.'

'Don't do it.'

'I have to.'

'No! Turn away from it.'

'I've tried. But I'm already evil. Can't you see it? But whatever it is, this darkness has claimed me. Now I need protection.'

Greven's tears arrived anew. He shook his head as fresh rivulets formed on his cheeks. 'If you pursue this, I am lost.'

Piven ignored his plea. 'I'm glad you don't deny me any longer; how you resisted me for so long is a miracle. Fear not, now we will always be together.'

'Hating each other,' Greven snarled.

Piven poked at the smoking hand. 'The hate would be only one way. Towards me. I don't hate you, Greven. I could never hate you.'

Greven retched as he watched the child he loved tear off a piece of cooked flesh from the severed hand. To add to his horror, the raven swooped down to land near the appendage, which now looked like a blistered claw.

'Our companion may like to try some too,' Piven said lightly but there was no amusement in his voice.

'I won't witness this,' Greven said, desperately trying to stop himself from gagging.

'You will sit there and bear witness, Greven,' Piven ordered and now there was no lightness to his words or bearing. He placed the cooked flesh in his mouth and chewed, no revulsion in his expression. As he swallowed, Greven felt his world begin to spin. He couldn't believe it. It seemed impossible that Piven could be Valisar, and yet deep down Greven's whole body, his very soul, had known the truth; his own magic couldn't lie. It knew a Valisar when it found one.

He couldn't hear the words of binding but he could feel their effect. If the hacking off of his hand had hurt, this pain sucked all the breath out of his lungs. Through the screams he would later learn were his own, he could suddenly feel the hideous binding of two lives as Piven consumed him. Now their hearts were beating in tandem and the movement of their blood pulsed in synchronism. For a few moments of nerve-tingling darkness, in which he hoped he had died, there was only silence.

And then he heard Piven speak through the void. *We are bound.*

I hate you, Greven groaned.

I expect you do. As I warned, the hate will always move towards rather than away from me.

I will not help you.

You have no choice. You have no will anymore, other than to serve and keep me safe. Unlock your power, Greven. I can see it glowing within you like a river about to burst its banks.

I will not give it to you.

Again, I say, you have no choice. It belongs to me.

Then I will fight you.

And I will win. I own you.

The shadows surrounding Greven began to clear and with it all the pain left him, other than the throb where his hand had once been. As Piven's face swam into view and Greven was able to re-focus his eyes, he noticed with disgust that the raven was tearing ferociously at the withered hand. 'What now?' he growled.

'Once Vyk has finished with it, we burn the bit of you that you no longer need and —'

'So now you've become heartless, have you? Feeding me to a scavenger!'

'Not at all,' Piven said, frowning. 'I sense this was meant to be. Ever since Vyk consumed a part of you, he can talk to me. He asked me to tell you that he is honouring you by eating you.' Greven gave a sound of anguish. 'He is done,' Piven concluded.

'Burn it!' Greven demanded.

Piven sighed. Greven was sure the boy was talking to the bird at this moment. 'Did you want to say anything?' Piven asked, reaching down to pick up the hand by one of its roasted fingers.

'Like what?'

'Perhaps a blessing from Lo, or —'

'Lo has deserted me. Toss it on the fire.'

'As you wish,' Piven said quietly and placed the hand into the flames.

They both watched it sizzle and crackle for a few minutes in silence before Greven's attention was diverted by the nearby raven, cleaning its beak of his cooked flesh. Suppressing the desire to sicken at the sight of this, he tried to focus on what needed to be asked, but Piven spoke first.

'Who were you meant for?'

'Your father,' Greven snapped. 'How long have you known?'

'That you are an aegis, or that King Brennus was my real father?'

'Both, damn you!'

Piven shrugged. 'I knew of your magic almost as soon as I placed my hand in yours ten anni ago. I didn't know what it meant initially because I was still in my own stupor, but as my "madness" cleared, my intuition about life, who I was, who you were and so on, became clearer and clearer. As to your other question, I never doubted that Brennus was my father. From the moment I could think clearly enough to have logical thought I knew the truth in my heart.'

'But you continued the ruse with me.'

Piven nodded. 'Another Valisar secret. I was just continuing a fine family tradition. My parents wanted to offer their second heir as much protection as they possibly could. You have to admit, it was very clever.'

'But what about your madness?'

'Ah,' Piven said, a tone of resignation in his voice. 'That outcome they couldn't have foreseen.' He smiled sadly. 'Despite all his forethought, it must have grieved my father greatly to realise his grand plan was thwarted by what appeared to be a twist of nature, far more cunning than he. Now I realise, of course, it was not nature but the magic itself. You see, my father had none of the famed Valisar power and neither did his father. I think my great-grandfather might have been vaguely touched by it but even my great-great-grandfather missed out. No, we have to go back five generations to find a Valisar endowed with a level of magic that is spoken about as impressive.'

'Piven, how do you know these things?' Greven asked.

'I suppose I was listening. I was trapped in a prison of my mind and while I couldn't concentrate or even know what I was hearing, I was nonetheless always close by my father. Despite my so-called madness, he loved me and I felt his love. He kept me close, and he would often read to me from the books in his great library. I suppose during one of those sessions he must have shared the Valisar history with me. I think I learned plenty during those years without anyone realising it, least of all myself.'

'But you were such a young child! Even a healthy, normal five anni old wouldn't grasp what you did … surely?' Greven asked, his loathing momentarily set aside as his fascination with Piven's past sucked him deeper into his secret.

'Young in years, perhaps, but as we can both tell, I am endowed with a mind far more mature than is normal for someone my age. Even at five I suspect I was drinking in a lot more information than a normal child of that age, despite my incapacity.'

'And no one knew?'

Piven sighed and shook his head. 'Not even I. But you must have felt something, Greven. If I've understood what my father discovered from the writings in his library, an aegis is aware of his power and is drawn to the Valisars like a moth to a flame. You knew, and still you came to me. You didn't fight it.'

Greven held his head. He had guarded the knowledge for so long that the opportunity to finally admit his great secret served as a catharsis to the anger he'd harboured for all of his life. It cost him nothing to be honest with Piven for he was now bound to this young man until he died. He took a deep breath. 'It takes enormous willpower to resist the pull of the Valisar magic. It's like a sickness. I yearn for it and yet I know I must fight it with every part of myself. It's instinctive — no one had to tell me, I've just always known this. I kept testing and improving my resistance. Over the years I'd trust myself to get a little closer to the palace, constantly checking and double-checking my addiction to the calling but never wandering too close or too quickly. I practised and practised. I even once tried to stand on the fringe of the huge crowds gathered for one of the royal walks in the midlands. That went badly; I only just managed to escape the notice of King Brennus. As you rightly say, he wasn't endowed with any useful magic of his own but even dormant Valisar sorcery reacts to the presence of its own aegis. And only its own, I might add. I remember how distracted Brennus suddenly became that day, looking around him … looking for me! I was standing on a hill and could see him clearly, but fortunately I was shielded by a crowd of other wellwishers. I was able to get away. I never got that close again.' He looked up at Piven, a fresh gust of loathing washing through him. 'But, it seems Brennus's cunning and ingenuity caught me in its web all the same. I'm surprised you knew that you could trammel your father's aegis.'

'My Valisar magic was shielded and continued to be so while I emerged from my prison.'

'True,' Greven agreed. 'I sensed your magic at the beginning, but told myself I was imagining it, or that it was a shadow of you being around the Valisars for so long. I was confident of my invulnerability. I could, to some degree, control the call to the magic around you because I was not born for you. My reaction to your father was immediate — I sickened instantly, lost my bearings and most of my control. But I don't feel this reaction to you, nor did I with your brother.'

'I see. So the burden is on the Valisar to find his aegis?'

'Correct … or an aegis. It's actually far easier for you Valisar heirs to find your own because your magic and the magic of your aegis respond so dramatically to each other, as I've explained. Leo seemed to have no idea who I was and even if he did register something, I think he was in shock anyway; it would have easily slipped by him. I should add that I'm still very glad he spent the night in the crawlspace beneath our hut, however, and left the next day.' He shook his head. 'With you, it's been so different. I have been on my guard constantly this last decade. The smell of your magic — I have no other way to describe it — began to intensify as you grew and I subsequently had to intensify my control with each passing year. I wanted to convince myself you were adopted, not blood. It was too much to believe that your madness was a ruse.'

'Not my madness. My birth was the only ruse,' Piven corrected.

'Yes, it's all crystal clear now. Nevertheless, you were not the Valisar that I was born for, so in this respect I had the upper hand. I knew as long as I continued to guard my secret with care I was safe. And I loved you by then, child. I could not have turned you out.'

'Now you despise me.'

Greven nodded. 'You have robbed me of the freedom I spent my life protecting.'

'Is it really so vile?'

Greven didn't answer directly. 'I went to the Academy at Cremond once in the hope of finding a cure for my disease. I met a very old scholar there, who had once had access to the royal library. He had helped your grandfather decipher some texts and had enjoyed the opportunity to read about —'

He was unable to finish his sentence. Vyk suddenly gave two big hops and lifted from the ground to flap into a nearby tree. Greven frowned and he and Piven were both looking around to see what had frightened Vyk when a man crested the small rise and stopped, staring at them dumbstruck.

Piven was on his feet in a blink. 'You!' he yelled. 'You followed me?'

The man looked nervous. 'I had to. You saved my life, Petor ... or should I call you Prince Piven?'

And Greven, without needing to be asked, without even realising he was doing it, pushed and the invisible impenetrable shield instantly cloaked them ... and the pain disappeared as he allowed himself to acknowledge the force of his magic. Piven turned and their gazes met. Piven's expression was grateful; Greven knew his reflected only resignation. And in their minds they heard a voice, one neither had heard before but both instinctively knew.

Aegis magic, the voice said in an awed tone. *I will return.* And then Vyk was gone, a dark smudge swooping through the forest, melting into its shadows.

Piven returned his attention to the man who was walking towards them. 'Stay back,' he said.

The man stopped. 'Is it really you?'

Piven scowled. 'Whoever you think I am, you are mistaken.'

The man shook his head, his expression one of wonder. 'It's you. But you are talking, you are healthy? If I didn't know I was seeing you standing here, I would not believe it.' He regarded Greven. 'We meet again,' he said.

Piven looked between them, shocked, then pointed at the man. 'Stop your babbling,' he ordered. 'Explain yourself!'

The newcomer ignored the command. 'I was so close to death I was letting go. I couldn't breathe. The fire scorched my insides and flesh was hanging from me. Look at me now. I'm whole. The magic you used was so powerful I thought I was experiencing the presence of Lo himself, until you restored my sight.'

'Why did you call me by that name?' Piven demanded.

The man pointed at Greven. 'He tried to keep me away but I know you. I recognise you.'

'From where?'

'From Brighthelm, Prince Piven.'

'Stop calling me that. I am Petor Lark.'

'You are Valisar. You are royalty.'

Greven so far had remained silent but fearful. He intensified the shield, as Piven demanded, 'Who are you?'

'Ask your companion,' the man said.

Tiring of the standoff, Greven answered without further prompting. 'His name is Clovis. He has been following us … he and his wife, Reuth … the whole family, in fact,' he said sourly.

Clovis nodded. 'I am now alone. Your highness, I was sent to find you ten anni ago after your parents died and Leonel escaped Loethar's clutch. I have never stopped looking. Never. It would have been prize enough just to find you. But to discover you unshackled from your afflictions is too much to imagine. How can this be?'

'Who sent you?' Piven demanded.

'Master Freath … you may remember him?'

Piven considered this. 'The servant.'

Clovis nodded. 'He pretends to serve the usurper, your highness, but he is loyal to the Valisars. He saved my life, my wife's and many others through his courageous deeds. He was devastated when you were lost.'

'How was I lost?' Piven asked and Greven knew this was something the boy had always niggled at.

'From what I gather, Loethar forgot to take you back into the castle. You were outside playing in the queen's herb garden. Freath told us you were with the emperor — he used to keep you on a leash — and he was called away. It is our assumption that he thought you would be brought in by his mother, who was also present, and perhaps she thought you would follow her, or perhaps she didn't care. Either way you remained outside alone.'

Piven nodded. 'And Greven found me.'

'Ah,' Clovis said. 'I understand now.'

Greven spoke up. 'I was already in the forest, but I was drawn to its edge near the palace by the raven.'

'The raven! You mean Loethar's bird?' Clovis asked, surprised.

Greven nodded. 'That was him you just saw.'

The newcomer's mouth fell open. 'I didn't see it properly. I just saw a large bird fly away — nothing more than a shadow and movement, really. So he's now your bird?'

Greven began to shake his head but Piven answered for them. 'Yes. How did you find us up here?'

'I was trying to follow you, your highness. But it was the screams that helped me find you. What happened?'

Greven held up his arm. 'An accident.'

'Accident?' Clovis looked shocked. 'I thought someone was being murdered. How bad is it?'

'He lost his hand,' Piven said.

Greven scowled. 'He doesn't need to know this,' he said to Piven.

'Know what?' Clovis asked, advancing.

'Nothing!' Greven replied.

'I'm not scared of him, Greven,' Piven admitted. 'I promise you, he can't touch us.'

'No, but he can tell others about us.'

Clovis frowned. 'What are you talking about? I am not your enemy and anyone I tell anything will be your ally as well.'

'The mere fact that you have found Piven and will want to share this knowledge with others is dangerous to us,' Greven countered. 'Leave now while you can,' he offered.

'Are you mad? Did you not hear what I'd just told you about Freath? A decade of searching, a promise, duty … ?'

'Perhaps you didn't hear the threat in his voice, Master Clovis,' Piven said. 'I have to admit, I thought Greven was a mild person but he seems aggressive today, potentially violent.'

Clovis looked from Greven to Piven as though they were both acting simple. 'I don't understand this. I've been searching for you for a decade. You're still a mere youth but you're whole. You have everything to gain by reuniting with Leo. Two heirs — that would give Loethar pause for thought.'

'Firstly, Master Clovis, we are not heirs in the eyes of the people. I'm known as the adopted halfwit brother. No one is going to rally to my cause.'

Clovis leapt in eagerly. 'You're so wrong. The people of Penraven will rally to your name, I'm sure, when they see you are far from a halfwit.'

Piven continued, ignoring Clovis's remark as though he hadn't said anything. 'Secondly, Leo is not an heir.'

Clovis's frown re-appeared. 'Not an heir?'

'No. If he lives he's king, or hasn't that occurred to anyone yet? It doesn't matter what Loethar calls himself, Leo is the 9th Valisar, the true sovereign. Go away, Master Clovis. You should never have followed me. What I did, I did for selfish reasons you could never understand, not even if I tried to explain. Forget your search, forget you've seen me, forget what I did for you. Go back to your wife and your family and forget about us. Get on with your life.'

'This is wise counsel, Master Clovis, even if it is given by a youth,' Greven warned.

'I don't understand,' Clovis repeated, sounding helpless and suddenly lost. 'And for some reason I feel frightened by you both and I don't know why. I am loyal to your family, your highness. I was there in the palace soon after all the terrible events. I worked alongside your allies, who risked their lives to preserve the Valisar name. I don't understand.'

'Master Clovis, I tire of you. I think we have been fair. Leave now.'

'No, highness. I will not. I ran away from my duty once before. I was too weak, too filled with fear. I have regretted it ever since and it's part of why I have never given up hope of finding you. I want to reunite you with those who would wish to know of your safety. I promise you I will expect nothing of you, force nothing upon you, but let me fulfil this one desire on behalf of those who gave their lives for the Valisars.'

'It's a pity, Master Clovis, that as a Vested, you haven't put those skills to better use. If you had, you might have sensed I was beyond saving,' Piven said. *Do it, Greven!*

Greven knew that poor Clovis hardly noticed his arrival, or the blade in Greven's good hand, or even that his throat had been slashed. Indeed, even when the blood came spurting from his neck, his face looked mystified, not angry, not scared.

'I'm sorry for your family,' Greven said and meant it, hating how he had now become a helpless, witless servant.

Clovis dropped like a sack of potatoes, crumpling in on himself, first to his knees then curling inward, clawing at his neck. He bled out within moments and then all was still, the forest surrounding Greven and Piven eerily quiet.

'I hate you,' Greven said, not turning, staring sadly at the corpse of a good man.

'I know. I hate myself,' Piven replied, sounding equally melancholy.

'Let's go,' Greven growled.

'Where to?'

'Who cares? Away from here.'

There was nothing to pack. All that remained to tell anyone that they'd been there was the remains of a fire, the remains of two rabbits and the remains of a man. And, in fact, the gruesome events that had occurred might have been lost forever, had it not been for a child, who had witnessed everything, wide-eyed and terrified, hidden from sight.

15

Faris hadn't spoken to him for hours. He didn't need to talk to the outlaw, however, to know the man was seething. Beyond seething, in fact; he was all but foaming at the mouth, his fury burning hot below the controlled expression. Everyone, bar Jewd, was travelling well ahead of him and Jewd was giving him plenty of space too. Leo kicked his horse forward to catch up with Faris.

He was used to the man giving him a wide berth. He had never understood the yawning gap between them both emotionally and physically for he loved Faris. And though there were occasions like yesterday at the inn where Kilt was in high humour and they seemed as close as friends could be, those moments were not frequent. Leo had learned to enjoy them when they presented themselves and had become used to Kilt's more usual remoteness. Lily had assured him repeatedly that Kilt didn't permit himself to get too close to anyone. And though Leo worshipped Lily he considered her naive to think that he could not work out that Kilt deliberately avoided him.

'Kilt, I know you don't want to talk to me but —'

Faris exploded. 'It's not what I want, Leo. This is all about you. You're a king, you can do just what you want! You can commit murder in broad daylight against a loyal man who had likely laid down his life many times for you already; had clung to your life like a beacon for ten anni, wishing and hoping that his dream to see

you again might come true. What does his life matter, when you —
great and brave King Leonel — want revenge? A man's life clearly
means nothing to you. Even as he died — with your back turned
to him — he had only the highest regard and care for you. Talk to
you? I don't even want to look at you, Leo. Get out of my sight,
your majesty.'

Leo was stung deeply by the emotion driving Kilt's words, but
his heart refused to back down. 'When you have lost as much as I
have, Kilt, perhaps you'll glimpse the depth of my despair.
I watched my father die horribly while people laughed at him.
Loethar hacked off his head to present to my mother. And
perhaps you think a boy of twelve can stomach watching his
father roasted and eaten without carrying that memory forever
within a dark place? And how about watching his mother flung
from a high window? In the space of a few days, Kilt, I lost both
my parents, my new sister, my brother, a great friend called
Corbel, his father, who was second only to my own father as the
man I most admired, and any number of other people I had grown
up with and loved. I lost my family, I lost my crown, I lost my life
as I knew it in those few blood-laden, terror-filled days. And the
only constant in those dark hours, apart from my fear and Gavriel
de Vis, was Freath! Freath sucking up to the invaders, helping
them hunt me down, saying the most terrible things about me
and my family. I killed him — yes. It's done. By all means pass
judgement but don't ever forget this: I am a man of my word. If I
make an oath, no matter the consequences, I'll keep it. You know
that scar you've seen on my chest?'

At last he had Faris's attention. The outlaw finally turned his
angry face to look at him, still filled with loathing.

Leo pressed on. 'Well, I'll tell you what it is. That wound was
made by my own blade when I was in hiding, witnessing all these
brutalities. I made a blood promise to end Freath's life. And today I
killed him because he murdered my mother and I swore an oath
that he would pay for that with his life. His reasons for what he did

may well have been honourable but he murdered a queen. And now he has paid the consequences in front of his king.' Leo felt himself breathing hard, driven by passion and anger. 'You're an island, Kilt. You've said often enough that you don't have anything to lose. But one day you will lose something precious to you and you'll know just a fraction of the despair I have felt.'

Faris didn't soften his glare but Leo knew his companion had paid close attention to his impassioned speech. 'War is never fair, Leo. In times of war people behave in a manner that often seems unthinkable. I could hear the admiration in Freath's voice for Loethar. Even you admire him! But that same man who is now winning so many hearts and so much respect — just ten anni ago was roasting and eating those he conquered. War brings out the very worst in people, and Freath was in an impossible situation. But he wasn't trying to save his own life through his actions; he was trying to save yours!' Faris gave a groan of despair. 'Your father demanded this of him. Freath hunted us down, no doubt risking plenty, in order to try and save your life once again, and you reward him with a painful execution.' Faris shook his head. 'Honour be damned. You Valisars with your oaths and secrets and magics and wretched duty. What about the lives you ruin? What about the people who have given and would gladly give their lives to hold on to that precious crown for you?'

It was Leo's turn to be infuriated. 'What do you want me to say?' he yelled, aware of the others stealing backward glances at them. 'Do you want me to apologise for being Valisar … for being the king? I didn't choose this path. It chose me.'

'Then grow up, your majesty!' Faris hurled back at him. 'I liked your father and I respected his · courage and commitment but I didn't and don't agree with his methods. Life cannot be seen in simplistic terms of black and white. Poor old Freath lived in shades of grey, risking his life for ten long, hard anni on your behalf, you ungrateful, petulant prat! If you think I'm going to support a revenge mission, you've got another think coming.'

'Faris, I —'

'Hush while your elders speak, Leo,' Jewd said quietly from behind and Leo closed his mouth, stunned by how viciously Faris was addressing him and so publicly.

'I will not let you bring death and destruction through your spontaneous and thoughtless behaviour simply because you're too young and delusional to realise that owning the title of king does not guarantee you safety or immunity from my rule. While you live under my protection, you follow my rule. That wound in your leg should be a timely reminder to how tenuous your situation is. And without Freath we wouldn't know anything about this new threat. His risks, his courage have forewarned us and we can now try and take some precautions.' Faris stopped his horse, forcing Leo to do the same. He noticed, uncomfortably, that everyone else had stopped as well and was watching them in awkward silence. 'But all of that aside, your majesty, you have now risked my life and those of my men.'

Leo frowned. 'What do you mean?'

Faris regarded him as though Leo had lost his mind. The king felt the rebuke as keenly as a slap. 'Did it enter your vengeful mind, filled with only what was good for you, that in killing Freath you would focus imperial attention on us? As far as Loethar is concerned, his aide had travelled north on imperial duty to inform taxpayers of new obligations. So I'm sure he's not going to ignore the fact that his counsel was not only murdered but that it occurred outside of the town where he was supposed to be. Loethar is no dullard. He will investigate Freath's death, putting my men in peril.'

'I didn't think —'

'No, that's my whole point. You didn't think! You didn't think about *anything* but your selfish pursuit, and now your brutal act will bring the full weight of the empire's scrutiny into the north and give Loethar the excuse he's so badly wanted to tear this part of the world apart. Everyone else will think he's searching for a brutal murderer, but you and I know that Loethar is really searching for me, Leo, because he doesn't even know you exist. Congratulations — you've all but given us to him. And you killed a good man in the bargain. Get out of my sight.' Faris didn't wait for a response. He clicked at his horse and the beast moved forward. One by one, the men followed him and gradually the main party had drifted away, leaving Leo with rage and hurt, his damaged pride and a dawning disgust at what he had brought down upon the people he loved, the people he called family.

'If it's any consolation, he doesn't stay angry long,' Jewd commented from behind. Moments later his horse drew alongside Leo's. 'I know it hurts but he's right.'

Leo felt sickened. 'I hadn't thought it through, Jewd. I'm an idiot.'

Jewd reached across and squeezed Leo's arm. 'You know, I could share some tales with you about Kilt Faris when he was your age. Now that he's reached his wise fourth decade, he has plenty of experience and wisdom to draw upon. If I reminded him of his reckless youth, he might well cringe. But, your majesty, the key here is learning from a mistake. I think Kilt feels far more responsible for you than he lets on.'

Leo looked at Jewd uncertainly, his cheeks still burning from the harsh conversation. 'You really think he humiliated me for my own good?' he said, irony in his tone.

'Most definitely. Kilt Faris doesn't do anything reckless anymore. Surely you've grasped that by now?'

Leo shrugged. 'There are times when I could believe he is repulsed by me.'

Jewd's gaze was filled with reproach. 'He wouldn't waste the words on you if he didn't think the breath was well spent.' He gave a small gesture of resignation. 'Don't get me wrong, he's as angry as I've ever seen him and your killing of Freath was ill-inspired and very dangerous, no matter what your reasoning was. But most of his fear is for you.'

'That's not how it felt,' Leo groaned.

'This fellow called Vulpan is unnerving him. He seems to recall him from his brief time at the Academy in Cremond. He is seeing much danger in this whole turn of events and Freath's death will now intensify the precariousness of keeping you safe.'

'Then I will leave. I don't want to cause any more danger.'

Jewd stared at Leo, a wry expression creasing his face. 'Now that's just the very petulance he was referring to.'

'No, I mean it!' Leo said earnestly. 'I don't want any of our band captured or hurt or in any way singled out. I've always been a liability, Jewd.'

'No, not really, because no one has ever known about you, other than us. And your secret has been ferociously protected by Kilt, or hadn't you noticed?'

Leo nodded sheepishly. Jewd was making him feel worse than Faris had.

'Very few people know you're even alive,' the outlaw continued.

'And now there's one less,' Leo said, feeling miserable.

'Indeed, one we could have made such good use of. Imagine what Freath could have told us if he'd spied directly for Kilt.'

Leo considered this. 'I'm an idiot. Piven isn't the simpleton Valisar. I am.'

'No point in taking that attitude. And also no room or time for self-pity, please — that's another attitude that will get Kilt's ire up. You're better than that, your highness.'

'Don't. You know I hate the title.'

'Then don't act high and mighty. You might think that killing Freath fulfilled an oath you made many anni ago but, Leo, you were a child then and thinking like a child. You're a man now. And you're a king. You have to start thinking like a sovereign, which means thinking about what is best for your people rather than just you. Your people are right here,' Jewd said, pointing at the retreating men. 'We're all the subjects you have for the time being and you weren't putting us first or even your crown first when you took Freath's life. You've always told us Brennus put the throne before anything. In your situation, he too might have wanted to kill Freath, but search your heart and ask yourself whether he would have.' Jewd straightened in the saddle and looked towards where Faris had gone. The men were no longer visible. 'But you're still young. Hopefully you've learned an important lesson today. Kilt is true to you and his wrath today was testimony to how badly he wants you to act as the king you must become if you're going to challenge Loethar.'

'How, Jewd? With what? Our small army of twenty?'

'Don't judge too hastily. Who knows what can be achieved with the right timing and the right plan? Loethar used cunning to destroy the Denovian Set's rulers. He's now applying that same cunning to re-build the set. You will have to match his cunning.'

'What will happen with Freath?'

'Jorn's taking him back down. I think he'll try and leave his body somewhere near to the mountains rather than in the town centre. He has to be found, so we might as well choose where.'

For the first time since he'd drawn the blade, Leo felt the utter futility of his own actions. 'I hadn't thought about all that,' he admitted. 'Where to leave the body, how it should be found, how the death should be made to appear … it's overwhelming. What do I do now?'

Jewd sighed sadly. 'Ride through the storm with Kilt and perhaps say a prayer for Freath's soul. He deserved better.'

Roddy was scared. He'd never seen a dead person before. He'd seen his fair share of animals slaughtered but that usually involved a lot of activity and squealing. This man had died silently; he hadn't even seen death coming. Roddy felt frozen to his spot in the tree he'd climbed to get a better view of what was happening between the three people.

His mother would be furious with him. Perhaps she was past angry now and was just scared that he was nowhere to be found.

He felt badly about that, especially in the light of already having given her the worst fright in almost burning to death.

He remembered seeing the barn on fire, and running inside for Plod, unprepared for the sheer force of the flames. The heat and the suffocating smoke burned his eyes, forcing him to close them almost immediately. And then he had lost all sense of direction.

Strong hands had grabbed him, he recalled, but within moments he and his would-be rescuer had been engulfed by the flames. Roddy could remember the lick of their heat and the instant, shocking pain as his shirt disintegrated and his skin began to bubble.

His next memory was waking up in his mother's cottage, the youth who had called himself Petor bending over him. Roddy would never forget Petor's smile, filled with warmth and so much affection. Roddy could still feel the tingle of a mighty magic fizzing through his blood, the magic of life over death. The magic of opposites, Roddy thought, for how could Petor give Clovis life and in the same day take it so brutally? Roddy pushed away a tear that had welled.

After he'd been brought back to life, his mother and Aunty Fru had stolen out of the room to fetch water for his parched throat and probably to discuss the event out of earshot. Roddy had seen the man next to him cast him a single glance before he, too, left the room, moving swiftly. Roddy knew where Clovis was headed because he too inexplicably felt the same driving desire. He had slipped from the window soundlessly, and he too had begun following their healer out of the town.

Roddy stared down at Clovis's corpse. He'd lost sight of Petor and the man missing a hand. But he knew he could track them if he moved fast. Digging deep for courage, he lowered himself carefully from the tree before moving to stand over Clovis. He knew he should be revolted by the blood but he was just sorrowful for the death. If he felt revulsion, it was towards himself, for this driving need that he didn't fully understand. Piven — as the man had named him — was the link to what he wanted, what he now realised he was seeking.

He'd never told his mother about this feeling he'd always had, this restlessness. It wasn't until he'd seen Piven, locked gazes with him, experienced the beauty of his magic, that he realised his compulsion had a focus. One side of him begged him to ignore it, to stay safe; the other urged him to leave his mother, his home, and follow.

Petor will provide answers, the whispers assured him. *Petor will lead you to where you need to be*, they insisted. But another part of him hinted that to follow Petor meant only misery and pain. Roddy didn't know which side of him told the truth, who he should trust. Up until this day he'd always erred on the side of caution, banishing the whispers as best he could. But feeling the touch of Petor's magic had dismantled that fragile shield. Now, suddenly, he didn't have the strength to deny his desire to learn the truth.

He closed Clovis's eyes. There was nothing he could do except commit the man's slackened face to his memory. Roddy hated to rifle through the dead man's few possessions so he took the small sack and slung it around his own body. It hung low on him but its weight felt reassuring.

'May Lo speed you to his gates,' he whispered over the corpse and then he knelt and kissed the cooling cheek of his rescuer. 'Thank you, Clovis, for my life,' he said gravely, before he covered the dead man's face with a hat he found nearby. He wasn't sure who it belonged to but it would do and no one needed it.

He looked around to check there was nothing else here for him. As he spotted the cooked rabbits his belly grumbled. Roddy trotted over to the small fire, now just glowing ash, and retrieved the meat. Clearly no one wanted this either; it would not be stealing.

He ate as he walked. Soon he would run. He had no idea where he was going or why. All his instincts told him was that the young man Piven might provide answers. And he no longer felt as though he had a choice — not now that Piven's magic had awoken his.

16

Loethar undid his shirt, a sheen of sweat glistening on his forehead from his exertions to return to the palace swiftly. The messenger had found him enjoying the surrounding landscape as a mist rolled across the moors, the threat of the morning sun promising to burn it away. The trio of minders had permitted the messenger through their protective ring to the emperor.

'What is it now?' Loethar had exclaimed, peeved by the youngster's arrival.

The youth had looked understandably nervous. 'Urgent news, Emperor Loethar.'

'It always is,' Loethar had said wearily. 'What is it?'

'I was sent by the empress to bid you to return to the palace immediately. It is not the child, I was instructed to tell you.'

Loethar had taken a deep breath. His wife knew better than to summon him without just cause and he was relieved there was nothing wrong with his son. He had nodded, resigned. 'I'm on my way.'

The rider had turned immediately and urged his horse back to the palace.

'What is it?' Stracker had galloped back from where he'd been ranging ahead. 'I saw a messenger?'

'Valya has requested me urgently back to the palace.'

'The baby —'

'No, nothing to do with our child. Something else but she didn't say what, other than it was urgent. She would not call me back from a ride without very good reason.'

They had ridden back to Brighthelm at full gallop, which had gone a little way towards clearing the cobwebs of tedium in Loethar's mind. But now, as he impatiently awaited Valya in his salon, he found himself irritated by inactivity and generally annoyed at the world for no good reason.

It was his mother who had noticed his discontent, she who had suggested he leave Penraven, even leave the shores of the empire for a while. 'Take an ocean journey,' she'd suggested. 'Go meet your fellow rulers in Galinsea or Percheron, or sail south to Lindaran or northwest to Briavel and Morgravia. All the sovereigns would be intrigued to meet you again, I'm sure — and on their ground, all the better.'

'It's tempting,' he had replied on one of their many slow walks near the herb gardens.

'Do it, Loethar. You're driving everyone mad with your mournful expression. It's clear you're bored. The empire is running itself beautifully, you have reliable people in place, the cities are flourishing and so are your people — all of us, Plains and Set. You are not needed here, so do something!'

It was sound advice. 'Not until Valya is pregnant again,' he had remarked, knowing in his heart that siring his heir was truly the last obstacle to feeling his work was done. Once he had a son, or perhaps a pair of sons, he could stop fretting about the security of the empire and start to live more selfishly.

His mother had sighed and nodded, understanding. Since that conversation nearly one anni ago, his mother's physical condition had worsened dramatically. His mother was frail now, needing two sticks to walk and requiring 'carriers' on hand day and night to attend to her whims and her ablutions. Now they no longer went walking together and she emerged from her chambers infrequently.

In a strange way he missed her confrontations and her controlling nature. Now he found himself surrounded by people overly eager to please. If not for Stracker, whom he could never fully trust, and Freath, who, despite being a servant, gave him the only intelligent conversations he enjoyed, life would be interminably dull. And now Freath was gone to the north. Loethar sorely missed his dry humour and wise counsel.

Valya arrived in a cloud of perfume and groans at her swollen ankles, even more swollen belly and the whole tiring nature of trying to give him the son he craved.

'Valya,' he acknowledged with a perfunctory kiss to her hand. 'I trust this is not trivial. My daily ride is very important to me.'

He noticed she ignored his barb but her eyes flared with pleasure at his dishevelled state. 'I'm so used to seeing you neat and tidy, Loethar, that I forget that the barbarian lurking beneath all this finery still excites me,' she drawled.

Unfortunately, Valya had never fired any genuine lust within him. Even at the beginning, it was more her fiery determination and propensity for revenge that had attracted him; that and her knowledge of the Set. He'd married her because he didn't know what else to do with her. He knew that she loved him, revered him even; there were moments when he briefly felt badly about the way he did not and never could respond in the way she dreamed, but she seemed to be able to overlook those shortcomings in their relationship with ease. Loethar knew much of her ability to see only the bright side of being together was connected with the riches and power her marriage afforded her. He forgave her that. So long as he never heard of her abusing that power so that it lowered people's esteem of him, she could do what she liked. Her only use to him now was to be a provider of sons. Set sons. And in that she had failed … so far.

'Why have I been summoned? Make it good,' he warned, moving her hand from his chest.

'My darling, I have unhappy news.'

His gaze narrowed. She looked breathless and excited. Something in the cruel slash of her mouth told him she was excited for all the wrong reasons. 'Tell me,' he ordered.

'It's Freath.'

He frowned. *Freath?* 'What's happened? Is he unwell?'

'You could say that,' she smirked. 'We have news that he is dead.'

'Dead?' he exclaimed.

She nodded. 'Murdered, apparently.'

Loethar blinked, not at all sure he'd heard right and hating that Valya seemed to be enjoying his discomfort. He took a moment to gather his wits. This must be some sort of mistake. 'Who brought this news?'

'The soldiers who escorted him. I haven't even let them rest. They await your pleasure. Freath is in the chapel, pale and cold.' He could see the delight dancing in her eyes at the last comment.

'That will be all, Valya. Best you get back to your confinement. If Stracker's around, I would speak to him.'

Valya's lips pursed. She moved to the outer chamber and he heard her fling the door back, barking an order. She returned sullenly. 'He's being fetched. Aren't you going to ask how I feel?'

'I can see how you feel. Elated.'

She shrugged. 'That's most unfair, Loethar. I am about to deliver a child. I have far more important things on my mind than the death of a mere servant. I shall leave you now.'

Loethar forced himself to say nothing. He didn't want to upset her and threaten the baby. Nothing mattered more to him right now, not even Freath's apparent death. But he could feel his wrath gathering. How could Freath be dead? 'Come!' he yelled at the sounds of footsteps outside his chambers. He marched into the private salon area as the door was opened and Stracker entered.

'I've only just heard,' he admitted. 'It seems your wife got to you with the news first.'

'Have the other escorts sent to the chapel,' Loethar ordered, his expression like a thunderstorm.

A man — the lead escort — was shown into the chamber.

'Is is true?' Loethar demanded, ignoring his obeisance. 'Is Master Freath dead?'

The man nodded miserably.

Loethar pointed at him, furious. 'Tell me what occurred and keep it to the point.'

The man swallowed, showing how fearful he felt. 'Highness, we accompanied Master Freath, as instructed, into the town of Francham in the north. He was staying at an inn called The Lookout.'

'What do we know about the inn?' Loethar interrupted, looking at his general.

Stracker shrugged. 'Nothing special about it. Most popular inn in the town. The population is transient so plenty of strangers are coming and going through the inn's doors.'

Loethar's expression darkened further. 'Go on,' he said to the warrior.

'Er, my lord, we took the horses for stabling while Masters Freath and Felt went directly to the inn. To my knowledge there was nothing out of the ordinary. They ate a meal at the inn and —'

'Wait! What do you mean *to your knowledge*? Were you not there to see with your own eyes what was going on?'

'Er, well, you see, my lord, Master Freath told us that he had no plans to do anything more than eat a hearty meal, share a flask of wine with Master Felt and take an early night.'

Loethar blinked. He knew what was coming, felt a familiar rage rising. 'And the trio of soldiers I sent to escort my aide into what we believed might be hostile territory were where this night? The local brothel?'

'He insisted, my lord,' the soldier replied.

'Insisted what?' Loethar demanded. He impaled the younger man with a stormy gaze. 'What did he insist upon?'

To his credit, the man spoke evenly, confidently. 'That we should eat where we wanted and, er, take the night for ourselves.'

'And you did just that, didn't you?'

The soldier looked down. Stracker's expression now matched his half-brother's. 'You unreliable swine!'

Loethar held a hand up to prevent the tirade. 'Do we know what happened?'

'We arrived at The Lookout well before closing time, my lord. I saw Master Freath but not Master Kirin. I'm sorry to say I assumed that the Vested had already retired. It seems he had left the inn but we do not know why. We never saw him again.'

'And Freath?'

'He was sitting at the back of the inn, talking with someone, just another guest. I never saw the man's face — he had his back to me — but he was not memorable by his clothing or build.'

Loethar sighed. *How obvious*, he thought.

The Red continued. Freath saw us and nodded.' He shrugged. 'That was enough. We knew where he was and that all was well.'

'When did you lose track of him?' Loethar pressed.

'That's just it, we don't know. We were all watching this big man trying his luck at a game they play in the north called Arrows. Everyone was betting, the atmosphere was very lively. It was —'

'A diversion,' Loethar cut in, his voice weary.

The man frowned.

'Deliberately done, I'd say. I'm sure the next time you looked for Freath he'd disappeared.'

The Red nodded. 'Exactly so, my lord. We never saw him leave and to be honest I thought he'd escaped the noise and revelling to retire.'

'Finish this tale!' Loethar said, a wave of his hand accompanying his snap.

'Yes, my lord. The next morning we couldn't raise either Master Freath or Felt. We spent several hours questioning people and following every lead but to no avail. Then some travellers raised the alarm about a body found on the pass. It was not too deep into the mountains — almost at the gates, in fact. It was Freath, my lord. He had been run through with a sword.'

'He was dumped there, presumably?'

'We believe as much. He had no reason to be in the pass, had no way of getting there and there was no blood to suggest he'd been killed where the body lay,' the Red replied.

Loethar felt something die inside him. He already missed Freath. 'Before you are executed, make sure General Stracker has all the information you can possibly remember about the man Freath was talking to and the big fellow you mentioned who created the diversion. He was memorable, surely?'

'Yes, my lord,' the Red said. Stracker ushered him out.

Loethar noticed his warrior had not flinched at the news of his death and he felt a momentary prick of pride. It was short-lived, though; none deserved to live for failing in their duty to him. He wondered if the man had a family — whether any of the guards were married or were fathers. He was glad he didn't know, but at the same time he was angry with himself for even considering their situations. Ten anni ago it would not have even crossed his mind to wonder about the real victims of his tyranny — the family members left without their husbands or sons, fathers or brothers. He hated that he had turned more Set-like — some might say soft — in his approach to life. But then again, no one could accuse his predecessors of being soft. He was following in Valisar footsteps in putting Crown and duty ahead of family and personal feelings.

'Stracker,' he called, halting the general as he returned to the chamber. 'Let the Red live. He is young and was raised mainly in peace time. His elders led him down the wrong path; they were the ones who should have known better.'

'All three were guilty of —'

'The Red may live. Punish him however you see fit but do not take his life. And make sure the families of the other two are compensated for their losses. Pay them well.' He saw the look of disappointment creep across Stracker's face, laced with disdain.

Stracker pitied him. It would not be long now before his half-brother made his move. The man was bored. Bored by the fact that the realms had cleaved into empire with relative ease and were getting on with the harmonious business of being led by one man surprisingly well.

Ignoring Stracker's badly disguised contempt, he continued, 'Where is Vulpan right now?'

'Heading north.'

'Get word. He's to set up base in Francham immediately. And you go up there and meet him. Find who killed Freath but do not kill him. Bring whoever's involved here. Do you understand?'

'I do. Do *you* understand that it appears soft if you allow the Red to live?'

'Don't question me, Stracker.'

'Don't push me, brother.'

'Half-brother.'

Stracker smiled, and Loethar saw menace in his eyes. Perhaps he would have to take measures against his sibling sooner rather than later. He would have to speak with Dara Negev.

'What do you want to do about the Vested?' Stracker asked.

'He's not important to me but I would like to know what he was doing leaving the inn. Perhaps we will have some answers if we find Master Felt.'

'You think Felt has betrayed Freath?'

'It's possible, isn't it?'

'They seemed bonded.'

'All bonds are stretched sometimes,' Loethar replied quietly.

'Indeed, little brother. And sometimes they break.'

Their glances locked momentarily. *Yes*, Loethar decided, he would have to make a decision about Stracker soon. 'Find Felt if you can,' he said, deliberately moving away from the innuendo. 'He's the missing piece in this jigsaw. One more thing. I would talk to the oldest member of the party before he's executed. I'll see him at the chapel. You too.'

Stracker nodded and mercifully left.

Loethar sent a runner for his mother to be brought to the palace chapel.

Faris stared at his man. They were high in the forest again and meant to be feeling safe but Faris felt a knot of fresh anxiety forming. 'Say that again,' he demanded.

Coder obliged. 'Lily and the man called Felt were taken by soldiers.'

'To where?'

'I'm not sure, Kilt. We pretended to be brother and sister as we'd planned but Felt suspected we were lying, I'm sure of it. Not that it mattered. He only had eyes for Lily.'

Faris bristled. Jewd caught his gaze and raised his eyebrows, silently warning him to calm down. Leo walked into the camp and placed his saddle over the railings built for the purpose. 'What's going on?' he asked.

Jewd whispered, filling him in as Faris ignored the interruption. 'What happened?' he asked Coder.

'We were travelling with the merchants. It was a perfect cover and Lily and Felt had just fallen into conversation when we were interrupted by a party of imperial soldiers. Amongst them was a Wikken.'

'You're sure? He wore purple and was scarred?'

Coder nodded. 'I'm sure, Kilt. In fact, he was the one who kept whispering to the guard. I'm certain that he urged that Felt be taken.'

Faris frowned. 'What has Lily got to do with this? Why was she taken as well?'

'They pulled them away from the main party and I wasn't privy to what was discussed but I could tell the soldiers insisted Felt accompany them,' Coder said, visibly embarrassed, his eyes darting from Jewd, to Leo and back to Jewd, avoiding Faris.

'Why Lily as well?'

He shrugged. 'I can't tell you; she didn't consult me. Be assured,

Kilt, I would never have let her go. She was talking to Felt when the soldiers arrived and for some reason when they singled him out, she moved her horse with his.' He looked anguished at the unspoken accusation in Faris's face. 'I think she felt obliged to stay with Felt because of your instructions to stay close. I know he looked surprised when she began talking but unfortunately I couldn't hear what was exchanged. It happened in the space of such a short time, and I thought it made more sense not to follow but to get back here quickly and raise the alarm.'

'But why would they let her accompany him?'

'I'm sorry, Kilt. I really don't know how she managed to persuade them to take her with them.'

Faris spun away, fury mingling with his exasperation. 'Is she mad? Where have they gone?'

Coder seemed to take a breath. He glanced around at the others, especially Jewd, who took the hint and nodded. 'I found out a bit more later from one of the merchants. There's a man called Vulpan, he —'

'Yes, we know all about Vulpan,' Faris said, waving a hand irritably. 'He's all I'm hearing about it seems.' At Coder's anxious hesitation, he snapped, 'What about him, anyway?'

'That's where they're headed, apparently. They've taken Lily and Felt to where Vulpan's based at the moment — a town called Woodingdene.'

'Where the mint is?'

Coder nodded. 'They have no reason to hurt Lily. And the merchant believes they're taking Felt to be listed.'

'They were murdering people for less just a few anni ago and she's put herself right into the mouth of the dragon!'

'Steady, Kilt,' Jewd said. 'We'll get her back.'

Faris turned to stare at his friend, feeling suddenly lost. He was not used to this. He lived by his wits and was always so careful, so controlled, that no barbarian had ever even got close to him or his men. Even before the barbarian invasion he had prided himself on dodging the king's men. And now Lily was in enemy hands. He reminded himself why he and Jewd had often talked about enjoying women without falling in love with them.

As usual, Jewd sensed his mood. 'We suggested Lily tail this fellow. We should be praising her commitment, not wondering at her mental state. No more recriminations. Let's plan our strategy to get her back.'

'Before it's too late, you mean,' Faris said, uncharitably. He sighed. 'I'm sorry.'

'I know,' his friend replied. 'Seems like both you and Lily say the first thing that comes into your heads. Lo knows what she's told them but she was obviously convincing.'

The men listening smiled uneasily.

'I'll go, Kilt,' Leo spoke up. 'It's too dangerous for you but —'

Faris laughed ruefully, cutting him off and backing away.

Leo looked hurt. 'No, listen to me. As far as anyone else is concerned I'm a nobody. I'm young; I can act dumb. I can —'

'No, your majesty. With every due respect, no!' Faris growled. 'You forget he has tasted your blood.'

'But he doesn't know what that means, or who I am,' Leo protested.

'Loethar suspects it's one of us. That's all that matters. And he will pursue you until he has your body strung up from a tree or much worse. He thinks he's onto me, but doesn't know you're even alive. I intend to keep it that way. You will stay away from this man … this Vested creature. Jewd, you've been seen by the soldiers; we can't risk you, either. I'm leaving you in charge.'

Now Jewd looked cranky. 'I'd prefer to come along.'

'Too risky,' Faris snapped. 'Clear up here, everyone, we're moving back to the camp.'

His men drifted away, although Leo looked as though he wanted to have a fresh debate over his suitability to rescue Lily. But it was Jewd who grabbed his friend's arm and swung Faris around.

'Face me and tell me why, Kilt,' he said. 'We don't split up, you and I, not on something like this. And don't give me the caution about the soldiers from the inn. The chances of them being at Woodingdene is slim and the chances of those same soldiers not only being at Woodingdene but precisely where we might be is virtually nil.'

'It's a risk all the same, Jewd,' Faris persisted.

'One I'll take if it helps to keep you safe.'

'No.'

Jewd's gaze darkened and his brow creased in a mixture of irritation and confusion.

'Just leave it,' Faris urged and walked away. He had to prepare for his departure.

'What's going on, Kilt? What's this about?' Jewd called after the outlaw but won no answer.

'It's about fear, I think,' Leo said quietly.

Jewd looked around, surprised. 'What do you mean?'

Leo shrugged. 'He loves Lily. Has Kilt ever loved anyone before?'

Jewd paused, thinking. 'Not a woman.'

'Well, you said it. I reckon if he was prepared to confess, he'd own up to loving Lily, and he loves you. His two favourite people in the world are suddenly at risk. Perhaps for the first time in his life something worth losing is being genuinely threatened.' Leo swung his hand around in an arc. 'Look at the way he lives. His home is the forest, his closest friends are outlaws. He owns nothing. What money he needs he steals.' Leo gave a sad laugh. 'He doesn't even keep it. When my father used to talk about the highwaymen of the north, I imagined you were all rich and debauched.' Jewd gave a rueful smile. 'Now I learn their leader gives most away.'

'Aye, his favourite recipient is the convent in the mountains. Plenty goes to the Academy at Cremond, of course.'

'Did my father know this?'

Jewd nodded. 'He would have had his suspicions, I think, and I imagine that's another reason he came looking for Kilt in the first place. He probably reasoned that no one who gives so much away could be all bad. And he found that to be true, because he gave him his most precious possession of all.'

'His heir,' Leo said, a maudlin tone creeping into his voice.

'Are the relations any easier between you two?'

Leo shrugged. 'Not really. He's very angry. And he's hardly ever been affectionate towards me so I can't tell. I'm just Leo, the irritating burden. Lo knows why he protects me.'

'Loyalty to Valisar. I know he has a strange way of showing it but he's a king's man.'

'Not this king's,' Leo admitted.

'He has every right to be angry.'

'He does. It was stupid and impetuous. I know that now.' Leo shook his head. 'Kilt is right. My actions were the revenge of a child, not the disciplined action of a king.'

'All true. Did it satisfy you?'

'Pardon?'

'Do you feel relieved? Set free by Freath's death?'

'I feel hollow. Freath's death did nothing but answer a sort of primeval rage. Seeing him again made me think of those terrible few days in the ingress, but more than anything it made me realise how angry I feel at not knowing where Gav is — or even whether he's alive or dead. Seeing Freath has re-opened a lot of wounds. I wanted to make him pay for all that pain he caused me.'

Jewd sighed. 'It's a pity Freath had to die to make you realise that nothing will give you back what has been taken from you. Make sure his death counts for something, your majesty. Let it make you a better king, or all the lives he risked and lost were for nought.'

Leo nodded thoughtfully. 'In the meantime, what are we going to do about Kilt?'

'You're going to stay safe. I'm going to follow him.'

'If you disobey him —'

Jewd snorted with disdain. 'He's not my mother! Or my keeper. I go my own way.'

'All right, then. I'll tell him of your plan if you don't let me come too.'

'No! How many more times do we have to say that?'

'Plenty, because I'm not hearing it. Lily's my friend too. I'm the reason she's even here. And all this dangerous deception ultimately finds its way back to me anyway. Everyone is taking risks for the restoration of the Valisar Crown. I have to stand up and be counted, or what sort of worthy king am I?'

'Leo, you're twenty-two anni.'

'Old enough, for Lo's sake! I think you mouth twenty-two but you think twelve!'

'We're all doing this to protect you, not risk you.'

'But we have to stop the fear at some point and take action. I'm ready, I'm trained, I'm hardened. Let me come along just as someone who watches your back. I won't get close enough to give any trouble, I give you my word. I'll take it all in from a distance and report to you or Kilt.'

Jewd made a growling sound of displeasure.

'I will be very careful, I promise you,' Leo pressed.

'He'll kill me.'

'He will anyway if he finds out that you're going after him. And I will tell him.'

Jewd's lips twisted in a sneer but it was obvious he felt trapped. 'Get your weapons! We'll have to think of some disguises as well.'

17

Hurtle was a flourishing village, just on the very tip of turning into a town.

'Lo blind me, what a surprise,' Kirin said, looking at the busy square filled with people and stalls. 'I wonder what's going on?'

Lily's smile seemed to lift her spirits. 'I know what this is. It's the Blossomtide Festival. All the towns and villages will be swamped by it shortly.'

'Of course,' Kirin said, wondering at all the colour and frantic preparations. 'We've clearly lost track of time.'

Lily nodded. 'I know I have, living in the forest all this time. I've only enjoyed one festival in the last decade, I think. That was at Francham and because it's mainly merchants and transients, they don't make much of it.'

'Well, they take it very seriously in the city.'

'The barbarian permits it?'

'Oh, he's very much for it, actually. You know, for all his savagery and ruthlessness when he invaded the realms, you'd be surprised if you met him to see how sophisticated he is.'

'What do you mean?' Lily said, tearing her gaze away from a queue of little girls waiting to have flowers braided into their hair.

'Well, he doesn't sit on a throne, dressed in black and calling for the heads of people so he can drink their blood, if that's the image in your mind. He's not at all like that. If he walked into the main street of Hurtle right now, he'd pass unnoticed. He's actually a quiet sort of man. And by that I don't mean he's silent. He just doesn't need to hear the sound of his own voice.'

'So he's subtle, you mean.'

'That's exactly what I mean. He's also surprisingly retiring, very engaging when he decides he's interested in something and he has a mind that can soak up information like a sponge. According to Freath it's the empress who wants all the balls and grand events. Loethar's happiest on his horse riding around the moors. He even quotes poetry, for Lo's sake!'

'And yet we're all intimidated by him.'

Kirin nodded. 'As you should be. No one should be fooled by his demeanour. His intelligence is vast and history attests to what he's capable of. And his nasty half-brother is always waiting in the wings. Now there truly is an evil man. His name is Stracker. Likes to take the title of general.'

'Half-brother?'

Kirin nodded. 'Mark my words. He's shown remarkable patience but I don't understand what keeps Stracker in that second-in-command position. He could overthrow Loethar in a blink if he wanted to.'

'Truly?'

Kirin shrugged. 'Why not? He controls the army. Loethar may be emperor but Stracker is the voice of the warriors.'

'But they're not militant, are they?'

Kiring considered this. 'They haven't been allowed to be but they train hard. There's nothing soft about them. Loethar's just very keen to see them integrating so he agrees instantly to any mixed marriages and children of those marriages are given special considerations: money, schooling. I wouldn't be surprised if he doesn't start bribing them with land.'

'Bribing?'

'Freath says he calls it *encouragement*. These children grow up with a great understanding of east and west, both languages, both customs, a good grip on the two cultures, and so on. Loethar's clever, I'll give him that. He's slowly building a population that has known nothing but imperialism and thrives on that.'

'I see. You sound as though you like Loethar.'

'I hate him for his conduct of anni gone by. The killing of innocents was deplorable. Today he appears a completely different man.'

'He's reinvented himself, you mean?'

'Not really. I think he's always been this man. I think he's also the barbarian warlord. He's whatever he needs to be at the time.'

'So right now he's a loving husband and doting father-to-be.'

Kirin's mouth twisted. 'Definitely looking forward to fatherhood, I gather. I'm not so sure about the loving husband. From what Freath has told me, and from what I've seen, Loethar merely tolerates his wife. It was a marriage of convenience.'

'How sad. I know how it feels,' Lily said, looking away.

Kirin looked at her. 'How many more ways can I say I'm sorry?'

She shrugged. 'Forgive me. That was unfair.'

'This festival can help us actually.'

'How do you mean?'

'Well, the Blossomtide celebrations are essentially about love and fertility. They say couples who marry on the day of the festival are blessed. You'll find loads of lovers will be planning to wed today.'

'So how does that help us? Surely it only complicates things in terms of the priest being available and —'

Kirin laughed. 'You really have been in the forest for too long, Lily. They don't do individual marriage ceremonies at Blossomtide. They marry all the couples at once. I suspect they'll hold the ceremony on the village green — that would account for all the decorations going up. It means we can be married relatively anonymously. Few questions will be asked and no one will recall the strangers who took vows. Come on, let's go find a stable and also a place to stay. The inn is probably crowded to the rafters.'

As it turned out, The Miller and Magpie had a single, tiny loft room left.

'It's very small,' the innkeeper apologised. 'I feel obliged to tell you that it's normally reserved for children but there's a double cot ...'

Kirin slapped a joyful hand onto the counter. 'That's all we'll be needing, Master ... ?'

'Annis,' the innkeeper finished, watching Kirin pull Lily close and tickle her. She giggled helpfully before slapping away his groping hands.

'We're to be married today,' she said to Annis, beaming.

'I'd never have guessed it,' he replied with a wry smile. 'Just sign here,' he said, pointing Kirin to a line on his ledger. 'Evening meal's normally at sundown, though on a festival night anything seems to go.'

Kirin grinned. 'As I said, all we'll need is the bed,' he said, winking.

Annis sighed. 'I guess you'll be wanting to speak to Pastor Byron then. Better catch him soon and register. He'll want to see the ring and bless it beforehand. There are too many of you for him to do it later.'

'The ring,' Kirin repeated. 'Yes, of course. I'll find him right away. Thank you, Master Annis.'

'Happy nuptials,' the man said. 'Two flights up. There's only one door so you can't get lost. One of the girls will give you a key when you're ready. How did you come into town?'

'By horse,' Kirin replied.

'Stabling is just out the back. Hay is included in the room price.' Kirin nodded. 'I see you're travelling light. Do you need help upstairs with anything?' When both Kirin and Lily shook their heads, he said, 'Enjoy your stay,' adding, 'and congratulations. I hope you're both very happy.'

They murmured thanks before Kirin pulled Lily back outside. 'We need to get you a ring,' he said urgently. 'I'm just not sure I have enough money to —'

She bit her lip and frowned before reaching down under her bodice. She pulled out a ribbon from which dangled a pretty silver ring, engraved with leaves. 'My mother's wedding ring,' she explained at his look of query. 'I, er, I always planned to get married with it.'

'You don't have to give up that wish. Save it, I'll find us something.'

'No, Kirin. Use this. It's … well, it's just silly not to.'

There was pain in her voice and Kirin hesitated, but he didn't have much money with him. The room at the inn would eat into most of what he had and he still needed to consider food and drink. 'Thank you. It will be a great help. Shall we go?' She nodded and he offered an arm. 'Time to pretend again, Lily. You did well in there. We just have to keep it going a bit longer.'

She pulled his arm around her more tightly and gave him a peck on his cheek, beaming widely. 'Like that?' she enquired lightly, the smile not faltering as people walked by them.

'Perfect,' he said, a little sadly. Suddenly he realised he had never loved anyone outside his own family. His closest friend had been Freath and his relationships with women were fleeting. As he walked beside Lily now, his arms tightly around her slim body, her warmth passing easily between their clothes, he felt an unfamiliar stirring of emotion.

'Kilt Faris is a lucky man,' he murmured.

'Let's hope he sees it that way,' Lily replied, and somehow Kirin was sure she'd missed his point.

Pastor Byron, when they finally had their few moments with him, looked addled and apologised before Kirin even had a chance to explain their presence.

'Forgive me but today is not my favourite of days. I like what it stands for but it wears me out and sucks at my tolerance like an insatiable leech. You don't even have to tell me why you're here. It's written plain on your faces; I can see you're a couple in love and old enough to know it.'

Kirin closed his mouth.

The pastor continued, 'I've tried to turn away so many youngsters today. They think they love one another but I can tell it won't last. They're too young, they still have so much to learn about themselves. But you two must both be past your third decade?' They both nodded dumbly. 'Neither married now or previously?' They shook their heads. 'Excellent! The ring, please?'

Lily untied the ribbon and handed the pastor her mother's wedding band.

'Very nice,' he said. 'I like older pieces. Your mother's?'

'Yes,' Lily replied. 'I'm Lily and this is —'

'No need, my dear. Forgive me if that sounds rude but I have dozens more to see today. I won't remember your names past the next pair of lovers.' He began to bless the ring, dipping it into Lo's Bowl at the front of the chapel. Finally he opened his eyes. 'There. Now you'll take your vows publicly with everyone else. Please be on the green at start of fourth tide. Thank you and bless you both.' Kirin patted Lily's hand affectionately and they both withdrew. 'Er, you're most welcome to leave an offering,' the pastor mentioned over his shoulder, his back already turned to them. 'Oh, and don't forget the veil. That's one tradition I will insist upon.'

Outside in the sun once again, their eyes adjusting from the chapel's shadows, Kirin aimed for a lighter mood. 'Well, that was painless. Let's go get you a veil, shall we?'

'Kirin. You go back to the inn. I, er ...' Lily shrugged. 'Well, I wouldn't mind a little while on my own and I feel a bit funny about your coming along to help me choose a veil. That's something that the bride should do with other women. I'd rather do it alone.'

He understood. 'All right. Where and when shall I see you?'

'I'll meet you on the green.'

Kirin nodded. 'Lily, are you planning to run away? I'm sorry I feel compelled to ask you that.'

She looked at him with shock. 'It hadn't crossed my mind.'

'Forgive me for putting it into your mind, then. I could pry, of course, but I'd prefer not to, given that I've already gone blind today on your behalf.'

Now Lily just looked sickened. 'I'm aware of my precarious situation, Master Felt, and I will go through with this. I just have to come to terms with it.'

He gave a small bow. 'Then I shall see you shortly.' Kirin took her hand and kissed it. 'For the sake of those watching,' he assured her, and then he turned and left her.

18

Loethar had banished everyone from the chapel, including Father Briar, who, to Loethar's annoyance, seemed unable to contain his grief. 'You may admit my mother when she is brought here,' he said to the weeping priest as he shooed him away, bolting the doors behind him.

Finally he turned to regard the pale, thin body. He couldn't believe that Freath was dead; realised he was holding his breath as he regarded the man who had become such an important counsel to him ... someone he might even have called a friend in his innermost thoughts. Freath's death was so random, so unexpected, so wrong! He pulled back the rest of the shroud abruptly and stared at the ugly wound. There was no doubting it had come from a sword; both sides of the wide cut were neat, the flesh had been sliced through with ease and with no jagged edges. A big sword too. Freath would have known it was being drawn, he had been facing his attacker. Loethar checked Freath's hands. They looked like the white stone quarried in Gormand, but with a mottled pattern of blood, and they certainly felt as chill as marble. He balled one of his own hands into a fist, unconscious of the rage building because inside he felt as cold as Freath did. *Cold rage*, his mother often accused him of possessing.

Freath's hands showed no sign of lacerations. So he had put up no fight, and it didn't seem as though he had gripped the sword sticking from his belly as most people in shock might do. From what Loethar could tell Freath must have seen his attacker, did not resist him, took his death without a real struggle. Why?

Other questions bloomed behind this. *Why was he found in the mountains, not in the inn? Why did he leave the inn in the first place? If he was taken by his attackers, against his will, surely he would have put up some sort of struggle? And where did they take him? Where did Freath die? The mountain gateway was too busy, but then again that sort of activity would have provided good cover if the assailants had known how to make the best use of crowds.*

Loethar walked around the body, lost in contemplation. He circumnavigated Freath a dozen times perhaps, slowly pacing, thinking. And then he came to a final dread conclusion. *Freath had known his attacker.*

A soft knock at the door distracted him. He looked up, vexed, but he knew who it would be and could not ignore it. Loethar returned to the door and unbolted it. Father Briar stood next to two servants who carried Dara Negev in a special chair Loethar had had constructed for this very purpose. She looked like one of the royals he'd heard stories about from the exotic land of Percheron, carried around in covered seats by slaves.

'You summoned me,' his mother said, her voice cutting through the thick silence.

'Thank you for coming,' he replied.

'As if I had a choice,' she remarked. 'Set me down and leave me,' she ordered, obviously sensing that her son wanted total privacy. As the two servants did so, Loethar addressed the priest.

'Father Briar, you cleaned up Freath's body, am I right?'

'Yes, my lord. It was my unhappy pleasure to do this for him.'

Loethar nodded. 'Did you notice anything?'

Briar blinked. 'Such as, my lord?'

Loethar blew out his cheeks. He wasn't sure what he was searching for either. He shrugged. 'I don't really know, anything that might give us a clue as to where he was when he was ultimately attacked.'

Briar began to shake his head. 'His clothes were —.' Then he hesitated.

'Were what?'

Briar looked back at him. 'Sorry, er, his clothes were dusty, which I'd expect from his travels, but now that you mention it I did notice a few pine needles clinging to the folds of his garments.'

'Pine needles?' Loethar repeated.

The priest nodded. 'Is that helpful, my lord?'

'I don't know yet. Send a runner to fetch General Stracker, would you?'

'Of course,' Briar said. He bowed to Loethar and nodded graciously at Dara Negev before departing.

Loethar's mother didn't notice; her attention was riveted on the corpse. 'I thought it was a mistake when I was told.'

'I hoped it was,' he replied.

'How?' she wondered. 'He wasn't young but he was barely into his sixth decade, surely, and spry?'

'He didn't die, Mother, he was murdered,' Loethar snapped. Angrily, he hauled back the shroud again to reveal the wound. Dara Negev's mouth opened in response but no words came as she regarded the deep wound. Finally, she spoke. 'Who knew that Freath was going north with this news of increased taxes?'

Loethar had to admire his mother. She had cut through all of the obvious exclamations and pointless jabber, straight to the heart of what mattered most. 'No one. Only myself, Stracker and the men who accompanied him.'

'Did his wizard go with him … if you could call him that? I've seen no sign of any magics with that one,' she said with disgust.

Loethar smirked. 'I think that was the point of why we allowed Freath to have Master Kirin in the first instance. His powers are so weak — if he has any — as to be negligible. But Master Kirin is intelligent and I've found his help around the library and with the new academy of learning we've established in Penraven to be extremely competent. I have no gripe with him. But you raise an important point.'

'Well, he's the first person you should interrogate. I can't say I'll be mourning Freath, Loethar. I don't like traitors and the man betrayed his own with barely a look over his shoulder.'

'You know as well as I do how valuable Freath has been to me.'

'I've never quite let go of the notion I had when I first met him that he was not entirely honest. He struck me as being more than simply a man arriving where the wind blew him.'

It was an old Steppes saying and Loethar nodded. 'I'm sure he wasn't, considering that barbarian invaders were spilling through the stronghold of the famed Valisars.'

'No, it was more than that, son. Freath was calculating. He was charming and eloquent, his intelligence was vast, but he was a man of shadows.'

Loethar shrugged. 'Any man who betrays his king would have to become careful. He hadn't given me any cause this past ten anni to consider him anything but committed to the empire, if not necessarily devoted to us.'

She nodded thoughtfully. 'So if no one but you and Stracker, the wizard and his escort knew of his arrival in the north, who could spring such an attack?'

His mother's suspicions were talking directly to his own. The whole notion of a random attack felt less and less likely.

'In fact,' she continued, 'for him to be found anywhere but where he should be ... am I right that he was discovered out in the open?' When he nodded, she continued, 'Well, it suggests to me that in the first instance, that whatever reason he was outside of the inn and perhaps beyond the town's centre, he was there willingly.'

Loethar's eyes narrowed. 'That's how I feel. My suspicions are that Freath went willingly from the inn where he was supposed to be staying. In fact —' He paused as Stracker entered. 'Ah, there you are.'

'Mother,' Stracker said, 'you look well today.'

She gave him a look of disdain. 'I'm eighty-one anni, son. This is how I look.'

Stracker's tatua moved as he grinned. He glanced briefly at Freath. 'I've got the eldest of the trio of escorts outside.'

'Go ahead,' Loethar said.

Stracker paused. 'I had no time for Freath but I'm angry anyone under our escort is dead. That said, I have no reason to mistrust his escorts and neither have you. All of them are handpicked and reliable. At Freath's bidding they took a couple of hours' relaxation before returning to The Lookout. The Blue checked with the staff and according to them Freath and his sidekick did not leave the inn during that time. They emerged later from their shared room for an evening meal. We even know what they ate. As you heard, our men returned to the inn during the evening and saw Freath. There was nothing untoward, nothing unusual.'

'He was talking to a stranger,' Loethar reminded him.

'Yes, but in broad view of everyone. The serving girl said they didn't seem to know one another. From what she could remember, they simply began passing the time of day as she offered to refresh their ales.'

'Perhaps that's how it was meant to appear,' Loethar said.

'Our men only left him alone a short while.' Loethar frowned and opened his mouth but Stracker held up a hand. 'And before you ask, the time between when they last noticed him and noticed he was gone was just moments. The time it took to take a few sips of ale.'

'So he was bundled out of the inn, possibly?' their mother offered.

'I doubt it,' Stracker replied. 'Imagine trying to steal a man away in front of dozens of others in a busy inn! His reluctance to go would create a disturbance. And they didn't drug the ale; our men tasted what was in Freath's cup. It's just not feasible to get him out of the inn easily —'

'Unless he wanted to go,' Loethar finished.

'Well, yes,' Stracker conceded, frowning, 'but why would he want to go?'

'I can't tell you, I wasn't there,' Loethar replied, his tone bordering on acid. A glare from his mother wiped away the scowl he had directed at his half-brother.

Stracker didn't seem to notice either of them. 'All right, then. But how would he leave without our men noticing him?'

Loethar sighed. 'I told you. They created a distraction. It's the oldest trick going. What were they doing when this was occurring, sitting around a table chatting?'

Stracker shrugged. 'Let's ask.' He walked to the door, opened it and mumbled something.

Loethar recognised the experienced, senior member of the Blues who entered. 'Hello, Jib,' he said, the man's name coming to him.

'Emperor,' Jib said, nodding politely. 'Dara Negev,' he added, bowing to the old woman. His fist went to his heart. 'General Stracker.'

Stracker nodded. 'Jib, tell us what was occurring when you and the men arrived at the inn.'

Jib shrugged as though it wasn't worth even mentioning. 'The usual sort of Denovian recreation. It was crowded and the mood was jovial. Everyone was drinking, even Master Freath. He had finished his meal and was sitting not that far from us across the chamber at the back.'

'He was not alone, though,' Loethar confirmed.

'It was crowded, my lord, and he was near a lot of people because of the happy mob. At one point he exchanged a few words with the man next to him, who had his back to us. From his gestures I think he looked to be explaining the game that was underway.'

Loethar nodded at Stracker, who took up the questioning.

'From what you told me before nothing, was unusual and Freath appeared relaxed.'

'Yes, general. He raised his mug to me to acknowledge us as we entered. We pushed through to the counter, ordered some ales and then moved to a table.'

'A table?' Loethar quizzed.

'Yes, my lord.'

'If it was so crowded, how could you so easily find somewhere to sit?'

Jib nodded. 'It's true, it was shoulder to shoulder in there because it is the most popular watering hole in the town. But everyone was on their feet watching a game of arrows. I haven't seen this game before; I think it's only played in the north. A big man was taking his turn, and doing very badly. He was very amusing and everyone was betting against him.'

'Did you?'

'No, my lord. We only watched, we didn't gamble.'

'I see, and then when you moved to find Freath he was gone?'

'Yes, my lord. When the contest was over and everyone was moving back, I decided I should work out the plan for the next day with Master Freath, but he had disappeared.'

'All right, Jib.'

The man glanced over at the shrouded body, only now perhaps fully realising who was laid out and covered. He looked instantly sorrowful. 'I'm sorry that he slipped us, my lord. We were diligent and I'm at a loss to imagine why or how he got past us.' The emperor nodded. 'You may go.'

Jib stole a glance at Stracker and bowed to the emperor and Dara Negev before leaving.

Once the door had closed Loethar rounded on Stracker. 'Let them all live. Even our men sense that Freath went willingly. He used the words *slipped us*.'

Stracker looked incensed. 'They let you down.'

'And nothing will be achieved by executing them,' said Loethar.

Stracker threw an I-told-you-so glance at his mother, then returned his attention to Loethar. 'So you believe Freath deliberately sneaked out of the inn, using the contest as a diversion?'

'Of course. I have no other explanation. The question is why? Who was he going to meet? How does he know these people? Why are they important to him? Exactly what was Freath up to in the north? Clearly not taxes!'

'A romantic tryst?' Dara Negev offered, then laughed. 'I jest, of course. Freath was like a dry old stick.'

Stracker sighed. 'I'll leave for Francham now.'

'Find the Vested,' Loethar repeated. 'Master Kirin must know something. Why else isn't he dead alongside Freath?'

'We've got the realm covered. We should be able to place him within a few days.'

Loethar considered this. 'He was initially brought here against his will. I worry that the lure of freedom is seductive.'

Dara Negev gave a sound of derision. 'That man of magic seemed happy enough here.'

'He did,' Loethar agreed. 'I always liked him, to tell the truth.'

'What magic did he possess anyway?' she demanded.

'Low level stuff. He could judge people relatively well. I know that sounds vague but apparently that was his skill. He was based at the Academy of Learning in Cremond to match students with the right sort of education. As he put it, someone might present as a person who wanted to study the stars but he would know very quickly that the student would make a better adept as a physic, or perhaps as an architect.'

'How odd,' she commented. 'Nothing really useful, then?'

'No, and that's why we didn't need him or fret about his connection with Freath in those early days. He didn't give Freath anything back when I wasn't in a position to trust him. That's what is so galling. I trusted the man!'

'I don't know why you needed any of them. You should have had them all killed.'

'We've been through this, Mother,' Loethar said, his tone suggesting how tedious she was.

'Well, we might have, but I can't help but remind you, Loethar. People with any skills, low level or otherwise, are dangerous. And you've got them all packed away together. What makes you think they won't use that power against you?'

'I've explained before, Mother, that to waste the power of the Vested is short-sighted. I'd rather harness it and use it to my own ends. And rather than cooping them up and making enemies of them, I'm now doing a controlled release of them throughout the realm so I know where they are. Some have extraordinary powers.'

'Like that wretched blood taster of yours. He makes my flesh crawl.'

'Like Vulpan, yes. Speaking of whom, Stracker, have you sent word ahead to get Vulpan moved immediately up to Francham?'

'Yes, but I have to question if Freath is really so important that we're going to drop everything and chase after his killer? He's not going to be mourned by anyone.'

'This is not about Freath. It's about the death of a key member of my retinue and the mystery surrounding it. Why would someone Freath willingly met kill him in cold blood? And why all the secrecy? Whatever your personal opinion is, Freath has worked closely alongside me for the past ten anni. What if this is connected to a plot against me? Freath must have lost a lot of blood. If Vulpan can follow the trail, he might be able to find where Freath died.'

'He'd need to taste his blood first,' Stracker remarked, looking bored.

'It doesn't have to be fresh, does it?'

Now the general grinned. 'No.' He reached to his waist, unsheathed a dagger and strode to where Freath's corpse lay.

Staring at he mottled, grey face of the aide, he plunged the dagger into the middle of the body's chest, just below the sternum. 'Ah,' he groaned with pleasure. 'That is very satisfying. I've wanted to do that for years.'

His mother chuckled, unaffected by her son's ghoulish behaviour. Loethar, however, ground his jaw as he blinked, his lips slightly pursed. 'Done?' he asked with forced politeness as he reached for the corner of the shroud.

Stracker withdrew the blade and stared at the dark, sticky mass that coated it. 'Vulpan will enjoy this.'

Loethar's bland expression hid his concern at his family's lack of finesse. 'Take whomever you need,' he told Stracker. 'Get Vulpan to Francham and hunt down where Freath died and get onto the trail of the person or persons who did this. And find me Master Kirin. I need to know why he and Freath did not suffer the same fate.'

'Can I use whatever means I need to fulfil your orders, my emperor?'

Stracker was baiting him. Loethar took a moment to consider his reply. 'No killing, Stracker.'

He watched his half-brother glance at their mother before he nodded. 'When did you turn so soft, brother?'

'These days a more subtle approach is prudent,' Loethar replied carefully.

'Don't change too much,' Stracker warned, turning to leave.

'Or what?' Loethar asked in a quiet voice.

Dara Negev's gaze flicked anxiously between her sons. They both ignored her. Stracker turned around and regarded his younger sibling. Loethar's stare impaled him, unflinching. For the briefest moment Loethar believed Stracker was finally going to share what he was really feeling, what was really building within that huge barrel chest of his. But it seemed the influence of their mother was still too strong.

Stracker shook his head slightly and then smiled wryly. 'Or

you'll disappoint your true people,' he answered. This time when he turned his back on the emperor, he left, although Loethar would have put money on the guess that Stracker's expression was far from smiling as his broad body moved across the threshold of the chapel and closed the door behind him.

Loethar glanced at his mother. 'Trouble is brewing.'

'Always has been between you two.'

'Oh, I don't know. I think we handle our differences rather well.'

'It's easy to say that when you're emperor.'

'Should I be worried?'

Dara Negev sighed. 'Not as long as I'm alive, son. Beyond that I cannot say. But Stracker isn't a deep thinker; you know that. He's someone who reacts. Keeping him under such control for this long is a miracle.' Loethar nodded. He knew his mother was right. 'He thinks you have forgotten what the struggle was all about.'

'Mother, Stracker never knew what my struggle was.'

She regarded her son. 'He could be forgiven for assuming you both shared the same vision.'

Loethar looked down. 'Yes, he could be. But he doesn't know.'

'And if you want to keep your throne, child, he must never know. Remember who answers to him. You are emperor and our people respect you — always have, even when you were a mere barbarian warlord. But now the Set people respect you, too. It's quite an achievement and I never doubted you could attain this goal. But Stracker doesn't share the same ideals.'

'I know,' Loethar said, tiring of the obvious.

'An heir is critical now, Loethar. If the monster you call a wife doesn't give you a son, kill her and take a new wife. Bearing heirs is all she was ever good for and if she can't do that for you, she is a pointless waste of time. Daughters will not protect this throne. As soon as your son is born, move to protect him.'

Loethar looked up to the chapel's ceiling, where sparrows flitted in the rafters. 'Curious, isn't it, how history repeats itself?'

'What do you mean?'

'Brennus. He did everything to protect the line of the throne. And now here I am, suddenly finding myself in the same precarious situation.'

'It's how it's always been.'

'Not for the Steppes people. We fight for our throne.'

She smiled. 'Don't you ever forget it, son.'

'Come,' Loethar said. He glanced once more at Freath, then turned away to call for the runners to carry his mother back to her chambers.

Crouching beneath the shrouded table that held Freath's corpse, holding his breath, a young page prayed to Lo that the emperor and the crone would leave quickly. He was sure his trembling was shaking the linens that hid him.

Empress Valya stared out of her window, so overwhelmed by her frustration that she felt rigid, her thoughts fractured. Her marriage was a sham. Her love seemed to hit the wall of stone that her husband had become, bouncing back sharply to pummel her with silent derision.

She felt the baby inside her belly shift, and marvelled helplessly at the strange little shape that pushed against her body. An *elbow*, she thought, just for a blink, amused and transported by the wonder of it.

'I always loved your father more than he loved me,' she began, stroking where her child stretched, finding a small measure of comfort in talking to her unborn. 'And if I'm honest perhaps he never did make a promise to love me. That's a pity, for I love him more intensely now than ever and my unrequited affection is more damaging than his unspoken words. I realise now he married me simply for show, so that he would fit the mould of the Denovian he strived to be. And you are the reason for our marriage. You're not the first, of course. But it seems I am inadequate as a breeder. I have failed every time, until now. You must hold on. You will be my triumph, and my bartering stick. For he wants you more than he wants anything in this land. Don't be a girl, sweet child. You must be a male, or all of us are lost. I might even have to kill you myself if you are born female. I would be showing you a mercy. He will not want you; none of them will want you. And I will be cast aside as their patience wears thin of my —' She stopped her murmurings at the sound of the door. 'Who is it?' Valya snapped.

'It's Fren, empress,' came a small voice through the door.

Valya hated the new gait her body had adopted as her pregnancy had edged closer to its finale. Her once lithe, trim body was hugely misshapen, forcing her to waddle. She had known women who had been smug and proud of the swollen outline produced by these moons of childbearing, but she hated it; hated that she couldn't ride or move with elegance, that her ankles were twice their normal size, that fat had seemingly layered itself all over her body. Like a sea vessel in full sail she drifted in a swaying motion towards the door and pulled it open, scowling. 'Do you have news?'

The boy nodded.

'Come,' she ordered.

The child stepped inside her chamber.

'Did you take care?'

'Yes, empress, very good care.'

'Tell me.' At Fren's hesitation, she grabbed his thin arm. 'Tell me!'

He was frightened, she could see that now. What had he heard? 'Fren, where have you been?'

'In the chapel.'

'Chap— Why?'

'You told me to take every opportunity to eavesdrop on the emperor.'

'And?'

'I knew a runner had been sent to summon Dara Negev regarding Master Freath's death and I thought he might talk openly to her about it.'

'Hurry up, Fren,' she said. 'Why are you drawing this out?'

Fren flinched as she snapped her fingers before his face. 'I ... I heard the emperor talking to General Stracker and Dara Negev.'

Dawning spread on Valya's face. 'Really? So they had a gathering without me.'

'All I know, empress, is that he summoned both once he'd arrived in the chapel.'

'What was said?'

'They discussed Master Freath's death. The emperor is very angry about it.'

'I don't know why,' Valya said, waving a hand dismissively. 'Good riddance, I say, to the oily old coot.'

'I believe that is how the general felt, empress.'

'But not my husband.'

'He is angry. He wants answers. He said Freath's not important. Er, I just have to remember this properly, empress.' The boy frowned, presumably running back over his recollection of the conversation. 'It's not about Freath, he said, it's about why Freath was lying.'

'Lying?'

'Yes, empress, that's what I understood although I didn't really follow what —'

She flicked back her golden hair with irritation. 'Fren, remember the words themselves, what he did say.'

'He said: "*that's what is so galling, I trusted the man*". I don't understand galling but the way he said it, it sounded as though he was lied to by Master Freath.'

Valya pondered this information, her thoughts racing. Had Freath really lied to Loethar? 'Why do they think Freath might have lied?'

The boy shook his head. 'They said Freath must have known

his attacker or at least willingly left the inn with him. The emperor spoke with one of the soldiers who had escorted Master Freath to the north. The soldiers were in the inn with Master Freath, and had seen him drinking ale. Then he disappeared, under their noses from what I could tell, empress.'

'I see. So if he hadn't been a willing victim, there would have been some sort of disturbance to alert the soldiers?'

Fren beamed. 'That's exactly what they were saying.'

'Interesting,' Valya said, her brow creased in thought, one hand on her swollen belly. 'And how was the mood in the room, Fren?'

'Mood?'

'Yes, you know, how were the two men talking to one another? I know my husband never raises his voice but he can still make his listener understand when he's threatening them.'

'Then the mood was awkward, empress. The emperor and the general seemed … um…'

'Angry?'

Fren shook his head.

'Argumentative?'

'Sort of. What's the word when the conversation sounds as though everyone's trying to keep his temper in check?'

'Tense?'

He beamed. 'That's it, empress. Yes, it was tense between those two.'

'Tell me, did the general challenge my husband? You know, lay down any sort of threats?'

The boy looked back at her, wide-eyed. 'Not really, empress. But after the general had left, the emperor asked his mother if there was a problem. Trouble, he called it.'

'And he was referring to his brother?'

'Yes, because she said …' The boy paused again, his face creased in concentration. 'She said the general could be forgiven for believing they shared the same vision. She also said that if he was going to keep the throne, Stracker must never know.'

Valya had been pacing but now she swung around, astonishment on her face. 'Those were her words?' she demanded.

Fren nodded. 'I have a very good memory, empress, as you know.'

She feigned a conspiratorial smile. 'That's why you're my favourite and most handsome spy,' she assured. 'This is very intriguing, Fren. Very intriguing, indeed.'

'Is that good, empress?'

'Probably,' she said. 'And Dara Negev didn't say what this secret might be?'

Fren shook his head. 'From the way the conversation went, they both seemed to know what it was.'

She smiled for his benefit, turning away so he wouldn't see her fresh expression of outrage and confusion. Why, after all she had been through with them, would she not be privy to some great secret being shared between her husband and his mother? 'Was I mentioned at all during this conversation?' she said absently, merely for something to say as she puzzled over Loethar's secret.

Fren cleared his throat. 'Yes, you were, empress.'

She stopped pacing and turned back. Cocking her head to one side, she asked, 'Really?'

He nodded but Valya noticed he looked suddenly fidgety.

'What was said about me?'

Fren bit his lip and ran a hand through his hair. 'Well, empress, they were talking about an heir for the empire.'

'They being Dara Negev and the emperor?'

'Yes.'

'Go on. What about the heir?'

'Just how important he is.'

'He. Yes,' she said. Almost to herself, she added, 'I wonder what will happen if it's a she?' She didn't expect an answer, began returning her thoughts to Loethar's secret, and so was shocked to be given an answer.

'They would kill you.'

Valya rounded on the boy. 'What did you just say?' she hissed.

Fren swallowed. 'Dara Negev said you should be killed, empress, if you can't produce the heir needed.'

Valya blinked. 'You're quite sure she didn't mean a daughter should be killed?'

'I'm sure, empress. Her words were: *kill her and take a new wife.* She said that *bearing heirs is all you were good for and if you can't do that, then … then you are a pointless —*'

'Stop, curse you!' Valya exclaimed, her breath suddenly shallow.

'I'm sorry, empress.'

She paced, wringing her hands. 'Kill me?' she said, testing the words aloud. 'How did my husband reply?'

'He didn't, empress. He changed the subject to something about how history repeats itself. He seemed more concerned about his general's intentions than the need to secure the rule with an heir.'

Valya sneered, enraged that Loethar had not even pretended to stick up for her. 'Well, of course he would be.'

'Dara Negev did say, now I think about it, that as long as she was alive, the emperor was safe, but beyond her death she couldn't say.'

Valya pulled aside a tapestry and from a shelf recessed into the stone behind it took down a small wooden chest. Opening the chest, she took out a few coins. 'Here, Fren. This should feed your family for a month at least.'

The boy's eyes shone as the heavy coins landed in his hands, and he immediately tucked the money away in a pouch around his neck. 'Thank you, empress.'

'There's more of that for you. Keep your eyes and ears open. I want to know everything you hear immediately. Do you understand? No matter what time of day or night.'

'I understand,' he said gravely, then bowed. 'Thank you, empress.'

She flicked a hand at him, hardly noticing his departure as her mind fled to how she might protect herself. Well, she thought, rubbing at her belly, she wasn't that easy to do away with.

19

Kirin stole a glance at Lily, glad that he could, thanking his luck that it was his left eye that was blind. She looked like a picture, standing here on the village green with dozens of other young couples. Her veil was not nearly as elaborate as some of the other girls' veils but going by those he could see through the gauzy head coverings, his bride was by far the prettiest. Her cheeks looked flushed and she'd found a suitable dress from somewhere — he couldn't imagine where. It looked old, the embroidered rosebuds slightly faded, and yet it wasn't tatty and Lily made it look fresh and perfect. Her boots were muddy but he rather thought that summed up Lily — the little he knew of her, anyway. For a moment Kirin felt breathless. He was getting married.

'Stop staring,' Lily admonished out of the side of her mouth.

'Sorry,' he murmured.

'Concentrate. Our bit's coming up.'

He took a deep breath, listening as names were read out by the droning voice of the priest, clearly wearied by his role.

'Master Kirin Felt and Maiden Lily Jeves?'

Maiden? Kirin thought and had to stifle a smile, as did Lily, he noticed. How quaint. 'In Lo's presence, we solemnly swear,' they both answered. Kirin noticed Lily's smile fade as she proclaimed her vow. He felt a pang of regret. It was a pity she was not in a position to mean it.

Kilt Faris was on a mission. He had already left the main camp and was hurrying back down from the high parts of the forest, ignoring the draw of Francham, where he had last lain with Lily, and heading furiously to Woodingdene, where Coder had overheard the breakaway party was headed.

While Leo's threat echoed loudly, it was Faris's mother's words that burned in his mind: *you never realise the preciousness of what you've had until it's lost.* Leaving his mother was the hardest task he'd ever had to face. When he had gone to the Academy, all his siblings had long ago left home and his father had been dead for many years. She had never made him feel guilty, had never asked him to stay, but he had known she had wished he would. When she'd laboriously embroidered those poignant words onto a kerchief with his initials she had nearly undone him. But he had left, as he knew he must, and despite his best intentions had not returned home to visit. Receiving the news of her death had made him feel broken, and, if he were honest, was probably the reason that he ultimately lost his way at the Academy, striking out instead for a completely different sort of life.

He had no idea where his two brothers lived or whether they even thought about him. He doubted it. They were twins and they had never needed him; they'd always had each other for companionship. As the younger brother he had been an encumbrance and their teasing had been relentless, especially over his differences. But he'd always been his mother's favourite; she had reassured him time and time again that it was his very difference that made him so special. It was his mother who had suggested he keep his talent hidden and had counselled her twin sons to protect their brother's ability. And she had recognised Faris's intelligence from an early age; she had not been surprised when he had first broached the subject of moving to Cremond to educate himself. She had even given him the solid silver cup his father had given her on the day of their wedding.

'Sell it,' she'd said. 'It will fetch a handsome price melted down.'

He hadn't wanted to take it but she'd pressed it into his hands, insisting. 'It's no good to me, son, but it can do some good for you.'

Leaving Jewd had been equally tough. Jewd was a brother to him — even back then — and the separation had been terrible, with Kilt feeling as though he'd been cut adrift from everything familiar, everything he trusted. When Jewd had brought the news of Kilt's mother's passing, they'd both felt a similar urge to disappear from all that was familiar.

It was reckless, the action of youth, but it had felt wonderful to leave the Academy. They'd bought two horses and, with no plan in mind, moved in whichever direction had taken their fancy, making their living as highwaymen. From their first theft Kilt had made Jewd promise that they would keep no more than what they needed to eat and clothe themselves. The rest he anonymously donated to the convent in the east, two orphanages — one in the midlands and another down south — a small leper community on Medhaven, and so it went. Any group of people that he and Jewd felt were trying to help the less fortunate received a share of their spoils. The recipients were never told who their benefactors were although Kilt felt the wily Abbess had her strong suspicions.

There was not a happier time for him. At least not until ten anni ago when Lily had arrived in his life with a king in tow. And now his priorities had shifted. It had happened slowly at first, so gradually that he hadn't noticed until Jewd had quietly mentioned that as he and Lily were like an old married couple they might as well make it official.

'Are we really?' Faris had remarked, dismayed.

Jewd had looked at him with a wry expression. 'Well, it's either old age or it's Lily.'

'But what do you mean? What's so different?'

They'd been sitting on a log not far from the Stone of Lackmarin, staring down the incline at the carpet that leaf-fall had laid. Jewd had shifted to regard his friend. 'You jest, right?'

Faris had frowned and shaken his head.

'Kilt, are you aware of how many precautions you now take before each raid? You're driving the men nuts. And we raid so rarely now that sometimes I wonder how we'll get through the winter on the few supplies we can afford.'

'We make do, don't we?'

'We make do, indeed. But we don't have much to spare. You may recall we used to give a lot back to the convent. Can you remember the last time we took coin to the Abbess? Or when we last sent money to the leper colony? Or gave to the orphanage at Talren? You always said you wanted to spread Penraven's wealth around the whole Set, especially now it had a usurper for a ruler. Guess how long it's been since we've given anything away!'

Faris shook his head.

'Nearly four anni. Since then, we've lived pretty much hand to mouth.'

Faris felt his mouth fall open in shock.

'No one's complaining,' Jewd continued, 'because we all chose this life but —'

'I understand,' Faris had interrupted, for the first time realising how things had changed. 'I think I've turned too cautious.'

Jewd had laid a beefy hand on his shoulder. 'Lily's a great catch, not someone to lose or to risk by living too dangerously. Plus, you're grooming a king. You've done a grand job with Leo. When the time comes he will be prepared for whatever is thrown his way. He shoots an arrow as hard and as straight as any of us; his sword skills are dazzling, he —'

'I know, I know, but still …'

'What?'

'I wish de Vis was still around. He had all the courtly graces and skills that Leo should have been taught.'

'Leo already knows them. His education began the moment of his birth. When he came to us at nearly thirteen he already had sound, well honed skills.'

'Yes, but de Vis would have polished them. Stupid fool. I'll kill him myself if I ever clap eyes on him again. What possessed him to take off like that?'

'You know what possessed him, so don't play dumb. He was jealous over Lily's obvious infatuation with you.'

'But I didn't —'

'I know you didn't,' Jewd had interrupted. 'I didn't say you did. But, Kilt, you always stole the best girls from us lads even in our youth. It's just who you are, how you look, how you act.' He had shrugged. 'And you do it without much effort, damn you.' He had grinned. 'De Vis reacted predictably — I should have seen it coming, anyway — but I'd certainly like to know who took him, or how he disappeared when he was so badly injured.'

'Someone took him all right, and the arrow Leo found tells us it was a Davarigon. But why he was taken is a mystery.'

'We've never followed that up properly, have we?'

Kilt had shaken his head. 'We've been so preoccupied with keeping Leo safe.'

'That's a poor excuse. Let's make ourselves a couple of promises. I'll start some gentle enquiries about the arrow.'

'And the second promise?'

'You marry Lily and make her happy.'

Faris remembered how he had looked at Jewd that lovely leaf-fall morning. 'I don't want to stop our life —'

'No one's asking you to, least of all Lily.'

'Has she said something to you?'

Jewd had squirmed. 'She doesn't really have to. I'm just not as dense as you.' They'd laughed sadly. 'But I suspect she wants more than to just be your woman in the forest.'

'You're right.' Faris had laughed a little. 'I think at the back of my mind I've always believed I might not survive much longer.'

Jewd had grown serious. 'Yes, me too.'

'I feel so guilty about the men ... about you —'

'Don't! We can all think for ourselves. We've all chosen. Life was easier for us before imperial rule, but none of us want to see Loethar's reign continue.'

'Married.' Faris had tested the sound of the word. 'Sounds nice.'

'Doesn't have to change anything. Lily won't want to leave the forest and frankly, Kilt, if you don't ask her, I'll marry her.'

'All right,' he'd said, grinning. 'But you keep your end of the bargain. I've been remiss in not following up the de Vis mystery. Let's start tracking that arrow more aggressively.'

That had been the plan. And then Freath had suddenly entered their lives, changing everything. *Damn the young king's impetuous move!* Faris thought. He could have made good use of Freath's obvious cunning and position in the palace.

He shook his head. Now that burning question had to take second priority. Lily going missing had pushed his mind into chaos. In fact, his whole life felt suddenly out of his normally very tight control. He was slipping badly if he hadn't sensed all that anger in Leo, or seen what he was capable of. The youngster had little remorse in his heart for the killing; no matter what was coming out of Leo's lips, Faris saw only satisfaction in the king's eyes.

He was Valisar all right. Cold, ruthless, a blinkered view of what honour meant. Faris shook his head again with disgust.

Lily first. Then he would deal with the king. 'I'd better find Lily soon,' he muttered to himself, 'because very soon Leo will work out for himself that his authority trumps mine.'

Lily stared at the bed, mortified.

'Hope you like it?' the innkeeper's wife said, beaming widely.

Strolling around for hours on the green, trying to enjoy the festivities but really just killing time before the inevitable walk back to the inn had been bad enough. What awaited them turned out to be so much worse. They had been faced by an uproarious welcome of festival revellers eager to view any of the newlyweds. Within moments Kirin was dripping, his head doused many times by ale in a curious ritual that was supposed to make his seed strong.

And it seemed that every man this night was permitted to kiss Lily. Strangers felt emboldened to kiss any bride they met. She had done her best to avoid the wet, slobbery smooches from the more drunken fellows, whom she was now convinced travelled into Hurtle just for the opportunity to freely kiss the girls. She'd lost count of the number of times she'd pursed her lips together to shut out a roaming tongue, or turned her head just in time so that a kiss was smeared on her chin instead of her lips.

Kirin had looked equally dumbstruck by the rituals, apologising every other minute, his hair, his nose, even his rather long and lovely eyelashes dripping with ale. She was staring at those same downcast eyelashes now, her face no doubt thunderous even though she knew none of this was his fault. There was so much to like about Kirin. She could tell he didn't consider himself brave or strong and yet there was a quietly heroic quality about him that she found irresistible. With him there was no bluster, no muscles, no bravado. Kirin just seemed to possess courage and it was all the more poignant because he seemed such a lonely, somewhat sorrowful individual. And yet his smile and the dimples it produced were deliciously sunny. He was not smiling now, however.

'Well?' the innkeeper's wife prompted.

'Er, it's a wonderful surprise,' Kirin answered for them, when he clearly realised that Lily was too shocked to respond.

The woman's smile widened, Lily noticed, if that were possible.

'We like to make a fuss for our wedding guests, especially on festival night. My girls have done a lovely job, haven't they?'

Lily stared at the bed strewn with petals and the fresh lavender stalks carpeting the floor. A scented candle was burning alongside the bed and a heart had been formed from dried and jellied fruits left in the middle of the bed's counterpane on a platter.

The innkeeper's wife nudged her. 'Eat the brambleberries, my girl. On your wedding night, it is said they will make you a son. If you want a daughter, go with the sugared verberries.'

Lily felt dizzy. 'Thank you,' was all she could force out.

'All right, you youngsters, I know you're in a hurry to be alone,' she said. 'I'll —'

'That's kind of you,' Kirin said, moving to show her the door, glancing anxiously at Lily.

'Not so fast,' the woman chortled. 'You strangers, I don't know!' she said in feigned indignation. 'I was just going to say I'd better send up the Kissing Party.'

'Kissing Party?' Lily felt faint.

The woman nodded. 'We'll get this over and done with quickly so you can have some peace.' She bustled out of the room.

'Kirin, I —'

'I don't know what she means, Lily, but I promise we'll get through it quickly. Just hold on a bit longer,' he begged.

They stood rooted to the spot in silence. All Lily could think of was washing her face using the bowl of water and flannels that she could see on the sideboard, sluicing away the slobber of men's kisses. Poor Kilt. If he knew …

Her worried thoughts were interrupted by the merry sound of a stampede of people up the stairs, all singing wildly about love and fertility and being blessed by many years of affection and children. She moved closer to Kirin, instinctively clutching his arm. Kirin, Lo bless him, remained calm for both of them.

'Someone will have to explain this to us,' he said brightly, his arm wrapping around Lily in protection.

The innkeeper's wife couldn't wait to do the honours, it seemed. She held up a length of tiny pink, mauve and violet seaside daisies strung together. 'Well, the marriage is now officially blessed not only by Lo but by the townsfolk. Now we need to wrap you both in simple flowers of love and witness what's known as the Lovers' Kiss, and then we shall leave you to your wedding supper and whatever comes after.' She giggled.

'Lovers' Kiss?' Lily asked nervously.

'Get on with it, you shy young things,' the woman urged. 'Lo, strike me, you're both too old to be playing so coy.'

Kirin held up his hands in mock defeat. 'You need to understand our decision to marry was hasty. We were in love a long time ago as youngsters. The intervening years have made us hesitant and yet seeing Lily again I knew there would never be another woman for me. Never has been.' Lily realised Kirin was making a speech that he hoped they'd all remember if the townfolk were ever questioned about the marriage. *Clever Kirin, trying to ensure their safety.* She heard him finish with: 'I'm just so blessed she said yes.'

'I'll say!' someone called out.

Kirin smiled self-consciously and Lily could see how hard he was trying to keep the pretence going. 'And I presume as we kiss, you will wrap us in the daisies?' he clarified, before adding, 'and then you will leave me alone to my bride?'

'Exactly,' the innkeeper's wife confirmed, beaming as the revellers cheered.

Kirin turned. 'Lily, dear one. Allow me to express my love for you,' he said theatrically and although Lily was dying inside, she adored him for trying to help her through this difficult time. He leaned close to her ear and whispered beneath the raucous noise, 'Kilt will forgive you. Make it look real.'

She had to trust him. Reaching up, she put her arms around his neck and closed her eyes to block out her shame. She would let Kirin kiss her and she would pretend to respond. So why was she feeling so much heat in her cheeks? It wasn't guilt, it wasn't the humiliation … it was something else she was refusing to openly admit.

A roar went up as she felt his soft lips gently touch hers. She was aware of people moving around her, could feel the daisy chain beginning to wrap them closer in their embrace. What she hadn't expected was her eagerness to respond to Kirin's gentle kiss so quickly and while she convinced herself she was simply playing her part of the deception skilfully, she found herself wrapping her arms more tightly around his neck, her lips moving in tandem with his. She was aware of his ardour in another place and dismissed that her own body was reacting to it, answering it.

She inwardly begged for the cheering to stop and for the daisies to be done with, and especially for the kiss to end … yet still she clung to him, her tongue treacherously beginning to tentatively explore his mouth. Suddenly, and to her shock, Kirin pulled away from her, a huge roar of approval accompanying his huge, feigned grin.

'Now look what you've all caused,' he said, pointing below his waist.

Lily didn't need to look; she had felt his desire, could feel her own tingling through her. She was breathing hard and could feel her cheeks flushing, and although she tried to force a smile to match Kirin's she couldn't. Her mind was a roiling mass of confusion.

'I think we need to let these newlyweds finally have some peace,' the innkeeper's wife said. 'Everyone out! You both make me want to be young again,' she added, tapping Kirin on his behind and winking suggestively at Lily.

As the last person finally trooped out, the door shutting behind her, Kirin and Lily just stood there, trapped in part by the daisy chain but mostly by their combined distress. Kirin broke the spell and the chain by turning away.

'Please forgive me, Lily. I couldn't —'

'Don't,' she begged, pulling away as well, the flowers dropping to the floor. 'It wasn't your fault. It wasn't mine, either.'

'We did what we had to do,' he assured, storming over to the window and placing his hands on either side of it, staring out, no doubt to compose himself.

She was sure he was aware she hadn't held back. She prayed that she had fooled him. 'Kirin, you've probably just saved my life again with that kiss, so please don't feel bad.'

'Dad?' he groaned. 'I feel ill. I feel dirty.'

'Dirty?' Lily repeated, unsure whether she should feel insulted.

'I feel as though I took advantage of you,' Kirin continued.

'Don't be ridiculous,' she said, rushing to the window and placing a hand on his shoulder.

He reacted as if stung, twitching away from her. 'Touching me doesn't help.'

'I'm sorry.' She stood beside him, feeling as guilty and as wretched as he seemed. 'We did it to keep ourselves safe. You told me that.'

'I know why we did what we were forced to do, Lily. I just didn't expect to —'

'I know. I know. Look,' she began, desperate to repair the situation. 'Let's eat something, let's plan what we'll do next and then let's sleep. We need to be fresh. I presume we ride for Brighthelm tomorrow?'

Kirin shook his head. 'I'm not sure I can face the palace immediately.'

'Oh?'

'I might take one extra day — even if I have to ride around aimlessly. I just need some time to think. I wanted to find Clovis and I know if I go back to the palace now, I'll never get this chance again.'

She nodded. 'All right. We'll leave early so we don't have to face anyone.'

He turned to face her and she saw that his distress had melted. Kirin took her hand and kissed the back of it. 'I'm sorry. It's not you, Lily. My life is a mess,' he admitted. 'And now I've just complicated it further.'

'We'll sort it out, Kirin. This is all my fault. No, not mine, in fact, it's Kilt's. So when he starts throwing around accusations, I'll remind him that following you was his idea. We'll blame him for the fact that we now find ourselves married to each other.'

He actually smiled and once again she privately acknowledged how handsome he was when he did so.

'How are you feeling anyway?' she asked.

'Exhausted,' he admitted. 'But those seeds did a damn good job.'

'We'll find some more. Come on, eat something. We might as well devour all this food they've left for us.'

He let her lead him to the bed.

20

In broad daylight Sergius could make out the terrain, could even recognise some plants. He wasn't sure why he'd begun picking the pink, mauve and violet seaside daisies today but he'd been collecting a few of the pretty pink flowers of love when he'd heard a familiar caw. Looking up, he recognised the shape of his favourite friend.

Friends were few these days — just a couple of people from the closest village, who brought supplies to keep him going for moons on end. He wanted for little and grew a lot of what he needed anyway. But whenever he could make out Ravan, his heart lurched with joy. Ravan always brought real news from the outside, well beyond the boundaries of this cliff face or even the surrounding villages.

'Ah, Ravan,' he murmured. 'You seem to know when I most need your company.' He waved and before long the bird had landed effortlessly on the ground, leaping almost immediately to Sergius's shoulder. 'You're such a show-off,' he accused, stroking the bird as he walked into his hut.

Hello, Sergius. Got some food for me?

'No, wretched bird. You're the one with the sharp eyes. You'll have to hunt, I'm afraid.'

The hospitality's not as good as it used to be, Ravan complained mildly.

Sergius chuckled. 'Arriving unannounced, you must have some news?' he enquired eagerly.

I do. Troubling it is, too.

'Oh? Come in, come in. Do you need some water?'

I can't stay.

Sergius frowned. His friend sounded uncharacteristically nervous. 'What bothers you, Ravan?'

Piven.

'Ah. Now fifteen anni. Is he giving Greven some grief? It's to be expected in a lad of his age.'

Ravan hopped onto the familiar table so his friend could sit down and look at him at close range. *Grief? Yes, you could call it that.*

'Why didn't you just talk to me via the seam?'

I didn't want to risk it. I think I shield my thoughts better when I am far away from him.

'Loethar?' Sergius asked.

No. Piven.

'What do you mean?'

Piven is changing. I've sensed that for a long time and I seem to be in tune with his moods. Lately he's been plunging into a darkness I can't really describe other than to say it feels like evil.

Sergius frowned. 'Evil? I don't understand.'

Neither do I, fully. But I feel it. And he and I have always been connected.

'You've always felt connected to Loethar too.'

I still do. I'm connected to both of them, but in different ways. With Loethar I feel it's my duty is to be a friend to him. With Piven, it's different. I am drawn to him. And then there is another.

'Leonel is —'

No, Sergius. While I was glad to help Leo and his injured friend to get assistance from Lily and Greven, I don't feel connected to the Valisar king in the same way as I do to Piven, nor did I feel it for his father. Helping Leo in the forest seemed the right thing to do, yet I never understood why I helped Loethar's enemy.

'Tell me the news,' Sergius suggested. 'You seem troubled.'

I am. I felt Piven's spirits plummet and I went in search of him. I found him easily enough, running towards a village that was suffering a fire in one of its store barns.

Sergius looked puzzled. 'Alone?'

He'd left Greven behind on a small ridge, having just healed him of what I later learned was a sickness of the heart.

Sergius shook his head in wonder. 'He's amazing. So what happened with the fire?'

Piven gave back life.

'What?' Sergius exclaimed, frowning deeply.

We've known for a while now that he can restore health.

'But you said he restored a life.'

By the conversation I can only assume that two lives were lost to the fire, a man and a boy. Both came back from death.

'You mean from the brink of death ... that he healed them?'

No, I mean he gave them life when they were newly dead.

Sergius stood and paced, digesting this revelation. 'You're sure?'

Only of what I heard. And what I then witnessed. And later what I experienced.

Sergius's head snapped up, his eyes narrowed. 'Tell me everything!'

He listened in awed silence as Ravan recalled what had happened in the forest, from the moment he alighted on the branch to the moment Piven attacked Greven.

'An aegis?' Sergius said finally. 'Truly?'

Tell me about an aegis.

Sergius rubbed his face in a gesture of excitement as much as fear. 'An aegis, Ravan, is the ultimate champion. He ... or she ... can use magic to combat any aggression towards their bonded, and can shield the one to whom he is bonded from death or injury. But an aegis is also a slave — he has no will of his own. Once trammelled they have inordinate strength and can be commanded to use that strength against another.'

And they have no choice in the matter, I'm guessing.

Sergius shook his head. 'None at all, which is why an aegis will hide his true nature with great care. I've not actually seen one in action. Cyrena granted Cormoron that for every Valisar heir born, so would be an aegis. Not necessarily at the same time either — some are older, some are younger. Finding your own aegis is like looking for a needle in a haystack. Even though they are always born in relatively close proximity to their Valisar, they hide their true nature with great effect. For the most part these people are born and die without being bonded, without ever having to tap into the power that is only fully available to them once they are joined through magic to a Valisar. The bonding process is called trammelling and it is repulsive.'

Why are there so many hurdles to the process?

Sergius shrugged. 'Well, I suppose that even though Cyrena wanted to protect the Valisar line, she also knew the bonding is life-changing for an aegis. She put controls in place to ensure the Valisar would really need to trammel someone in order to do it. You've witnessed it; you understand why. Greven is now owned. He has no control over his own desires. He is compelled to protect Piven whether or not he wants to. Whatever Piven suffers, so does Greven — but not vice versa. It's a life of slavery but so much worse because the last frontier of privacy is invaded … one's own will.'

I watched Piven command Greven to kill a man called Clovis, who I recall from the palace. He did so without question, although I can assure you he suffered badly for it.

Sergius looked shocked. 'What do you mean? What did he say?'

He didn't say anything.

Sergius frowned. 'Then how do you know?'

Ravan shifted, cleaning his beak on the table. *I tasted his flesh,* he finally said, reluctantly.

'You ate part of Greven?' Sergius groaned, disbelief mingling with revulsion.

I felt compelled to.

'By what?' Sergius demanded, still repulsed. Standing, he angrily began preparing a herbal tea.

By Piven, Ravan said calmly.

Sergius swung around and regarded the raven. 'He controls you, too?'

No, Sergius, I promise you. Our bond is not like the bond between him and Greven. But it is a strong connection all the same. Forgive me for tasting Greven.

Sergius softened. 'And you think they killed Clovis because they didn't want him telling anyone that Piven was alive?'

It was more than that. I told you, Piven is changing.

'You've lost me,' Sergius admitted, frowning as he poured the boiled water into a large mug. Immediately a fragrance of herbs filled the room.

There are two things I have to tell you. The first is that since tasting Greven, I can now talk to both him and Piven.

'Like the seam that we use?'

Yes.

A thrill of shock passed through Sergius. 'What did they say?'

I think they were more surprised to hear my voice in their minds than the other way around. I didn't linger because Clovis had arrived.

'So you didn't see them kill him?'

No, but I heard it all unfold.

'Can you hear them now?'

If I wanted to, I suppose. But only if Piven wants me to, also.

'Why do you think Piven encouraged you to share Greven with him?'

Ah, that's something I don't fully understand. It probably has to do with the second detail I want to tell you about.

'Go on.'

Piven is turning bad.

'Explain bad.'

I saw darkness within him. Piven is far cleverer than any of us have ever imagined and he has probably long suspected that a magical bird

258

doesn't just come along for no reason. He must assume that I am around him for a reason and that I don't communicate only with him.

'He knows about me?' Sergius asked, aghast.

No. He presumes by my comings and goings that I go back to Loethar. He is not interested in that, I don't think. But I think he needed a witness to the trammelling. He needs a witness to this change. I know from my glimpse into him that he fights this darkness with all his being.

'Ravan, assure me he can't eavesdrop on this conversation.'

I would know if he were listening. He is not. He cannot, because I can shield myself. He doesn't take care to shield his thoughts from me. That's my very point; he wants me to know what he is thinking.

'This darkness you speak of. What is it? What do you see?'

Evil. As he explained to Greven, for every good deed he does, or tries to do, for all the goodness in his soul, there is a debt of darkness. And as he uses his power to give aid, the healing power that leaves him is exchanged by the gloom of evil.

Sergius frowned and sank his chin onto his cupped hands. 'As goodness moves out, darkness moves in?'

That's it. That's almost exactly what he was trying to say.

'When did this begin?'

I told you, he experienced that sort of awakening when Brennus died. I know that from the day Greven found him Piven could actually make out my call. He turned toward me that day in the woods. I know he recognised me, walked toward me. And everything about him started improving from then. He started healing birds and animals a few years after he left the palace, and even though he's only been using his power in small ways, every time his efforts to give or improve life have been repaid with the shadows that have lengthened over him. When he's in a bad mood, milk sours, herbs die ... even water tastes bitter.

'Do you know where his power came from?'

I just assumed it was wild — like the Vested.

Sergius said nothing, sipping his tea quietly, but he watched Ravan closely as the bird continued to move through his thoughts.

But an aegis doesn't make sense for Piven, the raven finally said, sounding exasperated.

Sergius nodded. 'As you know, there is an aegis born for each Valisar, and now Piven is —'

Wait! Wait! Ravan said, swooping now around the table.

Sergius pursed his lips. 'That took longer than I thought it would.'

No! That can't be! Ravan paused, then he hopped to stare at Sergius. *Why didn't you tell me?*

Sergius sighed. 'Because, while I suspected it, I didn't know for sure until you mentioned trammelling Greven.'

How did they hide it?

'The Valisars are all about secrets and there was no better practitioner of secrets than King Brennus. He had no magical endowment to speak of that I knew of, but he more than made up for it with his shadowy plans and plottings … this is another of his masterstrokes.'

Piven is Valisar!

'Indeed, or Greven would simply be a very angry man without a hand.'

He's a true heir?

'Yes, I'm astonished to say he is. I imagine Brennus would have been distraught, after all the trouble he must have gone to to keep Piven's birth a secret, for his son to be so disabled.'

Why do that in the first place?

Sergius shook his head. 'For all his lacking in magic, Brennus was more Valisar than any other I've known since Cormoron. He took his duty as sovereign deeply seriously — perhaps it's his lack of magic that drove him to make up for it in other ways. He must have forced Iselda to give birth to Piven in secret as a form of protection. Now I think of it, they said Iselda lost a baby son and very soon after, as a means of helping her to get over yet another death, she adopted the newborn Piven.'

How devious.

'It is, but history has proven his actions to be well advised. In keeping Piven's true identity a secret, no one but us — outside of the boy himself and Greven — know who he is. Loethar wanted to kill all the Valisars. We know he would have, given the chance. He spared Piven only because he was adopted, and his simpleton status no doubt helped. Does the boy look like a Valisar?'

Ravan pondered this. *He's dark and doesn't look much like Leo. I don't think he resembles Brennus, though. If anything, he could be Loethar's son.*

Sergius waved a hand. 'I just wondered why no one had picked a resemblance previously but then again when you're not looking for the resemblance you can be fooled. Either that or Piven takes after ancestors no one has seen. Cormoron possessed dark, brooding features.'

So no one but Brennus and the queen knew.

'Well, that can't be right. They would have needed at least one other ally. A wet nurse, presumably, someone to take care of the baby until they contrived to stumble upon him and bring him back to the palace.'

What about Freath?

'He gave no sign of knowing, did he?'

Not that I could ever tell.

'Knowing Brennus, I imagine he would have shared this secret with only the people who needed to know. Perhaps Freath was only privy to the journey the heavily pregnant Iselda took but not its outcome.'

Freath's been away with the one called Kirin. They went north. I followed them for a while.

'Ah yes, Kirin. You've never felt his magic again?'

I haven't but that doesn't mean he hasn't used it.

'True. His is a skill they would need to keep incredibly secret.'

It sounds like the Valisar Enchantment you've spoken of.

'No. From what you've told me, Kirin has the ability to plant a thought in someone's mind and make that person believe it. Correct?'

That's my understanding.

Sergius shook his head. 'The Valisar Enchantment has the ability to coerce not just one but many. If it exists, it will make Kirin's magic look like a parlour trick.

'And furthermore, the Valisar Enchantment is only granted to females and it kills them with remorseless frequency — that's the price they pay for possessing it.' Sergius frowned in concentration. 'Cyrena once mentioned to Cormoron that the Valisar magic, should it manifest itself in a woman, would be more potent than anything ever known to the male line. She said the female would have absolute control over the land. I can recall her laughing at his sourness; she reminded him that he worshipped a goddess, but Cormoron demanded that the power be made somehow impotent. He refused the idea of a queen as a ruler in her own right. Cyrena agreed that the Valisar dynasty would be better served by kings, and she agreed to limit the female power in the most devastating way.'

By killing the female line, Ravan finished.

'Exactly. Mightily powered, but seemingly unable to survive it.'

Too much magic for me to understand, Ravan said sourly. *So no daughter of the Valisar line has ever survived. What a pity.*

Sergius knew it was high time he shared his great secret, but still he kept it.

21

The two figures approached the convent on foot, leading their horses.

'Are you sure you want to do this?' the woman asked. 'Because there will be no going back, you realise that, don't you?'

Her companion nodded. 'I love my life but no man should live without knowing his past.' He dug in his pocket. 'This is all I have that links me to who I was before.' She stared at the shiny seeds in his kerchief, still none the wiser for their purpose. They'd even planted one to see what occurred, and though a plant had emerged briefly, it hadn't flourished in the mountains. He put the seeds back in his pocket. 'I know you understand.'

She nodded sadly. 'Go on, then. Bang on the door. I'll wait here with the horses.'

The man squeezed her hand before giving her his reins. He left the tall woman with the animals and walked in his signature, slightly lopsided but nonetheless long gait to the enormous oak door of the magnificent stone building that nestled among Lo's Teeth. He raised the iron knocker, resisted the urge to look behind him at the woman who had not only saved his life, but given him a new one for the past ten anni, and banged it twice.

The man who called himself Regor knew that once this door opened, he could potentially re-open his old life. Elka had done all she could to dissuade him from trying to trace the past. 'You have a good life here among my people,' she had warned. 'What you may go back to might be terrible.'

'I know, I know,' he'd replied. 'But I have to do this, Elka, or it's going to eat away at me.'

He recalled how Elka had ensured the journey through the mountains had been deliberately slow. She'd tried everything to persuade him against this trip. His cheeks began to burn again as he waited, remembering the moment of such terrible awkwardness for him and humiliation for her when she had attempted to tempt him with her body. And now an uncomfortable ravine had opened between them that had not existed before.

A small shutter opened near his chest. 'Yes?' a disconnected voice asked.

'Er.' He bent down. 'Forgive my intrusion, er, sister. My name is Regor and I would appreciate an opportunity to talk with the Mother.'

'Why?'

They had rehearsed this. Elka had made it clear to him that he had to convince the nuns of the convent of his need. 'Sister, I am an honest man. I was ambushed alone a decade previous in the Penraven forest, beaten senseless and injured so badly that I lost my memory. If not for my companion, who you see beyond with our horses, I would have died. She saved me from my attackers and saved my life. Her name is Elka and she is from the Davarigon people. The Mother knows Elka and I'm sure will want to see her, as well as myself.'

'And what was a Davarigon doing in Penraven all those anni ago?' the nun asked, her tone waspish, suspicious.

'Would you believe me if I told you she was collecting herbal supplies only found in our Deloran forest range?'

'I would not,' the woman said.

'I speak the truth. I would see the Quirin, if it is possible.'

'She sees no one, least of all a man.'

'Please, I beg you —'

'Go away!' The tiny trapdoor slammed shut.

He turned around helplessly and stared at Elka. She gave him a shrug as he limped back to her.

'They won't even listen.'

'I expected this. Apart from being very secretive, the nuns of the convent live remotely from society. The fact that you're a stranger, clearly not from these parts, and a man, would make them even more determined not to get involved with your problems.'

'I need to speak with the seer.'

'She may not have the answers you seek.'

'Elka,' he said with such a resigned tone that she flinched, 'I've resisted this for years but it's been building inside me recently. I think I will go mad if I can't take the pain away.'

'Pain?'

He nodded. 'Mental strife. There are moments when I feel so close to rediscovering who I am that I physically reach my arms towards it in my sleep. The truth eludes me but it draws near time and again to tempt me to keep trying. I must go back and I must do everything to rediscover who I was ten anni ago … or I might as well be dead.'

Elka's head snapped up, her dark brown hair shiny beneath the sunlight, the leather of her waistcoat creaking as she pulled herself around to face him. 'You would be dead if not for me and my people.'

He immediately raised his hands in a defensive gesture. 'Don't do this, Elka, please. I …'

But Elka surprised him, thrusting the horses' reins into his hand and yelling over her shoulder, 'Wait here!'

He watched, stunned, as she strode to the convent's entrance and hammered not once but several times on the iron knocker, until he saw the shutter fly back again. Elka was quick, reaching in and presumably grabbing whichever unfortunate nun happened to be standing on the other side. He couldn't hear what she said but was amazed to see Elka pull back her hand as the door swung open.

If the situation hadn't felt as dire, he would have laughed, as he had laughed many times before at Elka's intimidating manner.

In the open doorway stood a tiny woman, bent and gripping her wrist, which presumably Elka had twisted to make her point understood. A scowl twisted her features. Elka said something and the woman pointed behind her. Elka beckoned for him. 'She says to bring the horses through.'

He didn't need to be asked a second time; within moments he was leading the two beasts across the threshold of the convent. He bowed to the little woman, acknowledging her presence and hoping he could convey some thanks but the scowl remained on her face and she ignored him.

'We have to take the horses to the stable across the courtyard. Then we come back and wait by the fountain,' Elka said, pointing to the magnificently sculpted structure in the middle of the grand, very large courtyard. 'If I take the horses by myself, can you wait here and stay out of trouble with the women?'

Ah, there was that humour back. He thought it had deserted her for a while. 'Thank you, Elka.'

She said nothing but her expression was tinged with sorrow and he understood why. She led the horses away, the sound of their hooves echoing around the terraced courtyard. There wasn't another person in sight. He took the peaceful opportunity to wash his face and hands and run water through his hair in an effort to tidy himself from the long, dusty journey. A voice startled him as he dried his face with the tails of his shirt.

'You are Regor?' she said.

He dropped his shirt-tail and wiped his hands on his trousers. 'It's the name I use, yes,' he admitted.

'But it is not your name?'

He stared at the tall, slim woman dressed in a dun brown habit. Her eyes were sharp and genial; her lined face filled with enquiry. 'I was beaten and —'

'So I've been told. You've lost your memory, is that right?'

He nodded with a sigh. 'Yes, er, sister. I don't know why I didn't just say so. I have no idea of my true name, who I belong to, or where I come from. Elka,' he pointed at the familiar figure re-emerging from the shadows, 'rescued me and her people have returned me to good health.' He stopped abruptly as Elka arrived.

The old woman turned to Elka and held out a hand. 'How are the Davarigons?'

Elka smiled, kissed the woman's hand. 'As we have always been.'

'You look like your grandmother, but I'm sure you know that,' the woman remarked, surprising him.

Elka shrugged and nodded self-consciously. 'She died when I was young but my mother reminds me of our likeness regularly.'

'She was a fine woman, your grandmother, and she too used to take pity on helpless creatures.'

They both turned to regard him, seemingly sharing a private jest. He tried hard not to show his offence, schooling his expression to remain enquiring, and slightly baffled.

'He tells me his name is Regor?' the nun said.

Elka shrugged. 'He chose the name for himself when I found him. He speaks the truth, Mother. He has no memory of before the attack but we suspect he is more than a simple forest dweller.'

'Because of the way he speaks?'

Elka nodded. 'That, the clothes he was wearing when I found him, his sword skills, and lots of other small clues I've gleaned over the years. His gracious manners attest to his being noble at least.'

He glared at Elka. 'I can speak for myself.'

'Elka,' the woman said, 'find the food hall. Take some nourishment and rest. Allow me to speak with your companion alone, will you?'

Elka hesitated; then, at the Mother's gentle hand gesture, she acquiesced. 'Thank you for your hospitality.'

The woman smiled warmly. Elka smiled back, scowled briefly at her travelling companion, and departed.

'You seem to have upset Elka,' the woman said.

'Yes, it's a special talent of mine,' he replied and she smiled.

'Come, let us talk openly.' She led and he followed, surprised at how briskly the older woman moved. He drew alongside her as they moved into the cloisters.

'This is such a beautiful place,' he commented.

'And you've hardly seen any of it.'

'It's a pity more people cannot appreciate its beauty.'

'We do. It is enough.'

'How many women live here?'

She considered this as they walked. 'I think we must be around one hundred now.'

He was taken aback. 'That many?'

'Women come here for many reasons. Some want to escape their lives, others want to make peace and prayer their lives, and there are those who simply need a helping hand.'

'And men? Is there a similar place for them?'

'There is, or was, a monastery, I think, in the far south of Dregon on the coast, looking out to the Canuck Islands. I don't know much about it.'

'But no men are permitted here?'

'We're aiding you, are we not?'

He grinned back at the soft tease before looking up to admire the magnificent painted ceilings of the cloisters, depicting beautiful scenes of people at play in the heavens. 'Lo's Garden,' he murmured.

'So you remember that much,' she remarked.

'Pardon?'

'Well, you couldn't have learned about Lo's Garden with the Davarigon folk.'

He faltered, stared at her. 'You're right. Absolutely right!' He hugged her and she regarded him archly. 'I beg your indulgence. That's the first insight I've had into my previous life in ten anni. The ... the murals must have reminded me.'

She nodded. 'Losing one's memory does not mean it is lost forever.'

'I've just forgotten where I've put it, you mean?' he asked hopefully.

The Mother gave him a look of sympathy. 'Misplaced might be a way to look at it, yes. And it may be, Regor, that the more time you spend among your own people, the more memories will be jolted, and returned to you.'

'That's what I've been thinking about recently. It's why we're here,' he said. They'd arrived at a door, and the Abbess stopped in front of it.

'And no doubt why Elka feels angry,' the nun remarked.

'She's tried to talk me out of it.'

'It's because she's frightened for you, I imagine.'

'Yes, she doesn't want to learn the truth about me.'

'And perhaps you will regret it when you do,' the Abbess commented.

'I might. I'm terrified to find out if I'm some sort of law-breaker. Considering how she found me — tied up, beaten, a prisoner of the emperor's soldiers — it seems there is every likelihood that I could be someone on the wrong side of the law.'

'This occurred ten anni ago, you say?' He nodded. 'That was a time of vast upheaval for the Set. We were not an empire then. The various realms were trying to come to terms with slaughter and devastation, with their royals slain and the kingdoms in disarray. Emperor Loethar may well be a magnanimous ruler now but he was nothing more than a bloodthirsty tyrant at the time of your troubles, young man. Who is to say that you were not a rebel, fighting back on behalf of one of the crowns — Penraven's, maybe?' She squeezed his arm for reassurance and gave him a conspiratorial smile. 'Take heart. You came here for help. You want answers. Do not enter this doorway if you're not sure you want to hear them.'

He hesitated at the query in her expression. 'The sister who first met us said the Quirin sees no men. How come —'

'She doesn't see many people at all. And we discourage men entering our convent. You are special.'

'Why?'

'Because of who brought you. She knows our rules. She knows to ask this is a mighty request.'

'Then why would you permit this, Abbess?'

'For that very reason, my son. Elka knows what she was asking, but still she asked. She must love you very much.'

He stepped back.

She regarded him with a narrowed gaze. 'You didn't know?' she enquired gently.

'I've never really considered it,' he admitted, shaking his head, feeling his mind move into a momentary chaos.

'Has it not been obvious?'

'No!' he said quickly. 'Not at all. We are the closest of friends and her family, her whole people, have been so generous to me that I owe all of them my gratitude … my life.'

'But you don't love her,' she said, without query or damnation.

'Yes, I love her, Abbess, but as I would love a sister or a brother. She is family, she is my closest companion. I trust her, I adore her, I would see no harm come to her. She has never given me any indication of this … until …' He scratched his head, feeling fidgety, suddenly uncertain of everything again.

'And yet I only had to see how she looks at you to know that Elka would give her life for you.'

'And I for her, Abbess!'

Her face creased into a serene smile. 'You would do it out of duty and respect. She would do it because her heart beats only for you. But until you know who you are, you will not be much of a partner, lover, or husband to anyone. Elka will accept you as you are because she loves you, but even if you did feel the same way, she would be destined for unhappiness until you discover your history. The Quirin can put you back on your rightful pathway, I suspect.'

'And the Quirin is prepared to assist me … being a man I mean?'

'She makes no distinction but she is contrary and her way is the only way. She will not walk another path so don't try to control her.'

'I don't understand.'

'You will, my child. Now, some facts you need to know. The Quirin is deformed … and old. So old, in fact, I wonder how much longer she will be with us. I see that shocks you.'

'I suppose you never think of such gifted people being mortal.'

'Oh,' she smiled. 'She is very mortal, I'm afraid. She can do nothing for herself. We feed her, bathe her, we are responsible for her every need and desire. But she wants for little, and asks for even less, so a lot of the time we have to guess what it is that is best for her. She has been with us since she was a little girl. She is much older than me.' The Abbess beamed. 'Even though I know that's hard for you to imagine.'

It was a small jest but he couldn't enjoy it. 'Who comes after her? I mean, who will take her place?'

The Abbess shrugged. 'No one, at this point. Quirins are born, not made. We may live decades, perhaps centuries before we see another. Or a new Quirin may find her way here tomorrow, born Vested, realising she is more.'

'Vested?'

'The people who —'

'Yes, Mother, I know what it means. I haven't heard that word in a long time.'

'That's because it is a Set word. I think, Regor, you were definitely born and raised in the Denovian Set. But rally your courage now and learn all that you can.' She gestured at the door handle. As he reached for it, she added: 'I should warn you, she is blind. She is also deaf and pratically mute.'

'How will we communicate?'

'She has her ways. Go now, Regor. I hope you find answers.'

He didn't know why he embraced her, or even why she permitted it, but he bent and kissed her cheek. 'Thank you, Abbess.'

'I hope you'll feel the same way later.'

He returned her sad smile. 'Will you reassure Elka that I can't help this?'

'She already knows,' the Abbess said, nodding gently with encouragement.

There was nothing else to say. He gripped the iron ring, twisted it and pushed the door open. It was dark and cold inside. When he turned to say something, the Abbess had gone. Taking a deep breath, he stepped inside, wondering why they would keep this woman in such dark surrounds.

I have no need of light, a tetchy voice spoke into his mind. Surprised, he staggered backwards, grabbing for the door. The voice laughed. *I startled you. You shouldn't think questions so loudly if you don't want them answered.*

'Quirin, I'm sorry for acting afraid. I don't know what to expect.'

What? You've come here and now you've got nothing to say? she demanded.

Of course — she was deaf! He frowned in concentration and thought his response to her. *Forgive me. I said I was sorry for acting afraid.*

He heard her chuckle, not unkindly. *So they've given me a man.* She made a sound of pleasure. *I haven't heard one of your kind since I was a young woman. How old are you?*

I don't know. He was getting the hang of how to think his responses even though it was tempting to answer in the more natural way.

Guess.

I would estimate I am in my third decade, though where in it I cannot say.

Come here. Let me feel you.

He obediently moved forward gingerly, with no real idea where he was headed. He must have thought his uncertainty because a flame suddenly erupted and a single tiny candle was lit.

The owner of the dislocated voice was hunched in robes, her head covered by a caul. She felt her way along a wall, back into the gloom of the shadows, and sat down.

Is that easier?

Yes, thank you.

You have a nice voice over the seam.

The seam?

That's what we call speaking across minds.

How am I able to do this?

Because I permit it. You are drawing on my power.

Then I thank you again.

You are a polite man. Raised well. Noble, perhaps?

I have no idea. Do you have a name?

He could hear the smile in her mind-speak. *I did once. You are the first person to ask me for it in a long time.*

I would have thought the nuns would know it.

I am older than most of them. They know me simply as Quirin. But Quirin is a title, not a name. And names are so important, aren't they? They unlock secrets.

Yes, he said, *my name is very important to me.*

I know. I have been told of your predicament. So come, let me touch you.

He approached her. *Why do you hide yourself?*

Because I frighten people with my appearance.

You do not frighten me.

You have not looked upon me. You will need to bend down, my friend.

He went down on his knees so she could reach out and feel the contours of his face. They both fell silent as she touched his cheekbones and chin, felt the length and texture of his hair, which hung loose today.

Finally, she sighed. *A beard, so you are not so youthful but you are hardly an old man. I think you are right in your estimation, although I would place you at twenty-seven or twenty-eight anni. And you are handsome but I don't believe you've had many lovers.*

He cleared his throat. *Why would you assume that?*

I am told you have lived with the Davarigon folk for ten anni. Before that you would have been a young man, still a youth almost. Not enough years beneath your belt for much sexual adventure — although I suspect you are no virgin. He knew he reddened, could feel the heat on his cheeks. She was right. *But living with the mountain folk probably means you haven't engaged in much —*

None.

Why?

I have not felt inclined.

A man of twenty -seven or -eight not inclined to —

Hush, Quirin, you make me blush.

He heard her amusement. She sighed, as if making a decision. *My name is Vervine and I like your discomfort. I am blind but I see no pretension in you. And your embarrassment is like a small gift to one who has been starved of the opportunity to flirt.*

How old are you? he said, his tone filled with bemused wonder.

Now she laughed deeply in his mind. *I will help you, Gavriel de Vis. Ask me your questions.*

Gavriel rocked back. As soon as she spoke it, he knew the name was correct. It was as if a door had been unlocked and pushed open the tiniest crack. Through it he could see a thin glow of light. All the answers lay behind the door. All he had to do was push it open.

Where do I belong? he asked.

And Vervine began to speak.

22

Kilt Faris was rounding the same bend in the road that Lily had only a day or two earlier. As Woodingdene came into view, he was struck by the beauty of the town. What the ancient Valisars had begun, Brennus had continued here but Faris hadn't seen the region in the last six or seven anni and it seemed Loethar was the ruler who had made the real difference. All the buildings looked cleaned, freshly painted, and generally in such good repair that he stopped his horse, shocked, to gaze upon what had once been a village struggling to become a town and was now a thriving town destined to become a city. With the weather moving into easily the most temperate and enjoyable time, the sun made the pastel-coloured buildings sparkle. Faris smiled in spite of his mood.

He immediately looked for the inn, recalling it had once been called the The Golden Coin. It had been re-named The Emperor's Head and displayed a portrait of a man, presumably Loethar, on its sign. Funny, he'd never seen the emperor in all these years. He cocked his head, wondering if the depiction was a true likeness; if so, it intrigued him with its strong jaw, dark looks and serious expression. He left his horse at the stable, paying for her to be rubbed down, fed and watered and for his saddle to be oiled.

Inside the inn, he began his mission of research, first ordering a jug of ale to please the innkeeper at this time of the morning when business for ale was slow. A group of soldiers, bearing tatua, was drinking in the corner. But they were quiet and hardly looked up at his entry. Kilt deliberately didn't let his gaze linger as he took off his distinctive hat.

'You must be thirsty,' the man commented as he banged the full jug down.

'Oh, I think my eyes are always bigger than my belly,' Kilt admitted, forcing weariness into his tone. 'I've been dreaming of this ale for many hours.'

'Ah, a long journey then?'

'Yes, I'm up from the south,' he lied.

'Do you want a room?'

'I'm not sure yet.'

The man nodded. 'You let me know.'

Kilt poured himself a mug of ale and, although he wasn't in the mood for it, made a big show of swallowing at least half the contents, burping politely but loudly enough that all heard and grinned. 'That tastes good.'

'That's because it's made here. We don't take that stuff from Vorgaven … that overly yeasty brew,' the innkeeper admitted with a conspiratorial air. 'We brew right here. Well, the brewery is actually at Overdene just in the next town but it might as well be here.'

'It's excellent,' Kilt said. In truth, he was unable to distinguish one ale from the next. He and his men were grateful to get any whenever they could.

'How long are you here for?' the man asked, making conversation as he hung up tankards in preparation for the busy evening ahead.

'Again, I'm not sure,' Kilt said, sipping again, acting nonchalant. 'I'm actually here to find my … er, sister.'

'Oh? She's local?'

'No. But I've news from home for her and I believe she passed through here recently. She might still be here if I'm lucky.'

The man frowned. 'What's her name?'

'Lily Jeves.'

The man shook his head. 'We've had no one in here of that name — staying, I mean.'

Kilt nodded. It had been a long shot and he hadn't expected her to have been a guest at the inn but he hoped she might have been seen or heard of. He had to start somewhere, he told himself, feeling suddenly morose; it didn't matter if his first probe drew a blank.

A soldier came to the counter and banged four mugs on the surface. 'One more round, Arwin, and then we'll be on our way.'

The innkeeper nodded. 'Where are you off to?' he asked the soldier as he filled the mugs.

'Dregon.'

'You haven't heard of a Lily Jeves, have you?'

The man shook his head. 'Should I?'

'This ... er, what's your name?'

'Rik Jeves,' Kilt said, only at the last moment remembering that he was meant to be Lily's brother. He swallowed some ale to hide his expression of relief. Then as an afterthought he held out his hand.

'He's looking for his sister,' the innkeeper explained.

As the soldier was staring at his proffered hand, Kilt felt obliged to act more eager for information. 'Er, long dark hair, about this tall,' he said, indicating with his other hand. 'Very pretty, although I would never tell her that.' The man shook his hand and Kilt, relieved, continued, 'Greenish eyes, probably wearing a blue cloak with —'

'I think I have seen her,' the man said, frowning, slightly confused.

Kilt's heart flipped. 'Really?'

'Yes, well, it could be her. We brought her here, if it's the same woman.'

Now Kilt's heart began to hammer. 'Brought her into Woodingdene, or to this inn?' he asked shaking his head, deliberately looking muddled, trying to keep his expression even.

He knew full well Lily had been to this town. He just needed to know precisely where.

'Into town. She was travelling with a man, right?'

Kilt shrugged. 'Probably her —'

'Husband, yes,' the man said, his frown deepening.'

The mouthful of ale Kilt had just swigged stuck in his throat. He had to force himself to swallow. 'Er, yes, probably.'

'They were definitely travelling as a couple, this pair I'm thinking of.'

'Yes, that's right. She's married,' Kilt blurted. Was Lily pretending to be married to Kirin Felt? Why?

The soldier swung around. 'Ho, Brimen, what was the name of that couple we escorted here the other day? You know, the one that the Wikken Shorgan was interested in.'

Wikken. Kilt's stomach clenched.

The man called Brimen shrugged. 'Not sure I caught their names. Ronder will know, though. He spent most of his time talking with them.'

'Ronder?' Kilt queried. 'Where can I find him?'

The man at the counter shrugged. 'He's coming with us later today so I know he's here. He's probably over at the barracks.'

'Can I go over there and ask?'

The man nodded. 'I don't see why they'd give you trouble.'

Kilt smiled and tossed some coins across the counter. 'That should cover my jug and the round for these good men,' he said with a feigned grin at the innkeeper. 'Thank you,' he added to the soldier.

The soldier's tatua moved as he smiled in return. 'Tell anyone who may try to stop you that Shev said it was all right to let you speak with Ronder.'

Kilt squeezed the soldier on the arm in farewell. 'Our mother's very ill. I have to find Lily quickly. I know it's probably meaningless to you but Lo blesses you.'

The man nodded and shrugged. 'I don't mind who blesses me, so long as I'm blessed,' he said, grinning in the direction of the innkeeper, who had been following the exchange and who returned the grin.

Once outside Kilt asked a passing woman for directions to the barracks, glad of his disguise as a member of the clergy. This costume always worked wonders at loosening people's tongues … even barbarian tongues, it seemed, he thought.

The barracks was on the fringe of the town. Kilt walked there, marvelling once again at the beauty of the buildings he'd forgotten, reminding himself that the coin of the Set was now all minted here. Woodingdene was a wealthy town for sure, going by the number of people busy at their daily business and the number of elegant carriages plying the town.

At the barracks he was confronted by a huge soldier bearing the green tatua.

'Ah, I'm Pastor Jeves,' Kilt said genially.

The man didn't look in the slight bit impressed. 'And?'

'And I'm trying to find one of your soldiers by the name of Ronder.'

'Why?' the man asked, his sombre expression unchanged.

'I need to talk to him.'

'About what?'

'Well, I feel it's best explained to him.'

'Except I'm the man in charge of the gate, Pastor Jeves.'

'Yes, indeed. Well, Shev, who I met at The Emperor's Head, seems to think —'

'Shev?'

'Yes, wearing the green tatua.'

'I know who he is. He sent you?'

'Yes. We've just shared an ale together,' Kilt said, skirting the truth. 'He told me to tell whomever was on duty that it would be all right for me to speak with the soldier.'

'Wait here,' the man said. He called over a young lad and muttered something to him. The youngster ran off and the guard returned to the gate. 'Ronder's being called.'

'Thank you. It's lucky I ran into Shev.'

'He's one of General Stracker's lieutenants.'

'Ah, what a stroke of luck for me, then.'

'Shev must have been in a good mood to offer help.'

'I couldn't tell you,' Kilt said, his words genuine. 'He didn't look any different from his companions.'

'General Stracker doesn't look any different from us. He prefers equality.'

'Truly. How very … er … spiritual,' Kilt said. The man frowned at him. 'Well, what I mean is, it's not a creed one comes across often. I admire it.' He smiled. 'Naturally … being a man of Lo,' he added.

'General Stracker is a man to be admired,' the Green said.

'I'm sure. Have you met the emperor?' Did he detect a soft sneer that was gone as quickly as it arrived?

'Know him. I played with him as a boy.'

'Really? How extraordinary. Our old system of kings and queens, well, they never played with commoners, I don't believe.' Kilt reached out and slapped the man playfully on the arm.

'Too high and mighty,' the man growled.

'Mmm, well,' Kilt contrived a self-conscious smile, 'we've had ten anni of the emperor's rule now and I have to say it's —'

'And turning too much into a Set man,' the soldier continued as though Kilt hadn't spoken. 'Forgotten his roots.'

A spike of fresh interest moved through Kilt. 'Is that an issue for the men?' he asked, keeping his voice low, trying not to disturb the man's musings.

'We hate his wife,' the man said. The venom in his tone surprised Kilt.

Faris nodded. 'A Set woman, I gather.'

'Worse. A noble from the old days. He should have taken a Steppes wife.'

'I understand,' Kilt soothed, seeing someone approaching in the distance. He looked down, not wanting to challenge the big soldier with his gaze, but wishing he could keep exploring this conversation. 'Perhaps the general would make a better leader?'

'I'd follow him into the sea even if I had boulders tied to my feet,' the guard helplessly answered. 'Many of us believe it is time to overthrow our former ruler. It is time for change.'

'You want General Stracker to be emperor?'

'Stracker has not given over his heritage. He is Steppes through and through, which is more than we can say for Emperor Loethar these days.'

Kilt had run out of time. 'Ah'. He tapped the man's arm, releasing him. 'Is this Ronder?'

The huge guard turned, looking momentarily confused. 'That's him.' He beckoned to the approaching man, who hurried up to the gate.

'You're looking for me?' the newcomer asked.

He was younger than Kilt had expected. Holding out a hand in welcome, he said, 'I am. My name is Pastor Jeves.'

Ronder didn't seem to notice the salutary gesture. Nodding at Kilt, he said, 'We can talk over there. What is it you seek?'

Kilt inwardly sighed at his touch being ignored. *The hard way then.* As he and Ronder walked a little away from the gate of the barracks, he explained, 'I'm looking for my sister. Her name is Lily Jeves and I was told that you might have escorted her into Woodingdene.'

'I did. She was with her husband. They were only here a short time, just for their listing.'

'Listing?'

'Where are you from, Pastor?'

'The south. I've been travelling a while, though,' Kilt said carefully. He could feel a familiar tingling in his nose. It would happen soon. He would try once more. 'Forgive me, could you hold this?' he asked, handing over the small rucksack that he was carrying. 'I'm going to sneeze,' he lied, digging furiously in his pockets.

Astonished at the request but presumably feeling unable to ignore it, the soldier took the bag. Kilt miraculously found his kerchief. 'Thank you,' he said and as the sack was returned to him, he touched the man's hand in a move that was made to appear inadvertent. 'Er, you were saying,' he added. 'About the list?'

'Yes,' the man said. 'We are keeping a list of the Vested for the empire. Your sister and her husband were brought here to be listed with —'

'Lily? Why?' Kilt interrupted.

The man looked vaguely irritated. 'Why would you ask? You're her brother! Because she is Vested, of course.'

'I see,' Kilt said, grateful that his voice sounded normal.

'Although we were mostly interested in her husband,' Ronder added.

'I can imagine that,' Kilt remarked mildly.

Ronder nodded. 'They were tested and permitted to leave.'

'Tested? How so?'

Ronder smiled. 'His name is Vulpan. You must have been away a long time not to know of him.'

Fear crept through Kilt's body, beginning at the tip of his spine and working upwards and outwards. 'Master Vulpan, that's right, I have heard of him. The blood taster, right?'

'That's the one. He was here for a while.'

'And now he's gone?'

'Preparing to leave, heading north.'

'Why?'

'General Stracker has given orders.'

'Who are you hunting?'

'The outlaw called Faris.'

'No one's seen him, to my knowledge.'

'We don't need to. We think Vulpan's tasted his blood.'

Kilt knew he couldn't push too hard. 'Anyway, that's not any of my business,' he retreated. 'So Master Vulpan "tasted" my sister?' He tried to make it sound like a thoroughly normal query.

'I assume so. They were certainly permitted to leave by Master Vulpan and that wouldn't have occurred if he wasn't satisfied.'

How in Lo's name had Lily passed the test? 'Where does Master Vulpan stay when he's in Woodingdene?' Kilt pushed.

'In the mayor's residence.'

'I see. I don't suppose you know which direction my family headed?'

Ronder shrugged. 'I presume back to the palace. Master Felt told me quite firmly he was expected there.' The man looked suddenly taken aback. 'Your nose is bleeding, Pastor Jeves.'

Kilt shook his head, feigning disgust. 'Oh dear. This happens from time to time. Anxiety, I think. Well, I'll be on my way,' he said, holding the kerchief to his nostrils. He could feel the blood flowing. 'Sorry about this.' He held out his hand. 'Thank you.'

The man looked uncertain. He had no desire, clearly, to take Kilt's bloodied hand. Wiping his hand on his knapsack. Kilt re-extended it. 'My apology. Thank you again. Shev was right, you were extremely helpful.'

Ronder shrugged, and shook hands reluctantly. 'Your sister is nice. Her husband was a bit strange, though.' He shook his head as if slightly confused.

When he looked back, Kilt Faris was gone.

Lily was surprised how late it was when she woke with a start. She'd had an unsettling vision that she'd wake to find herself in the arms of Kirin Felt, believing him to be Kilt. Even worse she had the even more disturbing notion that she might have permitted him to treat her as every inch his wife.

She sat up, her heart thumping, and realised that not only was she still fully dressed but the other side of the bed was empty, barely disturbed. Now she felt ridiculous. But as she sat up she realised the real nightmare still existed. She was married ... and not to Kilt. Lily rubbed the sleep from her eyes and shook her head. The two men's names even sounded similar! But that was where the similarities ended. Kirin was Vested, and although their build was not so different, their looks were. Kirin was fair in contrast to Kilt and had finer features. Kilt had a more distinct jawline, and preferred a very close shaved beard — when he wasn't in one of his disguises — and that quiet, controlled, remote and often intimidating manner of his was in direct contrast to Kirin's gentler, more open way. Actually, now that she came to consider it, she felt she'd learned at least as much about Kirin in the short time they'd been thrown together as she knew about Kilt from the ten anni they'd shared. And, frankly, what she'd learned about Kilt had mostly come from Jewd. Kilt never offered information and was certainly cagey about his past.

Secretive. Yes, that's how she'd describe Kilt. No wonder King Brennus had decided he was the perfect choice to guard and raise Leo. Poor Leo. He had been deeply troubled by Kilt's decision to meet with the man Freath. She had privately agreed with Leo that it was madness to let that traitorous snake anywhere near them. But there was no one more slippery than Kilt and despite his guarded manner she trusted him and his judgement implicitly. If Kilt believed that Freath was worth listening to, she was happy to go along with the plan.

She'd warned Jewd, because Kilt wasn't listening, that meeting Freath might push Leo over the edge. This would be his first contact with the world of his childhood and she imagined it would bring back a wealth of bloody, brutal and fearful memories. And the young king was as skittish as she had ever known him. He was a man now, eager to make his own decisions, very aware of his position even though he so rarely mentioned it, and driven by a deep need for revenge. She'd mentioned this several times to Kilt but his only response had been that what Leo really needed was to lie with a woman for the first time.

Kirin, on the other hand, had been sensitive about her situation, although his wedding night kiss had been far from careful ... or contrived. Lily stood and stretched. Granted, he'd had to make it look real. They'd had an audience cheering their every move, after all. But there had been passion in that kiss. Lily pursed her lips, remembering it now; recalling with a flush of discomfort that she'd hardly held back either.

Lily moved to the jug and bowl, grateful to find the water was still fresh and unused. She poured out some water, lathered up some of the soap leaves and washed her face of the sleep ... and her embarrassment. Reaching for a small towel, she dried her face, staring into the small mirror. There she was — as traitorous as the man called Freath, pretending to be faithful.

As the thought crossed her mind, Lily stepped back, shocked. That wasn't true! No! She loved Kilt. In order to protect her life, and their secret, she'd had to marry Kirin publicly and then kiss him publicly. Nothing else had happened. They'd talked through the night until they'd both fallen asleep. She was sure she'd closed her eyes and lost track of the conversation first. And Kirin had covered her with blankets and left her undisturbed. That was all. He hadn't laid a hand on her, nor she him.

But the kiss? It felt so real, whispered a small, treacherous voice in her mind.

'The kiss was a ruse!' she hissed quietly at her reflection, flinging the towel at the mirror.

'Lily, my darling?' said a hesitant voice, accompanied by a gentle tap on the door.

'Kirin?'

'It's me,' he answered, more normally.

'I ... er, I'm just tidying myself.'

'I've ordered some breakfast for you. Will you be long?'

'I'll meet you downstairs shortly,' she said, her cheeks burning again. She hoped he hadn't heard her talking to herself.

'All right. Be quick or your oats will cool.'

She pulled off her clothes and washed herself properly, taking extra time that she knew she really didn't have to dampen and smooth down her hair as best she could. She grabbed at the few sprigs of burned rosemary left for guests and quickly cleaned her teeth, rinsing with the mint vinegar that had also been laid out the night before. After re-dressing in her riding clothes, she felt she looked presentable again. Her wedding attire she folded neatly and carried downstairs where Kirin rose to greet her, moving around to pull out a chair at the small table he'd chosen.

'Good morning,' he said, smiling. 'Just in time,' he added as the serving girl arrived with a steaming bowl of oats. 'I've eaten. You go ahead,' he urged as the girl set down honey, some nuts, and dried fruits.

'I'm starving,' Lily admitted.

'And very beautiful,' he replied, glancing at the serving girl, who grinned back.

Lily recognised her from the evening before. 'Thanks for all that you did,' she said.

The girl giggled. 'Hope you had a lovely night.'

'We did, thank you,' Kirin said, covering Lily's hand with his.

She felt the warmth of his touch and knew she couldn't pull away. But worse, she didn't want to. She wasn't used to all this romantic attention, and it was quite pleasant. And thoroughly innocent, since it was simply for show.

When the girl left them alone Kirin withdrew his hand. 'Sleep well?'

She shook her head. 'Well? I'm not sure. I certainly slept. Deeply, I think.'

'You did, I assure you.'

'Did you sleep?'

He shrugged. 'I dozed.'

'Were you even on the bed?' she whispered.

'I didn't want you to feel uncomfortable.'

'So you slept on the floor?'

'Dozed in a chair. Eat up,' he said, nodding at her bowl.

She picked up her spoon, ladled in the first delicious mouthful. He let her eat for a while in silence.

'You'd been through enough shock for one day,' he finally said, with a soft sigh.

'Thank you, Kirin. You're being very decent about this.'

He shook his head and shrugged.

She reached over and took his hand. 'Well, even for your rough night's sleep, you look much better than you did yesterday.'

'I could use more of those seeds but I do feel much brighter, it's true. This is how it is. I suffer and then it gets better.'

'Your eye —?'

'No,' he cut her off. 'That will not regain its sight. I will have to get used to turning my head to see in all directions.'

The moment felt suddenly awkward. Lily pushed her bowl forward. 'Most delicious, thank you. So, what's the next part of your grand plan? Please don't tell me we're going to the palace.'

'We'll have to at some point, I'm sure. But not immediately. I was on a mission when I met you and although in the space of a day I've been captured, married and had my blood tasted by a ghoul, I'd still like to complete it.'

She took a sip from the cup of dinch that he'd poured while she ate. 'To find this man, Clovis. You mentioned him last night.'

He nodded. 'I'm sorry I talked so much.'

Lily smiled. 'You have no idea how pleasant it was.'

'Truly?'

'Yes. I've lived with a man who says little. All the information I glean, I learn from his closest friend who knows everything about him.'

Kirin nodded. 'But you love him,' he finished.

'He's a good man.' She smiled ruefully. 'I know that sounds odd given his occupation but …'

'You don't have to explain,' Kirin said gently. 'He's a fortunate man.'

'An irate one now, I imagine, looking for me. He won't leave any stone unturned. I know Kilt.'

'He's going to have to chase us across the compass then,' Kirin warned.

'Kirin, why can't we part now? I can head back and —'

He shook his head. 'I'm sorry, I know it seems unfair but Vulpan warned he was going to mention us to the emperor. We have to stick together for now for the story to work. We have to act married, for a bit longer, Lily. Vulpan is suspicious and also vicious. Once the dust has settled on the surprise of my sudden marriage, we can have a huge public argument and you can be rid of me.'

She looked down, feeling ashamed. 'I didn't mean it like that.'

'I know you didn't but I need to impress upon you that this is only the beginning of our ruse. If we are to keep your life safe, and mine, we have to continue this charade for a while longer.'

'Then why not go straight back to the palace now?'

'Because I have to find Clovis. I told Freath I would. And as he's probably back at the palace already, having made up a story for my absence, it would be unwise for me to turn up so soon. No, it's best I press ahead and try and find Piven. At least it helps the cause.'

She looked at him sadly. 'Last night you seemed unsure of whether the cause was worth it.'

He looked self-conscious. 'I was obviously in a maudlin mood. This morning I feel as though I need to be more supportive of Freath, of Faris ... even you. You've given up your life to protect a child.' He shrugged. 'I must finish what I began.'

'What if you don't find Piven?'

'I have to believe we will. Clovis was sure he had found him. We simply have to find Clovis.'

Lily nodded. He was right.

'All done?' a voice asked. The innkeeper's wife stood by their table, smiling down at them.

Kirin reacted quickly, beaming at Lily and then at the woman. 'Thank you, it was all very nice.' He kissed Lily's hand, staring at her as if he couldn't bear to tear his eyes away. 'We'll be on our way now,' he said finally. 'Back to real life.'

The woman laughed. 'Not staying for the Newlywed celebrations on the green?'

'Er, no,' Lily replied, pushing back her chair and standing but maintaining an indulgent smile for the woman. 'I think my husband and I have celebrated long and hard.'

The woman chortled and Lily blushed at the innuendo she hadn't intended. Even Kirin grinned. Lily recomposed herself. It didn't matter what this woman thought. 'It's time to head home,' she said firmly.

'Where's home?' the innkeeper's wife asked.

'South,' Kirin said, cutting off any further enquiry by taking Lily's hand again. 'Come, Mrs Felt. I see you're all packed,' he said, glancing at Lily's small bundle. 'I've had the horses brought round. Good day to you,' he said to the woman, 'and our thanks again for all the festivity. It was memorable, wasn't it, my love?'

'Indeed,' Lily admitted.

'Well, you're all settled,' the woman replied, referring to their bill. 'And if you're sure?'

Kirin nodded. 'We are.'

He hurried Lily out to the animals that were tethered ready for them outside the inn. Someone had tied a flower into their reins and a long daisy chain trailed behind each of the horse's tails.

'Lo save us,' Kirin whispered. 'When will it end?'

Lily smiled. 'Come on, husband, let's go. Where are we headed?'

23

Empress Valya had organised for Dara Negev to be brought out into the orchards. Neither noticed the dark shape of the raven, whose sharp eyesight had likely picked out their movement, flying to the tops of the fruit trees to watch.

'What am I doing here, Valya?' the old woman grumbled.

Valya smiled. 'Well, I've barely seen you recently. I thought it was time that I found out how you are and what's happening in your life?'

'As you see,' the woman replied, scowling, reaching for a rug.

'Let me help you with that, Dara Negev,' Valya offered. 'It's not cold today, though.'

'I am never warm anymore,' the old woman snapped.

You don't have to tell me, Valya thought. 'It's an early summer's day and the sun's warmth will be good for your bones. Loethar tells me you have aches.'

'Valya,' Negev said, impaling her with a cool stare, 'at my age, everything aches.'

'I'm sure,' Valya sweetly agreed.

'I don't see why we couldn't have had this conversation indoors in my chambers.'

'Well, I thought you'd like being outside, especially in such a wonderful setting. Look at all the fruit exploding on the trees — you were always one for appreciating the changing seasons. Besides, I thought we might take some dinch together.'

'Dinch? Bah! You know I prefer the Steppes brew.'

'But we're in Penraven now, Negev, and as your son is now more Set than Steppes, I thought you should at least make an effort with the local customs.' Valya snapped her fingers and nodded at a nearby servant.

'Empress?' the servant enquired.

'Have some dinch served immediately. And perhaps bring some of those sugar biscuits I made for my husband yesterday.' At the servant's frown, she clarified, 'They're in a tin on my desk. I was going to give them to him today but he left early and I made too many anyway. A few for us will be a treat. Just take a handful from the top layer.'

'Highness.' The man bowed. 'Is there anything else I can do for you?'

'Yes, Roland, you can tell those men that we will call for them when Dara Negev is ready to be carried indoors but they may leave us now.'

'Your highness, someone must remain. The emperor —'

'I understand,' she cut him off. 'But we wish to speak privately. Withdraw far enough away that you may watch.'

He nodded and withdrew as instructed.

Negev gave a sound of disdain. 'There is nothing we have to say that can't be heard by a servant.'

Valya returned her attention to her mother-in-law but ignored the jibe. 'Nevertheless, they have to learn.' She made a tsking sound with her tongue. 'In my days in Droste, my father would have a servant whipped if they lingered too close.' She sighed. 'Anyway, aren't you going to ask how I am?'

'I'm old but my sight is still good enough, Valya.'

'Oh come on, Negev. I rarely see my mother and frankly don't want to now that she's become a fawning parent only because of who I married. So you will have to do … and as much as you dislike me, I am about to give birth to your first grandchild.'

'What do you want from me?' Negev asked. 'You have my son, you have my grandchild, you have the title you've craved, you have all the wealth a person could need.'

'And still I feel lonely.'

'Lonely? Am I supposed to feel sorry for you?'

'Maybe not sorrow, but how about some sympathy? I've been loyal to you and your family, I can't —'

'Valya, you are not loyal to anyone. You were not loyal to your own family and you are certainly not loyal to mine. You are what we call shakken.' Valya scowled at the old woman's offensive comparison to the animal but she said nothing as Dara Negev continued. 'The shakken has no territory of its own, as you know. It roams the Steppes alone, mating but not remaining with its partner to raise young, scavenging its food.'

Valya bristled but kept her expression impassive. 'And how do you relate a creature of the Steppes to me, Negev?'

'You are an opportunist. Your own people disowned you and so you found us. And as long as we provide what you need you will remain but I have never suspected you to be loyal to anything but your own needs.'

'That's very cruel of you.'

'Am I lying?'

Before Valya could answer, Roland arrived.

'Ah, set the dinch out here,' Valya instructed. 'I can pour.' Roland placed the tray and its accoutrements on the table between the two women. 'You may go, Roland. I have a bell and can ring for you,' Valya dismissed him.

'As you wish, highness.' He cast a glance at his mistress, Dara Negev, and at her nod he walked far enough away that Valya could not make out his features and she nodded, satisfied.

Negev's gaze narrowed. 'Did you really bake those yourself?' the old woman sneered.

Valya sighed. 'I did. I've noticed Loethar likes them whenever cook sends some up for him. I wanted to learn how to make them myself, so cook taught me.'

'Buying his love through his belly?' Negev queried, disdain dripping from her words.

'I will never understand why you have to treat me with such contempt. I would have thought my adoration of your son would impress you and the mere suggestion of grandchildren would make us closer,' Valya admitted, busying herself as she poured the drinks.

'Valya, you have lost more children than I have birthed. I will reserve praise until you actually deliver a son.'

Valya hadn't thought anything Negev could say could truly penetrate her mental armour; after all, she had been wearing it and strengthening it for years now at the end of this woman's harsh tongue. But this jab got through, stabbing right at the heart of Valya's greatest fears. She noticed her hand tremble slightly with rage as she handed her mother-in-law a beautiful porcelain cup from the imperial dinner set that was designed at the time of Loethar's coronation. 'I hate you more in this moment than I have ever hated you before,' she said, glad to snatch her hand back from where she had set down the cup and saucer near the old witch.

Negev smirked. 'Well, that makes two of us.' She shook her head. 'Not for me,' she said, refusing the dinch. 'I'm ready to go.'

'At least taste Loethar's biscuits,' Valya said, sipping her dinch to cover her fury and anticipation.

The emperor's mother could never resist a sweet temptation. Valya had counted on this and had deliberately poisoned only the top layer of biscuits. Dara Negev began chewing as she sneered, 'Ring for my servants.'

Valya obeyed the command, ringing immediately but continuing to sip her tea, leaving her own biscuit untouched. By the time Roland had hurried over, Dara Negev was already in her death throes, Valya turning in a stunning performance of a daughter-in-law in despair, screaming for help as the old woman choked and foamed at the mouth.

'Hurry,' she shrieked, 'she's choking. Fetch help, I'll try and clear her passageway.' But Valya only made a pretence of clearing the old woman's airways, waiting until she knew it was too late and she could see that Dara Negev knew it too. As Roland rushed white-faced from the death scene, Valya smiled. They were finally alone.

'I heard you suggested to your son that I should be killed.'

Dara Negev was intent on vainly gasping for air. Even so, Valya could see the shock that flared in the old woman's eyes.

'You've underestimated me. And now you're paying for it with your life. I baked poison into the biscuits, you old fool. Ah, here comes help now,' she said, glancing up, pretending to flap helplessly around Negev. 'See how concerned I look, Negev? They'll never suspect me. I'll leave you with this one last thought: perhaps I'll poison your son too as soon as my son is born. I can rule as regent for him. Die happy, you old witch.' She looked up, feigning terror. 'Roland! I think she's dying!' she screamed. 'Help, someone, help!'

In the tumult that followed Valya tipped the remaining two biscuits into the silken pouch she carried. She would dispose of them later. She knew what would unfold now and she had to keep her nerve.

Valya watched Loethar stare silently at his mother's face. Dara Negev looked surprisingly as though she were sleeping; her expression was peaceful, belying her final struggle to remain alive. The servants had given Loethar a vivid description of what had occurred and Valya imagined he was, in this uncomfortable silence, trying to conjure a vision of his mother's final moments. Valya, of course, had deliberately cleaned up Dara Negev's mouth. The servant thought she was making her presentable to the emperor but her true aim was to remove all clues to the woman's death.

She could feel the terrible tension building in the room. Loethar was unpredictable and not easily fooled; she would not be surprised if he simply accused her of murdering his mother. Still, she'd made her choice and would not regret it.

Finally the silence got the better of her. 'Does that bird have to be here with us?' she said, motioning to the raven.

'He chooses where he goes,' Loethar answered.

'It's disrespectful,' Valya said, making sure her eyes were misty, her lips slightly trembling. 'Where's Stracker?' she asked tearfully. The weeping wasn't hard to achieve; she was genuinely terrified of the brothers. Loethar had walked around his mother's corpse a dozen times already; the creak of his leather boots and waistcoat the only clue, up until a moment ago, that someone else was alive in this chamber with her ... other than her baby. She touched her belly. He was alive. Claiming the throne from the womb. Securing his mother's future.

Loethar glanced up at her, startling her out of her thoughts. 'How is our child?'

'Thank you for asking. Today has been very unnerving. But he ... he is fine.'

Loethar nodded. The silence lengthened again before he sighed. 'This is the second time in as many days that I've had to view the body of someone I care about here in this chapel.'

He cared about Freath? He'd never said as much before. 'I don't know what to say to you,' she admitted.

'She died choking, I'm told.'

'Her heart must have given out. She was struggling to breathe.'

'She came from people who lived well past their tenth decade. Her mother was ninety-eight anni, her father ninety-nine.'

Valya shook her head. 'I'm no physic. She could have choked on the biscuits she ate.'

'Biscuits?'

She nodded. *Stick close to the truth*, she'd told herself. 'I think she might have eaten two. You know how she is about sweet things.'

'And drank nothing?'

'No, that's my point.' Valya sniffed, and dabbed a silk square to her expertly running nose. 'She refused the dinch we served. I did say to her that she should take a swallow of it.'

'Who served it?'

'Er … it was Roland.'

'Roland?'

'Yes. He's attached to your mother's retinue.'

Loethar strode to the door, opened it and gave a muffled order before returning. 'Why don't you sit down?'

'I can't. I can't be still. This is so terrible. I felt so helpless.'

'Helpless? You, Valya?'

'Oh don't you start now, Loethar, please. And stop repeating what I say. I'm weary and your mother is dead. Let's show some respect.'

He stared at her, expressionless. 'I presume my mother was her usual charming self?'

Valya nodded. 'She was wicked to me. But I would never wish this on her.'

Vyk flapped his wings and made a loud cawing sound. He lifted from Loethar's shoulder and swooped near Valya's head. Shrieking, Valya slapped at the bird, which found purchase on an archway, staring menacingly down at her.

'What possessed you to seek her out today?' Loethar continued. 'You've ignored each other for several moons.'

She tossed her hair in a vexed manner. 'As I tried to explain to Dara Negev, I am about to deliver her grandson. I have no family that I care about, I have no one close to talk to — you …' She shrugged. 'Well, you're always busy. I just thought she might talk me through this whole business of childbirth and I really rather hoped that our son might bring us all closer. I wanted her and myself to find a level of friendship. I know we come from different worlds but we have you, our son, the empire in common. We are family.'

He did not seem moved; in fact, he regarded her with a look that was so veiled she couldn't tell whether he was amused or startled by her suddenly impassioned manner.

At the sound of a knock, Loethar turned. 'Come,' he called.

Roland entered, looking terrified.

'Your highnesses,' he said. 'I ... words can't ... I'm sorry.'

'We understand,' Loethar comforted. 'This is a very difficult time for us all. Roland, you are attached to Dara Negev's retinue, am I right?'

'Yes, my lord, since her arrival in the palace.'

'Did you make the dinch?'

Roland looked startled. Then he frowned. 'No. It was made by the kitchen staff. I could —'

'That's not necessary. Were you present when the dinch was made?'

'Yes, I was.'

'Were you present when it was poured for my wife and my mother?'

'No, my lord.'

'So who did pour?'

'I did, Loethar,' Valya said, adding a freshly weary tone to her voice. 'I also drank it,' she added before he could move to the next obvious question.

'Did my mother drink any?' Loethar turned to Roland, ignoring Valya.

Roland shook his head. 'I watched two cups poured and only one was drunk from. Your mother's cup was full, her dinch untouched. I noticed the empress sipping from her cup before and in her anxiety after your mother ... er ...' He looked too terrified to say any more.

Loethar turned. 'We checked for poison, did we, my love?'

Valya sighed. 'Ask Roland.'

'The empress instructed me to take the tray immediately to the apothecary, my lord. The physics have tested the pot, the cups, the remains of the dinch in both cups and pot and can find no trace of poison.'

Loethar nodded. 'The biscuits, Roland. Where did those come from?'

'From a tin in the chambers of the empress.'

'I see,' he said, glancing at Valya.

'Did you bring them to the table?' he asked her.

'I baked them for you. I brought none to the table but I asked Roland to fetch some when your mother decided on something sweet.'

Loethar returned his attention to the servant. 'Tell me about the biscuits.'

Roland looked baffled. 'They were freshly baked. I brought a few on a plate as instructed. The rest I left where they were in the empress's chambers.'

'Were all the ones you brought to the orchard eaten?'

Roland frowned, looking down. 'Yes, I believe they were, my lord. There were only crumbs left.'

'I ate one,' Valya lied, glad that Roland hadn't noticed the leftover biscuits. 'Your mother ate the rest rather greedily,' she added sourly.

Loethar ignored her. 'Go and fetch the tin of biscuits, Roland, and bring them back here.'

The man nodded and walked to the door. To Valya's discomfort, Loethar followed him and quietly muttered something before Roland left the chapel.

'Biscuits?' she snapped, moving into the theatrics she knew were now necessary. 'You don't honestly think I would —'

Loethar cut her off. 'I don't know what to think, Valya. Yesterday my mother was hale. Today she lies dead before me.'

'You don't seem terribly upset.'

'Neither do you. And the difference is, I don't share my emotions with everyone. How I feel is nobody's business. You unfortunately do show your every mood, which is why these fake tears and quivering lips have me baffled.'

'Loethar!'

'No, let me finish,' he said, holding up a hand, his voice annoyingly calm and even. 'You and my mother were not friends; you were not even good companions. But as much as you disliked her, Valya, she disliked you.' She noticed he ignored her look of indignation. 'I feel no sympathy for either of you. We can't be forced to like one another but I did hope you could get on.'

'We did. In fact, today was my effort to try and build some bridges. As I explained, I thought if she could give me some advice, perhaps take more interest in our child, we might go a long way towards being closer. But she said the most cruel things.'

'Surely that didn't surprise you.'

Valya realised she couldn't win. She made her voice sound weary. 'I suppose so, Loethar. I'm very, very sorry for your loss, truly I am.'

Vyk swooped back to Loethar's shoulder, calling again. Valya scowled, wishing she'd thought to poison the bird somehow as well.

There was a second knock at the door and, after Loethar's command to enter, Roland re-appeared, bearing the tin she recognised. He bowed. 'Here is the tin of biscuits, my lord.'

'Good. Open it.' When Roland did so, Loethar leaned in and inhaled. 'Mmm, lovely. You baked these?' he said with surprise, turning to Valya.

She nodded, and maintained wearied tone. 'They were for you. I know you like those buttery things. Me, I can hardly bear to smell them in my condition,' she said, rubbing her belly. 'Certain foods make me feel ill.'

He regarded her now with even deeper scrutiny, his expression creasing into a quizzical one. 'And still you managed to eat one only today.'

Valya blinked, but recovered instantly. 'I was being polite,' she said. 'I'm quite sure it's why I feel so unwell now.'

'Ah, and there I was thinking that it was having to sit this close to my mother's corpse.'

'Loethar, I don't want to play your games. I ate a biscuit, I feel ill, your mother's dead. Where is this going? You think the biscuits are poisoned? You think I killed her?'

He stared silently at her. Vyk stared intently at her too.

Valya gave a long sigh. 'Loethar, please select a biscuit. Any one.'

When his gaze narrowed, she sighed again. 'I'll have to hurry you, my love. I really don't feel terribly well. I make no jest.'

Turning and staring into the box, Loethar pointed to a biscuit.

'Roland,' Valya said. 'Bring me that biscuit the emperor has chosen, would you?'

The servant did as he was asked. Valya took the biscuit and very deliberately ate it. As both men watched in silence she made a show of swallowing the final morsel. 'Now I shall need a drink and a rest. If I should start to foam at the mouth or suddenly writhe all over the chapel gardens, you will know I am dying from the poison that I put in the biscuits I made for you!' Her voice had turned wintry. She curtsied. 'Now, if you'll excuse me, my lord, I shall retire to my chambers.'

Valya swept to the door, Roland only just getting there in time to open it. Silently she strode out, her head high in feigned self-righteous indignation.

It was only when she'd ascended to her chambers, closed the door to her salon and leaned back against it, that she permitted herself to breathe evenly … and to smile with triumph. She'd beaten them. And the old hag was dead.

Her waters broke moments later.

Loethar had paced before the same balustrade that ten anni earlier another king had paced for an identical reason. Both had awaited the birth of their son.

Both had been given daughters.

'What?' Loethar exclaimed.

Valya had banished the tribal women from her chambers; she had wanted a Set midwifery team. The eldest of those women now looked lost for words as she stood before her emperor.

'You have a daughter, my lord,' she said, as reluctantly as she had spoken the words the first time.

Loethar placed two fists, balled tightly, on the balustrade that overlooked the private courtyard, once a place of play for the Valisar dynasty. He lifted his chin and let out such a roar of anguish that the midwife not only stepped back, but turned and fled into the birthing chamber.

Loethar placed his fists against his forehead. 'I am indeed cursed,' he murmured, his eyes closed.

The silence lengthened. At last a physic appeared, awkwardly and unsure, from Valya's chamber.

'Do you wish to see your daughter, my lord?' he asked, his tone soft, his manner careful.

'No,' Loethar growled.

The man cleared his throat. 'Perhaps you should, my lord. She is ...'

'What?' Loethar said, opening his eyes, spinning around to face the hesitant man. 'She is what?'

The physic looked pained. 'She is sickly, Emperor Loethar.'

A rueful smile of acceptance ghosted fleetingly past Loethar's lips. 'Will she die?'

At first the man didn't reply. Finally he said, 'Probably, my lord, if my experience is guiding me correctly.'

'Then my child is already lost to me. I have no reason to stare at someone soon to be a corpse.' Loethar turned and strode away.

'My lord ... your wife?' the physic risked calling after him.

'She was lost long ago!' Loethar yelled and all but ran down the palace steps. He ran all the way to the chapel, where he ordered an immediate cremation of his mother's body.

Father Briar looked alarmed. 'Emperor Loethar, surely a more public mourning time, a proper —'

Loethar's expression darkened like a sky gathering for thunder. 'My mother was not a public figure. None of the Set people cared about Dara Negev and will not mourn her, Father Briar.'

'But your brother and —'

'My half-brother and I will mourn our mother in our own way, Father Briar. Burn her today. I will witness it. I want her ashes by tonight.'

'My lord, that's not —'

'Tonight!' Loethar roared. 'Or you'll go on the pyre with her,' he bellowed and stormed from the chapel.

Elka could see he knew everything again. She saw it in the blink of an eye as he walked towards her now, looking tense and embarrassed but also like a man unburdened. Ten anni of her life she'd dedicated to this man, a stranger. He had built a new life while learning to walk again, convalescing and returning his body to the fit, strong person he was today.

Only tiny snippets of his past had revealed themselves over the many moons he had lived in Lo's Teeth. He had readily admitted that although Regor was definitely not his name it nevertheless resonated with him, so perhaps it was meaningful. He was convinced that he belonged to a family. And they'd all worked out easily enough for themselves that Regor was not of common stock.

Regor's wit and charm had worn away her brothers' reserve and suspicions. They had taught him to ride bareback, to shoot arrows accurately over long distances, and to drink copious amounts of the mountain brew they called Lo's Fury. Regor had been accepted by her family as a new brother. Even though he was overshadowed in height — even by her mother — and looked nothing like the tall, powerful people he'd joined, he had effectively become one of them.

The Abbess reached her before he did. 'Are you ready?'

'He already looks different,' she remarked, trying to hide her disappointment.

'No, Elka, he was different with you. Now he is back to the person he truly was … is.' The woman squeezed her arm and Elka felt the conveyance of sympathy, the older woman's urging to be strong. 'After your grandmother lost your grandfather, she joined us here. Her memory lives strongly among us. You know you are always welcome, if just to talk.'

'I know, thank you.'

'He will need to return to where you found him. You must let him go — wherever that is.'

'I just want to take him home,' she said, finding a soft smile for her companion of the last decade as he drew closer across the courtyard. He did look changed.

'His home is not in Lo's Teeth, dear one. Be warned.' The older woman took her hand away and turned towards Regor. 'Welcome back.'

Elka watched his embarrassment deepen. 'Thank you,' he said. 'I am back, in more ways than is obvious.'

Elka felt her composure slipping but she kept it hidden, determined to let the unravelling happen only inwardly. 'So what's your name?'

He regarded her with bright eyes that, despite all his recent sadness, could never hide their mischief, or their openness. Suddenly, in that pause, she wished she had told him everything: all that she'd felt for him these anni past, the fact that it didn't matter that he was Set or short, or didn't know his real name. She loved him. She couldn't help it.

'My name is Gavriel,' he said, his voice shaking slightly. 'I have a twin brother.' She saw his eyes mist and he looked down. 'I … my father was killed, murdered.' He returned his gaze to her and she felt her heart break.

The Abess stepped away. 'You two have much to discuss. Welcome back, Gavriel. I'm glad our Quirin helped you.'

He turned. 'She is wonderful. I am so grateful to the convent and will find a way to repay your generosity.'

She nodded, smiling, before turning to Elka. 'Look after each other,' she said and withdrew.

'Elka,' he began.

'No wait. Not here,' she said, finding her courage again. Her own voice was back under control, as was her mood. She was Davarigon: a strong, independent member of the tribe who needed no man to fend for her, least of all a puny Set man. They were friends. She had saved his life once, helped him forge a new one, and that was that. Now he must return to his life, perhaps his wife! She was afraid to know. 'Let's leave. You can tell me as we travel.'

'Travel to where?'

'To the pass. At least that's where I'm going. I am going home, Regor ... sorry, Gavriel. I don't know what your plans are now.'

'Stop, Elka. Don't talk like that.'

Their horses had been brought from the stables. Her Elleputian — the bigger species of horse the Davarigons bred specifically in the valleys — dwarfed his.

'I'm being realistic,' she said, forcing herself to sound strong.

'No, you're acting like a woman.' She gave him a look that would have made most men step back but Gavriel had seen it before. 'Don't scowl at me. This attitude is so typical.'

'So typical of whom?'

'Women.'

'Oh, you remember them now, do you?' He laughed, only making her angrier. 'You know where we live ... if you ever want to visit,' she said, trying to disguise her heartbreak.

But Gavriel grabbed her wrist as she climbed onto her beast. His grip was surprisingly strong. She paused, shocked. He never touched her. 'Ride with me,' he said. 'I have lots to tell you.'

'I don't think I can.'

'Elka, ride with me,' he urged, his tone matching his grip.

'To where?'

'Back.'

'Home?' she asked, keeping the hope from her voice.

'Not yours. Not even mine.'

'Where then?'

'Where it began for us. The Deloran Forest.'

She began shaking her head, but Gavriel persisted. 'You yourself have told me that Davarigons travel through the empire more easily now.'

'I'm not worried about that.'

'What is it, then?'

'I fear what you'll discover.'

He shrugged. 'I have to do this. It's important. No, listen,' he said when she began pulling away again. 'I really mean it. It's not that I'm important. But what I was doing before you found me, before they attacked me, was. It was critical to the security and future of Penraven.'

She frowned. 'What are you talking about? Who are you?'

'Ride with me. I will tell you everything.'

Kilt found himself standing before a beautiful building of elegant proportions, currently accommodation for the man known as Vulpan, the emperor's latest weapon against the Vested.

'He doesn't take visitors,' the guard repeated.

'You've already said that. I simply have a question for him. Perhaps someone could take it to him and bring me his answer?'

Before the guard could respond, the door was flung open and a tall man appeared, his dark eyes matching the colour of his trimmed beard. He looked like a magistrate. 'What is this? Your voices are disturbing my work.'

'Are you Master Vulpan?' Kilt asked. The man sounded too impressed by his own importance to be anyone else.

'I am. And why does a clergyman need to know?'

'Pastor Jeves, Master Vulpan,' Kilt said by way of introduction. 'I believe you might have met my sister recently. I'm trying to find her with some urgency. Please forgive my interruption of your work.'

'I know of no woman called Jeves.'

Kilt hated having to even say the words. 'She's married. My apologies. Master and Mrs Felt. Her name is Lily.'

'Lily!' The Vested nodded. 'Ah, the beautiful Mrs Felt. Indeed, I do recall her,' he said, licking his lips, making Kilt wince inwardly. 'She never mentioned a brother.'

Kilt shrugged. 'I can't imagine why she would. She hasn't seen me for many anni.'

'How did you know she was here, then?'

'I've been tracking her movements. It's taken me an entire moon to get to this point. I sense I'm close; I must have missed her by only a short time.'

'So close I can almost still smell her,' Vulpan said.

Kilt forced himself to look deeply disappointed. 'Ah, pity. But,' he said, adding a fresh vigour to his voice, 'that means she is within striking distance.'

'What's it like to grow up around a Vested?'

'Er, well, Lily kept her skills very much to herself, Master Vulpan.'

'Is that so?'

Kilt had assumed far too much, he realised. This man was no easy target and while the disguise gave him a measure of protection, Vulpan was already suspicious. But Kilt knew he couldn't flee now. 'She didn't care to share it and our parents didn't encourage it,' he blustered. 'Which brings to me to my reason for being here, Master Vulpan.'

'Why don't you come inside? Perhaps we can discuss your —'

'No, no,' Kilt said, waving a hand. 'You're a busy man, Master Vulpan, I can tell that much. I simply wondered if you had any information on Lily's whereabouts. I have to find her because our mother is gravely ill. I was hoping that they could see each other before she died and —'

'Do come in, Pastor Jeves. Let us discuss this inside.'

'I'm actually in a bit of a hurry, sir, if you'll forgive my ungracious behaviour.'

'Pastor Jeves, I really do insist.' Vulpan smiled, not a skerrick of warmth in his expression.

Kilt smiled back. 'Well, all right, then. Just quickly.' With a sinking heart, he followed the man inside the elegant house.

As Vulpan closed the door behind him, the cold smile still not failing, he added: 'Pastor Jeves, are you aware that you have blood smeared across your face?'

24

Kirin and Lily had travelled all day, pausing only to rest the horses, eating four small sugarloaves between them as they journeyed. By the time they had reached a village called Green Herbery, they were exhausted, but Kirin felt a measure of comfort that they had put so much space between themselves and Vulpan.

He climbed down from his horse and stretched long and leisurely, groaning as he did so. 'Lo save us, look over there,' he said, pointing at a structure that looked as though it had collapsed.

'Fire,' Lily breathed. 'Oh, how terrible. It looks as though it was serious. I hope no one was injured.'

'I guess we'll know soon enough,' Kirin replied. 'Let's get these horses stabled for the night,' he said, adding, 'I'm sorry, Lily, but I'll need to dip into your purse again if you can spare some money. I have only a little coin left.'

She made a dismissive sound. 'Money is the least of our problems, Kirin. You can have whatever I have. I'm sure it's enough.'

'Just like an old married couple, eh?' he said, grinning as he helped her off the animal. As she slid from the horse and twisted in his arms, their gazes met and for just that tiny moment something passed between them. It was gone as quickly as it had arrived, though, and he felt self-conscious for letting his gaze linger. 'We'll have to pretend again,' he said, clearing his throat to cover the awkwardness.

'I know,' she said. 'But we're getting the hang of it now.' Suddenly she stopped, startled. 'Oh!' she exclaimed.

Kirin swung around, following her gaze, and noticed a small line of people following two men, who carried between them what looked to be a body slung in a sheet.

'Is he dead?' Lily asked.

Kirin looked at the limp arms swinging over the side of the hammock. Although he couldn't see the man's face, he could see blood on his front. 'Yes, I'd say so. Let's find out what's happened.'

Lily baulked. 'No, thank you. You can, if you're ghoulish enough. I'll go see if there's room for us at the inn. Here, you can take the horses. Let me just get my knapsack.'

Kirin watched her leave. Did she feel something for him? He'd made a promise to himself not to invade Lily's mind again. But he had to know. He trickled a modest stream of his prying magic and entered Lily's thoughts effortlessly; his arrival felt familiar, as did the accompanying sense of nausea. The sickness was claiming him faster, he noted; it was adjusting to his restrained use of his powers. He would not have long.

He mentally tiptoed around her thoughts, grimacing at the cacophony relating to Kilt Faris but there, right in the middle of the swirling mass of love and recrimination surrounding the outlaw, was the indecision over him. Kirin smiled. He was in her thoughts — and not for concern for his health, or gratitude for his help, not even fear over their situation. Right now he could hear Lily's angst over her behaviour just a moment or two ago. She was confused, unnerved by the way she had reacted to the look they had shared.

She liked him! Kirin nearly skipped as he walked between the horses. As she walked further from him she was admonishing herself for harbouring feelings for him. The bile rose; Kirin spat. He let go of Lily, but he had already outstayed his welcome and he fell to his knees, still holding the reins, and lost what paltry food he'd eaten earlier in the day. 'Never again!' he growled. 'Not with Lily.' He coughed and spat again.

'Hey!' a voice yelled and Kirin looked up. 'Are you all right?'

Clearly he wasn't but Kirin raised a hand and nodded. 'I'm fine, fine.'

But the man was not to be so easily dissuaded. He ran up to Kirin, reaching for the reins. 'We saw you stumble and then fall. What happened? Oh,' he said, noticing the mess. 'Are you sickening?'

'It's nothing serious,' Kirin said. 'A slight stomach upset. Bad milk, I think, in the previous village.' He allowed himself to be helped to his feet. 'Please don't trouble yourself.'

'No trouble,' the man said kindly. 'Here, let me help you.' He took one set of reins. 'Are you heading for the stables?'

Kirin nodded.

'I'll show you where they are. That way you can get to the inn quicker. Are you alone?'

'No.' Kirin took a deep breath to steady himself. 'My wife has gone ahead to see about a room.'

'She won't have any trouble securing one — ours is a quiet village,' the man said, and held out a paw of a hand. 'Deren Cannet.'

'Kirin Felt,' he replied, shaking the proffered hand of friendship. 'Thank you.'

'Don't mention it.'

'I couldn't help noticing your small procession just now,' Kirin said, eager to change the subject.

'Ah, but it's a sad thing,' Deren said, shaking his head with obvious regret. 'That man died twice.'

'Pardon?'

'It's true,' Deren confirmed, then pointed. 'Over here to the stables.'

Kirin followed, intrigued. 'Tell me how a man dies twice.'

'It's too curious to credit. That man you saw being carried, he was a stranger like you. He came into our village just a day or so ago. Do you see that barn?' At Kirin's nod, Deren continued. 'That was going up in flames, as you can tell. A lad ran into that burning

310

barn, trying to save his pet cat. And this stranger — we didn't even know his name at the time — blow me down if he didn't run straight in after the boy.'

Kirin's curiosity deepened. 'So what happened?'

'We're here,' Deren said. 'Hold on, I'll finish my tale. Let's just get these horses in. Ho, Neal, are you there?'

A brawny young man emerged from the shadows. 'Deren,' he said, then nodded at Kirin.

'We need stabling for this pair,' Kirin said.

The man reached for the reins. 'How long?'

Kirin shrugged. 'Overnight. They've had a long journey today so they'll need lots of rest and some careful handling.'

'I'll have them fed, watered, and rubbed down and I'll make sure they get fresh hay,' Neal said, taking both reins from the men. 'We'll take good care of your beasts.' He led them away.

'Neal's a good boy,' Deren said, pointing over his shoulder as he led Kirin away. 'His dad's recently been taken by the shaking fever so he's got to run the stables himself now and take care of his mam.'

'He looks young.'

'He is but he's strong and he knows his horses. Come, I'll walk you to the inn. There's only one so you can't miss it.'

'Finish the story of the dead man,' Kirin said, keen to head off any curiosity about his and Lily's story.

'Well, he ran into the barn, as I said, and he found young Roddy, don't ask me how. But he brought him out and then they both collapsed, horribly burned, it looked like. I thought they were both dead, to be honest. And then the barn began to collapse and we all rushed away. When I returned, he and the boy were gone.'

'So he survived?'

'It seems so. I can't explain it to you, Master Felt. My eyes saw a badly burned man. Roddy's mother won't discuss it. She said another stranger appeared and took charge, taking the injured pair back to her cottage where he healed them. She's been quite addled ever since, so she's not making much sense. Roddy disappeared the same day, you see.'

'He was burned, survived and then he disappeared?' Kirin clarified, not able to believe this tall tale.

'He wasn't just burned. He was crisped. His clothes were scorched, his hair was shrivelled, his skin had blistered. And still he stole out of the cottage and ran away.'

'Lo's light, I can't credit that. Where to?'

Deren shrugged. 'No one knows. The village went looking for Roddy. His mother was inconsolable. She thought she'd lost him once to the fire and then he was mysteriously and miraculously healed and then he disappeared. She's having to be sedated. But when we were out looking for Roddy, we came across the stranger.'

They had arrived at the inn. Lily stepped out of the front door and smiled. 'Hello, my love,' she said, sounding ever more practised at it. She even kissed his cheek as he arrived and took his hand. It felt wonderful and he suddenly felt insanely guilty. 'Is something wrong?' she frowned, staring deep into his face.

'Ah, Mrs Felt, your husband wasn't very well a moment ago. But I've got him safely here. He should rest.'

'Kirin?'

'Don't fret, my sweet. It was just a headache.'

'You said it was bad milk,' Deren remarked.

'That too,' Kirin said quickly. 'I've been feeling seedy all day, to tell the truth.' He could see that Lily didn't believe him.

'Let's get you upstairs,' she said, eyeing him suspiciously.

'Er, well, thanks again, Deren, I hope they find young Roddy.'

Deren sighed. 'Well, I hope we don't find him dead. The man who saved his life was killed viciously — it seems he was destined to die by misadventure.'

'Killed?' Kirin frowned. 'I hadn't realised. I thought he'd died from his injuries. That's terrible.'

'And very strange. We found him in an isolated part of the forest fringe when we were searching for Roddy. I can't imagine what he was doing there alone or who might have murdered him. Ah, I've remembered his name. Roddy's mother told us it's Clovis.'

'Clovis!' Kirin exclaimed, grabbing at his sleeve. When the man looked instantly alarmed, Kirin let him go. 'Forgive me. I ... er, well, I know a Clovis. How old would this man be?'

Deren shrugged. 'Search me. Come and have a look for yourself. Your friend hasn't gone missing, has he?'

'Show me,' Kirin said, glancing at Lily's worried face. 'Wait here,' he suggested, knowing a corpse was the last thing she wanted to see.

She nodded, clearly grateful. 'I'll be upstairs.'

Kirin followed Deren once again, this time grimly. His heart, which had been light such a short time ago, was now heavy with fear.

Deren led him to the church. 'We've put him here until we can decide what's best to do.'

A small group of people had gathered around the body. A woman was being consoled. Kirin's hopes flared. She didn't look like Reuth. This woman was slight of build, definitely shorter and her hair wasn't as dark as Reuth's had been. Reuth's hair by now would surely be peppered with grey. But when the woman began wailing about Roddy, Kirin's hopes were dashed. She must be the mother of the missing child.

Deren shouldered through the small group of people clustered around the body, laid out in front of the small altar. As they parted Kirin caught sight of the dead man's face and felt something give inside. Dear, unmistakeable Clovis. Older, paunchier, and covered with blood, but definitely his friend and fellow Vested. He choked back the sound of grief that he knew was about to erupt from his throat.

'Is this him?' Deren asked, seemingly insensitive to Kirin's despair.

'Unbelievably, it is,' he groaned, bending down on one knee to take his old friend's lifeless hand, trying not to look at the wound, focusing on his friend's kind face. 'I haven't seen him for anni,' he admitted, all the regret of the past decade coming home to roost in his heavy heart. 'Who found him?' Tears ran helplessly down his cheeks, not just for Clovis but for himself, for Lily, for their seemingly relentless struggle on behalf of a cause he constantly questioned.

'I did,' a man replied. 'There wasn't much to see, just the remains of a deserted fire. We didn't linger. Jory helped me carry him down to the others, who were searching below the ridge we found him on.'

'He's been stabbed,' a woman commented, although Kirin did not need that information to understand how Clovis had died.

Faris wiped at his mouth and nose but knew the blood was dried. Without water, the telltale stain would remain. He had been careless. Vulpan was eyeing the bloodstain like a man famished.

'What has occurred here, Pastor Jeves? Please, have a seat,' Vulpan said, casting an eye over paperwork on his desk.

Kilt could see the man was feigning only casual interest in him. The fire in his eyes was sparkling with fascination. 'A nosebleed, I'm afraid,' Kilt said, ignoring the offer of a seat but making a polite gesture of decline.

'Do you get them often?'

'No.'

'Really? So what prompted this one, do you imagine?'

'Truly, Master Vulpan I have no idea,' Kilt replied, allowing himself to sound fractionally testy. 'I really must —'

'Actually, Pastor, you really can't insist on anything.'

'What is that supposed to mean?' Kilt asked evenly, feeling all his internal alarm bells ringing.

As if he could read his mind, Vulpan reached over and plucked a small handbell from his desk. Ringing it twice, he said, 'A moment, Pastor Jeves.'

Kilt blinked in surprise as the door opened and a scarred man entered the room, two imperial soldiers remaining outside.

'This is Shorgan,' Vulpan introduced. 'He is our Wikken.'

Kilt froze, then tried to cover his fear. But he wasn't sure he had been successful. His gaze was riveted on the raised, purple network of scars that traversed the newcomer's face.

'I can see that his presence disturbs you, Pastor Jeves.'

Kilt inhaled carefully, calming himself. This was dangerous but he'd faced dangerous situations before. 'Aren't you going to introduce the soldiers as well?' he asked.

Vulpan smiled at him. 'Ah, a clergyman with a sense of humour. Very good. But are you really a clergyman?'

'What a preposterous question!'

Vulpan shrugged. 'I think you lie.'

'I don't know how to assure you, or even answer such a claim.'

'Well, moving on to the matter at hand, our revered Wikken —'

'He's not your Wikken, Master Vulpan. Wikkens are of the Steppes. You, unless I'm mistaken, are not.'

'I work for the emperor,' the Wikken replied as though that answered any query.

'Many do. Most do not claim to be Steppes people.' Kilt was playing for time, his mind racing for a way out of this dilemma.

Vulpan shook his head, appearing irritated by Kilt's argument. 'Your objections are irrelevant,' Vulpan dismissed.

'You have no right to keep me here,' Kilt blustered, deliberately sounding deeply offended.

Vulpan took a slow breath, and straightened his coat. 'Shorgan assures me you are Vested. He knew it when you first spoke outside.' Kilt swallowed. Vulpan gave an expression that suggested he was forcing himself to remain polite. 'You possess powers that cannot be rationally explained.'

'What of it?' Kilt said, allowing his annoyance and frustration to come through loudly now. 'I insist on being on my way.'

Vulpan clearly had not expected the admission. 'You admit to being Vested?'

'I never denied it,' Kilt replied, taking them all in with a single glance as if he was surprised anyone had thought differently. The soldiers looked very large and unmoved by the conversation. He might well be able to fight off Vulpan and his ugly companion but the guards would smash him to a pulp. And he noted that the door had been left open so they could be easily called. 'What actually is the problem here?' he demanded.

'I …' Vulpan hesitated. 'There is no problem,' he finally admitted.

'Good. Then call off your dogs at the door, Master Vulpan. I am a man of Lo and I don't take kindly to being threatened with violence, or being held captive, or being intimidated by your Wikken. That was your intention, wasn't it?'

Vulpan gave a gesture of dismissal and the soldiers disappeared. It was a small win, but even so Kilt's hopes soared. 'I came here seeking details of my sister. Do you have any?'

'Only that she is mildly Vested with healing powers and is now officially in our records. She left the same day with her husband.'

The word husband cut deep inside Kilt; the suggestion of Lily's being Vested rankled even deeper. Surely he would have known if she'd had more than the ability to simply wield her herbals with such stunning effect. 'Where were they headed, sir?'

'Back to Brighthelm was my understanding.'

'Thank you. I will take your leave.'

'Not so fast, Pastor Jeves.'

Kilt turned back to the man. 'I really must catch up with her.'

'Of course. First, though, we would like to keep a record of you as well. You are Vested, after all. You could have saved us a lot of time if you'd simply told us as much.'

'You never asked.'

'Indeed.'

'Do you hide your power because it is so strong,' a gravelly voice piped up. It was Shorgan, talking in perfect Set.

Kilt swung around; the man's face was scary but his voice was worse. Deep and unaccustomed to being used, it rasped in a manner that Kilt was sure could scare children.

'I wouldn't call it strong, sir.'

'I would. I can smell it on you. You hide it well, though.'

Kilt tried for a smile, lacing it with feigned self-consciousness. 'I don't know what to say. I don't use my magic. I have no use for it. I'm a clergyman, guiding folk in the path of Lo. I have never considered it strong, in fact —'

'When did you last use it?' Shorgan asked.

Kilt was taken aback. 'Well, I ... I honestly can't remember.'

'That long ago?'

'So long ago I really couldn't tell you,' Kilt said firmly.

'Could you give us a demonstration of your skill? What is it you do?' Vulpan enquired.

'Demonstration?' Kilt stammered. He hated himself in that moment. More than three decades of practice and discipline had just been undone.

Vulpan's head shifted. He regarded Kilt with a dark stare. 'Was that a stutter I just heard, Pastor Jeves?'

Kilt cleared his throat and smiled sardonically, using the moment to regain control of himself. 'Just a childhood affliction I thought I'd conquered.'

'But it comes out in times of anxiety?'

'Not really. Just now and then when I don't concentrate.'

'Interesting. Nosebleeds and stutters.'

'Master Vulpan, I'm not going to give demonstrations. I told you, I don't use my magic. You want a sample of my blood, presumably. Shall we get on with it?'

'Shorgan?' Vulpan asked.

'He's lying. He's very strong in his magic. He used it recently. I think you'll find that would account for the nosebleed.'

'What?' Kilt said, turning on his heel and roaring at the Wikken, who regarded him placidly. 'I demand to speak to someone who can grant me an audience with the emperor. This is ridiculous.'

'I can organise that,' Vulpan said. 'General Stracker, the emperor's most trusted confidant and brother, will be here shortly.

You're most welcome to discuss an audience with him. Until then, you'll remain here.'

'I'm a prisoner?' Kilt asked.

'I prefer the word guest,' Vulpan replied and smiled. Kilt could hear the Wikken chuckling behind him. 'I will, of course, still require a sample of your blood to taste.'

'Why don't you lick it off my face?' Kilt said, feeling angry and incredibly helpless.

'Oh, I prefer it fresh and running. Hold out your hand, please, Pastor Jeves.'

To Lily he looked like a broken man. He'd arrived in their room ashen, slump-shouldered and unable to talk. She noticed his eyes were watering.

'It was *your* Clovis?' She couldn't believe it.

'He …' Kirin sounded choked. She moved around the bed, watching him swallow hard to regain control of his composure. 'He'd been stabbed in the throat. Murdered and left to die alone in the woodland beyond the village.'

'Oh, Kirin.' Lily covered her mouth with a hand. His sorrow was threatening to make her weep now. 'I'm so sorry,' she managed to say. Her heart broke for him. He was so alone, desperately in need of comfort and affection.

Lily took a deep breath and put her arms around Kirin. She felt his initial shock and then he seemed to melt around her body. She knew he cried, and she wept too, stroking his back and hair, until his softly given tears subsided. They stood like that for a long time. It felt warm and secure and comfortable, and Lily hated herself for beginning to appreciate how well their bodies fitted together.

'I'm sorry,' he mumbled from somewhere at her shoulder, his face buried in her hair.

She pulled back softly. 'Whatever for?' They were close enough that she would only need to lean forward slightly to touch her lips to his.

He seemed to search her eyes. 'For compromising you like this.'

Lily felt an inward tug of guilt. 'Are you always this careful and responsible, Kirin?'

He shook his head. 'Only around you.'

She frowned. 'Why?' He still wasn't looking her in the eye, she noticed. 'Am I that hard to look upon?'

Now his eyes flashed up; his expression was disbelieving. 'The opposite.'

'Why do I make you feel so awkward, then? Why are you always so careful around me?'

'Isn't it obvious?' he said, pulling away, but she held him fast. She could almost see Kilt sneering over Kirin's shoulder, saying to her: *this is your fault. You created this scenario.* Kilt was like that: so tough, always demanding so much of those around him. She could accept that he ensured everyone took responsibility for their own actions and that made each of his men exceptionally careful — as he was — but sometimes she despaired for him to show some sensitivity. Kirin seemed so helpless at this moment and just her touch, she could tell, was giving him great solace.

'I shouldn't have said that,' he said, her hesitation embarrassing him.

'Kirin —'

'I can't do this, Lily. I thought I could but I'm going to fail spectacularly and do something one of us will regret.'

'What do you mean?'

She could see him looking at her as though she were dense. Perhaps she was … or perhaps she just needed to hear a man express his feelings of affection, feelings she had prompted.

He stepped back, away from her touch. 'Thank you for the embrace. It helps, it really does. But it has its own set of complications and I think it's better if we —'

'I needed to do something. You looked so broken. We're friends. Can't friends offer comfort?'

'What did you have in mind?' She was sure it was meant as a jest, a response to lighten the suddenly awkward atmosphere that had settled around them.

She shook her head, feeling trapped. She wanted to say that she had little in her head but stupidity, but instead she stared at him, saying nothing.

Kirin smiled gently. *Had he pried? Had he listened in on her thoughts,* she suddenly wondered? *I'll kill him.* In that blink of startling revelation, Kirin pulled her to him; suddenly he was kissing her. It wasn't gentle but it wasn't aggressive either and there was nothing unpractised about it, and yet she knew he had acted entirely spontaneously. And, Lo save her, she returned his passion helplessly.

Kirin deepened the kiss, his arms tightening around her, and Lily came to her senses. She broke the embrace, pulling away from Kirin, horror ghosting across her face. He stared at her and she could see only pain in his expression.

Without another word, he turned on his heel and left the chamber. She didn't stop him, couldn't stop him. Her mind had already fled to another bedroom in another inn where another man embraced her and talked of marriage and a future. She hated herself.

Kirin stormed from the bedroom, his body tingling. He'd kissed Lily and this time there was nothing feigned about it. It was wrong and it was doomed but it had been delicious. Her mouth had been soft and welcoming; she had responded, he wasn't imagining it.

He was angry too, though. And it was a good idea to get out of that room. Lily had hardly discouraged him and while he had made the move to kiss her — which he had known even was ill-advised — she had made the move to show him affection. He wasn't a monk. Having to look upon lovely Lily and live alongside Lily and pretend to be married to Lily — well, it was bound to happen, he growled privately as he stomped from the inn, ignoring the innkeeper's puzzled look.

None of this mattered! Not him, not Lily, not Kilt Faris's feelings. All that mattered was that Clovis was dead. Stabbed, abandoned ... murdered. Why? That's what mattered. Who had killed him and for what reason? What had Clovis stumbled into or upon?

He found Deren in the bakery, where he had said he would be for the rest of the day. He was covered in flour, pushing loaves into the clay oven. 'I need to see where he died,' Kirin said, before Deren could even open his mouth.

Deren looked around. 'I can't leave the bakery. These are loaves for tonight's meals in the inn.'

'Is there anyone else who could show me?' Kirin appealed.

Deren regarded him for a moment before sighing and nodding. 'I'll ask young Tod to take you. Roddy's his friend. He was helping to look for him.'

'Thank you.'

'Wait here,' Deren said and disappeared out the back.

Kirin strolled to the doorway and looked across the street. The barn would have to be rebuilt. To its left he saw the Widow Kenyan's cottage that Deren had pointed out earlier. He frowned, cocking his head to one side. The cottage's roof looked scorched, too, and next to it the trees looked damaged. What had occurred?

Deren returned. 'Tod says he'll take you for a couple of trents.'

Kirin nodded. 'It's the least I can pay,' he agreed. 'Have you noticed that the Widow Kenyan's cottage is scorched?'

Deren was back to banging out hot loaves. 'Yes. It was damaged in the fire.'

'How? Nothing else around the barn is damaged. Why and how would the fire choose that cottage?'

The baker shrugged. 'I don't really know. Haven't thought about it.'

'Well, look at it.'

Deren stopped to look out the window. 'The trees are damaged too,' he observed.

'I know. So they caught fire and they somehow ignited the cottage roof? That doesn't make sense. The barn is too far away.'

'Embers, perhaps?' the man said, sounding increasingly less interested.

'But … oh, it doesn't matter,' Kirin said as a child ran in through the door. 'You must be Tod.'

'Got my trents?'

'I do,' Kirin said seriously, reaching into his pocket and fishing out one of the last of his coins. He flipped it to Tod, who caught and pocketed the coin with dexterity.

'Come on then, sir. I have to be back to bring the cows in or me da will whip me.'

'Lead the way,' Kirin said, looking over his shoulder and nodding a farewell. 'If my wife's looking for me, let her know where I am, will you?'

The man nodded but frowned as if to say *why didn't you?* Without looking back, Kirin left Green Herbery and the memory of kissing Lily behind.

25

Greven and Piven were approaching Berch. They'd walked solidly most of the day with Greven deliberately hanging back. He didn't want to talk to Piven ... couldn't. His hand throbbed. *Hand!* He sneered inwardly. He could still feel it. It was as though he were still whole and yet the intense pain told him differently. Piven had promised that tonight they would brew a strong painkiller but there had been no time to stop during daylight. They had needed to put distance between themselves and the murdered man.

Piven dropped back to walk next to Greven. 'We'll get help for you at Berch.'

'I don't need help. I know as much about healing as anyone in that town.'

Piven nodded. 'Then we'll push on to the coast.'

'Why?'

'We can stay out of sight for a while.'

'What are we doing? What in Lo's name are you doing?'

'I'm not sure yet. I'm following Vyk.'

Greven had been so lost in his thoughts and the pain that he hadn't realised that the raven was still travelling with them. He looked around, and found it watching them from a tree ahead. 'Lo curse the creature! How does it always find us?'

'He means us no harm.'

'Where does this end, Piven? In your strange mind, where does this reckless behaviour lead you?'

Piven frowned, considered the question seriously. Finally he blew his cheeks out. 'To the throne, I suppose.'

'Throne!'

Piven shrugged. 'I'm an heir,' he said, nothing defensive about his tone.

'And we now have an emperor with a well trained army specifically marauding to keep all memories of Valisars at bay. The Valisar line ended with Brennus! Accept it. The Valisars are simply history. And, besides, everyone thinks you're dead!' Greven spat as cruelly as he could.

'And that's my greatest weapon ... apart from you, of course.'

Greven scowled. 'I need to rest.'

Piven didn't look as though he wanted to but he paused and then shrugged. 'We can sit in the lee of this tree. But you don't really need to rest, do you?' he asked.

Greven shook his head. 'Until you die, I'm in a strange state of immortality. I don't need to drink, eat, or sleep.'

Piven nodded. 'Can we talk about this?'

Greven didn't reply.

'There's no going back now. What's done is done. You are my aegis. You have no free choice.'

'How do you know?'

'I told you. My father used to talk around me as though I were invisible, which to all intents and purposes I was. My father wanted to find his aegis ... he wanted to find you.'

Greven nodded sadly.

'It began about ten moons before Loethar struck. I'm amazed I can recall conversations in such detail. At the time I wasn't even aware of the words being spoken but now I understand that I heard everything. My mind was sound; it was just trapped.' Piven sighed when he could see Greven was not interested in his awe. 'The king became very insistent about it, sending de Vis off on missions to the

Academy to learn more about magic, hoping it might lead him to his aegis. In the meantime he got serious about training Leo.'

'What do you mean?'

Piven smiled secretively. 'Of course I tagged along, holding my brother's hand, lost in my madness. But obviously I was hearing everything, retaining it, too. You know, I really grew up around adults. When Leo was off playing with the de Vis brothers I was considered a nuisance. I couldn't fight or shoot arrows or get involved in swordplay. They didn't mind my being there as we all got older but as an infant I was an encumbrance to their play, so I was either at my mother's skirts, or where I preferred to be, which was close to my father.'

'Do you hate your father?'

'No! I worshipped him. He loved me. I know it. It would have been so easy for him to be disappointed, exasperated, even angry at me for being less than perfect. But he was always kind and loving.'

'But what about the fact that your parents kept your real birth a secret? Doesn't that anger you?'

'Why should it? I was the second heir. My father felt he had to protect me. It is an odd method, I'll grant you, but their intentions were sound. And they're both dead. I have no one to level any anger at, so it's a pointless emotion.' Vyk swooped down to land between them and Greven snarled at the bird. 'And neither have you anyone to level anger at,' Piven counselled. 'You were born to this. It's not Vyk's fault.'

'But I avoided it. I avoided your father. I ignored the magic constantly stirring within me, choosing instead the life of a hermit, choosing plants and know-how over magical healing.'

'Well, that was your choice. But you also chose to help my brother. You chose to come down from the forests. You chose to follow Vyk. You chose to take me in. Don't bleat now; it sounds to me like the inevitable outcome of your choices has occurred.'

Greven stared at him with wonder. 'Perhaps you should be king, talking like that.'

'Perhaps I should.'

'Is that what you want?'

'Greven, I just wanted to be left alone in a hut on the outskirts of Minton Woodlet. But what I want, I can no longer have. Now that people like that couple you were running from know of my existence, they won't be the only ones who can put together a few stray facts and come up with the truth that a Valisar is on the loose.'

'But no one knows that you are Valisar.'

'It no longer matters. The fact is, I am. The other fact is that Loethar would hunt me down if word got back to him that Piven the halfwit was alive and well. He'd want me back, and this time he may not be so happy to put me on a leash, not when he realises I am no longer the sweet, tragic, vacant Piven he recalls. So I have to protect myself with you. And it seems an awful waste not to use my immunity to seize back the throne for the Valisars.'

Greven took a deep breath. 'So that's the plan?'

Piven looked back at him with a soft frown. 'I suppose it is. I hadn't really thought that until now but it sits well in my mind. Loethar must pay for his sins.'

'And so you see yourself seizing control of the empire,' Greven said, not stifling his scorn very well, 'a mere youth, returning your older brother to his throne and —'

Piven blinked. 'Whatever gave you that idea? I've decided I hate Leo.'

'I don't understand,' Greven murmured, holding his breath.

'He left me. Deserted me. He's my brother. And older brothers are meant to protect their younger siblings. He escaped from the castle and he left me to my fate, and he has not tried to contact me.'

'He doesn't know where you are!'

'Or even if I'm alive,' Piven finished for him. 'He doesn't know because he doesn't care. He saved his own life and I imagine he was able to justify leaving me behind because I was so witless. I would have been the same encumbrance I was when we were children; I would have posed too much of a risk to him and Gavriel. I might even have given away their hiding spot. No, all in all, he worked out that it was better to leave me to Loethar's whims than to risk his own skin to save me.'

'And how might he have retrieved you? His escape was a sheer wonder on its own.'

'Well, you got me out.'

'He was twelve!'

'I'm only fifteen now. Age is irrelevant. Blood is what matters. Blood, loyalty, and duty.'

'Piven, your own father must have reached the same conclusion as Leo, and —'

'I think even my beloved mother did as well. But they've paid for their sins. Leo and I grew up together; we were close in our own strange way ... and he betrayed me by leaving me. I would never have left him. Never!'

Greven shook his head. 'And you're going to make Leo pay for being a terrified, traumatised lad who probably had little say in the matter of escape?'

'Oh yes, indeed. Leo and Loethar deserve the same fate. Loethar may have used me but at least he was honest about it. And I have to say, there were moments when Loethar really enjoyed me, I think.' Greven watched as Piven frowned, digging deep into his memories. 'He felt a sort of empathy that I can't fathom. Meanwhile my brother essentially left me to die. If Loethar had felt even a moment's threat from me he wouldn't have hesitated to put me to the sword. Leo would have known that. Still he ran from me, even knowing both our parents were dead and I had no one.'

'He was a child himself.'

'And I was five and helpless in every sense. He should have tried. If I knew he'd even tried to help me and failed, I could forgive him.'

Greven didn't know what to say. Finally he asked quietly, 'What are you going to do?'

Piven considered this. And while he was lost momentarily in his thoughts, Greven felt a pang of sorrow at losing his beautiful boy. The Valisar magic must be somehow tainted in his child. Piven had tried to use it well — he really had — but he was right: the more he'd used his powers to aid others, the darker it had made him. Greven didn't think he was lost fully to his darkness, not yet anyway, but unless Leo found an aegis of his own, the real heir to the throne was vulnerable ... as was Lily.

'The problem, of course,' Piven continued, and Greven realised he was still pondering the previous question, 'is if Leo finds himself an aegis. There's one of you for each of us.'

Greven shrugged, masking his fright and wondering if Piven could know his thoughts.

'If Leo's smart enough — and I know he is — he will likely be looking for his.'

'He may not know about the aegis.'

'But Freath did.'

'Freath? Ah, yes, the treacherous servant.'

'Not so treacherous. I remember everything about him now. I think he risked his life each day, first trying to keep my mother safe, and then making sure I was.'

'Leo told me otherwise.'

'Leo only knew half the story.' Piven smiled secretively again.

'So if Freath can find Leo, he can tell him about the aegis,' Greven said, trying to follow Piven's thoughts.

'Exactly. And since I've stolen you, that gives Leo a choice of at least three others.'

'At least three? How come?'

'Well, there's mine, his and my sister's. And my mother had several children who didn't survive, but that doesn't mean the aegis born for each isn't alive and well. Did you not know that an aegis could be trammelled by any Valisar?'

'I thought you were a lost soul — an invalid halfwit.'

Piven laughed. 'I'd surprise them all now, wouldn't I, Greven? Especially Leo and Loethar.'

'I think you intend to.'

'I'm going to turn people against both of them.' Piven smiled, got up and continued heading west. Greven had no option but to follow, for to be too far away from his bonded made him sicken.

26

Loethar had watched his mother's body burn. It had taken most of the day and had been done in the traditional Steppes manner in a remote, disused courtyard of Brighthelm. He'd ensured that his own people had built the fire so it was assembled correctly around his mother's corpse before he had dismissed everyone, including Father Briar. He had held the burning torch that would ignite the first flames of the pyre and alone he had committed her soul to the gods, with none of the usual rituals or lengthy prayers.

The castle had fallen silent. He wondered about his daughter, whether she had died during these last hours. He'd lost track of time; only the sky told him it was night. The full moon illuminated the remains of his mother. He had stood in the same position for hours and now, finally, he stretched, sighing at the creak of his bones and the tightness in his muscles. Reaching for the huge mallet, Loethar hefted it onto his shoulder before striding to the embers that had cooled only just enough to permit him to get close. He took aim and with a few determined blows he smashed up his mother's bones — everything but her skull.

Loethar retrieved a box from where he had stood for most of the day and with a small broom he scooped as much of his mother's ashes as he could into the box before sealing it tightly. Lifting her skull, he placed it into a sack he had also reserved for this purpose. The skull would need to be prepared properly: cleaned of all flesh, baked in the sun and then returned to the Steppes to be placed amongst the ridges and caves of the region of Dara Negev's birth. She would share eternity with her forebears; he would do this much for her. Negev might well have married the right man to claim her legal position but somehow Loethar felt sure that if women were permitted to fight for supremacy and leadership in the same way, then his mother would have claimed rulership of the tribes. She had been a forbidding woman all of her life and he imagined had she not been beautiful in her early years, no man would have taken her on.

He heard footsteps behind him, and turned to see Father Briar. 'I have kept a vigil for your mother in the chapel through the night,' the priest said.

'That was not necessary, Father Briar. She is not a believer of Lo.'

'But I am, my lord, and this is how we pray for the souls we farewell.'

Loethar nodded. 'I'm touched by your compassion. Thank you.' He sighed. 'An era died with her.'

'You have created a new era, my lord.'

'Is it the right one?'

Father Briar blinked. 'Do you doubt it?'

Loethar shook his head. 'I felt it was important ten anni ago. But sometimes now I wonder.'

'About what?'

'Whether we couldn't have achieved the same result without so much bloodshed. But, then again, I am reminded of my rage.'

Father Briar didn't understand him, but Loethar didn't intend for him to.

'What will you do with Dara Negev's ashes, my lord?' the priest asked. 'Can I —'

'I shall take them to my half-brother. He and I will scatter them to the four winds, as is the custom.'

'Very good. Is there anything else I can do for you?'

'Yes, Father Briar. You can tell my wife not to wait for me.'

Briar looked uncomfortable. 'Your daughter succumbed, my lord.'

'I knew she would. Have her body entombed in the chapel.'

Briar looked shocked. 'With the Valisars?'

'Yes. You may also conduct a Set ceremony for her funeral according to my wife's wishes. There will be no need to include any Steppes formalities for her.'

'As you wish, my lord,' Briar murmured. 'What shall I tell the empress about your departure?'

'Nothing. Just tell her I've gone to find General Stracker. And that I suggest, when she's well enough, she make her way to the convent in the northeast. She'll know which one. She has been there before.'

'Convent, my lord?'

'Tell the empress if I should see her again I will kill her. And that only my mourning is preventing me from doing so now.'

'My ... my lord. I don't understand.'

'You don't need to. But she will. You might care to mention that while she has spies, I have suspicions. I cannot prove them so I cannot deal with her as I would like, but I am giving her an opportunity to escape my wrath. Tell her she is to leave as soon as she can sit a horse and she is to go to the convent directly, or I will hunt her down.'

Father Briar looked deeply shaken.

Loethar moved. 'I am heading north. Alone. Tell no one, Briar, or your head will roll as well.'

Stracker barged in unannounced. It was early morning and the household was only just stirring. Fortunately Vulpan was an early riser and had been awake and dressed well before dawn. He had been unable to sleep peacefully, the taste of the pastor's blood lingering in his mind as much as his mouth. He knew the man was lying but he was good at it and Vulpan wanted to know what the pastor — if he was one — was hiding.

Although, unlike Shorgan, he could not gauge the power

available to a Vested, his refined skills could sort between bloods and taste differences. He had tasted blood like the priest's only once before. It wasn't recent but it was also not so long ago that he couldn't recall the taste with clarity. He couldn't recall the person precisely yet, but he knew she had been a woman … the taste of the blood told him that much. She had also been Vested, endowed with an immensely strong power, according to Shorgan. Vulpan racked his mind for details but he couldn't remember. He would know her, of course, if she crossed his path. He was just thinking he would need to mention it to Stracker when he heard the telltale sound of the general's booming voice.

He stepped out from his private chambers and walked down the stairs. 'General Stracker. How good to see you,' he lied. 'Welcome back to Woodingdene.'

'Vulpan,' Stracker said, nodding, Without preamble he baldly continued, 'We have orders. We leave immediately.'

'To where, general?' Vulpan asked, surprised, arriving at the penultimate stair and stopping to avoid being completely dwarfed by the huge man.

'North.'

Vulpan frowned. 'But we'll get there. I haven't finished in the midlands yet. I thought —'

'New orders, Vulpan. Don't question them.'

Vulpan nodded an apology. 'Of course, general. Can I offer you some refreshment?'

'We're waiting for fresh horses so I will take some ale and perhaps your cook can rustle up some food for my men.'

'I shall organise it immediately. Please go into the front salon.' Vulpan gestured towards the room before calling orders to a nearby servant. He followed the general into the elegant room. 'I have some intriguing news, too.'

'Where is Shorgan?'

Vulpan blinked, disguising his irritation at being ignored. 'Still sleeping, I imagine. Dawn is a while off.' He glanced out the window at the softly lightening sky. 'He rarely arises before the cockerels begin to call.'

'So, you've listed the Vested we sent here?'

'All of them.'

'Good. Where are they now?'

'They've been taken to the Dragonsback Mountains as ordered.'

'Excellent. Now, you said you had news. What else did you have to report?'

'A married couple was brought here. They were on their way to Brighthelm. Both Vested. I have listed them.'

The general looked understandably unimpressed. 'Did you send them with the others?'

'No, general, I did not.'

Stracker raised an eyebrow. 'We have strict guidelines.'

'I realise this, but–'

'But nothing! You take your orders from me. You do not make your own decisions that contravene those orders.'

'No, general. But in this instance the man in question was in the direct employ of the emperor. Forgive me if I have made an error in judgement, but I presumed the emperor's wishes were of the utmost importance.'

Stracker stared, frowning at Vulpan as though he were simple. Before he could respond there was a knock at the door and two servants arrived, bearing food and drink.

'Set it down there for the general,' Vulpan directed. 'And then leave us.'

Once the door had closed again behind the men, Stracker exploded. 'Who was this man?'

'He used the name Kirin Felt.'

'Felt? Aha, and so he turns up!' Stracker said gleefully, his wrath evaporating.

'So you do know of him?'

'Yes, he does work at the palace. He is a declared Vested and works alongside a man called Freath, an aide to the emperor.

Freath was a slippery character I never trusted. I don't trust Felt either but he's quiet, avoids attracting interest.'

Vulpan nodded. 'Then I'm glad I trusted my instincts and let him return. I would not have wanted to risk the anger of the emperor in holding up his own staff.'

'Except that very man is now wanted by the emperor. We have reason to believe he is connected with the death of the aide.'

'What? No! He did not strike me as a man on the run. He was on his way with a merchant caravan back into Penraven city, to Brighthelm.'

'He didn't seem nervous, agitated?'

Vulpan shook his head. 'Unhappy at being brought here, of course, but otherwise he was keen to oblige. He and his wife both —'

Stracker had been picking at the savoury pastries but he spun around now, the food halfway to his mouth, his face full of query. 'Wife?' he asked, puzzled. 'He's not married.'

Vulpan felt the stirrings of fury. 'Kirin and Lily Felt. They were travelling from Francham to Brighthelm and we intercepted them during the night.'

'He is *not* married, I tell you. He's lived at the palace for the past decade. I don't believe he's left the city once in that time. This was the first occasion he'd travelled beyond the city walls.'

Vulpan inwardly fumed, unsure of who was lying. Stracker had no reason to. That much was certain. 'Well, we shall see. I have her brother under lock right here. Eat your food, general, I'll be back shortly with an interesting person for you to meet, someone I definitely do not trust.'

Leo and Jewd had shared the vigil through the night, keeping watch on the house into which Kilt had disappeared the previous day. Leo had taken the early morning watch while Jewd grabbed a few hours' sleep, but now the big man was back at his side.

'Here, loaves were just coming out of the ovens. I grabbed you one. Cheese too.'

Leo's eyes widened with pleasure. 'Thanks. I'm famished.'

Jewd gave a nod of understanding. 'Did you see anything?'

Leo shook his head as he bit into the small warm loaf. 'All quiet but he's definitely a prisoner, Jewd. Otherwise he wouldn't remain in a place like this. He's too vulnerable there.'

'Kilt wouldn't even stay at an inn if he didn't have to. He definitely wouldn't linger in a private house, especially the one being used by Vulpan.'

'I wish we knew more about him.'

'We know he's dangerous.'

'But he's no threat to Kilt. He's not interested in him, surely?'

'I wouldn't think so but my gut tells me something's wrong. He shouldn't still be there.'

They were sitting on the porch of a small dincherie that was open all hours and was conveniently opposite the house under scrutiny. As Leo sighed at Jewd's comment, and reached to refresh his mug of dinch, riders galloped into the relative silence of pre-dawn.

'Lo's bollocks'! Jewd exclaimed. 'They're going in.'

Leo blinked and stared, feeling his emotions wrenched back a decade. 'Jewd, that's Stracker.'

Jewd dragged his gaze from the house to his companion. 'Are you sure?'

'He is unmistakeable. Look at him. Do you think that's a man I'd forget?'

Jewd shook his head. 'I've always wondered what he looked like. He's as big as I am.'

'And far more ruthless, I can assure you. He hasn't got a single bone of empathy in his body.'

'We've got to get Kilt out of there.'

'What can we do?'

'For now we watch. If they're genuinely imprisoning him, they'll move him from the house, which is not an ideal gaol. When they move him, we have to act.'

'Us against all those guards?'

'I've come prepared.'

'For what?'

'A diversion,' Jewd replied cryptically. 'Keep watching,' he growled, 'I'm going to get our horses.'

Kilt was led out of the room he'd been locked into by a new set of guards. He was dishevelled and hungry but, more pressingly, disrupted by lack of sleep and the anxiety that with each slow passing hour Lily moved further from him. He was slightly comforted by the knowledge that she was travelling with Felt but confused about why she was pretending to be his wife. Something must have scared her, forced her into the disguise. He had to find her and apologise for asking her to play a role that should have been given to one of his men.

The guard banged on the door to Vulpan's salon. 'Come in!' Vulpan called and Kilt was marched in to be confronted by a powerful man proudly bearing his tatua with a warrior-like air.

'Pastor Jeves, may I introduce our revered General Stracker.'

Stracker! Kilt had to hide his natural inclination to baulk. 'General Stracker,' he said, bowing his head, glad to hear his voice was steady, 'I'm honoured.'

'Why?' the general snapped.

Good question. 'Your reputation precedes you, general. Why, only a few moons ago my village greeted you. In fact, you stayed overnight during our Harvest Festival.' Kilt remembered hearing on the tall grasses of Stracker's visit south. Word had bubbled up to the north that he acted every inch a royal, expecting hospitality without payment for him and his men.

Stracker grunted. 'So why has Vulpan got you trapped in his web, eh?'

Kilt adopted an air of innocence. 'I'm waiting to hear all about it myself, general. We shall have to ask him; I can't fathom why I've been detained. Has he told you I'm trying to find my sister, sir?'

'He has. And we're certainly interested to catch up with her too.'

Kilt's stomach clenched. 'Why's that?' He frowned, looking perplexed.

The general picked at the debris of what looked to be the remains of a breakfast. He threw a fig into his cavernous mouth, chewing while he spoke. 'Well, firstly, she's apparently married to a man we're looking for.'

'I see.'

'How long have they been married?'

Kilt shrugged. 'I don't know, actually. I learned of her marriage only recently and I have no idea when it occurred. I've never met the man. Perhaps Master Vulpan explained my situation —?'

'He did. You see, the intriguing part of all of this, pastor, is that Master Felt, to my knowledge, was not married. He has been living at the palace for the past decade and I know this because I captured him originally. He is Vested.'

Kilt's stomach did a flip. 'Really? I had no idea,' he lied calmly.

'Yes, Vested and working indirectly for the emperor.'

Kilt feigned being impressed. 'I'm most upset she's told her family none of this. But I still don't understand why.'

'We're hunting her husband in connection with a possible murder.'

'I told Master Vulpan that's ridiculous.'

'How would you know if you haven't seen your sister in many anni and don't even know who her husband is?'

He was right. Kilt had to talk quickly. 'It's just too unbelievable,' he blustered, 'but irrespective of what he may or may not have done, why am I being held against my will?'

'Ah, well, that's another story. You are Vested, yes?'

Kilt nodded, unsure of this path. 'Nothing spectacular, I can assure you.'

'What is it you can do, Pastor Jeves?'

'A helpful but rather tedious skill of being able to gauge weather. I can tell you when the rains are coming, for instance.'

'My knees can tell me that, pastor.'

Kilt forced a smile as he shrugged. 'I rest my case, general. My skill is dull, irrelevant and practically pointless … unless you're a farmer.'

'Except Shorgan assures me that you possess very potent power,' Vulpan chipped in.

Kilt laughed. 'Then I'd like to see proof of it. What is it that I'm supposed to be able to do?'

Vulpan shook his head. 'That's just it. We don't know. But we intend to find out,' the general added. 'You can come with us to the north.'

'North?'

'Francham,' Stracker added. 'Then we'll be sending you on to a special place in the Dragonsback Mountains.'

'Wait! Absolutely not! I am going in search of my sister.'

'We'll find her,' Stracker said with a tight, sinister smile. 'I hear she's pretty. The men will enjoy escorting her back to Brighthelm, where Vulpan suspects the emperor would like to know of her talents.'

Kilt ignored Stracker's threat. 'Why Francham?' he asked, knowing he was a dead man if they escorted him there.

'That's where we believe a man called Master Freath was murdered. Your sister's husband knows something, if not about his murder, then certainly his movements. We know they ate together on the evening of his death.'

'But this has nothing to do with me!'

'I didn't say it did,' Stracker said, leaning close to Kilt's face. 'But your magic does and we want to know what that part of you is all about. Don't fret, we'll certainly reunite you with your sister soon enough.' He looked at Vulpan. 'We leave at light's break. Get organised.'

27

Gavriel sat beside the stream and stared at the silent Elka. They had ridden for what was left of the day and finally they had stopped to water the horses. He had talked for the entire journey, a torrent of information spilling from his memories.

The pause felt brittle and filled with hurt. 'Talk to me, Elka, say something.'

'What can I say?' she said mournfully, not looking at him. 'You're a noble. Attached to royalty. Our lives feel suddenly so far apart.' Gavriel gave a pained expression. 'You were escorting the young king when I interfered, for Lo's sake!'

'If you hadn't, I'd probably have died.'

She shook her head. 'They would have killed you long before if that had been their intention.'

'Then Loethar would have killed me. Freath would have told him who I was and then ...' He made a slashing sign across his throat.

'So why go back now? Why risk it?'

'Surely you don't have to ask me that?'

'How do you know he's even alive?'

'Because he was with Kilt Faris. Leo will now be twenty-two anni.' Gavriel shook his head. 'How incredible. He's a man; probably drinks Rough and enjoys a tumble with a girl.'

Elka regarded him. 'You sound envious.'

His gaze snapped up. 'Do I?' At her nod, he explained, 'I don't mean to but … well, what's past is past.'

'I think now that you know what you've missed, you want it back … your old life, I mean.'

Gavriel shook his head. 'I haven't had enough time since learning who I truly am to think about what I've missed. And the life I was living when you found me was one filled with trauma and danger. There was nothing enviable about it; nothing about it that I'd want to return to. But it's the people who matter, Elka. I have a brother, my twin. And he disappeared. I'm going to find him. And I'm going to find Leo.'

'And help him claim the throne?'

'Whatever makes you say that? Ten anni ago all I was doing was following my king's orders and protecting the heir, who became sovereign during that time. When I was injured, King Brennus had only been dead for days. A decade on, Loethar has carved out his empire. The Valisars are a memory now.'

Her gaze narrowed. 'I don't think you truly believe that.'

He shrugged. 'Believe what you want.'

'I believe that all you've learned today has re-ignited you. You even sound different, Regor, you —'

'My father's name was Regor. I suppose in my confused state the name came to me. But my name is Gavriel. I would be known by that name from now on.'

She nodded and he could see grief in her face. 'So, where does this leave us?'

'Us?'

'You are part of my family.'

He considered taking her hand but thought better of it. 'I will miss them all more than you can imagine.'

'I see,' she said, her resigned expression telling him he didn't need to say more. She found a small smile and stood. 'I've always said I prefer travelling at night. I might be on my way, then.'

'Elka, wait!' he said, getting to his feet. 'Don't rush away.'

'Gavriel,' she began, her mouth twisting into a rueful grimace. 'That name sounds strange,' she admitted. 'And you are a stranger to me now. It's best I return to the mountains. Perhaps you'll visit.' She moved to her horse. 'Come on, see me away. Let's not drag this out.'

'Why do you have to go?'

'Because you do. And I don't belong where you're going. Our paths crossed accidentally and the Abbess is right, I must let you return to your people and your life.'

'I'm not returning to anything. Everyone's gone. But I have to try and find Corbel, find Leo, make some sense of what occurred, find some peace. Will you ride with me a few more days?'

'What's the point?'

'Because we're friends,' he said quietly. At her wince, he moved towards her and was surprised when he hugged her; was even more surprised that she let him. 'Elka, I do wish I could look you in the eye as I do this,' he admitted with exasperation.

She impressed him by laughing but he could hear her sorrow. She pushed him away and he understood. 'I just want you to know that I love you, you're my best friend, you're my hero and my protector — and not just because you're so much bigger than me,' he said. She laughed again, tears misting briefly in her eyes. He continued, 'That will never change. We will always be best friends. Love of the romantic kind can be fickle; love of the friendship kind rarely is.'

She wiped the tears from her eyes and punched him lightly. As he staggered backwards, she asked, 'When did you become a philosopher?'

Gavriel was grimacing, breathing out. 'Oof! That hurt!'

'Pathetic,' she sneered, not unkindly.

He was relieved and glad that the emotion she had permitted him to glimpse in its rawness was now smothered again, and her strength — the aspect of her he admired so much — was back in control. 'Stay a while longer,' he begged. 'We'll part tomorow, or another morning. It will be so much easier.'

'Why?'

'Because your breath is bad in the morning,' he quipped, raising his hands in defence when he saw her make a fist. 'I jest, I promise. Your breath is in fact like the fresh dew of the morning.'

'Not that you would know!' she parried back. 'Fresh dew of the morning? My arse.' She pushed him gently and once again he staggered.

'You've got to stop manhandling me, my sweet. I'm no match for you. Stay, Elka. One night. We'll talk about all the good times and part in good spirits.'

She didn't look convinced but she sighed and nodded. 'I hope you plan to cook me something.'

'Rabbit coming right up, my lady,' he said, bowing. 'Just let me get my bow.'

'Get on with it, then. I'll build a fire.'

He gave her a soft smile and winked. 'Thanks, Elka.'

'Hurry up!' she said, trying to snarl. 'I'm famished.'

'And when you say you could eat a horse, I think you really could,' he said, just managing to dodge the small branch she hurled at him.

Loethar had said farewell to no one. There was no one, after all, to care about. His daughter had died, as predicted by the physic, and he had not even seen her. Valya had sent so many messages since the birth that he had stopped admitting the messengers, flicking his hand irritably at them and sending them away before a word was exchanged.

Valya had murdered his mother. He didn't need proof. His instincts told him enough.

And now he was fulfilling the final act that was expected of him as a member of his family. He had already changed horses twice. He would be at Woodingdene by mid-morning if he kept this pace up.

343

He dug his heels into the horse to urge it faster. He had stolen out of the palace in the dead of night, not even waking the stablehands when he'd led the nearest horse out of its stall. With only the help of Roland, now his conspirator, he had disguised himself and left anonymously through one of the side gates, just another of the many visitors and dignatories making his weary exit. Roland had kept the sleepy guards in conversation; had almost half-heartedly waved goodbye to the bearded Master Frank, whose large hat and cape covered his identity further. Before he knew it, Loethar had slipped the castle perimeter and was moving through the city streets, the mourning bells sounding for his mother.

He didn't care that it would appear strange that he would not be present in the city to take the inevitable flow of commiserations. Perhaps the death of his daughter would suggest to many that the family did not want to be seen publicly. That excuse was fine with him. Once he had cleared the city's perimeter he had hit a gallop that he had maintained since.

What would he say to Stracker? Stracker would want to kill Valya with his bare hands, and there was nothing to be gained from that, and, further, such an act would only enrage Droste. He needed nothing to prompt unrest just now. Banishing Valya to the convent had been the safest response, and he hoped Valya had taken his advice and fled as fast as she could. Once their initial grief was shared and done with, Loethar knew the tenuous relationship he had with Stracker would change irrevocably. His mother had warned as much. *As long as I'm alive*, she had counselled. Now she was dead. He should heed her advice.

Deep inside, Loethar knew it was madness to be out and alone and so vulnerable like this. Stracker might take this opportunity to end his half-brother's life. Loethar could beat Stracker in hand-to-hand combat, he was sure, but Stracker rarely travelled alone. Even if the tribes stayed loyal to their figurehead ruler, Stracker would have his Greens and enough angry men in that clan to do his bidding.

Frowning, Loethar ignored the voices of warning. He had to do this to fulfil his code of honour. Stracker was currently travelling alone. Perhaps he could get through these formalities and then escape, riding swiftly back to the Brighthelm stronghold before Stracker's slower mind began to consider overthrow. And when it did, he could confront Stracker on his own terms. Now that their mother was dead, Loethar would have little compunction about killing his half-brother if he was forced to.

'We shall see,' he said into the wind. 'Hah!' he bellowed, urging the horse still faster. Dawn was approaching.

They had watched with anguish as Stracker had re-emerged, this time with Vulpan, a strange-looking man with vicious purple-coloured tatua, and Kilt, flanked by several guards.

'Oh, Lo, you're right. They're taking him somewhere, Jewd. He hasn't been able to talk himself out of it.'

'Be still, Leo. If they wanted to execute him, he'd already be dead. They're obviously still interested enough in him that they're taking him with them. Let's follow them. I need to get an idea of where they're headed and I need some time to think.'

'Where do you imagine they'll go?'

'My gut tells me Francham. I don't think Stracker's sudden arrival is coincidence. I think he's here because of Freath.'

'But Kilt —'

'Kilt's presence here *is* coincidence, and bad timing on his part. He's being haplessly caught up in something and we just have to pray that Stracker doesn't make any connection between him and Freath.'

'But what if he already knows?'

'He can't.'

'How can you be so sure?' Leo demanded, slamming down his near empty mug of dinch.

'Easy, Leo. We don't want any attention. If you recognise Stracker, I can't be sure he won't recognise you.'

'I assure you, he won't.'

'Even so, be still until they've gone.'

'How can you be sure he doesn't know about Freath?' Leo repeated.

Jewd sighed and drained his mug. 'Because if they'd seen through his disguise, he would be looking a lot less like a pastor than he still does. I don't think they've put him together with Freath. But I do think they want him and that's what's got me baffled.'

'How are we going to get him away from ...' Leo took a moment, squinting. 'From seven men?'

'Only Stracker and his four guards matter. Vulpan and the Wikken couldn't swing a sword if their lives depended on it. So we're two against five. I like those odds. And they get better if we can somehow get a sword into Kilt's hands. Fortunately, he's not bound. They're still treating him with a small amount of respect — which is another reason I don't think they've made any connection between him and Freath, or even who Kilt really is.'

'But they will.'

'We'll have him by then,' Jewd said but Leo heard the note of false bravado in his voice.

'Saddle up,' the big man said. 'Remember all the training on how to track silently?'

Leo nodded. 'Once we know the road they're taking, we'll use the surrounding woodland as cover, bind the horses' hooves and tie swords and bows, anything that rattles,' he said dutifully.

Jewd nodded. 'We taught you well, my king. Let's go. Keep it casual, don't watch them. We're just two travellers finishing our dinch and setting out again.'

Leo drained his mug as Jewd had and made a show of standing, stretching and yawning before following his companion to where the horses were tied up. He didn't want to admit it to Jewd but he was feeling excited. The notion that he might finally be able to sink an arrow into Stracker's chest was irresistible enough to make him smile inwardly.

28

Greven could taste the salt on his lips. The coast was close now. They had been walking non-stop, but he needed no sustenance or rest. And he would remain in this state of non-life until Piven died … and Piven was a young man.

'I feel you drawing it,' Greven said into the long silence that had stretched since leaving Tomlyn.

'I don't have your seemingly-immortal status. Did you think I would be capable of walking without rest for days on end?' Piven snapped.

'No, nor did I ask you to.'

'How does it feel?' Piven asked, clearly intrigued.

'I suppose a bit like I'm bleeding. I can't think of a more appropriate way to describe it.'

'Does it hurt?'

'It's not comfortable, if that's what you mean.'

'And is your power limitless?'

'I have no idea. I don't care.'

Piven remained quiet for a moment. Greven couldn't tell whether he was considering Greven's attitude or working out how to insist he make all of his power accessible to him. He didn't care either way.

'We're nearly there,' Piven announced. 'Or so Vyk tells me.'

'Where?'

'He wants us to meet someone.'

'Why?' Sergius asked.

Ravan hopped, irritated. *I thought you'd like to see Piven and I also thought you'd like to meet an aegis.*

'But here? Ravan, this is dangerous. Who am I to them?'

You are someone who can answer questions.

'But that's —'

Piven deserves to talk to someone who knows something about this strange life of his. I know you know more than you have told me. I think you're as bad as the Valisars you watch over with your secret-keeping. But I am worried about Piven. He escaped his prison of madness only to be plunged into a new sort of madness. I think it is claiming him, Sergius.

'I cannot help him.'

Perhaps not. But you can explain things to him.

'I know so little —'

I think you're underestimating what you know — either that or you're lying. And I deserve better than lies. You will meet Piven and you will tell him what he needs to know ... and you will be honest.

'Or what?' the old man asked, dismayed.

It's not a threat. I am no warrior, I have no weapons and I cannot punish you in any way but this: I promise you that if you are not true with him I will leave you and I will never return. I will no longer be your ears and eyes. I will forget I ever knew you. You have used me and I can forgive that, but I will not forgive you if you do not give Piven this chance to understand himself. He is so young and there was always so much goodness in him.

'But, Ravan, you yourself said he's turning bad.'

I don't really understand what's happening. The point is, neither does he. He needs a guide.

Sergius shook his head. 'I will answer his questions as best I can.'

Sergius was being typically evasive, Ravan realised. He felt disappointment spike through him, but he had no intention of letting Sergius avoid this meeting. He allowed his mind to reach out to the youngster, and sensed that Piven was calm, almost happy.

Piven felt his touch. *Vyk. Hello. We can smell the sea.*

Then you are almost here. I shall come now. Re-opening the seam to Sergius, he alerted the old man.

Sergius looked deeply unhappy but he said nothing, grabbing only a cloak and his staff, and mumbling about not wanting to climb the cliff steps again. Ravan ignored him, swooping ahead to fly high, hoping to catch sight of the approaching pair. He picked them out with ease, the forest as a backdrop to their arrival, the sea facing them. Piven looked glad to be alive but he could see Greven wore the expression of a condemned man.

Piven saw him first and waved, his face breaking into that beautiful smile of his. Ravan wondered how long it would last. How much more time did Piven have? He hoped Sergius would provide some enlightenment.

Jewd's gaze narrowed. 'Well, if they follow the road, I reckon they're headed to Francham. If they turn off it at Four Points, then your guess is as good as mine.'

They had already entered the sparse woodland and were using it as a hiding place from which to watch the small party of riders. They held their breath and waited, both holding their horses' reins close to the beasts' chins, their hands each cupping the muzzles. Not even a shake of the animals' heads or a whinny could alert Stracker to their presence.

'Here we go,' Leo breathed, watching anxiously.

Both men were silent, the horses were silent and it seemed even the birds had stopped their chittering. In the near-distance they could hear the men's quiet talk. Kilt was wordless, looking down. Stracker led.

'I could take him, Jewd,' Leo whispered, pointing at his bow.

'And they'll be on us in moments. Be patient, lad.'

Leo sighed inwardly. It would give him enormous satisfaction to end Stracker's life. He didn't know when he'd become so ghoulish, or so capable of violence, but even now, though he was still openly ashamed of his decision regarding Freath, privately he praised himself. He knew his father would have been proud of him — not of the consequences of his actions, of course — but he could imagine his father nodding his head in ackowledgement that Leo had made an oath and seen it through.

'It's Francham,' Jewd murmured.

'So what do we do now?'

'We're heading up as far as we can and then we're on foot, dragging the horses behind us. We'll need them tethered and ready to flee. We'll go across the woods while they take the longer route on road. Come on.'

'But what are we actually going to do?'

Jewd grinned tightly, mirthlessly. 'Ambush,' he replied. 'It's our only chance.'

Loethar arrived into Woodingdene not long after dawn. He was weary and he was glad the town was relatively quiet, yet to fully wake. He could smell food on the wind as people's morning fires were stoked, and oats being cooked and bread being baked. His belly rumbled in answer but he ignored it. He walked the equally tired horse up to the gates of the old mayor's residence.

'Stop,' a guard said. 'State your name and business.'

Loethar knew his expression was one of bemusement. Had he really changed so much? This was a relatively young soldier, though, proudly bearing the blue tatua. Perhaps he'd never seen his ruler.

He slid off the horse and handed the young man the reins. 'I am your emperor, boy. Where is General Stracker?'

The guard looked astonished, his expression coalescing into fright as his mouth opened and closed twice. It was obvious that he couldn't be sure of what was best to do, torn between following his orders but also not wishing to risk his emperor's wrath. Words failed him.

Loethar sighed. 'Find your superior and be quick about it!'

The young guard yelled for his captain over his shoulder and Loethar was impressed that he hadn't turned tail to run and find someone. The young guard, finding his voice, apologised. 'Forgive me, my lord, I shall have to ask you to wait here. May I take your horse, though?'

'What is your name?'

'Darly, my lord.'

'I know I frighten you, Darly, and that's a good thing. But even better is your composure. I shall mention you to the head of the Blues.'

The younger man bowed his head slightly, trying not to beam. 'Thank you, my lord. Forgive us for keeping you waiting. I can tell you, though, that General Stracker is not here.'

Loethar frowned. 'Not here?'

Darly shook his head. 'He left at first light, my lord.'

'Headed where?'

'Er, perhaps you should talk to Captain Ison.'

As if on cue, an older man approached, a senior member of the Greens, and Loethar saw the flare of recognition just a blink before the man halted and dropped a low bow. 'Emperor Loethar, forgive us for not being ready to —'

'Captain Ison. It is no one's fault but my own for arriving unannounced.' He could see Darly was even more surprised to have confirmation of his status and he was privately amused to realise that the youngster, despite his gracious approach, hadn't really trusted him. Good. 'I'm here on urgent business with General Stracker but Darly here tells me I've missed him.'

'He rode out at dawn, my lord, for Francham. He took Master Vulpan, Shorgan, three of our men and a stranger who arrived in town yesterday.'

Loethar frowned. 'Who is this stranger?'

Ison gave an expression of apology. 'He was a priest. I'm sorry but I don't know anything more about him. I don't think he wanted to spend the night here, my lord, but Master Vulpan detained him.'

'Is he Vested?'

'Most likely, my lord, although I don't know for sure. Can we offer some —'

'No, I must reach my brother quickly. I'll need a fresh horse, and perhaps some food in a small sack.'

'Come, my lord, I will organise both. Darly, remain at your post.'

Darly bowed. 'Emperor,' he murmured as Loethar walked by him.

A fresh horse, food, a long draught from the well and a chance to refresh his face from a pail of water and Loethar was on his way again, his hair still dripping from the dousing. His clothes remained dusty and he knew he looked dishevelled but that had never troubled him; his tidy appearance was reserved for his palace. Suddenly he felt free again.

With a sense of anticipation, not dissimilar to how he had felt when he'd first set out with his marauding army towards the Denovian Set ten anni previous, he spurred his horse into a gallop towards the inevitable confrontation with his half-brother.

'This must be who he wants us to meet,' Piven said, and Greven was obliged to catch up with him. He immediately strengthened the power surrounding Piven, even though his heart desperately wanted to let it drain completely. 'I feel your despair, Greven. Stop fighting me. There is nothing you can do. Remember all the talk of love and loyalty? Now's your chance to show it.'

'I want to give you both, but freely,' Greven replied.

'Well, pretend,' Piven said, raising a hand towards the man who waited for them at the cliff's edge.

The man who greeted them was old, with a narrow, lined face. He was clean-shaven but his hair was long, tied back and mostly silver. He wore simple robes, leaned on a gnarled stick, and as they drew closer Greven saw that his eyes were rheumy.

'You'll have to come closer, my sight is misty at best,' the man admitted amiably.

'Who are you?' Greven asked, when Piven said nothing.

'I'm Sergius. Welcome.'

Greven nodded. 'I'm Greven, this is Pi —'

'Piven, yes. I've heard a lot about you, young man.'

Greven turned, expecting Piven to respond, but the youth said nothing. His expression had become shadowed; in fact, all of his previous happy disposition had given way to an ominous expression. Greven realised, distressed, that he could finally feel the darkness emanating from his charge, like a tangible mass.

He swung back. He had no defence if Piven gave any orders. 'Sergius, whoever you are, Piven means to hurt you.'

He glanced at his companion. Piven didn't seem troubled by either the admission or the seeming betrayal. And why would he be, Greven thought bitterly, hating the power simmering and awakened within himself, ready to be commanded by the youth.

Sergius looked appropriately taken aback. 'Hurt me? Why? He doesn't even know me.'

'I know you,' Piven answered for himself. 'You are a man of old magic. I feel it, I see it, I smell it, I think I can all but taste it, and it's raging around you. And there I was, concerning my thoughts with my brother, when my true enemy awaited me here.'

Enemy? Vyk spoke into their minds, echoing Greven's own question.

Piven ignored the query. He pointed at Sergius. 'You lie, you manipulate, you use people.' He stabbed his finger again. 'You have used Vyk. That's not even his name, is it? Old man, I can see straight into you. I can hear your fear rattling around your ancient mind. How long have you walked this land?'

Vyk again broke into their minds. *What are you talking about, Piven? Sergius is no threat to you. He is a friend.*

He is no friend to me! He is a liar. He means to hurt me if I don't deal with him.

353

Greven, Vyk said anxiously. *What is happening?*

Who can say what he's thinking anymore? You've brought this upon yourself, bird. You should never have led him here.

Don't talk as though I can't hear, Piven admonished them conversationally. *Ask me, don't ask Greven.*

Vyk hopped over to Piven. *Sergius has been my friend for a long time. As you can gather, I am no ordinary raven. I have lived a long life.*

You are my friend. I believe you are true to me. But he can never be my friend. He supports my enemies.

What? Piven, you do not know what you say.

Don't I? He can shield some but not all of his thoughts from me. He hasn't grasped that my magic is so tainted, it is beyond the bounds of control.

'What is happening?' Sergius asked, looking between them all, suddenly realising they were talking amongst themselves.

Piven snapped the link to Vyk and to Greven, turning to talk aloud to Sergius. 'I was just explaining to Vyk that you are my enemy.'

Sergius blanched. 'Enemy?' He repeated the word as though he did not understand its concept. 'But why do you say that, child? I —'

'I was telling Vyk that my magic does not follow the rules you are used to. It has no constraint, other than the limitations I put on myself.' Piven suddenly balled his fists. 'I was a good person! I wanted to use this magic to help, not destroy.'

Sergius looked around. Vyk could do nothing and it was obvious that Greven could not interfere. Greven looked up from the ground where he had been staring.

'I cannot help you,' he explained to Sergius. 'I cannot defy him. I'm sure you understand that now,' he offered sadly. 'I am sorry for this.'

Sergius looked worriedly towards Piven, who was glaring at him. 'What have I done to wrong you?'

Piven stared. 'Sit!' he commanded.

Sergius struggled down, and Piven also lowered himself to the ground. Vyk swooped over him. *Will you tell me what you fear? I will lay those fears to rest.*

I fear nothing.

Then why are you showing such aggression towards Sergius? He is an old man. I can explain everything you want to know …

Piven's eyes snapped over to the bird. *No, Vyk, you can't. He has kept secrets from you. Listen and learn.* He returned his attention to Sergius.

'Tell me about the serpent.'

The old man flinched, shaking his head slightly as if he didn't understand what was being asked.

'Do not play games. I see a serpent in your mind. You are calling to it now, pleading with it for help. Who is this serpent?'

'Cyrena,' Sergius replied, his voice thick with resignation. 'A goddess. She watches over the Valisars.'

'And what is she to you?'

'My mistress. She created me … and Ravan.'

'Ravan? That's your real name,' Piven declared, glancing over at the bird. 'It suits you.' He looked again at Sergius. 'Tell me his purpose.'

'Simply to watch. Originally he was given to Loethar. More recently he has kept an eye on all the happenings surrounding the Valisars.'

'He is a spy.'

'You could call him that. But I notice he has a genuine attachment to you.'

Piven nodded. 'I have looked into the bird's heart. He is honest in his friendships, unlike you.'

'What do you mean?'

'He is your friend, is he not?'

Sergius nodded. 'For decades we have been inseparable.'

'That does not answer my question. Ravan thinks you are his friend. Are you?'

'Of course!'

'Then tell him.'

'Tell him? What?'

Piven smiled. 'You are shielding well, Sergius. I'm impressed. But you cannot hide my sister from me. Tell your great friend of decades what you have hidden from him.'

The raven hopped up to Sergius. *Sister? What is he talking about, Sergius? He is mad, Ravan. We were right all along. The magic is eating away at what little sense he has left.*

No, that's the problem, Piven intervened, making Sergius flinch with shock. *Did you believe I couldn't hear you? Sergius, privacy is no longer yours. I am far from mad. The madness of my childhood has deserted me and left me with a brutal sanity that is dark at its heart and wants revenge. It will not be sated by placations. It demands action. I will bring down all the Valisars ... all of them!* he repeated, tittering.

'Your sister has done nothing to you,' Sergius railed, raising his bony hand, extending a finger of accusation.

'Oh, but she will if you have any say in it. Tell Ravan, Sergius. Tell him about my sister.'

29

Leo and Jewd were on opposite sides of the road. Leo watched Jewd working rapidly, tying a near invisible line across two trees that flanked the road.

'That's not going to achieve much.'

'It will when they're galloping, trust me,' Jewd murmured. 'How much time have we got?'

'I can't see them yet,' Leo replied, rising in the saddle to stare down the slight gradient in the road. 'But you know we've only won ourselves minutes.'

'Nearly there. Now, the best bit,' Jewd said, winking. He ran further down the road. Leo followed at his side. He'd never seen the trick that the outlaw band called witchflame. Kilt had once explained that they rarely used it, saving it only for times of extreme emergency. *When one of our own is in trouble*, he had counselled Leo when the king had first stumbled upon the stash of tiny blue paper packets, each formed into a small pyramid.

Jewd seemed to sense that Leo needed an explanation. He gave it as he worked. 'We got these from our travels through the northernmost part of Cremond. Kilt and I were returning from a trip to Skardlag. We were still young, you know, and far too reckless for our own good. We came upon an old woman accused of poisoning the local livestock. The people were desperate. Their cattle and sheep were dying daily. They blamed this woman, Meg, because someone had seen her walking through a flock of sheep, and he claimed that three of them fell over and died in her wake. Meg looked like Kilt's dear old mum so he decided we would save the old girl. It was madness; two of us against a mob. The mayor was a bad sort and had already determined that Meg should hang; we sensed he had a previous grudge with her and this was his revenge. I was terrified but Kilt just marched into the throng, found the mayor and persuaded him that Meg was nothing but a harmless herbalist.'

'And they just forgot about it, just like that?'

Jewd frowned as he put his final blue packet into place. 'It was very strange. Kilt explained that it was probably the sheep's food. Strange blue flowers — a weed — had begun spreading across the north, growing at an alarming rate across the fields and paddocks. Kilt suggested they should put their efforts into helping old Meg find a way to kill the flowers and make the grasses safe again, rather than killing her and watching their animals continue to die, and beggaring themselves.'

'What happened?'

Jewd grinned. 'We watched them release Meg. Kilt had suffered the most vicious nosebleed and she offered to staunch it. That's when we discovered her amazing firepowder. She gave us a sackload of these packets in thanks for rescuing her. We never saw her again. There, we're ready.'

'How do we light these things?' Leo asked. 'There's no time to start a fire or —'

Jewd grinned. 'That's the beauty of them. Look closely at the taper. Do you see the red end?'

'Yes.'

'When I give the signal, you scratch that. You'll ignite a tiny flame that will then burn through the taper. Get out of the way as soon as you see it lit. Understand?'

'Right,' Leo said, enjoying himself immensely despite the danger of what they were about to do.

'Leo.' The king looked up, grinning, but hesitated at Jewd's serious expression. 'If anything goes wrong, you run, all right? No heroics, no settling old scores. We haven't got you this far to lose you to some lowlife warrior's blade, do you understand me? These are orders from your elder. King's rank doesn't count here.'

'I promise.' Leo glanced down the road as a flash of colour caught his eye. 'Jewd, they're coming.'

His friend gave a thumbs-up and put his finger to his lips. 'The horses are secured and hidden?' he murmured. Leo nodded. 'When it all erupts, you make those arrows sink home. I don't care if you can't get a clear shot to kill but we don't want those soldiers getting up. Remember, aim for the soldiers. The others are not fighters and less of a danger. As soon as you can, grab one of the horses. I'll get Kilt. I'll have no time for anything but picking him up. Got it?'

Again Leo nodded. Jewd looked worried but he still found a smile. 'Good luck, your majesty. Have fun with your first real chance to strike back at the empire.'

Kilt's mind was in turmoil. This was the first time since they turned outlaw that he and Jewd had not been together on a task, and he was rueing the decision not to have Jewd at least tail him. He'd been bull-headed, his thoughts so blurred with fear for Lily and his pride so wounded, that he had lost his senses. Working alone like this was madness. It was little wonder he'd found himself in this perilous situation. He had no one to blame but himself for his petulant, arrogant behaviour. He was no better than Gavriel de Vis had been long ago, when he'd stomped off away from the group in much the same mood and got himself not only injured but also imprisoned.

Kilt had privately never forgiven himself for losing the young man. In his heart he had admired de Vis for keeping his head through a situation that most well-trained men would have quailed at. Gavriel de Vis had witnessed his own father's brutal death, had lost his twin brother to who knows what, had also had to live through the ghoulish murders of his king and queen — and all the while he had been responsible for keeping a twelve-anni-old calm and safe. Kilt had never underestimated what Gavriel de Vis had done for the crown; getting the boy-king away from the palace into the relative safety of the forest and then somehow navigating him to the security of Kilt's camp was a real test of anyone's mettle, let alone a seventeen anni old. *And then you do something petulant and totally stupid*, he thought. *Over a woman!*

Kilt felt an inner voice accuse him of hypocrisy. He felt a spike of humiliation. Not only had he taken the same petulant, stupid course of de Vis, running away from those who kept him safe, but he had also done so over a woman. *The same woman!* the inner voice reminded him.

'What are you grinning at so wryly, priest?' Stracker asked, interrupting his thoughts.

'Myself.'

'Why?'

'How stupid I've been to end up here … with you.' It didn't sound like something a man of Lo might say but Kilt no longer cared. And it seemed neither did Stracker, who smiled back at him.

'Not enjoying the ride, eh?' Stracker baited.

'Not one bit of it, least of all the company.'

'Look at it this way, priest. Your mother's probably dead by now so your sister's presence is no longer essential. Plus, as you haven't seen her in anni, it wouldn't matter if she were dead too.' His green tatua moved on one side of his face as he lifted a lip in a cruel smirk.

Kilt stared at the general. 'One day I'll make you regret saying that.'

Stracker made a tutting sound. 'Threats of violence. And from a man of Lo. Shame on you, priest.'

Kilt knew Stracker had probably seen through his disguise right away, but at least the general had no idea of his true identity. The problem was, he couldn't use his advantage because none of his own men knew where he was. And on top of that, his secret was in danger of being discovered … he couldn't risk that again, not yet. He was so out of practice, too; using his gift felt clumsy and cumbersome. He never thought he would have to consider its presence again, but now, in the space of a day, he had called on it twice. Would it ever leave again?

Kilt twisted in the saddle, trying to distance himself from the still sneering general, when a sound like a thousand thunderclaps exploded on his right, blue flames erupting from the trees. The horses screamed and reared. Kilt was aware of Vulpan falling off his horse, and an arrow striking a nearby soldier in the chest. He was struggling to wrestle his horse under control when a second explosion sounded to the left and this time all the horses panicked as one. Kilt definitely saw a second guard go down, an arrow pointing out of his chest, and suddenly everything fell into place. *Jewd was here!* Lo bless his disobedient but loyal heart. And Jewd would need his horse.

Pandemonium ensued and he lost his sense of direction as the horse twisted beneath him, smoke all around them. As Kilt struggled to maintain his grip on the reins, Stracker's ugly face leered out of the smoke. He was growling something unintelligible and then he was grabbing for Kilt's reins. Kilt tried to fight him off but the general was much stronger and a far more able horseman, than he. Leaning forward, Straker slapped Kilt's horse's rump and the animal leapt forward in a freshly panicked gallop. Kilt could see Stracker in front of him as they cleared the smoke, the general dragging Kilt's horse by its reins. It was all Kilt could do to keep his seat.

'You're coming with me, priest!' Stracker howled.

Kilt could hear Vulpan's high pitched-shrieks and hoped one of the arrows would hit home, into his throat, and end the vile man's life. He could see nothing over his shoulder, bent low like this as he gripped the horse's mane. Without reins he felt helpless. He looked towards the general and was surprised to see that Stracker was suddenly no longer in front of him. And then he too was falling.

Leo's heart was hammering but he was proud that although internally he was churning, his arms and legs still obeyed him calmly. Jewd's witchflame had been ignited first and Leo had counted dutifully to twenty before he ignited his own. Without pausing to watch its effects, he had emerged from behind the large tree and loosed his arrows with calm efficiency. The smoke had hampered his aim but he knew one guard had taken a shot high in his chest and would be unlikely to live to tell the tale. Another had got an arrow embedded in his leg and he hoped that the third might have been fatally wounded, though he couldn't be sure.

He despised himself for not aiming for General Stracker — but he couldn't see the general and Jewd had urged him to get as many soldiers out of contention as possible. Now he was running towards one of the loose horses. From the corner of his eye he saw two people bolting, and although one was definitely Stracker, he couldn't tell if the other was Kilt.

He could hear his own breath, was aware of his steps thumping over the grass. He crashed through the low hedgerow and grasped for the panicked horse's reins. Its eyes were wide and terrified.

Suddenly the Wikken stumbled through the clearing smoke, blinking and cursing. Without thinking, Leo dragged Faeroe from its scabbard and slashed the sword across the helpless man. The raised purple tatua on the man's face twisted in a snarl of pain and disbelief as blood spurted, hitting Leo. He watched the man go down, threw Faeroe back into the scabbard and then fled, pulling the horse behind. He didn't look back, didn't dare glance at the carnage.

In the woodland, his and Jewd's horses were waiting for him, dragging against their bindings, equally panicked. Leo sucked in gasps of air and finally turned, three beasts in tow, casting a prayer to Lo that Jewd was right behind him with Kilt.

* * *

Jewd had desperately wanted to finish off Stracker. The general was pinned beneath his horse, struggling and cursing; the line they'd tied across the road had worked perfectly. Jewd's sword was ready, itching to hack at the prone man's throat before he could release himself from the thrashing animal, but another man emerged from the smoke, running hard at him, ignoring the arrow sticking out of his leg, not even pausing to break it in half.

Jewd cursed the strength and resilience of the Steppes people but had no alternative but to deal with the wounded guard. He caught a glimpse of Leo in the background, leaping into the fray of men, horses and smoke, but had to give his attention to his own attacker. Kilt was somewhere on the ground near his feet, unmoving.

'Kill him!' Stracker screeched at his soldier. 'Or I'll kill you!'

Jewd had no intention to fight honourably — this was battle in the least noble sense. Kicking out with his long leg he connected expertly with the arrow sticking out of the man's flesh and the guard predictably doubled in surprised pain.

'Brave but stupid!' Jewd roared and brought his sword down in a vicious hack, killing the man instantly.

He looked up and though he couldn't see Leo he could see Vulpan emerging from the stinging smoke. Stracker had nearly pulled himself free of the dead or dying beast that lay on top of him. Jewd knew he had only seconds. 'You'll keep for another day, Stracker,' he warned, yanking Kilt's body up and heaving it onto his shoulders.

'And I know you now, big man. Consider yourself marked!'

Vulpan had collapsed to his knees, coughing and spluttering. Jewd risked a solid kick to Stracker's temple and felt satisfaction at the thud. Stracker's eyes glazed over. Settling Kilt's body into a better position across his shoulders, Jewd took off running towards the meeting place.

He caught sight of Leo's back disappearing into the woodland and sent a quick thanks to Lo that the king had been spared; as it was, Kilt would be furious that he had put the king's life in jeopardy. He couldn't think about that now, though; not until he knew whether his best friend had survived.

'Here!' Leo yelled as they approached, holding out the reins. 'Thank Lo you got him.'

'After all that, he can't even sit a horse! Get on your saddle and ride!' Jewd yelled, slinging Kilt across his own horse. He climbed up behind him and urged his beast on its way. 'We go as high as we can on horseback, Leo, then on foot. They'll never catch us if we can make it deep into the forest.'

He could hear voices shouting in the distance.

'Ride, your majesty! Just go north. Don't look back!'

30

Loethar galloped up and leapt off his horse as soon as he could make out the prone bodies in the distance. As he arrived he counted three soldiers dead alongside Shorgan. His fury rose. Ahead, Vulpan and Stracker sat at the side of the road. Loethar almost wished that whomever was responsible for this killing had included his half-brother in the body count.

Vulpan struggled to his feet and then bowed. Stracker sighed. 'What are you doing here, brother?'

'Lucky for you I am. What occurred?'

'An ambush,' Stracker growled. 'They were after the priest.'

'Get up, Vulpan,' Loethar said. 'Are you injured?'

'My eyes sting and I've hurt a shoulder,' the Vested replied.

'How about you, Stracker?'

'Don't worry about me. I've just got a sore head from a giant's boot. I'll see his big body swing from the gallows soon.'

'Tell me what occurred,' Loethar said, reaching for his water bag and offering it. 'How long ago?'

'Long enough,' Stracker said, gulping water, 'that it's pointless giving chase.'

'Where are your horses?'

'Bolted, my lord,' Vulpan replied, clearly desperate to be part of the dialogue. He looked longingly at the water bag that Stracker hogged. 'The explosions caused them to panic.'

'Explosions!'

Stracker nodded. 'Our attackers set off fire and loud noise on either side of the road, causing lots of stinging smoke. An archer took out the soldiers. I presume the same man killed Shorgan, though he died from a sword cut. I managed to get away with the prisoner but only as far as here. See the twine over there?' he asked, pointing.

Loethar squinted at the tree. 'Another old trick.'

'I was pinned beneath my horse long enough that they could get the priest. I hope he's dead. He certainly looked to be.'

'Who is this priest? Who would set up an ambush to retrieve him from you?'

'I'm asking myself the same thing,' Stracker growled. 'There were only two of them by my reckoning but they were good. Fast, ruthless. These were not peasants trying to rescue a priest. These were well-trained men, adept at ambush. They headed straight for the woods, even though it would have been much faster for them to ride straight down here and lose themselves at the next parting of the roads.'

'But they chose the harder, slower route. Because it could hide them, presumably,' Loethar finished.

'One of them is carrying a man on his back. Granted, he was a big fellow but he's going to be moving slowly all the same once they get off those horses. The animals won't be able to go very much higher.'

Loethar looked up, his gaze narrowing. 'Tell me about the priest.'

'Vulpan knows him better than I do.'

Vulpan straightened. Rubbing gingerly at his shoulder he told his emperor all he knew of Pastor Jeves.

'A man of magic?' Loethar queried.

'That's what I tasted, my lord,' Vulpan replied, slightly defensively.

'So he is Vested, chasing his sister who is Vested, who is married to the man we know as Kirin, who is also Vested and just happened to be travelling with Freath, who is now dead.'

'That's the sum of it, brother,' Stracker said, hauling himself shakily to his feet. 'We have to find the horses. Bah, but my head hurts.'

Loethar began to pace. Vulpan licked his parched lips, reaching for the cast-aside water sack, while Stracker ignored them both.

'This was no priest,' Loethar said.

Stracker laughed. 'Why do you think I was taking him north? I didn't trust him for a moment.'

Vulpan suddenly spat out water.

Both men turned. 'What's got into you?' Stracker demanded.

'Oh, Lo! My lord, forgive me.'

Loethar frowned. 'Well, speak up, man. What's wrong?'

'I ...' Vulpan hesitated, wide-eyed and clearly frightened.

Loethar took a step forward and Vulpan cringed. 'Please, my lord, I'm sorry. It all happened so fast. I fell off my horse, men were being killed. It's only now I ... Forgive me.'

Loethar grabbed Vulpan by the shirtfront and hauled him forward. 'What do you need to tell me?' he said slowly, quietly.

Vulpan's fear intensified; his face slackened and drained of colour. 'The taste of a man's blood has just come back to me.'

Loethar gripped him tighter. Vulpan was clearly struggling to breathe. 'Whose?' he demanded.

Vulpan pointed at his throat and Loethar flung him away. The Vested yelped as he hit the ground.

'Whose?' Loethar asked again, looming over the man.

'The archer. He was the man whose blood was found on the boulder.'

The half-brothers stared at each other. 'That was Kilt Faris?' Stracker queried. 'I never saw him properly, curse him!'

'We can't be sure,' Loethar warned. 'But it seems the priest was valuable to him or his men. The archer, describe him.'

'I can't, my lord, I really didn't get a look at him,' Vulpan quailed. 'My magic is not about vision. It's about presence. The man whose blood I tasted was definitely here.'

Stracker looked away from Vulpan with disgust. 'He was young, I know that much. Sandy-haired. Clean shaven.'

Loethar scowled. 'Too young for Faris, then, by our estimates. So he was one of Faris's band. Do we have any descriptions of Faris?'

Stracker shook his head. 'People whose palms we've laid money into, who claim to have met him, describe him differently. One minute dark-haired, the next he's fair or bald. The man's a starren.'

At the mention of the colour-changing six-legged reptile from the plains Stracker's and Loethar's gazes met and locked. 'Perhaps you actually had the infamous Kilt Faris in your grasp, Stracker,' Loethar said.

The big man nodded, his dirt-stained tatua twisted with disappointment. 'Perhaps I did. Has there ever been mention that Faris is Vested?'

'Not to my knowledge,' Loethar admitted. 'But we know the Vested like to keep their powers secret. What was his skill?'

Vulpan spoke up. 'He claimed to predict the weather.'

Loethar smiled grimly. 'We know that's a lie.'

Vulpan seemed to agree, his expression thoughtful. 'He tasted a lot like a woman I have tasted. I can't remember who, but she will come to me. You know, the more I taste — and my list is still fledgling, my lord — the more I'm beginning to realise I can discern the level of power. Everyone's blood tastes different, of course, but I am noticing a pattern in the tastes of people with closely aligned powers. Master Kirin, for example, is rich with power.' Vulpan hesitated as he saw Loethar and Stracker exchange a glance. 'The majority of people I have tasted can fit into perhaps,' he continued, making a tutting sound as he considered, 'perhaps three other levels. Pastor Jeves and Kirin Felt sit well away from the others, on a scale of their own. Very potent powers.'

'I see. And the woman?'

'Lily Felt?'

'If she is his wife. He certainly had no wife at the palace.'

Vulpan shrugged. 'She's a mystery. I tasted nothing that connected her to any of the other Vested and yet I felt the touch of her magic. It was very strange, almost …' He paused, licking his lips. 'She showed no discernible taste at all of magic, curiously, but I know she was empowered because I felt the touch of her magic.' He raised a hand. 'She healed a terrible scald, taking away the pain immediately. I told her I'd be mentioning her to you.'

'We are hunting Felt now, so presumably we will pick up this curious wife alongside him,' Loethar confirmed. He gave a grimace. 'And he's been around us for anni with us thinking he had so little magic.'

'I have a personal score to settle with Faris and his men now,' Stracker said.

'You two can take turns on the horse. Let's head for Francham. We'll make a decision there.'

'You haven't told us why you're here,' Stracker commented. 'And all alone?'

'I have plenty to tell you,' Loethar said, glancing at Vulpan. 'It can wait. Let's go.'

They'd ridden as high as they could possibly go with the two horses.

'Stop here, Leo. I need to see to Kilt.'

'At least he's groaning. We know he's alive,' Leo said, halting his horse. 'Shall I let the horses go?'

'Aye. They're no good to us here. Let them amble back down and find some water. I'm sure whoever finds them will be very glad to give them a home.'

Leo helped Jewd lower Kilt to the ground, then began unpacking the horses. Without being asked, he handed Jewd a water sack.

Jewd took out the stopper and held it to Kilt's mouth. 'Here, drink. Slowly. That's it.' He dribbled water between his friend's lips. Immediately, Kilt began to cough and Jewd gingerly lifted his head.

'Oh, Lo, my head!' Kilt groaned, but he drank thirstily.

'Slowly, Kilt,' Jewd warned again, 'or you'll choke. Anywhere else hurt?'

'Ribs, shoulder. I came down on one side.' Kilt opened his eyes to slits. 'Are my orders worth nothing anymore?' he demanded.

'A pinch of salt when I think they're stupid,' Jewd replied.

'You risked his life?'

'Aye, to save your scrawny neck!'

'Jewd, so help me ...'

Leo knelt down beside Kilt. 'I'm my own man now. You've got me this far but now I'm going to be making my own decisions, so stop talking about me as though I'm either not here or some sort of child you can push around. Remember who you talk to.' He glared at them both, defying them to challenge him.

The king looked annoyed when both men started laughing. Kilt immediately clutched at his shoulder, wincing. 'Got to get something to tie my shoulder up, your majesty. Don't crowd me.'

'You know, this isn't funny. I killed a couple of men back there.'

'Do you want a medal, your highness?' Kilt asked, his voice still dry and raspy.

'You can't have it both ways, your majesty,' Jewd added.

Leo's lips thinned. 'I just want you both to accept that I am now old enough to carve my own path. I am also a Valisar.'

'And Valisars don't take orders?' Kilt queried.

Leo gave him a look of disdain. 'Valisars are kings. I have to start acting like one if you want us to rule again one day.'

Kilt struggled to sit up, aided by Jewd. 'I am grateful to you — both of you — but it was stupid to risk your life,' he said, staring at Leo.

'Kilt, we have to be prepared to risk my life if we're serious about me claiming back the throne. You've got to stop believing you can protect me from all danger. Jewd understands, or he wouldn't have let me come.'

Jewd put both hands against his chest in defence. 'I couldn't stop you. You blackmailed me.'

'And lucky I did or we wouldn't have achieved what we have.'

'I'd have thought of something,' Kilt said.

Now it was Jewd's and Leo's turn to laugh. 'Get over yourself, Faris,' Jewd said, 'or I'll break your other shoulder. Now let's take a look and see how bad this is.'

'Don't touch it,' Kilt warned.

Jewd laughed. 'Have I told you, Leo, what a baby our trusted leader is when it comes to pain?'

'I just don't want you to touch it, all right?' Kilt sneered.

Leo grinned. 'Shall I hold him down, Jewd?'

'Looks like you'll have to,' Jewd said archly.

'I mean it,' Kilt threatened. 'Just let it be and ...'

'Kilt!' Jewd reprimanded. 'Am I going to have to knock you out again myself? It won't be good for your fat head if I do. That shoulder needs to be bound. If the joint has slipped, it has to be put back into place. If the —'

'All right, all right! Do it!' Kilt grumbled. 'Tell me you've got some bermine in that wretched satchel of yours, though.'

'You're lucky. I never go anywhere without it.'

'Is that the stuff you used for my leg?' Leo asked.

'That's it. We used to buy it but now Lily makes up her own version, which is far more potent. Here, drink it.' Jewd pulled the tiny stopper from a small bottle and handed it to Kilt.

Leo winced. 'Horrible stuff.'

'Better than the pain,' Kilt said and took a draught, his face wrinkling at the taste. 'Like a thousand farts,' he groaned.

'Go and check we're still all clear,' Jewd said, sensing Kilt wanted the king gone for a minute. Still grinning at Kilt's fart comment, Leo nodded and set off.

'Thanks,' Kilt said. 'I don't need him seeing me at my shrieking best.'

'Has it worked yet?'

'I want to say no.'

'All right then, let's see.' Jewd removed Kilt's shirt, glancing only briefly at the familiar birthmark beneath his shoulder blade as he focused on the injury. 'Good news or bad news first?'

'Get on with it!'

'We have to put right your shoulder joint.'

Kilt groaned. 'And the good news?'

Without warning Jewd manipulated his friend's arm and Kilt yelped as his shoulder slipped back into its correct position.

'The good news is, it's back in,' Jewd said, grinning.

'Oh, very funny,' Kilt choked out, breathing hard and wincing.

'Here, keep the bermine. I reckon you'll need it. We have to make up a sling.'

Leo returned. 'All clear. What's happened?'

'His shoulder was out,' Jewd replied.

'And now it's back,' Kilt finished.

Jewd winked at Leo. 'And he didn't even scream. How's your leg?'

'I hate the limp but at least I don't need the stick anymore.'

'Told you it would get better. Is there pain?'

'Nothing to scream about,' Leo replied.

'Get that sling onto me,' Kilt demanded, seeing that Jewd had finished turning a large kerchief into a workable hammock. 'And let's get out of here.'

Later, as they rested briefly for Kilt's sake, he spoke to them both in a grave tone. 'I haven't said thank you.'

'For disobeying you?' Jewd said.

'For action that probably saved my life.'

'They didn't know who you were, Kilt,' Jewd assured.

Kilt nodded. 'They can add things up, though, my friend. A limping archer, a huge man? Why would they appear out of nowhere to ambush the emperor's men in order to rescue a clergyman? No, we'll have pricked their curiosity. And we can't discount the fact that Vulpan was present. According to what Freath told us, once he's tasted your blood, he can recognise you again without having to taste you. Do you understand?'

Leo and Jewd shook their heads, after glancing, confused, at each other.

Kilt pointed at Leo's leg. 'He's tasted you, your majesty. We cannot overlook the possibility that amidst all that confusion he recognised you.'

Dawning spread across their faces. 'But he doesn't know me! Doesn't know who I truly am!' Leo protested.

'No, that's right. But if what Freath says is true, then he will have recognised the blood of a man from the north. They don't know which one, but they know you were one of the outlaw band and that's all they'll need. They now know that our men were rescuing Pastor Jeves. We know Loethar is too smart for his own good. He won't necessarily arrive at the conclusion that they had Kilt Faris in their clutches but they'll know they had someone who matters to the outlaw band. I reckon they'll now intensify their search.'

Jewd was nodding. 'Blind me! This is why you lead us. I just don't think this far ahead.'

'What about Lily?' Leo asked.

Kilt sighed. His expression became still more shrouded with gloom. 'She's obviously using this "marriage" as a cover but as Stracker's onto it I presume she and Felt will have to keep up the pretence in order to keep themselves safe. Especially as Lily has somehow passed herself off as Vested.' Both his companions opened their mouths but he continued, cutting off their questions. 'Don't ask how because I don't know, but she seems to have Vulpan tricked. He claims he's felt the benefit of her magical touch.' Kilt shook his head. 'For now we have to let her go or we could compromise her disguise. I think Felt will take her back to Brighthelm.'

'I'm sorry for you,' Jewd said quietly.

'Don't be. This is all my fault,' Kilt replied, his anger not well disguised. 'Come on, we have to get back to the hideout. We must warn our band that imperial guards are going to be stepping up their search for us.'

31

Arriving at the entry to Francham, Loethar allowed Vulpan's horse to move slightly ahead so he could speak to Stracker in relative privacy. 'People don't need to know I'm here. We want no fuss.'

Stracker shrugged. 'I can't stop them recognising you.'

'I've grown a beard, I'm deliberately wearing rough clothes. Besides, they won't be looking for me.'

'What's the secrecy for?'

'A precaution. I don't want Valya knowing I'm here, for instance.'

Stracker smiled unkindly. 'Has wedded bliss worn off, brother?'

'It was never present,' Loethar replied. 'Our child died,' he added as bluntly.

Stracker was unmoved. 'Son or daughter?'

'A girl.'

His half-brother made a sound of disdain. 'Then it doesn't matter, does it?'

Loethar bit back on the retort that sprang easily to his lips. 'I suppose not,' he lied.

'Is that why you're running away?'

'I've asked Valya to leave.'

'Banished the bitch, eh? Excellent news. So that's why you're here.'

'That and a couple of other things.' He moved ahead of Stracker. 'I'll make my own arrangements but I shall see you later.'

'Where?'

'You know this town better than me. Somewhere quiet.'

'How about the two-mile marker to the west?'

Loethar frowned. 'In the forest?'

'You said quiet,' Stracker said, shrugging.

'But I didn't say dangerous.'

'Don't you trust me?'

'Shouldn't I?'

Stracker grinned. 'Tell me now then. I don't care either way.'

'I would prefer you to have privacy when I give you this information.'

'So cagey, Loethar, one would think you were sensitive to my feelings.'

'In this instance I might be.'

'Then I'll see you at the two-mile marker. It's quiet, private … and safe.'

Loethar nodded, holding his half-brother's gaze. 'When?'

'Twilight.'

'I'll see you there.'

'What about Vulpan?'

Loethar shook his head. 'Right now he's your concern. But from tomorrow we're going to use him to track down the Faris gang once and for all.' He saw soldiers — Greens, mainly — melting out of the throng of people, having recognised their general. Loethar did not want to be seen by them. 'Until later, keep my secret.'

'Happy to, brother,' Stracker said to himself as he watched the emperor blend into the busy Francham main street.

It was nearing sunset when Gavriel and Elka led their horses out of the eastern foothills. They could see the activity of Francham ahead, chimneys smoking and lanterns beginning to be lit across the busy community. The town twinkled like a fairytale oasis in the gradually falling light, the Dragonsback Mountains rearing to the north and the forest a dark blanket to the west.

'Lo's wrath!' Gavriel remarked. 'You told me it was a town. This looks like a small city.'

Elka was shaking her head. 'If I wasn't seeing it for myself I wouldn't believe it,' she admitted. 'Ten anni ago it was little more than a large village on the verge of becoming a town.'

'Well, it looks like it's a thriving spot now.'

'My brothers have been through here. They said it was a busy place but I think in their usual way they've understated the fact!'

Gavriel looked at her. 'I know what you're going to say next.'

She gave him a superior glare. 'Then I don't need to say it.'

'Oh, but you must. I get such satisfaction out of knowing you so well.'

'Not as well as you think,' Elka cautioned.

Gavriel looked appropriately abashed and tried to change the subject. 'So, want to spend another night under the stars with me?'

'And there I was thinking you'd never ask,' she answered wryly.

His change in subject had failed miserably.

She seemed to notice his discomfort. 'Listen,' she began, losing all the sarcasm in her voice. 'You know that I don't like being so obvious.'

'Of course.'

'So sleeping in the forest is far more alluring to me than a night at an inn where everyone wants to compare their height to mine or have a drink with me, or worse, arm wrestle me.'

He laughed. 'I'd tell them not to bother. You always win.'

'And lose me a fortune?' she asked.

'Save you a night of tedium, more like.'

'So we're agreed. We'll stay in the forest?'

'I can't think of a better place. I really hate soft beds and ale and roasted meats,' he said sarcastically.

'Gavriel —'

'Well done.'

She looked at him quizzically.

'That's the first time you've called me by my real name without stumbling or wincing.'

'I had to get used to it.'

'I know,' he said, a sad note in his voice. 'And I'm grateful for it. The moment the Quirin spoke my name I knew it was right.'

'Have you remembered more?'

'I don't think there's any more to know.' He shrugged. 'I was escorting a king to safety from the threat of the barbarian warlord Loethar, now the emperor. We got as far as the outlaw band in the north led by an arrogant swine called Kilt Faris —'

'Was he really that bad?'

'No, probably not, but I'm delving into memories from when I was seventeen. My judgement was different then. Anyway, we got separated, I got captured, you know the rest.'

'How do you mean to find your brother?'

'I have no idea, not a clue where he went and so no inkling of where to begin. I'm going to start from where I left off and hope things will begin to piece themselves together from there. Perhaps Corbel is looking for me.'

'How do you know the king is still here? It seems highly unlikely,' she said, pulling a face of doubt.

'I agree but, Elka, I have to start somewhere. Faris's hideout was the last place I was seen. At least if I can find Faris, he can tell me what's become of Leo.'

She nodded. 'Right. So we have a plan. Let's go. Can we skirt Francham?'

'No. We will take the direct route and ride heads high. If Francham has grown up so much, seeing you is not going to be the novelty it once was. I think you're overestimating just how interesting you are, my lady.'

She gave him an audible sneer and kicked her horse forward. 'Come on then, runt. Let's go. We should have found our spot to camp by sundown.'

He grinned, and gestured with his hand for her to lead. 'Height before beauty.'

When Loethar arrived at the two-mile marker, the sun had set and the forest canopy ensured it already felt like night had fallen fully. As the moon's light was nearly absent due to thick cloud cover, Loethar had to depend on a single thick candle to illuminate the path. He'd left his horse tied to a tree at the end of the forest and had walked in, carrying only the small chest.

This was madness. He knew it in his heart. He was alone, vulnerable and very likely walking into a trap. He had to hope his half-brother still held enough respect for the memory of their mother to wait until her remains were properly dealt with before springing any attack.

Stracker was waiting for him. He was seated on a tree stump, pouring out a second goblet of wine. His own was half full. 'I can't remember the last time we did this, alone, in the wild. Here,' he said, offering the full goblet.

Loethar gave a wry smile and took it.

Stracker held up his goblet. 'To us!'

Loethar had never known Stracker to be sentimental but now was not the time to be churlish, he decided. He took the goblet and raised it, nodding. They sipped.

'Did anyone recognise you?' Stracker asked, standing.

'Not a soul.'

'Are you at The Lookout?'

Loethar nodded. 'I'll head back tomorrow.' The wine was decent and he drank deeply again.

His half-brother drained his own cup, sighed, and wiped the back of his hand across his mouth. 'Such a swift visit. So tell me what is so urgent, so private.'

Loethar followed suit and drained his wine. He fixed Stracker with a dark gaze. There was no easy way to say it. 'Our mother is dead.'

Loethar watched his half-brother's confident expression falter momentarily. The tatua twisted before it relaxed again.

'And that's her, I suppose,' Stracker said, nodding at the chest. 'Her ashes.'

'She was old but she wasn't ailing when I left.'

'She was poisoned, Stracker.'

Now the man showed some emotion. He stood and strode forward, looming over Loethar, his lips pulling back to reveal small, uncared-for teeth. The several rings hanging from one ear jangled angrily. 'Accidental?'

Loethar had not shifted stance nor expression. It was important to hold his ground here as he knew this was a watershed moment for him and his violent sibling. 'I believe she was murdered.'

'Who?'

'Valya.'

Stracker growled in an animal-like sound of despair. 'And you banished her, you didn't kill her!'

'I have no proof. Only my suspicions.'

'Why now?'

'I think Valya got wind that our mother suggested she was a useless wife if she couldn't produce an heir. I can't imagine how, but perhaps Valya was spying on us that day in the chapel. Mother suggested then that Valya should be disposed of if she didn't give me a son.'

Stracker stabbed a finger at Loethar, just stopping short of hitting his chest. 'Our mother was right! Valya failed again and gave you a daughter — a dead one at that. Why a convent when a grave would be so much more appropriate?' Loethar blinked. Stracker continued. 'She should be hunted down and answer for her sin. How can you permit our mother to die under these circumstances and not make someone pay?'

'I told you, no proof.'

'You're weak, brother. You've become so soft you can't even control the Denovian slut you married.'

'Valya is many things, Stracker, but she is not a slut. I think you should study the Set language before you use it. Perhaps you are better off back in the Steppes, speaking our tribal tongue?'

The tatua stretched as Stracker grinned with menace in the low candlelight. 'And there I was thinking it was probably you who should go back.'

At last. They had arrived at the point that Loethar knew had been coming for years. His mother had warned him. Her intuition had become fact. And he had misjudged Stracker's sense of honour.

It was Loethar's turn to smile. 'Is that a challenge, Stracker?' He blinked a few times, suddenly feeling a warm blurriness in his head.

'Certainly sounds like one. Are you surprised?'

Loethar shook his head in answer but also to clear his mind. 'Not really. I just thought you might wait until our mother was properly committed to her god. But, Stracker, nothing's changed, or have you been practising with that weapon at your side?' His tongue felt suddenly thick in his mouth.

Stracker laughed. 'I'm not that stupid, brother. I am well aware of your almost otherworldly sword skills.'

Loethar understood, decided to steal Stracker's surprise. 'And so it has come to this. Not even a fair contest but an ambush? Not very noble.'

'I never claimed to be noble like you, brother. I am of the Steppes. We use cunning. There is no room for honour.'

He shook his head again to clear it. 'That's what makes you so unfit for leadership. Honour is something your father tried very hard to impress upon you. Whatever you think of me, Stracker, honour is my code. It always has been.'

'I'm glad you have finally admitted that he was my father.'

'He was a father to me all the same. And he was an honourable man.'

'If he saw you now, I think he would be ashamed.'

'I doubt it. I think his only shame for me is that I let you live.'
Loethar shifted balance and staggered slightly.

Stracker's expression changed from smug enjoyment to
genuine menace. He didn't reach to help his kin. 'Perhaps you
should have killed me when you had your chance.'

'I've had many chances, but for our mother's sake I refused
them all.'

'And now you have no more.'

'So you don't plan to draw your sword on me?' Loethar baited,
listening for the inevitable sound he had been anticipating since
he realised the trap had been laid. He could feel the drugged wine
spreading its dulling, soporific effect far too quickly for him to do
much to help himself.

Stracker shook his head and a malevolent grin returned to his
face. 'I just want you compliant and unable to draw your own.
You'll be conscious for a while yet I'm assured by the physic who
prepared the brew for me. You'll even be able to answer back! He
laughed. They both looked over at the stump behind which
another flask of wine had been hidden and clearly the one Stracker
had used to pour his own goblet. 'And now you're going to endure
the punishment that you have earned for many years.' He nodded,
glancing over Loethar's shoulder. Loethar didn't bother to even
turn at the sound of the first twig snapping underfoot.

Neither of them had been hungry enough to go to the trouble of
lighting a fire, let alone trapping a rabbit. Instead, they had munched
on their plentiful supplies from the convent, happy to eat on the
move as they looked for an appropriate spot to camp for the night.

They'd led the horses in and up about a mile past the-two mile
marker when Gavriel had proclaimed himself spent and suggested
they not even bother to light a fire. 'I just want to sleep. It's a mild
night,' he admitted.

She'd smiled at him. 'Short and weak.'

'Whatever you say,' he'd muttered as he yawned, quickly

tethering the horses. They'd taken the precaution of watering them at Francham. 'We'll have to leave the animals tomorrow and proceed on foot.'

'Nothing changes in the forest,' she replied. 'I know a good spot where they'll be safe and protected.'

Gavriel nodded, yawned again. 'Faris will find us first, most likely.'

'What if you are not "found" immediately?'

'Then we'll have to return to Francham, perhaps leave the horses and I'll try again in a few days.'

'You don't think people in town will begin to be suspicious of all the going backwards and forwards?'

'If I have to return, I won't be leaving until I find him,' he warned. 'There will be no going backwards and forwards.'

She sighed. 'This is it for me, my friend. If we leave the forest empty-handed tomorrow, I'll be making my way back east.'

He nodded in the dark. 'I understand, Elka. I'm grateful you've accompanied me this far.'

Nothing more had been said. They'd drifted into silence on that mournful note, the haunting sound of an owl and the chirrup of crickets accompanying them into sleep. Gavriel rolled into his sleeping pack and was snoring gently before Elka had even lowered herself to the ground to unravel her pack. As she turned to settle down, a light in the far distance, down the incline, caught her attention. She squinted, at it, concentrating. There it was again, and it was moving. Who would be coming into the forest at this time of the evening and why with such a low light? She clambered agilely over to Gavriel and shook him. He mumbled something unintelligible as he turned onto his back. Elka pinched him. 'I said wake up!' she urged.

Gavriel's eyes flew awake, and he would have yelped if she hadn't been fast enough to clamp her hand across his mouth. 'Sssh!' she cautioned. 'We've got company.'

He nodded and she removed her hand.

'Ouch!' he muttered angrily.

She smiled in the dark. 'Over there.' She pointed.

'I see it. What is that, a single candle?'

'Looks like it.'

'Bit of an odd time to be coming up into the forest,' he mused.

'My thoughts exactly — and clearly wanting to be kept secret. Anyone meaning to be here and not worried about being seen would use a lantern or two.'

'It could be Faris's men,' Gavriel suggested.

'Yes, that's what I reckoned. Let's go take a look and make sure they're not about to stumble upon our horses.'

'If it's Faris —'

'And if it's not, we don't want that sort of company. Come on, Gavriel, try to move as silently as we've taught you.'

'Shut up, Elka. I move like a cat and you know it.'

She laughed softly and he realised he couldn't hear her tread at all.

Loethar was gripped between two Greens, their strong fingers digging into the muscle at the top of his arm, a trick used by the warriors to deliberately numb a man's body and his ability to fight back. He could already feel the telltale tingling in his fingers.

'Are you sure you want to do this?' he asked them. 'I am your emperor but before that I am your tribal ruler. Your death warrant aside, are you happy to go to your god as a traitor to the Steppes tribal law?'

The man to his right faltered. Loethar knew it was not because he feared death — none of his warriors feared death — but because he feared the recrimination of the gods beyond death.

'Aludane will never forgive your treachery,' he continued. 'You know the creed —'

'We all do, brother,' Stracker interrupted. 'But even Aludane will forgive us this. You are no longer a leader we respect. As I say, you are more Set than you are Steppes. You bear no proud tatua. You never wanted to be a true tribal leader. You used us to take the

Denovian Set because ruling here, in the western sovereign's way, was always your desire.' He nodded. 'Look at him,' he ordered his men. 'Our tribal leader looks more Valisar than Brennus ever did!' He laughed maliciously. 'Although, brother, I was impressed with your early ruthlessness. And while you have become complacent over the last ten anni, I am also impressed with your ridding yourself of your ghastly encumbrance of a wife. I will enjoy killing her on behalf of Dara Negev.'

'You can't see beyond the immediate, can you?' Loethar replied calmly. 'Did you honestly believe my intention was to slaughter everyone and simply take over the land?'

'Yes.'

'Then you are even more stupid than you look.'

Stracker's eyes turned to slits as his mouth thinned with fury. 'We have achieved nothing!'

'That's because you will always see yourself as a tribal yob, Stracker. You haven't evolved. Many of our people have matured and grown, they've become educated and eloquent. They speak two languages, sometimes three. It's not about us; it never was. It was always about generations to come. We have taken this land and infiltrated its people so that all people will benefit. Many of our children are half Set, half Steppes. A whole new generation is growing up, Stracker, and they are going to be stronger, cleverer, better than any of us could dream. They will do us proud. They will sail to new continents and discover amazing new cultures and practices that they will bring back here. That's how an empire and its people evolve and grow. But your idea of rule is to stay the same, to kill anyone who steps out of our primitive ways. Unhand me, you fools. This man will lead you and your families down the path to destruction. He has no plan. He is only happy with the smell of blood in his nostrils.'

Stracker punched his half-brother. His expression showed how much he enjoyed the sensation. Loethar slipped to his knees, breathing hard.

'You were once happy with the smell of blood. I can remember when you ate kings,' Stracker accused.

Loethar struggled to talk. He'd misread the fire in Stracker's belly to be rid of him; had thought that Stracker wouldn't even think of overthrow until Dara Negev no longer stood between them. But his half-brother had obviously been plotting for a long time. 'I was happy for blood when the spilling of blood was necessary. We are in more sophisticated times, Stracker, that require diplomacy and tact and intelligence, all of which you sadly lack.' He felt Stracker's fist connect with his jaw, a well-judged blow to make him black out only momentarily. When he regained his wits he could hear Stracker's jeers.

'You have turned us into soft-bellied, soft-witted Denovians. I think you want to be a Valisar, Loethar — is that why you ate Brennus?'

'No, you sad fool. I ate him for his magic, but I realise now that the Valisar magic doesn't work that way. You see, Stracker, I am capable of learning. You are not. Why don't you fight fairly? Let me draw my sword and we'll sort this out in the tribal way.'

'No, I already accept your supremacy as a swordsman. We fought for kingship once before the tribal way and you won. Now I'm fighting for leadership the cowardly Valisar way … I'm using cunning. And it seems I've won.'

'Do you truly believe people will follow you?'

'If they don't —'

'They'll die?' Loethar finished for him.

And Stracker laughed. 'The Denovians will become our slaves, our workers.'

'And what of the people who are tribal but have intermarried, have children who are half and half?'

'They can choose to die or become slaves too. There will be no mixed blood. The tribes must remain pure.'

'You are mad.'

'This was always my creed. I haven't changed.'

'What would our father think?'

'My father hated that you pitied me.'

Loethar knew this to be true. 'And what would our mother think of your ambushing me as I bring you her ashes?'

'She always knew I would kill you. Surely she tried to warn you?'

Loethar spat blood out. 'In her way, yes. But I never thought you would try anything with our mother still present,' he said, glancing at the chest containing her ashes.

Stracker shrugged. 'I'm not as sentimental as you are.'

'I can tell.'

The general grinned. 'It's good to see you humbled like this, on your knees before me.'

'Stracker, I'm not humbled. My mortal body crumples as anyone's would, but in my mind I laugh in your face at your pathetic intentions. The army follows you because it follows orders. But when misery takes a hold and you begin to lose control, that same army, these very men who do your bidding now, will rise up against you. You don't understand leadership; you only understand the blind obedience of a dumb dog. Oh yes, you feel you're taking initiative now but it is purely the snapping of that dumb dog railing against its master. A dumb animal doesn't survive very long without someone to control it, feed it, water it, train it. You —'

Loether never got any further; Stracker hit him so hard he bit off a piece of his own tongue, his mouth filling with blood as he hit the ground, unconscious. He never felt the beating he took.

'String him up,' Stracker commanded finally. 'He can die in the forest, hanging by his neck. No honourable tribal sword will tarnish its blade with his blood.'

Watching, hidden, Gavriel swung around, looking stunned. Elka turned to him, equally shocked.

'The emperor?' she mouthed.

Gavriel nodded. 'I can't believe it.'

'Should we stop them?' she whispered.

'No. Let them kill each other. I'll enjoy watching him die; he might already be dead. He looks it.'

Elka looked back as the men picked up the slumped, unconscious captive; she'd only recently heard her friend's chilling description of all, that this very man had inflicted upon his family, his friends and, more widely, his countrymen. The Davarigons, after all, had been spared the effects of the push for empire. And though she understood that Gavriel had suffered much at this man's hands, all she could see now was a helpless man who had been beaten senseless by thugs and was now about to lose his life.

'Gavriel,' she began, as the warriors dragged Loethar towards a nearby tree. 'This is what it looked like when the imperial guards were beating you. I sat in the shadows just like this and I made a decision to help you.'

'We're going to watch him swing.'

'No.'

He glared at her. 'Did you not hear anything I told you on our journey here?'

She laid a hand on his arm, feeling the tension beneath her palm. 'Listen to me a moment,' she urged. 'Everything we've heard back from the Set in the last five or six years has been positive, has it not?'

He looked away, scowling, but she knew he was listening.

'If not for your memory returning, you would be none the wiser about this man. You would feel as outraged as I do that he is about to go to his death with no fair trial, no way to defend himself —'

'He has no defence!' Gavriel hissed beneath his breath. 'He doesn't deserve a def—'

'He deserves to die, I agree, but perhaps he should be given the opportunity for a formal execution. He is an emperor.'

'He is a usurper.'

'He is a king in his own right. And his former cruelties aside, we've had many a conversation back home about how the Set has begun to flourish under his rule. You know the trade routes have opened up for us directly as a result of Loethar's new policies.'

'Elka —'

'No. Ask yourself, now that you're a Set man again, whether you want to be ruled by that evil-looking thug of a brother,' she said, stabbing a finger in Stracker's direction.

Gavriel turned sourly to regard Stracker. 'Half-brother,' he corrected, shaking his head.

'Right,' Elka said. 'So we are not going to permit Loethar's death today, even if we have to take him as our own prisoner.'

'Are you going soft in the head?'

'I would have thought bringing Loethar as your captive to present to your king would be a fine homecoming,' she baited.

Gavriel clearly couldn't dismiss her logic. She watched him consider, and hoped the Valisar king was still alive, and still in these parts. He finally nodded. 'What do you suggest?'

Relief coursing through her, Elka reached behind her. 'We'll stun them,' she replied, pulling her catapult from her belt with glee.

'Don't look at me like that, Bleuth,' Stracker growled in Steppes language.

'General,' the Green began reluctantly, 'I would advise you against this action.' Loethar hung limp between the two men. A third Green was throwing a rope over the chosen branch.

'Haven't got the stomach for it?' Stracker taunted.

'I think it is a rash move that you may regret. I am your friend; I hope I can say this to you without recrimination.'

'We are friends but you are also my subordinate. And you will follow orders.'

Bleuth nodded. 'I will indeed. But I am first trying to prevent you …'

'What?' Stracker demanded as the Green trailed off.

'This is murder, Stracker.'

The general laughed, pasting a feigned look of confusion on his face. 'That is no stranger to me.'

'Murder of tribe. Murder of family. Murder of a brother. Murder of a king. Murder of the emperor. Most of all, the murder of a man who spared your life once.'

'And has treated me like his servant ever since!' Stracker raged. 'I was prepared to walk in his shadow if he'd become an emperor I could be proud of. Instead, he has turned us into Denovians. Our blood is being diluted, our culture is being lost, our very memories of who we are and what we stand for are being diminished. He has let us down.'

'What will you tell people?'

Stracker shrugged, uncaring. 'Anything I like. My brother left the palace, grief-stricken at the loss of his child, rode into the north and was never seen again. He says he told no one where he was headed and I believe him; my brother is secretive. His disappearance can become one of the empire's mysteries.'

'I have to say this: I don't want to be a part of murdering our emperor.'

'I am not giving you a choice.' Stracker looked over at the man with the rope and added, 'Put it round his neck and hoist him. He's near enough dead now. He'll be none the wiser.'

Stracker saw the three guards share a glance. 'Are my orders to be disobeyed?' The two other men shook their heads, clearly more scared of their general than their broken emperor. 'Bleuth?'

Bleuth gave a wry half grin. 'I know you'll kill me if I don't.'

'You can choose to stick by your principles if that's more important to you than loyalty to your general, to your people, to your culture.'

'It's wrong.'

'Not in my eyes. We fight for leadership on the Steppes.'

'Only when our tribal ruler dies.'

'He's going to die very shortly.'

'By murder.'

'Choose your side, Bleuth!' the general ordered, tiring of the debate.

The man hung his head. 'I won't defy you, Stracker.'

'Coward!' Stracker said, laughing. 'Hang our prisoner!'

Slowly, the two Greens hoisted Loethar into the tree.

'That's it, boys,' Stracker urged, 'get his feet right off the ground. Good.' He clapped. 'Now tie him off. Farewell, brother.'

Elka took the leader out first, her pebble hitting him in the temple expertly. He dropped like the stone that struck him, his body crunching heavily to the forest floor. The three guards looked surprised and the pair holding Loethar above the ground had their mouths open comically when the other took the next stone, collapsing like his general with a shout of pain.

The two other guards let go of the rope but it had already been tied off and Loethar swung, his toes just missing the ground. Elka shot another stone, felling one of the remaining guards. His companion shouted in fear, drawing his sword. Elka, aware of her distinctiveness, remained hidden. 'Cut him down!' she called to Gavriel from behind the trees.

The guard thought she was speaking to him and backed away from Loethar, shaking his head. 'I have orders,' he stammered in Set. Gavriel emerged from the trees as Elka took aim with her fourth stone. The man began to babble at Gavriel, wondering where his slingshot was, but without pausing, Elka hit him in the thigh and he screamed and fell over. 'I didn't want him to have a slash at you,' she said to Gavriel. 'Quick, get him down.'

'I can't believe I'm doing this,' he growled over his shoulder.

Elka ignored Gavriel, and reloaded her catapult.

'Please,' the guard urged, still at Gavriel. 'You don't need to —'

'Oh, but I do,' Elka murmured to herself. She squinted, took very careful aim and let the sling hurl the stone straight at the man's temple. He made no sound but keeled over sideways.

'Is he alive?' she asked, finally emerging to help.

'I hope not.' Gavriel had cut the rope and Loethar's body had slumped once again to the ground. 'Another high body count, I see,' he said conversationally as he undid the rope from Loethar's neck.

She looked around. 'Last time I left men dead. I didn't want to this time. But they'll have horrible headaches, possibly split skulls.'

'How can you be sure they won't die?'

'Lots of practice,' she said, looking at her catapult before she put it away. 'Now, let me look.' She pushed Gavriel aside and placed her head close to Loethar's chest. Finally she looked at him. 'Bad news for you. He's alive.'

'Lo's wrath!' Gavriel replied. 'A half-dead emperor and my sworn enemy and now I'm stuck nursing him back to health. Is that your plan?'

'I nursed you.'

'I wasn't a war-mongering murderer.'

'Yes, but I didn't know that. You could have been.'

'This is typical of you, Elka. You think your calm reasoning will always win.'

'It usually does.'

'I wish you'd lived through what I had to. You wouldn't feel this way about this animal.'

'With him alive and captive, perhaps you give your king some bargaining power.' She shrugged. 'This way Stracker will know that someone witnessed his treachery, that he didn't clean up his tracks well enough. Even in their language I could see that this older soldier was not thrilled about killing the emperor.'

Gavriel nodded. 'So, before the thugs wake up, what do you suggest?'

'He's badly injured. But we have to get away from here. He's not even conscious to chew some seeds so he'll have to put up with whatever pain we cause.' She hoisted Loethar onto her shoulders. 'Ah, this feels familiar.'

Gavriel scowled. 'Let's go, wherever we're going.'

32

'... and that's all I know,' Sergius concluded. 'I have no idea where she is.'

Night had closed in around them. Sergius was shivering from its cool embrace.

You see, Ravan — may I call you that? — how devious your friend is? My father was no better. He planned my sister's death and yet it was all a ruse. He allowed my mother to hold a dead baby and think it was her own daughter. I was there when my father discussed it with the de Vis family.

Who was the little girl who died?

Who knows? Whoever she was, she was killed expressly to trick everyone — but especially the queen and so ultimately Loethar — that the princess had died moments after birth. But my father did not do this terrible deed with his own hand. Oh no, like all cunning men, he had another carry out his dirty deed. He chose Corbel de Vis; asking him, when he was not that much older than I am now, to kill a child that would be passed off as my newly-born/newly-dead sister, while my real sister was secreted away to your friend, Sergius. You know the rest. My father carried out this secret, murderous work, convinced he was doing it in the family's best interests and for the Crown. But he never considered the human cost — someone's child killed, Corbel having to carry a child's murder in his heart, Regor de Vis losing a son, my mother being tricked into losing her baby. She lost so many children in her journey to have Leo and myself and still my father forced her to declare me an unwanted orphan, convinced himself that risking my mother's sanity was worth the good for the Crown. She held on long enough just to defy Loethar but I can recall now how she whispered to me that it wasn't worth living any longer — not without her husband or her son. She loved me but I wasn't enough, not trapped in my madness. Death was a welcome visitor to Queen Iselda and she went to it believing all her three children were lost to her ... when in fact we all survived.

Sergius had been permitted to hear this exchange over the seam. *Ravan, my role is for the Valisars. I am loyal to them.*

The bird hopped over to his friend. *You told me it was in an observer's role.*

Ah, well, he lied to you again there, Piven announced. *I suspect Sergius plays a far more subtle game. I think his role has little to do with the Valisars themselves but everything to do with their magic. That's what he observes — the use of the magic: who has it, who is wielding it, and how.*

Is this true? Ravan asked his old friend.

Sergius nodded. *Piven is young but he is either well informed or incredibly sharp. The magic must not be wielded in a situation that is out of control.*

Piven began to laugh. *But it is! It is under no one's control but mine and no one controls me! The poor befuddled orphan invalid was blessed with all the power.*

Sergius said nothing.

'Is there anything else you wish to tell us, Sergius?' Piven said, switching to real speech. 'Perhaps how you plan to bring my sister back.'

'I cannot.'

'I'm sure that's a lie.'

'I told you, I have no clue to her whereabouts. The destination was chosen by de Vis. Even if he did so unwittingly, it was his mind that guided them.'

'Is Corbel empowered?'

Sergius shook his head. 'Not a skerrick. But the magic still permitted his navigation.'

'Your magic.'

'I suppose,' Sergius replied grudgingly.

'Then your magic brings her back!'

'Only if she wants to return. I cannot contact them.'

'So we have to make them want to come back. Perhaps I'm better off leaving them where they are. It's been ten anni after all.'

'And she is none the wiser; your sister likely has no knowledge of her power.'

Piven considered this, a soft smile playing around his lips as he looked directly at Sergius. 'I sense that you are lying to me again.'

Sergius shrugged. 'Believe what you want. You're the one with the power here.'

'Why don't you hurl some of your magic at me, Sergius?'

'Apart from the fact that my magic doesn't work that way, what would be the point? You have an aegis. You are protected from magic that can harm you.'

'But not other forms of magic?'

Sergius shook his head. 'If it doesn't want to harm you, you have nothing to fear from any other form of magic.'

'I don't fear anything, old man. Now, what else have you to share with us? Ravan still needs to be fully enlightened.'

'Only that there's an aegis for each of you.'

'Ah, I'm supposed to feel threatened by that. Except I don't because I doubt very much whether my brother or sister will look for theirs; they probably don't know much about it.'

'How is it that you know so much?'

Piven shrugged. 'The curse of my affliction. I was able to move amongst many without their caring about my presence. People spoke freely in front of me and I absorbed a lot of information that was useless at the time but is now highly valuable to me. I know about the power of an aegis. I doubt my brother does.'

'You should never be so sure.'

'I agree. Others could inform him. And perhaps you would make a special trip from this Loforsaken spot of yours to enlighten him, bad eyesight or not.'

Sergius's lips thinned. 'Perhaps I might,' he shot back.

Piven stretched and stood. 'Which is why we can't let you live.'

Greven looked up, alarmed, but Sergius didn't flinch.

'I see you were expecting that,' Piven continued.

Sergius shrugged. 'You will do what you will do. I am helpless.' He pointed to his bird. 'Ravan, be warned. Piven is no friend to you. The only friend you have here is about to be murdered. Flee, my long-time companion. Find a way to tell allies what this boy — nay, he is no boy; he thinks and talks like a man — has in store for them. Go, Ravan!'

The black bird swooped angrily overhead. *What are you doing?*

Piven sighed. 'I'm sorry, Ravan. Greven, throw Sergius off the cliff, would you?'

Sergius closed his eyes. 'Farewell, Ravan.'

No! the bird yelled into their minds. *No, Piven!*

Greven moved reluctantly towards Sergius.

I have made my decision. Sergius must die.

Ravan hopped towards him. *Sergius has walked this land for centuries. He has known all the Valisar kings. He travelled with the —*

Nevertheless, he must die now.

Why did I ever trust you? Ravan hurled with fury at Piven, watching helplessly as Greven grabbed Sergius. *Fight back, Sergius!* he begged.

No point, old friend. Sergius gave a soft sigh as Greven picked him up easily with a strength infused by magic.

'Forgive me, Sergius,' Greven mumbled.

'You are a slave. I understand.'

'Oh, get on with it. Throw him to his well-deserved death!' Piven said, bored. 'You see, Ravan, I've given up fighting my dark inclinations. I'm giving in to them fully instead, now. Let's see where this new attitude leads.'

Let him live! Ravan screeched.

He is my enemy.

Then you are now my enemy.

So be it. Piven looked over at Greven, who stood at the cliff edge. Sergius balanced in front of him, looking not down over the perilous drop but out to sea, to the far horizon, his eyes closed, lips moving in what appeared to be silent prayer. *Scream to your god if you want, Sergius, it may help*, Piven offered mockingly and then nodded at Greven.

With a sigh of deep regret, Greven pushed the old man, who disappeared quickly over the lip of the cliff to the sounds of screams — not his own, but the cries of despair from a bird.

Piven moved to the edge to join Greven and, illuminated by thin moonlight, they watched Sergius's body bounce down the cliff face, coming to rest broken and bloodied on the rocky foreshore of the beach.

'Good,' Piven said. 'Let's go. *Coming, Ravan?*'

The bird swooped past him, violently raking his clawed feet through the boy's hair. *I will see you dead for this!*

Piven touched the injury on his head, pulled his hand away to stare at blood that appeared black in the moon's silvery light and smiled. 'Looks like it's just us then, Greven.'

The former leper finally tore his eyes from the sorrowful scene on the beach and glared at his charge.

Piven looked bemused. 'Stop scowling. He threatened me. Your job is to keep me safe.'

'He was an old man.'

'He was a god's tool and a king's pawn, and far too dangerous to let live now that he has marked me and knows me for what I am. And you know it. Come, I think it's time we returned to Brighthelm and let everyone understand that a new ruler is about to take his crown.'

* * *

As if the land sensed the loss of one of its longest travellers, the clouds thickened overhead to block what little moon's light had filtered through earlier. A gust of wind off the ocean challenged the two torches lighting the steps and won the battle, their flames dying soon after Sergius's body crumpled on the beach. The foreshore was thrown into darkness but despite the limited visibility, Ravan's eyes were still sharp enough to pick out his friend. He swooped down to land next to the old man's head, and could see that it was leaking blood in several places from wounds inflicted by the cliff's unyielding surface.

Ravan concentrated and then a few moments later flapped excitedly. He threw up shields around his thoughts. *I hear your heartbeat, faint but there nonetheless. Can you talk to me?*

I can talk over the seam only, the voice he loved answered.

Sergius's link felt weak. Ravan intensified his own. *I have shielded us. Sergius, I —*

Listen, Ravan. Nothing can be done for me. Perhaps this is what Cyrena wanted for me.

Don't say that!

It doesn't matter. My life is over — but yours still matters. You must follow your instincts now. You know Piven's intentions and his powers. You have to let people know.

How?

That is your journey, my friend.

Why didn't you tell me about the princess?

I would have.

Sergius, that is not good enough.

It is all I can say. I have but moments now, and I must use them not on recrimination but on concentrating on my own death. They will feel it.

Who?

Corbel de Vis and the Valisar princess — if they have survived — will feel my passing. They are connected to this land through my magic.

And as a result of your death they'll know what?

That it's time to return.

How?

The same way they left us. Cyrena's powers will help them re-enter from whichever plane they come from.

How will Cyrena know?

She already does. Now leave me to my death, Ravan. I love you and I'm sad we must part but you have grave responsibilities now. We are counting on you.

Me! What for?

To stop the evil that Piven possesses. No one has ever fully understood the Valisar magic. Piven admits the more good he tried to give, the more his soul was filled with darkness. We don't know his power yet. If his sister has lived, she will surely possess the Valisar Enchantment — she will have the ability to compel others. She is the only hope against Piven and his aegis. Now go. I have nothing more to give the Valisars but my death. I hope it's enough.

Sergius!

Ravan ... go, little friend. And remember, Loethar was never your enemy. He sighed. *I am spent. I must let go now. Let me hear your wings once again; their sound will bear me away with them to a happier place.*

Ravan lifted sorrowfully, swooping near his old friend several times before lifting himself up into the night in spite of his desperately heavy heart.

Sergius died a moment later.

Far away a man sat bolt upright. He had been sleeping under the stars on a rare break from his usual labours and routine. He couldn't place or didn't recall what had disturbed him but it had been powerful enough to wake him fully and as he lay now on his back, staring up at the night sky, he noticed a shooting star. He frowned at its unusual brightness; the pattern it traced across its inky backdrop seemed to imprint itself on his thoughts. It was as though he could concentrate on nothing else but that blazing path — all other concerns, even his pressing need to empty his bladder, suddenly faded. All that mattered, all that resonated, all that counted in his life at this precise second was the burning passage of that star as it spent its energy travelling to death.

Corbel finally blinked, his frown deepening. He had an inescapable sense of certainty that the moment was upon him.

It was time to return the Valisar princess to her people.

33

Once they'd retrieved their belongings they abandoned the horses; they could move faster on foot in spite of being encumbered with Loethar's dead weight. Nevertheless, Elka was surprisingly light of foot even with the man prostrate across her back, with Gavriel bringing up the rear, making sure they were not followed.

They travelled in silence, putting their energies into their exertions rather than conversation. Gavriel was surprised and relieved to note that his time in the mountains had prepared him more than well enough for this sort of terrain. Where once he might have been out of breath, he now found he could travel the steep, slippery undergrowth with ease. His stride was long and only vaguely hampered by a limp from his old injury; his muscles were ropey and strong, and his endurance matched anything the Davarigons had thrown at him. His convalescence was well and truly behind him. Most importantly, his mind was sound, his memories returning in a constant stream of enlightenment.

He shook his head yet again at the notion that the man Elka carried was the despised Loethar. Where once his personal impression had been so twisted and skewed that Loethar had seemed invincible, now the barbarian appeared every inch a mere man. Gavriel despised the way Loethar had re-invented himself, swapping so easily from all-conquering, all-slaughtering invader to magnanimous emperor that people had begun to whisper had made the Set an easier place to live, trade, move around. The bitterest truth was realising that he had, in his ignorance, also unwittingly admired the man that he now remembered had murdered his father, among many other ruthless, unnecessary slaughterings.

Loethar groaned and Elka immediately stopped. Gavriel hung back, scowling. 'Good. I hope it really hurts.'

She threw him a glance of reproach as she turned. 'Let's set him down there,' she said, nodding at a ridge not far above them. 'Then we'll get a better sense of where we are and we could use some sleep ourselves. It will be dawn all too soon.'

Gavriel said nothing but took over the lead, quickly moving ahead and up to the ridge. 'This is fine,' he confirmed and Elka followed, Loethar now moaning softly from her back. They lay him down.

'Give him some water,' Elka suggested.

Gavriel handed her the skin. 'You can do it.'

Her expression told him she wearied of his stubbornness but Gavriel remained adamant.

'Here, drink,' Elka coaxed their prisoner.

Loethar's eyes flickered open. He clearly made no sense of what he saw; tried to speak but it came out as a croak. The water dribbled onto his lips and he grasped at the water sack greedily, Gavriel only noticing now, with a spike of satisfaction, how one of the emperor's fingers stuck out at an unnatural angle.

'Thank you,' Loethar finally managed, seemingly unaware of his wrenched finger. 'Who are you?'

'Not now. Save your injured throat. You are out of immediate danger, so sleep. I'm going to cook up a brew that will ease the pain ... in your hand, for instance,' Elka said, also just noticing the dislocated finger.

'Hand,' he repeated, even managing to achieve a dry tone. 'There's so much pain, I can't locate it to any specific area.'

She smiled gently and Gavriel's scowls deepened.

'I wish they'd killed you,' he murmured.

Loethar only now realised there was another person present. He shifted his head gingerly in the direction of Gavriel's voice, his eyes slitted in pain. 'My persecutors would agree. Who are you?'

'Someone with a grudge.'

Loethar rather impossibly managed a brief smile through his swollen, bruised lips. 'Then tell me which of my enemies you are. Are you sure you know me?'

'Oh, yes. Yours is not a face I'd forget.' Elka looked over with an expression of irony and Gavriel could see the dark humour in his words. 'Emperor Loethar,' he continued, 'we meet again.'

'We do? I don't recognise you.' Loethar blinked, grimacing through obvious hurt.

'That's because you haven't actually met,' Elka explained, glaring at Gavriel again. 'Let him rest, will you? He's no good to you dead.'

'No,' Loethar urged. 'Talk to me, stranger. Stop me from slipping into unconsciousness again. I want to remember this pain. I want to use it when I finally give Stracker the death he has long deserved.'

Elka sighed. 'I can't produce the brew in moments so enjoy your suffering.'

'Can I know *your* name at least?' he asked her. 'Lo's breath but you're a tall woman!' he remarked as she stood. 'Wait, did *you* carry me?'

'Well I certainly didn't ... or wouldn't. I'd have preferred to watch you swing,' Gavriel answered before she could.

Elka ignored him. 'I am Elka. From the Davarigons.'

'Ah, I've so longed to meet your people. The famed giants of the mountains. You are elusive ... and generous, it seems. Thank you, Elka.'

'Hardly giants. Just tall,' she conceded.

'And strong,' Gavriel reminded for Loethar's benefit. 'So don't try anything.'

Loethar wheezed a laugh at the very suggestion. 'Are you always so brave with your tongue when your female bodyguard is near?' Loethar baited.

Gavriel took a breath of calm. 'Be careful, Loethar. I'm the one with the sword, remember, and I wield it easily. I won't hesitate to plunge it into your belly.'

'Easy to say when I'm lying here helpless. I've obviously personally offended you, stranger. And yet while I never forget a face, I don't recognise you at all and why would I, for your friend has confirmed we have not met. So who in your family have I injured?'

'You killed my father, amongst many others.'

Loethar tried to nod, winced, and closed his eyes. 'I killed many people when I overthrew the Denovian Set. But since being crowned emperor are you aware that I have killed no one by my own hand? And the only deaths I've ordered have been those who have disobeyed imperial orders — either Set and Steppes?' He sounded breathless but his voice was improving.

'No, I doubt my companion is aware of that,' Elka said, fanning the flames of the small fire she'd been coaxing to life. 'He harbours a lot of hate for you.'

Loethar sighed. 'Why did he rescue me, then? So that he could have the pleasure of killing me himself?'

'You were rescued only because Elka insisted,' Gavriel replied.

'And so your brother wants to kill you,' Elka interjected.

'Half-brother,' Loethar and Gavriel corrected together. Loethar looked over at Gavriel, bemused. 'Who *are* you?' His efforts set off a coughing fit and he winced.

'Be still!' Elka commanded both of them. 'Focus on the pain and tell me where it is,' she told Loethar.

Loethar was breathing shallowly. Through gritted teeth he said, 'Ribs, mainly. My hand, as you pointed out, my throat, for obvious reasons, my head … even my arse hurts.'

She nodded. 'You're going to feel a lot worse, I promise you.'

'I'm rather enjoying seeing you in this state, Loethar,' Gavriel added. 'Your imperial guards treated me in very similar fashion a decade ago. Ask Elka how badly beaten and broken I was. In fact, you're getting off lightly. They were just going to hang you — and while you were already unconscious. Your animals broke both of my ankles just as a prelude to their fun, so that I was appropriately hobbled and at their mercy, fully conscious. If not for Elka I'd be long dead.'

'Or rotting in the gaol,' Loethar suggested.

'No, definitely dead,' Gavriel confirmed. 'You would not have let me live.'

'I'll ask again, why?' He sounded exhausted now.

'Tell him,' Elka growled at Gavriel. 'You remember the pain; he's going through the same and I don't know how he's still got the strength or inclination to talk.'

'Force of will, Elka. It's a powerful thing,' Loethar said, resting his head back and closing his eyes again. 'Come on, man, who was your father? Would I even remember his name? The invasion was a mad time. I killed a lot of noblemen and I can hear from your voice you are no peasant.'

'You'd remember his name, all right. His death was probably your most cowardly. He was Regor de Vis.'

Loethar's eyes snapped open. He tried to sit up but Elka's large, very firm hand, urged him back. 'I don't believe it.'

Gavriel nodded smugly, taking much pleasure in Loethar's shock. 'Believe it.'

'Which son are you?'

'Gavriel.'

Loethar turned to Elka. 'Is this the truth?'

'Can't you see how much he's enjoying your discomfort?

Gavriel continued, 'I carry ten anni's worth of vengeance.'

Loethar shook his head. 'Lo rot you! I never understood how you slipped our guard.'

'It was easy,' Gavriel lied. 'In spite of Freath's treachery.'

'Freath is dead.'

Gavriel gave a small whoop of delight. 'Don't expect me to mourn him. How did he die? Painfully, I hope?'

'Yes. A sword wound. His body was found at the entry to Hell's Gates.'

'Here in the north! Why was he here?'

'Imperial business. I presume you've heard of the outlaw Kilt Faris? We're hunting him down. And we're so close now he can probably feel our collective breath on his collar. Freath was working on finding him.'

'That cowardly turncoat was —'

'Curiously enough, my friend,' Loethar finished, 'I miss him already. I will find his killer and I will have Kilt Faris's head on a spike outside Brighthelm.'

Gavriel refused to look at Elka. 'I'm just glad another of my enemies is dead.'

Loethar smiled. 'And yet it seems our destinies remain entwined.'

'Don't feel so confident about that. They won't be for long.'

'I wonder where you will find another king? The alternative of my half-brother is surely unthinkable. And the Valisars are all gone, with pickings from the other former realms equally unpalatable.'

'Again, you may presume too much,' Gavriel replied with a sneer.

Loethar's gaze narrowed. 'Is that so? Then perhaps the de Vis family has delusions of grandeur that went unnoticed in your father's era?'

Gavriel stood and drew his sword. 'My father was the most loyal of all Valisar followers.'

Loethar nodded. 'I'm sure he'd turn in his grave to know his son slaughtered a wounded, unarmed man.'

Gavriel sneered. 'My father has no grave. Do not speak of him as though you would know anything about him, or how he would feel. You forget, barbarian, that you too slaughtered him as an unarmed man, who came in good faith to parley with you.' He advanced on Loethar, murder in his eyes.

'Gavriel!' Elka warned, standing. 'You fall right into his trap if you do anything but let justice take its right course.'

He knew she was right; her caution echoed his instincts. Pride aside, no matter how his father died, Regor de Vis would likely not have praised his son for ending a man's life this way.

'You are so much better than this,' she muttered for his hearing only, directing her glance down to the broken man who lay prone before them. 'He's going nowhere but to where you decide and as your prisoner.'

Gavriel nodded. 'Give him your brew. I need to walk!' He turned and strode away.

'He has good reason to hate me,' Loethar said, sipping from the proferred bowl.

'Yes, he does,' Elka replied quietly.

'And lots of good reasons to keep me alive — thank you for making him see that.'

'Be assured, I did you no favour.'

Loethar drained the brew, his bruised, swollen lips slick with the dark liquid. 'How does a Davarigon become such a close companion and ally of a noble from the court of Valisar?'

'I suppose in much the same strange way that the barbarian warlord from the Steppes finds himself in similar company.'

'And what is that way?'

'For someone who is so battered, you are very talkative.'

'Answer me. It takes my mind off the pain.'

She tipped out the dregs of the pain-killing liquor and wiped the bowl with some leaves, then slung it back in her sack. 'Circumstances.' She shrugged. 'We all make decisions, take pathways, choose our way forward. I chose mine, Gavriel de Vis chose his, and our paths crossed.'

'Fate?'

'Yes, something like that.'

'My presence here is not fate. Even my condition right now is not fate.'

'So you wanted to be beaten and killed by your brother?'

'My half-brother is predictable. I certainly factored in that he would do what he did.'

'And still you came to him. Why?'

'Honour.'

Elka, who had been re-packing a few utensils back into her pack, turned to stare at him now. 'Honour?' she repeated. 'Yes, I heard you spouting about that.' She expected a wry smile, or a sarcastic response, but she got neither. Loethar stared back at her gravely. 'You expect me to believe that?' she asked.

'Do you think I am not capable of it?'

She shook her head. 'Not from what I've heard.'

'You should listen again, then, and be sure that you are hearing only words you can trust. The truth will reassure you that I am a man of my word.'

She sneered. 'So you are honourable to yourself, you mean.'

'No, I didn't say that. But a man who keeps his word is honourable. A man who gives promises and keeps them, swears oaths and follows through on them, or remains true to himself, is honourable. I am all of those things.'

Elka shook her head. 'What was the honour in coming here to knowingly risk death at the hands of your half-brother?'

'I was bringing our mother's ashes to him. Stracker was close to our mother and though she could see his faults — of which there are plenty — he was her flesh, and she did love him.'

Elka faltered. 'When did your mother die?'

'Yesterday … I think. I fear I've lost track of time. She was poisoned by my wife, I believe. I cremated my mother and felt it was right to bring her to my sibling. It was my duty to give him the opportunity to pay his respects, and for us to scatter her ashes in an agreed spot. It wasn't wise, it wasn't clever or even brave, but it was the honourable way.'

'I want to say I'm sorry but I don't believe you deserve any sympathy after all that you've perpetrated on my friend and on the

Set. I do, however, respect that you have lost a parent and for this I appreciate your sorrow.'

He sighed. 'No sorrow. My mother led a hard life but she was a hard woman. As it turned out, revenge is always a cold satisfaction; it never quite lives up to the anticipation.'

'Revenge? For what?'

Loethar seemed to come out of a trance. He blinked at her. 'I have no idea why we're having this conversation. I haven't talked this much to a woman in years. Your brew is clearly having an effect on me, Elka, in loosening my tongue.'

She regarded him quizzically, then turned as Gavriel returned. 'Can he move?' he asked.

'Not on his own,' Elka replied. 'Looks like I'm stuck with you for a little longer,' she said to Loethar; then, turning back to Gavriel, she added, 'I'll carry him.'

'Are you numbed yet?' he asked Loethar.

'Do you care?'

'Not in the slightest. I hope it hurts far more than you can bear.'

Loethar actually smiled lopsidedly. 'I can bear plenty.'

Gavriel turned his attention to Elka, ignoring their captive. 'We haven't been followed. Are you sure about coming with me?'

'Well, you can't move him on your own.'

'Elka, there is no promise that anyone is waiting for us.'

'I know. But unless you have another idea, we have to try and find them. I'm not leaving him here or alone with you.'

Loethar had appeared disinterested in their conversation but now he spoke up. 'Who are we trying to find?'

Elka shot Gavriel a look but it was too late. He could show restraint for only so long. 'King Leonel,' he snarled.

For the first time since they'd encountered him, Loethar looked genuinely shocked.

34

They were moving slowly, tracking northwesterly, climbing all the time. It was nearing dawn and the landscape was unfolding before them once again in a thin, misty light as day began to waken.

'Not bad progress at all,' Jewd said, when they took a short rest. 'Slow but steady. How are all your aches?'

'Don't worry about me,' Kilt replied firmly. 'I'll take the bermine regularly and grit my teeth and ignore what it doesn't cover.'

'My hero!' Jewd commented, feigning a swoon.

Leo chuckled.

Kilt glared at them. 'Well, this is a jolly adventure for you both,' he sneered.

'All right, Kilt, you want us to be serious,' Leo surprised him by saying. 'Tell us this. What interest did Stracker, or Vulpan, for that matter, have in a clergyman?'

Kilt swung around to stare at Leo. 'What do you mean?' he replied, searching his mind for an excuse, absently checking the shields he was so practised at erecting in the king's presence.

Leo shrugged. 'Well, it strikes me as odd that they would have any interest in you at all. Why were they going to all that trouble to escort you alone with three guards, and Vulpan and Stracker in attendance? They were taking you north. Why?'

'How should I know?' Kilt said, knowing he replied a moment too soon. Even he could hear how it smacked of things left unsaid.

He sensed rather than watched Jewd's eyes narrow, his expression turning from amusement to a soft frown. He refused to look at his big friend, for Jewd would know immediately that he was telling a lie. 'I was given no reason,' he added.

Leo nodded but didn't seem convinced. 'It just seemed odd, that's all.'

'What happened with Vulpan, anyway?' Jewd asked.

'He incarcerated me. What did you think he did?'

Jewd shrugged too. 'Oh, I don't know, I thought he might have tasted your blood.'

'He did,' Kilt replied, realising too late — in the space of a blink of an eye — that he had made the most terrible admission. Two errors in a row after years and years of being cleverly secretive.

He watched Jewd carefully but his big friend simply nodded. 'And then what?'

Kilt forced himself to speak calmly and in an offhand way. 'Oh, you know, typical questions. Why was I interested in Mrs Kirin Felt, essentially; I found myself spinning the usual lies.' He frowned, showing his irritation. 'This feels like an interrogation.'

Jewd grinned but Kilt could see the gesture carried no sincerity. They both knew each other too well … and each knew the other was lying right now. Jewd looked at the king. 'Leo, run ahead, will you, and let me know what's ahead of us beyond this hill. I suspect we should be able to get a clear view of where we need to head and plot our path before sundown. Another night sleeping rough, I'm afraid.'

Leo gave a soft snort of disgust. 'That comment suggests that we sleep like royals back at the camp!' He winked at Jewd and was gone, oblivious to the manipulation.

Jewd returned his attention to Kilt, who regarded him steadily, anticipating the confrontation.

'We've been together too long to fool each other, Kilt.'

'I don't know what you're digging for.'

'Yes you do. I'm big, old friend, not thick. I told you a long time ago not to make that mistaken assumption.'

'Jewd —'

'The truth, now, or I walk away from this.'

'What?' Kilt felt shock like the water down his back.

'You heard me. You nearly died back there. We all could have died, especially the lad.'

'Jeopardising Leo's life was your fault, your decision! I told you to stay behind. You didn't —'

'We did. No one else was going to save your arrogant arse. What did you think? You could just walk into the viper's nest and come out unbitten?'

'I just wanted information.'

'Fair enough. But I don't understand your needing to go alone. I don't understand their interest in you. And I certainly don't understand your reluctance to tell the truth ... to me, of all people. Tell me the truth or I will walk away from you and from this strange life we've built alongside one another.'

Kilt stared at Jewd, feeling as though he didn't recognise his closest friend. 'I ...'

'Remember ... big, not stupid,' Jewd warned. 'And hurry, before Leo returns. He has no idea that you've been lying to us, although he too is smarter than you give him credit for. He knows something isn't adding up but he trusts you. I thought I did, too.'

'And now you don't?'

'I don't like lies between us. They compromise us. They lead to danger ... like today. Let me make this easier for you. Let me tell you what I know ... Vulpan is interested in one sort of person only. A Vested. That's what he's doing right now — compiling a list of Vested. He tasted Kirin Felt — Vested. He even tasted Lily because somehow she has convinced him that she too is Vested. And now he has tasted you. Why would he taste you, Kilt?'

'I ... really, I —'

Jewd stared at him, his eyes glittering with scorn. 'He wouldn't waste his time with you unless ...' He shook his head, seemingly unable to speak.

Kilt took a deep breath. He knew in his heart he should have explained it all many years ago … when they were children. He couldn't lose his close friend. 'Does it really change anything, Jewd?' he asked, his voice hoarse with the emotion he wasn't sure he had fully under control, his nagging pain momentarily forgotten.

Jewd blinked with shock. 'Doesn't it change everything?'

'Why?'

'Deceit is a poisonous ally.'

'I haven't deceived anyone.'

'How do you arrive at that conclusion?' Jewd's expression had turned to barely disguised scorn.

'Because it's never been used.'

'Until now.'

Kilt swallowed. 'Yes, until yesterday.'

Jewd swung and punched the tree. His knuckles bloomed blood.

'Ah, Jewd. Don't, please,' Kilt said softly, genuine remorse in his voice. 'If I could go back or change this, I would.'

'Me, Kilt. It's me you've lied to.'

Kilt looked down. 'I've been lying to myself, to tell the truth. I thought if I ignored it, if I refused to answer its call, I could beat it. And I did … I have. All these years I have never once fallen prey to its seductions. Not once, Jewd. I've been strong and utterly in control of it.'

'Am I supposed to be proud?'

'No, not proud. Understanding, perhaps. I do not want this. I never asked for it. It has been a permanent curse on my life, but I've beaten it day after day. You can't know what willpower it takes to resist its call. Why do you think I went to the Academy? I thought there I could understand this thing inside me. But that only made it worse.'

Jewd took a breath. 'What exactly is it that you can do?'

Kilt's face twisted into disgust. He looked away, then up into the trees, considering his answer. Kilt could see Leo, who had arrived at the summit of the hill they were ascending. He was scanning ahead and soon would be back. This conversation needed to be behind them by the time Leo returned, for Kilt had no intention of sharing his secret with the king. He sighed. 'I have an odd ability to elicit information out of people, that's all.'

Jewd regarded him suspiciously. 'Against their will. Is that what you're saying?'

Kilt nodded. 'I can't make it last for long. You see, nothing so special.'

'I'd give my left nipple for such a skill, Kilt!'

'No, you wouldn't, Jewd. That's the point. There's a price.'

'Such as?'

'Well, I get nosebleeds every time I use the magic.'

'I've never seen you with a nosebleed.'

'And now you have the answer to your next question.'

Jewd looked suspicious. 'So now you read minds?'

'No, I think it's obvious you want to ask me if I've ever used my ability against you. And as you've never seen me with a nosebleed, not only do you have the answer you want, but you can reassure yourself that I'm telling the truth when I say that I have not made use of the magic through our life together. The last time — before yesterday — was when I was barely a stripling youth.'

Jewd's expression turned to one of awakening. 'Nosebleeds, of course! It comes back to me now.'

'Yes, well, you only saw me with them once or twice as a child, I recall.'

They both glanced up and saw Leo making tracks back towards them.

'So you bled and Vulpan saw it, I take it,' Jewd said.

'Yes, damn it. It was the blood that attracted him to me. Once he tasted it, I had to admit my skills and naturally he refused to let me leave. I was being taken to join all the other Vested, presumably.'

'Aren't Vested supposed to be marked somehow?' Jewd queried.

'No, you're thinking of the legend of an aegis,' Kilt said dismissively. 'That's entirely different.'

'I missed the nosebleed sign, though, didn't I?'

'I never gave you any,' Kilt replied, his tone regretful. 'I'm sorry, Jewd. You're the last person I'd ever want to —'

His friend waved a hand. 'You've told me now. I'm shocked. I'd be lying if I said anything different but I must accept it. I can see you don't relish its company.'

'I hate it! I've been running from it all my life.'

'There's nothing else?'

Kilt shook his head, despising the lie.

'Well, we don't have any need to discuss it again,' Jewd said as Leo skidded down the final few paces.

'You two look very serious,' the king observed.

'Kilt's pain is intensifying,' Jewd answered. 'What did you see?'

'The landscape is still, no riders anywhere on the roads or paths below. We need to swing more west now and I've found a good track that should make the going easier for you, Kilt. We'll be back in familiar territory by nightfall if we make good time today.'

Kilt felt relief. 'I'm going to need a spectacular disguise.'

'What for?' both of his companions asked at the same moment.

'For when I go to Brighthelm and get Lily,' he replied, surprised they needed to ask.

Roddy was exhausted from trailing the pair. He knew their names now. Petor was not Petor at all but a youth called Piven. And his companion was an older man he called Greven. They were not happy travellers, he noticed. The man was mostly silent. Piven did all the talking whenever there was any talking.

Roddy was good at tracking. Being an only child, he'd taught himself how to play alone and play quietly. The forest had become his playground and its animals his playmates. He had learned how to creep up on even the most timid squirrel and be able to watch it from a close distance without it suspecting. Following Piven was easy, although Roddy could feel the magic bristling around the youth who had saved his life. He still couldn't understand why the compulsion to follow Piven was irresistible, stronger even than his anxiety for his mother and how bereft she would be without him. But he couldn't not follow the stranger.

Both Roddy and his mother had always known that Roddy was different to other children. The palsy in his hand had always fascinated his peers, while his mother's neighbours simply used to sigh, squeeze his cheeks and make exclamations like *poor little mite*, or *perhaps he'll grow out of it*.

Roddy knew he wouldn't grow out of it. Instinctively he seemed to know and accept that it was his burden in life, and while it didn't seem to stop him from leading a perfectly happy childhood, it did single him out. There was no pain, no discomfort at all; just a helpless tremor that was at times worse than others and that was completely out of his control.

When Petor had brought him back from the dead it had become worse. Whereas, before, his palsy hadn't always been immediately noticeable, now even Roddy was aware of the constant trembling. There was suddenly no stopping it. The touch of Piven's magic had awakened it.

Roddy tasted salt on his lips and was dragged back to the present. He had never seen the sea before. Though he had heard plenty about it, to be here looking at its vastness, its changing colours and its soothing monotony of constant movement, filled him with wonder. It felt dangerous but exhilarating and if he had not seen death just now, he might have been able to indulge his awe. But he felt the tug of fear as he looked again at the spot where an ancient looking man called Sergius had been flung from the top of a cliff.

Once again Piven had shocked him, ordering the death with such casual brutality. And what was more shocking was that once again the man called Greven had obeyed. Greven looked reluctant but he had still done as Piven demanded. Roddy considered this. He felt a strange kinship with Greven and a helpless fascination for Piven. He had to continue following them. In fact, he didn't believe he could resist the call of Piven's presence.

Dawn had broken, and beautiful she was, too, spreading across the sea as well as the fields inland. Roddy knew he would need to make a start if he was to catch up with Piven. He wasn't worried, given his strong sense of direction and ability to track, but he didn't want them to get so far in front that he lost their trail. Already they had several hours on him. But he had felt frozen to this spot, churning over in his mind what he'd witnessed and what he'd heard.

He moved at last, stretching from his crouched position in the hedgerow. He needed to eat something. He had deduced that Sergius lived nearby. Perhaps he should search for a hut. He didn't want to see the man's smashed body on the beach but he was helplessly drawn to the cliff's edge. He peeked over, feeling a keen stab of sorrow to see Sergius crumpled into a tight position — as though he'd died in agony — at the cliff's floor. As he stared sadly at the man he didn't know and yet could grieve for, Roddy felt a stirring of magic that was powerful enough to make him suck in his breath. It touched him deep to the core and it was from within that he responded.

'Where are you?' he yelled, his breath now coming in shallow gasps.

'Here,' said a beautiful voice and the body of a woman whose torso ended in serpent coils reared up before him. She seemed to hang in the air and he dared not look down or wonder whether those coils went all the way to the beach from his high spot. 'I am Cyrena.' She was translucent, as though there but not fully formed. 'Only you can see me, Roddy, if that's what you're scared of.' She laughed and it sounded like glass tinkling. 'Only you and Ravan, that is.'

'Ravan?' Roddy swung around to see that the large raven had settled nearby, watching him. 'Hello,' Roddy said tentatively, willing himself not to be frightened.

Who are you? the bird asked, the words blossoming in his mind. Roddy fell back, terrified and amazed at once. *Are you the person who has been watching us?* The raven continued. *I've been aware of you on the rim of my mind but so much has occurred that I haven't been able to concentrate fully on what has been nagging me. Have you followed us here?*

Roddy nodded, too shocked to say anything.

From where exactly?

'Green Herbery,' the boy murmured. 'I'm following Piven.'

Why?

'I can't help it. I am touched by his magic. I have my own, too.'

Ravan blinked slowly. *You are Vested?*

Roddy nodded. 'I've heard that name before. My mother whispered it with fear, although she never liked me talking about my ability, especially now. She said they would take me away.'

They would.

'Then I am right to have kept the secret. But then Piven made me well again using his magic and ...' He shrugged. 'I thought he might have some answers for me. He seemed kind.' He glanced at the serpent woman nervously.

You saw him order Greven to kill a man.

Roddy nodded. 'That old man. And again not so long ago — a man called Clovis.'

You shouldn't have followed Piven.

'I couldn't help it. I had to. I didn't feel as though I had a choice. It was my magic's decision, not mine,' Roddy bleated. 'Was the old man your friend?'

Why do you ask that?

'You seemed ...' Roddy tried to find the right way to describe what he had felt. 'To belong together.'

We did, in a way. Yes, he was my friend. My oldest friend.

'I'm sorry for you.' Roddy turned to face the enormous serpent-woman. She was so beautiful, he couldn't possibly be frightened of her, despite her size and those twisted coils. 'Are you my friend, Cyrena?'

She laughed softly. 'I do hope you are mine, Roddy. I chose you.'

His fear was lessening by the moment. 'Chosen for what?'

'You are on your journey now, Roddy. You took the first steps yourself and now I am going to tell you more. Ask your questions. You do not need Piven to answer them.'

He stared at her, his mind racing to understand. He would have to be smart in how he phrased his questions. 'Why am I following Piven?'

'You are right that you are connected to his magic, which has touched yours.'

'My mother has always believed I was touched by the fairies but I think she used that to explain away my tremor.'

'She is right in a way. You have a vast well of magic available to you, Roddy. Magic I have given you. Consider how you track, think about how silently you can move and the extraordinary wealth of information you can take in at a single glance.'

'Is that magical?'

She smiled kindly. 'I can assure you, no ordinary person can move as you do or follow a trail so accurately. And certainly no ordinary person has a perfect memory of everything he sees at any time. You do. These are the skills Vested in you by magic. But the rest of the magic you possess is yet untapped.'

'Why me?'

'You were the right soul.'

'What am I to do with this?'

'That's the important question, Roddy. While the magic is part of you and comes from you, it does not belong to you.'

'It belongs to you?'

'No, there is another.'

Roddy's face lit up. 'Piven!'

'No, Roddy. Piven is no friend to you. He is no longer the person he was.'

'But he saved —'

'I am aware that he saved your life. But that was a personal crusade. He has been fighting demons that take the form of his inclinations. Piven's magic is dark, Roddy. It is an angry, bitter magic, as you have witnessed for yourself.'

'So who owns my magic?'

Cyrena smiled. 'You will know in your heart when you meet. But you must find this one, Roddy. That is what you must do for me. It doesn't normally work like this but Piven's rage has changed everything. Ravan will help you.' Roddy glanced at the great black bird. 'Trust him,' she assured. 'He is your friend.'

'Who is he?'

Cyrena's coils twisted and her spectre shimmered above the cliff. 'He is a guide. Ravan is on a special journey of discovery for himself now. A great magic is about to occur and changes will result, especially for Ravan. Truths will be unlocked for him.'

'Will I see you again?'

'I'm not sure, child. The death of Sergius summoned me; I was able to use his moment of death to enter this plane long enough to speak with you. Unless another Valisar is crowned I have little access to the magic that permits me here.' She smiled sadly. 'We have not known times like these before. I shall rely on brave souls like yourself to make the right decisions to aid the land of Cormoron the Great. You will make me proud, Roddy.

'Remember, a magic has been unleashed. Sergius asked it of me, and his death has created a rift in the world that has allowed me to make it possible. I can tell you and Ravan only this. Go to the mountains. Ravan.' She turned to regard the bird who had not moved, made no sound during the conversation. 'Trust your instincts. Do not be afraid. Trouble is ahead but the Valisars are stronger than their enemies credit them. Make haste to Lo's Teeth and the Davarigon people. The storm comes.'

Cyrena began to fade.

'Wait!' Roddy begged.

'Farewell, child. The magic has begun,' she managed to say before her light and colours diminished until Roddy found himself blinking, realising the apparition was no longer there.

Roddy turned to the raven that regarded him. The air around them seemed to sigh and then swell. Roddy felt pressure at his temples and his ears began to throb. He put his hands to them as a great rushing sound overwhelmed him.

He closed his eyes as Ravan began to shriek.

35

Kirin was subdued and Lily felt incredibly awkward. Long before a raven had begun its raucous racket in the far west, he'd spent the last of their coin on a cart and an old nag to pull it, plus some meagre supplies. She thought they were on their way to Brighthelm but Kirin had ignored several roads that could have led them into the city. So far she'd left him to his silence, believing he was still smarting over her rejection but over the last two hours she'd realised he wasn't sulking. Kirin was distracted, deep in thought, but not about her, not even about them. She couldn't stand the quiet any longer.

'Kirin, are you going to tell me what this is about?'

For a blink he didn't say anything; then his expression turned to a confused frown of query.

'This hideous silence between us,' she prompted, emotion piling up behind the words she refused to vent because she didn't want an argument just now. Her throat felt tight and she swallowed hard.

He turned to regard her. 'You look very upset.'

'Kirin!'

He flinched.

'What is happening? We were kissing not so long ago and you looked happy. Now you're —'

'I didn't want to be reminded about that,' he said sadly.

'Oh really? Well, forgive me. I can't push it to the back of my mind as easily as you seem able to.'

Kirin sighed softly and looked at her gently and she hated herself more for winning his sympathy. 'Lily, I have nowhere to put it but the back of my mind. What would you have me do? There is nothing more heart-breaking than unrequited love — I'm sure of that now.'

'Love?'

He looked away, stared off to the side of the road.

'We hardly know each other, we —' she said.

'I don't need to know anything more about you. I love you.' He shrugged. 'But you love someone else and that's just my bad luck.' He turned back and gave her a sad smile. 'My bad luck to love my wife.'

Lily's heart melted along with her anger. She leaned her head against his shoulder, knowing it was wrong to encourage him but unable to help herself. She liked the way he cared for her and was so gentle around her. He seemed to treasure her in a way whereas Kilt just took her for granted. And he had a manner of talking that she found helplessly appealing. She couldn't understand it. Kilt's dry wit was the opposite of Kirin's studious, often serious way, and one would think she'd like the laughter more, but she was inexplicably enchanted by Kirin's reflective nature. He did not hide behind humour, as Kilt often would — and despite their closeness and obvious love for one another, Kilt hid from her. She didn't know why or what his secrets might be, but being shut out hurt far more than the lack of attention or being taken for granted. Kirin did not shut her out ... not until today, anyway.

'I thought it was ...' She smiled, instantly embarrassed.

'About us kissing? No. That was a wonderful moment I'll cherish ...' and as she started to say something, he added, 'and keep secret.'

Lily frowned. 'Then why this difficult silence?'

'Something very bad has happened and it's connected with Clovis.'

'All right. Can you start from the beginning? I'm really confused, Kirin. I thought we were going to Brighthelm to protect your cover until we work out how to get me back to the north without raising suspicions. Why are we moving west?'

'Did I tell you that Clovis had lost a hand?'

She shook her head.

'Well, I couldn't understand it so after you pushed me away I went looking for the baker. I wanted to see where Clovis was found. He organised for me to be taken to the spot where his body was discovered.'

'And?'

'And I found the remains of someone's hand.'

'Ugh,' she exclaimed. 'Where?'

'It was in the remains of the fire. The villagers hadn't even looked at it. I suppose the excitement and terror of finding a murdered man was enough to make them careless.'

'All right, so you found a hand. Why in the fire? Had the killer tried to burn the evidence?'

Kirin gave her a soft look of irony. 'Why leave the body of Clovis in plain sight then? No, only a hand was in the fire. Bits had been pulled off.'

Lily felt her stomach turn over. 'What do you mean, pulled off?'

'It had been cooked, Lily. Bits of the cooked flesh were pulled from the bones. A finger was missing. I found the bones of that finger in the grass nearby. They were picked at.'

She shrugged. 'You're being ghoulish, Kirin. Couldn't it have been animals?'

'Animals would have dragged the hand out of the cooled embers, probably eaten most of it. This looked to be carefully done, the hand was left mainly intact, apart from the finger in the grass and the meat that was pulled from it.'

'What are you surmising?'

'The killer did this.'

She looked at him as though he were demented. 'The killer ate the flesh of someone's hand and killed Clovis?' she said, then shook her head. 'He must be as mad as you are.'

Kirin looked away, said nothing.

Lily waited but he didn't respond, just fell silent again. She felt immediately uncomfortable again. 'All right. Tell me what you think has occurred.'

'I think I'll be wasting my time,' he replied.

'No, I need to understand what you believe. I know it's important to you.' She tugged at his sleeve. 'Please, Kirin. I won't jeer at whatever you say.'

Another thing she liked about Kirin was that he didn't hold a grudge. Kilt would have gone silent on her for the rest of the journey. Kirin seemed to have the wherewithal to not take her disbelief so personally that he needed to punish her.

'Tell me,' she urged.

'I don't suppose you've ever heard of the legend of an aegis?'

She shook her head and frowned. 'Should I know it?'

'No, not really. I honestly believed it was just an old story of our ancients. I've told you about Freath,' he began. At her nod, he continued, 'Well, he believed deeply in the existence of an aegis. So did King Brennus.'

'And an aegis is what?'

Kirin sighed. 'It is said that the aegis is one of the Vested; hugely empowered, although you would never know because an aegis would keep that magic secret from everyone.'

'Is it dangerous?'

'Yes, very, because it's so powerful. But he, or she, doesn't want anyone to know he possesses this. According to legend, it actually belongs to the Valisars ... and only the Valisars. It is said there is an aegis born for each heir. If the heir can find an aegis, he can bond him by a rather brutal method known as trammelling. To trammel an aegis requires the Valisar to consume some of him.'

'What? Eat him?'

'I'm afraid so. That's another reason why a Vested who knows he is an aegis will avoid recognition.'

'Wait, how is he recognised?'

Kirin shrugged. 'That's his only protection — secrecy. He protects his own knowledge if he can. It's tricky, though, because an aegis is helplessly drawn to the Valisars. It takes enormous will, apparently, to resist the call. I suppose a person who spends years avoiding the city or any place the royals go, becomes more adept as he matures at resisting the urge, or an aegis too young to recognise his inherent skill doesn't feel the attraction until later.'

'But they'd know from childhood?'

'I honestly don't know. I think one is born an aegis, so presumably, yes, they'd know of their difference, certainly.'

'But say an aegis can resist the call to the Valisars — can't he just hide and the royal would be none the wiser?'

'Well, yes, and that's what most want to do. They don't want to have bits cut off them and they don't want to be under someone else's will. But there's one more hurdle. Each aegis is marked somehow.'

'You mean like a visible sign — a birthmark or something like that?'

'Indeed, or it could be more subtle. I sound as though I am knowledgeable about this matter but in truth I know little — only what Freath told me and what I vaguely learned from my days at the Academy. My understanding is that if an aegis comes face to face with his own Valisar, both will know it instantly. But let's say a Valisar stumbled upon an aegis — not his own — then unless he is warned or touched by magic, he wouldn't necessarily know of the magical connection. I believe that's how it works. The aegis, however, always knows and so would have to work very hard to keep themselves secret and resist the call of the Valisar.'

'And you say Freath knows more?'

'Yes.' Kirin's face clouded. 'He will be devastated by Clovis's death. He was clinging to the hope that Clovis would deliver someone very important.'

Lily frowned. 'Who? Important how?'

Kirin slapped the reins on the horse's rump. 'It's a long tale ...' He began to tell Lily how he met Clovis, when they were delivered as prisoners to Brighthelm soon after the overthrow of Penraven.

Roddy watched in shock as the raven stretched its neck, its head pulled back. Its shriek turned into a keening that sounded like despair. His head was hurting from the pressure of the air around him, now throbbing with magic, visible magic that appeared to shake the air until it looked as though the world was trembling. He realised he could no longer hear the waves, nor the lonely call of gulls — just Ravan and his terrible cries.

Roddy was beginning to feel dizzy from the pain in his head and the noise. Instinctively he reached out to the bird.

Ravan! Ravan!

And in his mind he heard a groan.

What's happening? he begged of the bird, who, like the air, seemed to be expanding.

It hurts, Ravan cried.

Buffeted by what seemed to be swirling winds now, Roddy pushed against the air, forcing his way to Ravan. He was shocked to realise that the bird appeared to have swollen to ten times his normal size and was still growing. He could no longer recognise him as the raven; now he looked like a formless dark shape.

The screaming intensified, the pressure became impossibly worse and Roddy began to feel that he was losing consciousness.

Ravan! he yelled. *Forgive me.*

Roddy's world turned black.

* * *

'Piven?' Lily queried, her tone filled with disbelief. 'Leo's adopted brother?'

Kirin nodded. 'Piven, or perhaps someone who is protecting him. It doesn't make sense, does it?'

'Not at all. Why? More importantly, how? He's not even Valisar, is he?'

Kirin looked perplexed. 'No, you're right, logic says it can't be him. He was an orphan child taken in by the Valisars. But, if it was someone else, he couldn't trammel an aegis.'

'So, logic aside, what makes you think this was Piven's work anyway? He'd be about …' Lily frowned. '… about fifteen anni or thereabouts.'

Kirin shrugged. 'I don't know — instinct, I think. Clovis had found the lost Valisar, we know that much. I know, I know,' he said, raising a hand against the protestation that he could see leaping to her lips. 'But we think of him as Valisar. Freath and I have held out hope for the child for a decade. Clovis was excited and was going to meet the person he thought was Piven at a small place called Minton Woodlet in the far south. Originally, you see, Freath charged Clovis and me both with finding an aegis and Clovis additionally with finding Piven. Now, ten anni later, Piven is found, Clovis makes contact after a decade of silence, and he's discovered murdered in a lonely spot with what looks like the remains of a trammelling. Am I imagining it, or is this too close for comfort?'

'The latter,' she said, thoughtfully, her face filled with consternation. 'So a Valisar, presumably, has trammelled an aegis.'

'That's what it looks like. However, that supposition could be wrong. Someone else could have attempted to trammel a Vested. It is possible that the body that owns that hand is lying in the forest somewhere or someone is moving around minus their hand and pretty angry about it.' He shrugged.

'But your instincts scream differently?'

'Yes,' he said, frowning. 'Screaming loudly, in fact.'

'Could it be that Leo has found his aegis?'

'How? You said you only left him a day or so ago in the north.'

'Mmm, that's true,' she admitted. 'Who are the other Valisars alive?'

Kirin gave a lopsided grin. 'Exactly my point! I keep coming back to Piven. I've looked at this every way I can.' He began counting off fingers. 'Brennus is dead. Leo is alive but it's impossible that he could be here. The daughter died soon after being born — we even saw her ashes scattered from the parapet of Brighthelm. There are no heirs left, save Piven.'

'But Piven isn't Valisar!'

Kirin stared at her, his gaze narrowing.

Lily frowned as she watched him. She knew he wanted her to make some sort of mental leap with him but she couldn't work it out. An idea slithered through her mind ... but that was ridiculous, wasn't it? She glanced at Kirin. He refused to help, just kept looking at her with a glint of something dangerous in his expression.

'Say it!' he said.

'Say what? I'm not thinking anything.'

'You are. You're my smart wife, Lily. Say it!'

She took a breath. 'All right. What if Piven is Valisar?'

Kirin clapped and grinned. He leaned over and kissed the top of her head in his excitement. She returned his grin. 'Clever, Lily. But more so, clever, clever Brennus and Iselda!'

'You've gone mad, you know that, don't you?'

'Well, I could be laughably wrong but history tells me that the Valisars have been a secretive lot down the ages. Freath once said that he'd never met a more furtive man than Brennus. What if the whole notion of Piven as an orphan was one enormous and elaborate lie to protect the second heir to the throne?'

Lily shook her head with wonder. 'Who would know?'

Kirin looked equally awed. 'No one, I don't think. Everyone who might know is probably now dead. Perhaps only Freath is still standing who was close enough to the royals to share some secrets but I truly believe Freath was honest with me.'

'You can't be sure —'

'No, I can't. But the more I consider it, the more likely it seems that Brennus and Iselda masterminded a devious plan to give absolute protection to Piven at birth. Perhaps what they didn't count on was his illness. He was an invalid and that offered a measure of protection that Leo could never have enjoyed. Loethar liked the child, treated him as a pet.'

'But the ruse obviously worked, then,' Lily remarked.

'Spectacularly! Loethar didn't feel threatened by Piven; no one felt threatened by Piven. He was considered fondly by all — even our infamous enemy.'

'All right, I'll go along with this. Let's say Piven did do this trammelling.'

He nodded.

'Tell me how a youth who, according to Leo, has the mental capacity of an infant, can achieve what you're suggesting?'

Kirin's face clouded. 'That is my stumbling block. There are only two possibilities. The first is that someone else is controlling Piven's actions.'

She looked doubtful. 'Another person showing him how to hack off someone's hand, eat the flesh and bond another man to him? I can't imagine it.'

'Neither can I,' Kirin agreed.

'So what's your other suggestion, although I suspect I can guess,' she said disdainfully.

'Go ahead,' he invited.

'You now want me to believe that somehow in the intervening years of his disappearance, Piven has overcome his disability and is now a rational, intelligent fifteen-anni-old youth, strong enough to overpower a man and do this terrible deed.'

'That's about the sum of it,' he admitted.

She nodded, saying nothing for a few moments and they rode in thoughtful silence. 'Why would Piven want an aegis?' she finally asked, thinking aloud.

'That's what I've been trying to fathom. How does he know about one, how did he find one, why would he do this?'

'Did you come up with answers?'

He looked at her doubtfully. 'Only suppositions, I'm afraid. It's illogical, but the only rationale I can put together is that Piven either inherently knows, or has always had the ability to absorb information and thus understands the legend of an aegis and had the capacity to trammel him.'

Lily bit her lip in thought. 'But, Kirin, why? Why would he do this?'

'Fear. If he understands the concept of the aegis, he understands his own vulnerability at Loethar's hands if his new sanity is discovered. He needs protection.'

'But he was living in obscurity, obviously. Why would he come out into the open now?'

Kirin shrugged. He looked deeply perplexed. 'I don't know. I really wish Clovis were alive to tell us what happened.'

'So where are we going? We've come full circle. Why not back to the palace?'

'I now believe my cover no longer matters. I think Piven has nothing to fear anymore.' He turned and regarded Lily.

She looked dumbstruck. 'You are jesting, aren't you?'

He shook his head sadly. 'Why not? He's unstoppable. Lily, perhaps you haven't grasped the magic I speak about. A whole army cannot penetrate the defences of an aegis. If I'm right, Piven is now untouchable.'

She looked at him, feeling her stomach sink. 'Untouchable?'

'If he's decided to take the throne, not even Loethar's cunning or the might of his tribes can match the power that an aegis has to resist their onslaught.'

Lily couldn't believe what she was hearing. 'Why are you running, then? Isn't a Valisar on the throne what we've all been trying to achieve?'

'This is the wrong Valisar. And that aside, he's killed Clovis, which means he's likely acting purely in his own interests. Clovis was no threat and Piven, if his mind is as sound as we're suggesting, should have been able to work that out. He must have his own reasons for grasping the throne — if that's his plan.'

'So he's a new threat, you think?'

Kirin shrugged. 'I don't know.'

'Well, Kirin, we have to find out. We are the best placed to do this. You have good reason to be at the palace. Have you ever done anything that could possibly offend Piven?'

'I don't believe so. I don't even think he'd be that aware of me.'

'Then you have nothing to fear. We must turn back and head for Brighthelm. Where were you going, anyway?'

'I was taking you back to Kilt Faris,' he said softly.

'Oh,' Lily replied, feeling awkward. She wasn't sure she was ready to return to the north. Her feelings were very confused; she needed time to think through everything.

'That's what you want, isn't it?'

'Yes, of course,' she snapped, 'but this is more important. Let's find out what's happening in the capital and take that information back to Kilt. He'll know what to do with it. Besides, even your Freath won't know all of these developments yet. I imagine he's making his way back to Brighthelm now and you can warn him, or share everything you've discovered.'

'You're right, of course,' Kirin said hesitantly. He looked reluctant. 'Lily, you don't have to do this.'

'Listen, Kirin. This is not about me or what I want … or even us, our safety. We're involved in something much bigger and we have to play our part.'

He nodded. 'All right. If you're sure …'

'I am. We've come this far. We might as well use the cover we've set up to find out as much as possible.'

Kirin hauled on the reins. 'Back we go to the city, then.'

Lily ignored the inner voice that accused her of duplicity. She was insisting upon this move entirely for the sake of Leo and the safety of all those she loved … especially Kilt.

Have it your way, the voice of conscience sniggered, but Lily banished it, returning Kirin's sweet, almost shy, smile, as he urged the old horse around and headed them back in the direction they'd just travelled.

36

Roddy could hear the gulls again. The pressure of the air had disappeared, leaving a soft sea breeze that blew around him with a carefree abandon, tousling his hair and reassuring him that a sense of normality had arrived. Except it hadn't. The remnants of pain throbbing at his temple told him that he had not imagined the build-up of a powerful magic. And Ravan, crouched before him, told him much more.

'Ravan,' he finally whispered.

His companion sighed and Roddy watched him take a long, slow breath before he unfolded his limbs and straightened to stand erect. 'Yes,' he answered in a scratchy voice.

'Is it really you?' he asked, staring at the willowy man.

'Yes, but I don't understand it.'

'Cyrena said you were on a new journey. This must be what she meant.'

Ravan finally opened his lids and regarded the youngster through deep blue eyes. Trails of pain seemed to still tremor through his body. 'Yes, but why?'

Roddy shook his head and shrugged. 'You still look a bit like your old self.'

Ravan actually laughed but it came out like a squawk. He felt his face. 'I'll have to improve on the qualities of being a man — learning to laugh, for instance.'

Roddy watched him touch his nose. 'No beak,' Roddy offered. 'Actually, you are very fine and handsome. You look fearsomely strong.'

'I'm also naked,' Ravan replied dryly. 'That must be fixed!'

'You can have something of mine,' Roddy said, 'but I think you're too tall.'

'I know where I'll find clothes.'

'Where?'

'In the hut where Sergius lived. Follow me.'

Roddy hesitated. 'Can you change back?'

Ravan shook his head. 'If I can, I don't know how. This way,' he said, pointing. 'I hope you have good balance.'

'The best,' Roddy answered and grinned.

'I'm impressed how calm you are with all this death and magic.'

'I'm frightened by it but I feel as though I'm meant to be here. I'm not sure I can bear to look at Sergius, though.'

'We will honour him shortly. For the time being avert your gaze.'

Inside the bare hut, which Roddy noticed Ravan seemed to know his way around, his friend grabbed a blanket and pulled it around him.

'What about clothes?' he asked, wondering why Ravan was sitting down and staring at a bowl in the middle of an otherwise cleared and scrubbed table. 'What's wrong?'

'Roddy, how much do you know about magic? Your own magic, for example?'

'I don't know that I have any.'

'You do. I can sense it. And Cyrena confirmed it.'

'I know I'm different from the other children, that's all.'

'Do you trust magic?'

Roddy nodded, keenly aware of his trembling hand.

'Do you believe you can trust me?'

'Cyrena told me I can … and I trust her.'

Ravan tried to smile and Roddy could see he found it difficult, as though he needed time to get used to his new senses and abilities. 'I trust her too. So did Sergius. So with Cyrena our common bond, let us here and now pledge trust in each other. I will never do anything to harm you.' He held out his hand straight, palm up.

Gravely, Roddy placed his trembling hand on top; they linked thumbs and then in the Set manner of sealing a bargain, they rotated their hands so that Roddy's was now on the bottom.

'Done!' Roddy said.

Ravan echoed his sentiment. 'Done.'

'Why does that bowl fascinate you?'

'Because I know what it means. Do you see its contents?' Roddy nodded. 'That is called firedust. The dust is imbued with a powerful magic, which, when it is cast into a flame, will reveal something. I imagine Sergius has left behind a message for me.'

'And when you burn the dust we can *see* the message?' Roddy asked, catching on.

'Exactly. It must have taken much of his strength to cast the dust. To my knowledge he has never used it before but he did tell me about it not so long ago.'

'Perhaps he knew his time was coming.'

Ravan nodded sorrowfully. 'I wish he could have told me.'

Roddy looked over at the embers in the hearth. 'Shall I get the fire going again?'

'Thank you. I'll find something to wear.'

Both set about their tasks. Roddy immersed himself in rebuilding the small fire, so much so that he was surprised when Ravan finally spoke again.

'Yes, Roddy, I think we can safely say that Sergius knew his time was coming.'

Roddy turned to see his new friend dressed, not in clothes that looked makeshift or belonging to an old man, but that seemed unused, even new. 'He had these prepared for you.'

'I never saw Sergius wear any of these items, so I have to assume so. They are new and I think it's a small note of humour.'

Roddy smiled. 'Well, you look good in black.'

Ravan swelled his chest. 'It all fits well enough too.'

'You're moving better and your voice is smoother. I think you're getting used to your new form.'

'I will miss flying.'

'I would too,' Roddy agreed, his tone sympathetic and almost wistful as he imagined what it might be like to leap into the air and ride the winds. He shook himself free of the thought. 'The fire's ready.'

'Good, stoke those flames. I'm sure Sergius mentioned to me that the higher they burn, the better the result.'

Roddy nodded and tossed more kindling onto the fire. The flames leapt in response. Ravan reached for the bowl.

'Are you supposed to say anything … cast a spell or something?' Roddy asked.

Ravan smiled. 'I don't know any spells. Ready?'

'Go ahead,' Roddy said, sitting back and holding his breath. Ravan picked up the bowl and without hesitation threw its contents into the flames. They blazed purple, spitting and crackling and Roddy smelled a strange but not unpleasant fragrance. He hugged his knees close, utterly fascinated, but not frightened … not now that he had Ravan.

And out of the crackling purple haze he spotted a shape coalescing. As it drew itself together he began to recognise it.

'It's Sergius,' Ravan confirmed, lowering himself as though weak. He knelt next to Roddy and Roddy could feel his friend trembling.

Sergius shaped himself fully in miniature. Looking out from the glow of purple that surrounded him, his expression was apologetic.

'Ravan, my oldest friend. If you are listening to me now, it means I am dead. I am sorry for that — for leaving you alone, I mean. My death will trigger three events. I have much to tell you, so listen carefully as you can only hear this once. I dreamed that you would bring a visitor and that although you regarded him as a friend, he was

actually an enemy to me. This is no fault of yours, Ravan. Whatever thoughts may be darkening your soul I beg you to release them. Whoever he is, he meant you no harm and whatever he offered you, he did so in good faith. When he sees me, though, he will recognise me as a danger and he will act accordingly. I hope you found the clothes I left for you? I can't be sure they're your size but I have a good feeling they'll fit. Sergius chuckled, no doubt thinking of the colour of the garments, and his amusement made Roddy glance at Ravan, who looked as if his heart was breaking. Roddy leaned closer but Ravan didn't take his eyes from the image of his old mentor. *I wish I could see you. You have been made in Cormoron's image. Later, you must look at your reflection; I hope you approve. And while I am sure you feel disappointment in me for withholding this secret from you, let me assure you that I didn't know, Ravan. This was Cyrena's secret; it was revealed to me in a dream and only in the last few days. I have been dreaming a lot!* He smiled gently again. *Why is this necessary?* He shrugged. *I do not know. Perhaps, dear Ravan, she is simply returning you to what you always were ... a man. I cannot enlighten you any further. This is your journey.*

Sergius paused momentarily and Roddy thought he seemed to take those few heartbeats to gather his thoughts. He straightened, lifted his head and sighed.

And now, here is what you must know. My death will trigger a message to a man far away from here. His name is Corbel de Vis and although you have never seen him, you will know of him. He is the twin brother of Gavriel de Vis. Ten anni ago a baby was born; it was the eve of the invasion of Loethar's horde and King Brennus knew the child would be killed if found by the barbarian, or would likely perish if he tried to hide it. With his struggles to sire surviving heirs, Brennus was not about to let any child of his die if he could help it. Instead, midway through the queen's pregnancy, he came to visit me here. He told me he had dreamed of Cyrena and that she had led him to this place. He had experienced this dream repeatedly since the queen had first announced her pregnancy. We talked at length, sharing several pots of dinch, and we agreed that while neither of us knew why we were connected through his dreams, that he would await a sign. The dream seemed too powerful, too repetitive and too much like how Cyrena works for me to ignore its significance. I knew if she was communicating with Brennus, she would find a way to instruct him. And she did, presumably, because while he was dreaming of me, I was dreaming of Corbel de Vis. I didn't know why or what it signified but I have learned to trust these events, knowing they would show their true meaning in time.

Sure enough, the king must have been given a sign — although I am not privy to what it was — and on the night before Corbel de Vis arrived at this spot, I myself dreamed he would bring a child that needed protection, protection of the most magical kind. I gave it and Corbel de Vis disappeared not long after he arrived, into the sea. He took a Valisar princess into those depths with him, and while I have never seen them again I am aware that a mighty magic occurred that stormy night. I was the channel for the magic that sent this pair to safety, we hope, away from our world.

Sergius paused and smiled softly. *I know you have questions, Ravan, but I cannot answer them. I simply have to hope that what I tell you is enough.* He nodded. *So, to continue, I mentioned that three events will have been set in motion at my death. The first event, as I said, is that Corbel de Vis will have felt my passing as a message to return. How he will do that, I have no idea, but I suspect you, dear Ravan, will be connected with it and I pray to our goddess that you are ready. The second event you are already well and truly aware of. You have transformed into a man. I have only ever known you as a raven so I cannot tell you whether you were originally a man. That is for Cyrena to explain. But you will walk in this mortal form from my death. And, finally, my death will bring Cyrena to you. She can only reach us at times of change in the magical balance of our world and only when those times of change are connected with the Valisars. And be wary, Raven — others will feel the presence of this magic, friends and enemies alike.*

Sergius held out his hands, palms up. *And so that is all I can tell you, Ravan. Where you go now I do not know, although I suspect you will be guided by outside forces. The princess must return safely to Penraven and she must be guarded, her identity kept secret, particularly from the person who caused my death. He is an enemy now, until balance can be restored … if it can be restored.*

Once again Sergius straightened. He sighed. *And now, friend, you must burn me. Let my spirit rise, my magic be unleashed. But do not wait. Set me alight and then go. Two horses await you at the village nearby. Ride to where you must. Goodbye, beloved Ravan.*

Sergius raised a hand in silent farewell. The flames roared once again, just for a heartbeat, and then died down to their natural colour, their guest gone, his image dissipated.

Roddy and Ravan sat in silence for a while. Finally Roddy spoke up. 'Cyrena told us to make haste for the mountains.'

'Then that is where we must go,' Ravan agreed, his voice tight. He looked at the boy. 'Are you hungry?'

Roddy nodded, trying to quell his enthusiasm.

'Forgive me. Not much of a host, am I? Sergius always had food ready for me. He would not be impressed by me ignoring your needs. I must go down to the beach now. I will take some time alone with Sergius, but please help yourself to any food. There is sweet water in a canister at the back of the hut. Take all you need. I doubt we'll return here.'

'What about you?'

Ravan shrugged. 'Since tasting Greven's flesh I have not eaten a morsel and curiously I have no hunger now.'

'I watched you do that. Will you explain it to me on our journey?'

'What I can, I will.' Ravan stood. 'You may want to pack some food for the journey, but pack only for one.'

'Is it the magic?'

'I suspect so. Also that I am not real.'

Roddy sensed the new man's grief embedded in his remark.

'Ravan, you look and feel real,' he said, touching his arm. 'This means you are real ... to me you are someone I can count on. If you weren't real, how could I possibly think that way?'

'I'm glad we met, Roddy.'

The boy's face creased into the first genuine smile in a long time. His belly grumbled, as if on cue, and they both laughed.

'You see,' Roddy said, delighting in the sound of Ravan's laughter. 'You become more real with every moment.'

37

They made far better time than they'd hoped. The sun was low but nightfall was still well away when they entered a familiar area of the forest. Kilt was exhausted but had found it easier to walk than be carried, which dented his pride. He'd rather accept the pain. He knew he didn't have to tell Jewd this, his friend's instincts were keen enough to work it out, so he hadn't put up a fight when Kilt insisted on being set down some time previous.

They were resting, taking some water, before they began the next climb. Kilt had no idea how he would make it but he would, both for Lily's sake and to ensure Leo had the safety of the camp.

'It's good to have the canopy of the trees again,' Leo admitted.

'How will our king ever live in a palace again, I wonder?' Kilt asked Jewd mischievously.

The big man grinned and winked. 'Servants to cater to his every whim.'

'To dab his mouth after a meal.'

'To wash his hands and dry them on a dainty linen,' Jewd added.

Kilt grinned. 'Someone to blow his nose.'

'And kiss his arse,' Jewd finished.

Leo took it in good cheer. 'I haven't thought about it. I can never get past the vision of confronting Loethar.'

'Do you see yourself killing him?' Kilt asked, genuinely interested.

'Of course,' Leo replied. 'That's all I see. But ever since I took Freath's life and realised how hollow the satisfaction is, I don't know how I'll actually behave if given the opportunity with Loethar.'

Kilt sat up, while Jewd stole a sly glance at Leo. 'Do you really regret it, Leo?' Kilt asked.

'I didn't get a chance to say this to you but I do regret that Freath is dead, yes. The problem for me, Kilt, is that I've been raised to be a man of my word. I would shame my family name to be otherwise and while I do wish Freath wasn't dead now, I don't believe anything could have stopped me killing him. I know that's not answering your question but I'm trying to be honest. He had to die — out of duty to my king, to my mother, to myself … to Piven and our sister. Freath had to die for murdering the queen.'

Kilt wasn't convinced. 'Do you never see situations in anything other than right or wrong, black or white, Leo?'

The young king considered the question, then gave an awkward shrug. 'Corbel de Vis used to try and explain what he called shadows to Gavriel and myself. Actually it was for Gav's benefit — I was still so young — but I can remember it clearly. Corbel always viewed a problem in its entirety. He used to say to Gavriel that men should avoid judging a situation simply because of its personal effect but should rather aim to see it as a whole, and instead of laying blame, should try and find the right solution that benefits everyone.'

'Then Corbel de Vis had a wise head on his shoulders at seventeen. It's taken Jewd and myself our lifetimes to understand and respect that there are two sides to most stories.'

Leo nodded and Kilt could see he was listening seriously. 'Corbel used to force Gavriel to try and take a bird's position. He'd say: "Gav, hover above the issue and look at it from all sides. Soon you'll see there are different reasons for why people react in the ways they do".'

'He sounds very different to the de Vis we met.'

Leo laughed. 'They're twins but you couldn't have met more distinct personalities. Gavriel was fun and popular and very smart. Corbel was quiet — people hardly knew he was there at times — and he was smart in a different way. Don't get me wrong, Corbel could hold his own in any sword fight or fisticuffs, but he'd usually outsmart his opponent with cunning, while Gavriel was just simply brilliant with weapons.'

'I wonder what happened to them,' Jewd mused.

'Corbel disappeared on the day of my sister's birth, I think. It's hard to remember now. But I know my father put me in Gavriel's care and that whole next day has blurred into one with the days that followed. Thinking about Corb and Gav just triggers memories now of fear, blood, brutality, death … and escape. Finding all of you.'

'I don't know why we haven't considered this before,' Kilt said, 'but, Jewd, we should try to find this Corbel de Vis.'

Jewd shrugged. 'We've tried to find his brother with no luck. You'd think he would have come forward by now if he knew people were seeking Gavriel.'

'Yes, you would. But who knows what has befallen him? Perhaps he can't get to us — maybe he's injured somehow.'

'Then he's not much use to us, Kilt.'

Leo frowned. 'Well, I'd certainly like to know where he is and where he's been all this time. Frankly, I'd like to redouble our efforts to find Gavriel. Either he got away or the person the arrow belongs to has him. Why he hasn't tried to find me again is a mystery.'

'They beat him very badly, Leo,' Kilt admitted. 'I've never really told you everything. Perhaps he can't walk, can't talk. He could be an invalid.'

Leo shook his head. 'No, I'm not prepared to believe that. I will see Gav again. If it takes me the rest of my life, I'm going to find him. I'm going to find them both!'

Kilt glanced at Jewd. 'Don't lose sight of the real prize, my king.'

'When, though, Kilt? How?' Leo asked, his exasperation showing as he punched the tree he leaned against.

'When? Soon,' Kilt answered, surprising Jewd, who raised his eyebrows, regarding his friend quizzically. 'As for how, I think we have to look to our neighbour, Barronel.'

'Barronel?' Leo repeated, astonishment in his voice. 'Whatever for?'

'For your army,' Kilt replied in a conspiratorial tone. 'We have no resistance to speak of against Loethar's warriors. You yourself admit that the Set people are getting more and more comfortable with the notion of empire and the security of peace, so you'll get little or no support from your own citizens.'

'Army?' Jewd repeated, perplexed.

'Which army will support me in Barronel?' Leo added.

'They're called the Vested.' Kilt smiled. 'Shall we go, gentlemen? I'll outline my thoughts as we move. Let me just take another swig of the bermine.' He tipped the bottle to his mouth, licking the last drops from the top. 'True, that's the last of it. That will have to see me through to the camp.'

'We'll be approaching from the back, won't we?' Leo asked.

Jewd nodded. 'Don't worry, they'll still see us coming.'

'How long?'

'For Kilt's sake, I'm hoping we're there before the sun sets.'

'Let's go,' Kilt said, pushing away from the tree with a groan.

Loethar called a halt and Elka set him down. 'I can't stand this finger of mine anymore, sticking out at this odd angle. Elka, your brew has numbed me enough. Do you think you could … ?'

'Oh, let me help,' Gavriel said with a sneer. Within two strides he was at his enemy's side. He took Loethar's arm by the wrist and smiled into the emperor's face. 'Ready?'

'Enjoy yourself,' Loethar replied, his eyes slightly glassy, pupils larger than normal.

Gavriel didn't hesitate. He yanked the finger straight, not even feeling for the right 'fit' as his father had taught him. He was disappointed that Loethar made no sound; didn't even flinch as the finger slid back into place. 'That should ache for days now.'

'Thank you, de Vis, for your kindness.'

The man was infuriating! Gavriel showed nothing in his expression other than a smile of satisfaction. 'It was a pleasure,' he said, releasing Loethar's hand. They locked stares and Gavriel was aware of Loethar's injured hand moving. 'Don't even think about it. The dagger's long gone. We searched you.'

Loethar smiled. 'I would have been disappointed in you, de Vis, if you hadn't. However, it was not a blade I was reaching for.' He pulled out a kerchief. 'Just something to bind my fingers with.'

Gavriel glanced at the kerchief. A tremor ran through his body, a feeling like one of those nightsparkles was exploding — the kind that Brennus used for city celebrations, made by the famous Brinaday family for centuries.

Elka, never far way, noticed how rigid his body had become. 'Gavriel?' she asked, trepidation in her voice.

'Where did you get that?' Gavriel all but spat.

Loethar frowned momentarily and then looked to the kerchief. 'This? I don't know.' Then he grinned. 'Ah, but I do. Of course. This would be your father's kerchief.' He twirled it in his injured hand, suddenly smirking. 'It even has a monogram. I've never noticed that before. I took all your father's clothes when I first arrived. We were of a similar build, your father and I. He must have kept himself very fit and trim.' He laughed at the not-so-disguised insult. 'Of course, I've moved on from his wardrobe from then but here, by all means —' he tossed it at Gavriel — 'have it as a keepsake.'

It looked fresh, unused; Gavriel could imagine it might even still smell of his father. Once again, though, he exercised his will over his rattled emotions. He reached into his own pocket. 'No need. I have one,' he said calmly and glanced at Elka, who gave him a familiar look that spoke only of pride. 'Put it to some use, Elka,' he said. 'I'll go on ahead. It's beginning to look vaguely familiar up there.'

Elka and Loethar watched him go. 'You won't win, you know,' Elka muttered. She took the kerchief from Loethar.

'His father would be proud of him,' he said. There was no irony in his voice and Elka regarded the emperor thoughtfully. He shrugged. 'I mean it. He has every reason to ignore all the best advice and just run me through with his sword.'

'Gavriel's too controlled.'

'So it seems. I'm impressed.'

'Because you have your life still?' she asked pointedly.

He offered his hand, and she began binding the injured finger to its neighbour. 'No, because he's the kind of person I wish surrounded me.'

Gavriel whistled and beckoned from above them. 'Elka, you'll recognise this area.'

'Are we that close?'

He nodded and grinned.

'Close to what?' Loethar asked.

'Not what. Who!' She tied the knot. 'Kilt Faris,' she finished, smiling. 'You won't have to hunt him down at all. I'm sure he's going to find it deeply amusing to meet the prisoner we've brought into his forest.'

'This is my forest.'

She shook her head. 'While Kilt Faris might acknowledge it doesn't belong to him by law, he will still claim it's his through the mere act of possession. But he would never agree to its belonging to the empire, Loethar. Faris recognises the Crown, believe it or not. While you think he's a law unto himself, according to Gavriel he actually respects the Valisars. And this forest has always belonged to the Valisar kings, which you are not. Come on, I want to get there before sundown.' She made a gesture to suggest she was plucking a hair from her head. 'Old mountain ritual to bring about good fortune,' she explained, helping him up the incline. 'With luck our host already awaits us.'

A man high up in the trees signalled to his companion below and the man on the ground ran across the clearing. 'Tern,' he called.

'This better be good news,' Tern replied, turning from the small piece of mirror he was watching his reflection in as he shaved. 'Glad to get that beard off,' he added, reaching for an old linen to clean his face.

'Good and bad.'

Tern swung around, frowning. 'Tell me.'

'We've spotted our own trio. They should arrive by dusk, perhaps before.'

Relief spread across Tern's face. 'Thank Lo for that! So what's the bad news?'

'There are three others — all strangers to us — also approaching.'

'What do we know?'

'Dorv is coming down from the lookout. Should be here any moment.'

As he said this, the man who had been positioned in the tree arrived. 'You've heard?'

'Tell me what you know,' Tern demanded.

Dorv nodded. 'We need to get some help down to Jewd. Kilt's hurt, I reckon.' Tern nodded at the first man, who immediately left to organise men to offer aid. 'The others, well, they're a strange trio. Two men and, I promise I'm not dreaming this, but I think there's a Davarigon walking with them.'

'What?'

'A woman, well, I think it's a woman. I can't be sure.'

'You're sure she's Davarigon?'

'Either that, or the giants walk the land again. No, she's Davarigon all right. I've seen her kind once before near Hell's Gates.'

'And she's with two men. Set men?'

'Seems so. One's injured. She's helping him. The other man is ranging ahead of them. I could be mistaken but he's looking up all the time towards us. It's as if he knows we're watching.'

'He wants to be spotted?'

Dorv shrugged. 'Just my interpretation.'

'Grab a few of the boys. We might just head them off. If they do mention us, bring them back here. I need to know what they know and why. I'm going to check on Kilt and Jewd.'

Dorv nodded and disappeared. Tern sighed and reached for his quiver, strapping it onto his back. He picked up the bow and followed Dorv and a few others down to the incline, curious but also concerned.

Loethar was quietly wondering to himself how much worse the pain could get. When he was young he'd taught himself to set pain aside. It took immense concentration and when he was first acquiring the skill he'd had to find a trance-like state. Nowadays he could achieve the introspection he needed at will; he still practised what the Wikken called 'spirit focus' frequently, so the ability to find that special state of mind was always available to him. He used it to divert pain, fear, even sorrow, believing that his spirit was a separate entity from his body and that it could pull away from the mortal framework to avoid the repercussions of unpleasantness — physical or mental.

But on this occasion he was not winning. He stopped to take some deep breaths; that usually helped. 'Carry on,' he said to the others, 'I just need a moment.'

Gavriel doubled back. 'Not likely, Loethar.' He withdrew a blade from a belt around his hip. 'I'm not letting you out of our sight.'

Loethar grimaced. 'I have nowhere to stumble to. You'd be upon me in a heartbeat.'

'You can believe that.'

'Besides, only brandish that knife if you're prepared to use it, boy.'

'Boy?' Gavriel laughed. 'Once, perhaps, barbarian. A long time ago I might have inwardly quailed at your threat. But never again. Be very assured I'm not only prepared to use this knife, but I'm looking for an excuse to. By all means, give me one.'

Loethar could see the man — who, indeed, was certainly far from a boy — meant every word. The way his jaw ground told him de Vis was fighting his inclinations to kill him with every step of their journey. Despite his precarious situation he liked de Vis; liked his passion, his loyalty. Especially he admired his control. A lesser man would have gone for the transient pleasure of plunging his blade into his enemy but de Vis was exercising wisdom over heart right now, and that spoke droves for any man — young or old.

'Gav, hush!' Elka suddenly hissed. 'Someone's coming.'

As she said her final word, men melted out of the shadows, bows strung taut, arrows nocked. Loethar couldn't believe they hadn't spotted them until now; they were so close.

Elka immediately stepped in front of her two companions, reaching behind her for her bow.

'Don't. We'll kill you before you can even bring your bow to the front,' one of the men cautioned. Elka paused. 'You,' he added, nodding at Gavriel. 'Drop the dagger. And you,' he said, back to Elka, 'remove that bow — carefully — and throw it over here.'

Elka did as she was instructed. Gavriel hesitated. 'We're looking for Kilt Faris. I am —'

An arrow sped out of the trees and landed perfectly between his feet, cutting off his words.

The man smiled. 'The next one's in your gut if you don't obey.'

'They're not going to kill us,' Loethar said conversationally, 'or they would have done so. Look at their eyes. Dispassionate. They intend to question us.'

'Drop the blade!' the man commanded again.

'Don't, de Vis,' Loethar said 'Let's see what they do then.' He looked at Gavriel and winked and knew he'd struck a chord with the man, whose expression showed a glimmer of amusement.

Ah, a risk taker, Loethar realised. He liked de Vis all the more.

'Gavriel, do as they say,' Elka demanded.

Gavriel shook his head, looked over at the leader. 'Make me. I didn't come here to create any trouble. I just need to find —'

The sound of the arrow being loosed cut off his words. Loethar yelped as the arrow embedded itself into his chest, just below the left shoulder. Gavriel yelled and Elka began to move but once again the calm leader got their attention.

'Leave him!' he commanded. 'Next one's for you,' he said to Gavriel. 'And then a third will kill your wounded companion,' he added nodding at Loethar, who was lying on the ground.

'Animals!' Gavriel cursed. He ignored the warning and bent down to Loethar.

Loethar grinned at him. 'Told you they don't intend to kill us. But, de Vis, don't enrage them any more, eh? I'm near dead now. Another word would probably do it and I think you want to give Leonel that satisfaction.' He groaned and was surprised to see the consternation on de Vis's face.

The men of the forest surrounded them. 'Pick him up,' the man commanded Gavriel and Elka. 'Follow us.'

Kilt's strength had ebbed in synchrony with the dying sun, and he was now being helped along by Jewd, having turned down the help of Leo's shoulder. He was just managing to put one foot in front of the other. The sun was low but he remained optimistic that it would still be light when they hit the camp.

'You're serious, aren't you? Magic!' Leo said, half-scoffing, half-amazed as he loped along in front of them.

'There is no other way, Leo,' Kilt said, breathing rapidly to help the pain. 'We can't raise a credible army of fighters. A rabble of protesters, perhaps, filled with loyalist farmers or older men who still remember the glory days of Penraven. But a fit, well-trained army is beyond us.'

'But the Vested are —'

'Listen to me,' Kilt said, his vexation rising in tandem with the frustration of his injuries and his pain. 'No one has ever thought to unite the Vested.'

'Until Loethar.'

'That's right. Until Loethar.' He gave a resigned sigh. 'We might all hate him but the man is clever. Everything he does, he does with intelligence and cunning, even down to reinventing himself as the magnanimous emperor. And it's because of his cunning and intelligence that your people now see him as a man to be looked up to … he'll be remembered as a great ruler, I'm sure. So it's up to you, Leo. If you want to put a Valisar on that throne, you're going to have to show cunning and intelligence to match. You have no army and you have no prospects of raising one that can even begin to rival what he has in place. His men are tough and well trained and you know Stracker maintains the army to a very high level.'

'What makes you think the Vested can achieve what we need?'

'I don't. But the Vested are an unknown quantity with powers perhaps even they don't realise. None of us know what their magic can achieve, and while individually some of them are impressive, imagine all that individual power combined. Who knows how that power could be channelled?'

Leo nodded. 'I'd never thought of it like that.'

'No,' Kilt said, less aggressively, 'but your nemesis has. He's way ahead of any of us. But what he doesn't know is that you live and flourish and that if he can unite the Vested, so can you. Most of the Vested are now being carted off against their will to Barronel. They will be unhappy, hopefully angry. If we can infiltrate them, we can unite them.'

'How do you propose to do that?'

Kilt hesitated, and Jewd came to the rescue. 'Stop yabbering,

Kilt. You become heavier by the moment. Just support yourself and walk, Lo rot you!'

Leo looked over Kilt's bent head. 'That's a bit rough, Jewd.'

'Listen, let's just get him safely to the camp. Then I'll stop worrying, all right?'

Kilt glanced Jewd's way and smiled his thanks. He hoped he and his big friend were never separated again; it seemed he needed Jewd more than he'd realised.

It was Leo who heard them first. 'They've found us!' he called, pleasure oozing from his voice.

Both his companions looked up. Kilt had never been so pleased to see Tern in his life. The man wore a wide grin.

'Any sign of Lily?' were Kilt's first words.

Tern shook his head. 'I'm sorry, Kilt, nothing on Lily. But we have got company.' He slung Kilt's arm on his shoulder, taking over from Jewd. 'Hello, Leo, Jewd. Good to have you back.'

'What company?' Kilt growled.

'We don't know,' Tern admitted. 'Two men and a woman who looks like one of the Davarigons. One of the men looks to be injured.'

'What are they doing here?' Kilt asked, not protesting as the men made him lift his legs so they could move him faster up the hill in a sort of chair fashioned from their arms. 'Lo, I feel ridiculous.'

'Shut up, Kilt, let's just get out of the open and into the camp's cover,' Jewd rumbled, striding alongside. 'Are they being discouraged?' he said to Tern.

'Dorv's gone down to meet them. The problem is they seem to be making straight for us, as though they know where to find us.'

'Which direction are they coming from?'

'From town.'

'What orders have you given Dorv?' Kilt demanded.

'To feel them out. If he can dissuade them from their path, he will. Otherwise, he'll bring them close to the camp.'

'Bah! So much for our secret place.'

Jewd gave Tern a look that said just tolerate his bad humour.

Elka, Gavriel and Loethar were left under the shade of a huge old fir. 'Wait here, until we say otherwise,' Dorv said, turning to leave. 'The men have orders to shoot if you so much as look at them the wrong way. I suggest you don't test us.'

'Listen, I've been down this path before,' Gavriel began, feeling as though he was living his last arrival into this camp all over again. 'Tell Kilt Faris —'

'I suggest you tend to your friend and stop worrying about giving me orders. That arrow needs to come out and it won't be pretty.'

Dorv left them with five men watching them.

Gavriel swung around angrily.

'Why didn't you tell them who you are?' Elka asked.

'Because apart from not having the chance, it's meaningless. I don't recognise any of them and, besides, I suspect the name de Vis is long forgotten.'

'Don't you be so sure of it,' Loethar wheezed from the ground. 'I haven't forgotten it and you can be sure Kilt Faris would know it.'

Gavriel shook his head. 'I'm playing it safe. I'd rather tell Faris to his face who I am and who I have with me. I don't want to give that information to his minions. We don't even know if Faris is alive or still in charge.'

'Both, I reckon,' Loethar said, groaning and reaching for his shoulder.

'Don't touch it,' Elka warned. 'That needs proper care. I'm going to ask for some stuff.'

'They won't give it,' Gavriel said sourly. 'But don't touch it anyway, Loethar. If Lily is still here, she can work wonders with her potions. Best to let her tend to your injuries.'

Loethar smiled. 'I'm touched by your concern, de Vis.'

'Don't be,' Gavriel growled self-consciously. 'Just want you strong enough to meet your true enemy.'

'I can't wait.'

Elka began to move but an arrow landed to block her path. She stopped and glared at the man who'd loosed it.

'Another into your thigh if you move again,' he warned.

'I want to ask for some supplies to help him,' she said, pointing at Loethar.

'Just be patient,' he said. 'Be still. Drink the water we've left you and remain silent until we receive our orders.'

'Told you,' Gavriel said. 'I've done this before. These are not sympathetic men.'

'You said they were loyal.'

'Yes, loyal to the rule of Kilt Faris … and then Valisar, in their own twisted way. But the king of the forest is Faris.'

The trio were given an enthusiastic welcome from the men but Kilt, drained and weakened as he was, wanted to know about the strangers, with no time for celebration. 'What do we know?' Kilt asked Dorv, relieved to be back in familiar surrounds but wincing through the pain. He kept imagining how wonderful it would be if Lily bustled out of the trees, hurling anger at him for being stupid enough to get caught and injured.

'The younger of the two men, strangely enough, is the leader. The other one is injured, badly enough that they've been helping him. The younger is a noble for sure, by the way he speaks, but curiously he moves with the surety of a tracker. He's no soft noble and doesn't look to me like he's straight from the city. He's sunbrowned. The older one baits him. I think — I could be wrong — but this older one seems to be a prisoner. They are not revealing much.'

'And there's definitely a Davarigon with them?' Kilt asked.

Dorv nodded.

'Are you sure?'

'No doubt. I've seen Davarigons once before. She's tall and broad, and her skins and weapons are all of the mountain people.'

'What an odd mix,' Kilt said, frowning. 'All right. Where have you got them?'

'Half a mile away.' Dorv pointed.

'Right, let's go.'

'Wait, Kilt,' Jewd said. 'There's no need for you —'

Kilt glared at his friend. 'Find me some of Lily's restorative, Tern, would you? Jewd, help me down to where the strangers are. That's an order.'

Jewd sighed. 'You heard him,' he said to the men.

'Leo, you wait here. We can't risk your being seen.'

'Not on your life! I'll hang back, but I'm not skulking here, afraid of my own shadow. I warned you, Kilt —'

'All right, all right,' Kilt said, holding up a hand as though Leo's very words hurt him. 'You win. I don't have the strength to argue.' Tern handed him a small pottery cup, which Kilt took wordlessly, tipping the contents down his throat. He made a sound of anguish. 'Lo, but that tastes like hell.' He tossed the cup aside. 'Let's go. But I mean it, Leo, stay out of sight.'

38

Gavriel sat with his back to Loethar, his emotions torn and confused. How was he suddenly feeling sympathy and respect for the hated emperor! He could almost be grateful for his memory loss now; without it he knew in his heart that he would not have found the control to overcome the desire to kill the man who slew his father so callously. The distance of years and the lack of time to fester meant his grief had been diluted; it was fortunate for Loethar that while the immediate motivation to kill was there, maturity meant more wisdom and a cooler approach to fiery situations. He wondered if Leo was in the camp nearby, and whether the years would give him the same level of control when he was confronted by the slayer of his father.

Leo would be around twenty-two anni now. And Lily — oh Lo, Lily, for whom his whole sorry adventure from this place had begun — she would be a much older woman. Had she stayed here? He hoped not. Strange as it was, the candle that had been lit for Lily all those years ago burned just as fiercely now with the return of his memory. Unlike his memories of pain, the delight he had felt in her company ten anni previous had returned to him complete. He hoped with all of his heart that Lily had moved on, that no one knew where she was and that somewhere in the empire she was happily married with a family. To see her now would be too hard.

But in truth his greatest concern was seeing Leo again. King Brennus had entrusted him with arguably the most crucial role in the whole sorry saga of the invasion, and he had failed to fulfil it because of his pettiness over Kilt Faris and his lovelorn behaviour towards Lily. He felt devastated at letting down the Crown, his family name, and himself. Corbel would never have let anything get in the way of his duty.

Corbel. That was his next task, to hunt down his brother. But Leo had to come first. He cast a silent prayer now that Lo had watched over Leo in his absence and kept him safe. He knew he shouldn't expect the king to recall their boyhood fun or how close they'd been through that traumatic time of the overthrow, but he hoped his offering of Loethar's neck might go some of the way towards forgiveness.

'Are you all right, Gav?' Elka asked, sidling over.

He nodded. 'Just wondering what's next. I'm sorry I've dragged you into this, Elka. You would have been home by now in the mountains.'

She shrugged. 'You didn't make me do anything. I make my own decisions.'

'There's something I should tell you both,' Loethar interrupted from behind them.

'I don't want to hear it,' Gavriel replied. 'I don't want you to talk to me.'

'But it's important. It may be helpful at this point for you to know that I'm —'

'Here they come,' Elka cut across his words, standing. Gavriel followed suit and even Loethar struggled to lift his head, balancing on his elbows.

Gavriel grinned in relief. 'That's Kilt Faris,' he murmured. 'The one limping. He looks to be in as bad a shape as you, Loethar.'

'Good,' Loethar said, 'you can limp along together,' although his voice sounded choked. Gavriel glanced over at the emperor, whose eyes appeared slightly glazed and his expression unfathomable.

If Gavriel didn't know better he'd say it looked like greed, possibly joy. It didn't make sense. But he also didn't care about Loethar right now.

He turned his attention back to Faris, his grin returning and widening. Gavriel lifted an arm, yet more relief and even gladness surging through him to see the familiar, albeit older and — Lo rot him — even more handsome face approaching.

'Ho, Faris!' he called.

Kilt Faris stopped dead.

Gavriel continued, 'Good to see you, Jewd … Tern.'

'Who are you?' Faris demanded, clearly taken aback.

'I didn't think you'd recognise me. May I approach?'

Faris nodded.

'Stay here,' Gavriel said to Elka. 'Watch him,' he added, pointing to Loethar. 'Don't trust him.' She gave him a look of disdain and he returned his attention to the men.

As he left the shadows of the tree, Gavriel realised dusk had fallen. He didn't see Leo in their midst, and though his heart began to sink at this realisation, he forced himself to remain optimistic, striding towards the baffled group of men.

A cry went up from the trees. 'Gavriel!'

Everyone looked around, startled, as another man, young, tall and sandy-haired, burst from the cover of the trees, yelling and laughing.

It was Leo. No mistaking it! Gavriel leapt into the air with a cry of unrestrained laughter and then he too was running, ignoring the arrows trained on him and the men who tried to stand in his way. He vaguely heard Faris give Leo a warning but he and Leo were an unstoppable force, charging towards each other and then, as undignified as his father might have deemed it, Gavriel had his arms clasped around Leo.

'I'd recognise that arrogant stride anywhere!' the young king bragged, his eyes searching to see behind Gavriel's beard. 'It is you, isn't it, despite that slight limp I noticed?'

'Yes, Leo. It's me.'

They began to laugh again and then Gavriel pushed back. 'Let me look at you. Lo, but you're tall and so broad. And your voice is so deep!'

'Never as tall or broad as you, though. When did you get so old?'

They clapped each other on the back, unable to tear happy gazes away.

'So, de Vis, you finally return,' said a familiar voice.

Gavriel swung around, his arm still slung around Leo, who was wearing a lopsided grin. 'It's a very long story, Faris, which I will gladly share with you.'

'No longer the boy, I see,' Faris commented wryly. 'No longer the city noble, either.'

Gavriel nodded. 'That's true on both counts. I've spent all these years in the mountains.'

'But why did you take all this time?' Leo asked. 'Gavriel, it's been ten anni!'

Gavriel looked down. This was harder than he thought. 'As I said, it's a long story. Those warriors — I assume you saw them, they were left dead — they beat me badly enough that I lost my memory. It was returned to me only days ago.' He eyed Leo. 'As soon as I had my memory back, I had to come and find you.'

'We tried to find you,' Faris began. 'But I fear not hard enough.'

Gavriel stopped him with a hand. 'No need to explain. It's the past and I was impetuous. Nay, stupid! I blame only myself. Let us leave that now. There are more important matters.'

'Such as?' Leo asked, eyes shining, his smile seemingly immovable.

Gavriel stepped back and bowed to Leo. He'd almost forgotten he addressed his sovereign. His father would turn in his grave! 'Such as, the prisoner I've brought you, your majesty. Take a closer look, my king.'

All the men turned now to look at Loethar, who regarded them from a distance.

Leo stepped forward and squinted. Then he took another step, and another; his smile froze and then it disappeared. His expression moved from sunny to stormy in moments. And he began to shake his head.

'Stop him!' Gavriel murmured, leaping forward, realising that Leo didn't have the benefit of either his years or the memory loss to dull the impact of seeing this man again.

But Leo was too quick for all of them. He closed the gap between himself and the prisoner alarmingly fast. Gavriel watched with horror as the king paused only momentarily to draw Faeroe from its scabbard.

'Leo, no!' he yelled, chasing after him with no explanation to the shocked onlookers, determined that Loethar should not die like this.

Leo wasn't hearing anything, though. Gavriel, even running as hard as he was, knew he couldn't catch him in time. Even as he watched, Leo pulled back his sword arm, just steps away from the man leaning against the tree.

Loethar was helpless. Everything seemed to be happening so slowly he had time to take in that his killer was young, even time to notice that his death would be meted by the Valisar family sword he'd read about in the royal library. He recognised it, even from a distance, with its distinctive serpent snaking around the hilt. It was a fitting way to die, he decided as he adjusted his position so that he could at least look the young man in the eye when Faeroe descended. Without having to be told, he knew his executioner would be Leonel; no longer the boy, but a man. Curiously, his final thought, as death descended, was of Freath. Freath, his aide, his most regular companion … even his friend … had duped him. It was a shocking realisation. Freath had duped them all. Loyal to the Valisars all along, he had obviously led an audacious and dangerous double life.

And as the dying sun's rays glinted off Faeroe's blade, he smiled, privately congratulating the manservant for his daring and cunning.

But neither he nor Leo had calculated on the speed, long reach and powerful body of an angry Davarigon. Loethar watched with surprise as Elka appeared from behind the tree. It was too late for Leo to change his course and she knocked him over with ease; it occurred to Loethar it was as though she were swatting a fly.

He heard the would-be-king go down with a loud groan as Elka rolled over him, wrenching the sword and flinging it to the side as though it weighed nothing.

'Not like that, your highness,' she said, agilely rolling to her feet in a single move that astonished Loethar. 'I presume you are the king?'

She hauled Leo to his feet. Enraged, he instinctively swung a fist at her that she nimbly caught mid-air. Loethar couldn't help but be amused by her protection. He was sure he didn't deserve it.

'Forgive me, King Leonel,' she growled, staring down at him. 'But you will thank me for this later, I'm sure.'

Would he? I wonder, Loethar thought, enjoying the spectacle.

'Get your hands off me, you filthy —'

'Leo!' Gavriel said sharply, arrving at the young man's side.

'Whoever this Davarigon bitch is that you've brought, she will unhand me. *Now!*'

'Not until you calm down,' Gavriel replied.

Loethar saw that he masked his displeasure at Leo's offensive language. He glanced at Elka as a very tall man approached; she seemed unmoved by the Valisar's insult.

'You're very fortunate the men didn't fill her full of arrows, de Vis!' the newcomer said. 'What is she thinking attacking Leo and who is this man?' He swung around to regard Loethar, who was suddenly enjoying watching the theatre of these outlaws unfold. 'Kilt is asking.' He looked back and frowned. 'He's been badly injured but I don't know what's wrong with him — he seemed determined to come out and see for himself but now he's having to be helped back into the camp. He's really unwell.' He turned back to Elka and Gavriel. 'So you'll have to tell me instead.'

Elka looked hard at the king; once again Loethar was reminded that the Davarigon believed she answered to no one. He liked that about her and it attested to what he'd always believed about the mountain tribe: that they kept one foot in Set territory and the other firmly in the mountains, as though sovereign territory. Elka was Davarigon first, Set after.

'Your majesty,' Elka said, releasing Leo's hand, ignoring Loethar's scoffing sound at her use of the title. 'I apologise for treating you this way, but, as you can see, we have brought you Emperor Loethar for your punishment …' Her gaze narrowed. 'Your calm and calculated punishment,' she added.

'Loethar?' the big man echoed, swinging around.

Loethar gave a good attempt at a sarcastic bow, using only his aching head and a sardonic smile. 'Tell Faris I can't wait to meet him.'

The outlaw's attention flicked to Gavriel for confirmation. 'Is this a jest?' he asked, shocked.

'Jewd, it's Loethar, I can assure you.'

Jewd. Loethar stored the name. Perhaps it had been Faris they'd injured with the arrow. What wouldn't he give to have the blood-smeller now!

Jewd now looked both horrified and fascinated. 'Kilt is going to love this! How did you capture him?'

'It's a long story,' Elka replied.

Gavriel looked at Leo. 'You need to think on this, your majesty,' he said. Loethar could tell he was deliberately using the title to impress upon Leo his important role now as a king, not just a man with a grudge. 'Believe me, I have had to overcome my own desires to slit his throat for the murder of my father. You now have the opportunity to ignore revenge and instead deliver royal justice for the innocent people of the Set who died under his army's sword. That is what both our fathers would demand of us.'

Loethar was further impressed. He watched the youngster shake his head clear of all the rage and unsettling emotion.

Leo nodded at Gavriel, then impaled Loethar with his gaze. 'He is to be guarded day and night. Jewd, can he be secured?'

'Of course, *your highness*,' Jewd said, clearly picking up on Gavriel's language.

'Then let's get him shackled.' Leo began to move away, seemingly too disgusted to look upon the emperor.

'Your majesty!' Elka called after him.

Leo stopped but did not turn. 'Yes?'

'He is injured.'

'So what?'

'We would treat an animal better in the mountains.'

'None of you would permit me to put him out of his misery, which is how we normally treat a badly injured animal,' Leo snarled, impressing Loethar. He turned now to face Elka. 'Forgive my insult earlier. I can see you are a friend of Gavriel's. But please don't ever believe that gives you the right to treat me in a familiar fashion.'

It was obvious to all that Gavriel wanted to step in but, even knowing her for just a short while, Loethar was sure the Davarigon was too proud to have him fight her battles.

She didn't take a step back, he was glad to note. If he'd had the strength, he would have clapped Elka and de Vis for their honour. 'King or not, your highness, I will always treat all men fairly. This man deserves to answer for his sins but no one here would condone either his brutal slaughter or torture at the hands of the untended injuries. I believe, your highness, that compassion is what should set the Denovians above their barbarian conquerors.'

Loethar didn't agree but he enjoyed watching her noble words sting Leo.

'As you wish,' he said, after a difficult pause during which he regarded first Elka, then Gavriel, and finally the Davarigon again. He moved away without another word but to the sound of Loethar laughing at his back.

* * *

Roddy wiped the sweat from his eyes as he straightened. He looked at the sad sight of Sergius's broken body lying atop the kindling. It had taken them all day to build the pyre and Ravan had only just reverently carried his friend's once frail, now twisted body, to lay it in readiness for burning.

They'd worked in silence for most of the day, gathering the driftwood and whatever they could find to burn at the top of the cliff, both lost in their thoughts, neither eating but taking regular swigs from a flask of water that Ravan had brought down to the beach. Roddy noticed the tide was moving in.

'Have we enough time?' he asked, his first words in an age.

Ravan nodded reassurance. 'We will light the pyre at twilight.'

'Why not now?'

'It is said that twilight is a most magical time. The moment just before the sun rises and moments after she leaves us for the day — those times are when magic can be at its highest potency.'

Roddy was fascinated despite his fatigue. 'I didn't know that.'

Ravan continued. 'And we are in a position to wield a great magic, Roddy, because Sergius's spirit will be released where the land meets the water. It is believed that this meeting point of the elements also heightens powers. We are giving ourselves the best possible chance of success.' He looked out to the horizon, where the sun hung very low in the sky, burning a deep pink, spreading crimson slashes across the water.

'Then let us enjoy your friend's last sunset,' Roddy said.

The two new friends sat shoulder to shoulder on the sand and waited in companionable silence.

Roddy finally felt he belonged.

39

Leo and Jewd squatted by Kilt as he retched into the undergrowth, both desperate to give him the news. Gavriel hung back, unsure of his place here.

'What's happening, Kilt?' Jewd asked.

Kilt groaned, wiped his mouth with a linen. 'Search me. I feel light-headed. Perhaps I drank too much of Lily's brew.'

Gavriel flinched at the mention of her name. 'Where is Lily?'

Leo answered for them. 'She's safe, we think … but she's gone missing.'

This shocked Gavriel in two ways; that she was missing suggested alarm but Leo's admission meant Lily was still presumably living with the outlaws. 'Missing? What's happened?'

'We all have long stories to share, Gav,' Leo assured. 'The short answer to this is that we think she's with Kirin Felt.'

Gavriel stared at the king for a moment as the name filtered up from his memories. 'Felt? Freath's aide?'

Leo nodded. 'The very one.' He raised a hand. 'Don't ask why — I'll explain all later. She was meant to be here, meant to be marrying Kilt but instead she's having to pretend to be married to Kirin Felt, and she's travelling with him now, as his wife. We don't know the details, other than the fact that the ruse has kept her safe.'

It was too much information to take in at once. *Marrying Faris! But masquerading as Felt's wife!*

'Be careful what you say,' Leo warned, looking over his shoulder to where Loethar sat propped in the far distance. 'He knows none of this, of course. And we must protect her.'

Kilt groaned again and turned away, dry retching.

'You only took a single dose of Lily's brew,' Jewd assured. 'I checked with Tern. He used the correct amount.'

'I know,' Kilt said, wiping his mouth again, looking ashen. 'I don't understand it but this retching is killing my shoulder and ribs. Anyway, enough of this! Who is this prisoner?'

'It's Loethar,' Leo said.

Kilt looked at the king as though he had spoken in gibberish. 'Pardon?'

Leo nodded at Gavriel. 'It's true,' Gavriel explained. 'The man sitting against the tree is the emperor.'

Kilt blanched, staggering again. Jewd, frowning, caught him.

'I have so much to tell you but let me just briefly summarise how we came upon him,' Gavriel suggested. He recounted their passage into the forest of Penraven via Francham and how they stumbled upon Stracker attempting to murder his brother.

'You saved him?' Leo asked, aghast.

'Well,' Gavriel began laconically, 'I figured Loethar's rule was better than Stracker's. Until I knew that you were alive and we had the chance to put a Valisar on the throne, I thought it best to stick with Loethar's more peaceful leadership. Under Stracker I felt brutality would break out across all the realms.'

'Compasses,' Leo corrected with disgust.

Jewd glanced at Kilt, frowning at how pale and shocked his friend looked. It didn't make sense. Kilt had arrived into the camp barking orders and ignoring his injuries. Now he looked beaten, half the man he had been an hour ago. Worse, he looked frightened and he was saying nothing.

He'd have to do the talking for him. 'What's happened to Stracker?'

'I don't know,' Gavriel admitted. 'Elka's effective when she decides to go into a fray swinging. It was like that when she rescued me from Stracker's thugs all those years ago. I didn't even know what was in the undergrowth but her arrows pierced their bodies pretty effectively.'

'The arrow,' Leo murmured.

Gavriel glanced at him but continued. 'She didn't kill anyone this time, so Stracker will have a sore head and a lot of anger when he realises Loethar got away.'

'He's planning to seize power, you say?'

'That's my impression,' Gavriel replied. 'There was certainly no love lost between them. I'm gathering that the trigger of their official falling out was their mother's death. You can't imagine two more different people; from what I recall Loethar is subtle and cunning, full of secrets. As you can tell he has a quiet presence. And Stracker is all noise and brutality; he actually likes killing. I don't think Loethar enjoys it particularly, but he's not scared of taking a ruthless approach.'

Kilt shook his head, finally speaking. He sounded so weak to Jewd. 'But why did you bring Loethar here? Of all people, the emperor.'

Now Gavriel looked stumped. He sighed. 'I was so close to my goal, I wasn't going to turn back and re-think my plan. My priority was to find Leo. Loethar was a complication. As much as I would have happily watched him swing from that tree, Elka persuaded me that we should intervene. Personally, I couldn't care less if Loethar and Stracker kill each other but in those few moments we had to make a judgement.' He shrugged. 'As I said, Loethar alive is possibly more value to the Set than dead. Besides, I think I wanted to give Leo the decision ... and the opportunity, if he chose, to have Loethar executed.'

Kilt groaned, ran a hand through his hair. 'A complication indeed.' He looked at Jewd. 'Lily comes first for me, although she's even more vulnerable with Stracker in charge.'

'No, she's not,' Leo said, pacing. 'If my memory serves me right,

Stracker wouldn't even bother with someone like Lily. He'll have far bigger things on his mind.'

'I agree,' Gavriel said. 'In my opinion he's going to tear this forest apart looking for Loethar. He'll take him dead or alive but he'll want his half-brother in custody. Lily won't even register in his mind. If she's with Felt, I presume they'll head back to the palace, will they?'

Kilt shrugged. 'Felt won't know that Freath is dead yet. I know Lily won't let him near here. So I imagine he'll want to go back to Brighthelm.'

'Then she's relatively safe for now, Kilt,' Jewd said, picking up on Gavriel's thoughts. 'She's probably safer there than here, to be honest.'

Kilt considered this and nodded slowly, seemingly painfully.

'Let's go and talk to Loethar,' Jewd offered. 'If he and Stracker are now enemies, he's probably prepared to tell us how his kin is going to react.'

Kilt shook his head. 'I can't.'

Jewd stared at his friend. 'What do you mean, you can't? Come on, Kilt, get yourself together.'

'I'm not well, old friend. You'll have to do it.'

Jewd shook his head. He needed Kilt to show the leadership he was famed for, especially in present company. What's more, he needed Kilt's sharp mind. There would be no greater opponent to Loethar than his friend. And all the new magic he'd just learned his friend possessed was all the more reason to have him alongside.

'J-Jewd —' Kilt began but Jewd was already hauling him to his feet.

'Come on. I'll carry you if I have to, although I rather think you would prefer if the emperor saw you strong and in command.' He simply couldn't understand his friend. He could feel Kilt trembling. And was that a stutter he'd heard? Kilt had possessed a stammer when he was a very young boy, he recalled. But it had been a very long time since he'd heard it. Perhaps he'd imagined it just now?

Gavriel stopped them as they all moved forward. 'Well, let's agree on what our attitude towards him is. Leo?'

Leo looked at Gavriel with surprise. 'You have to ask?'

'I do.' He stared long and hard at his old friend. 'Consider your answer carefully, your majesty. This is not a decision you make as an aggrieved son, or even as a royal in exile. You make this decision with a coldness in your heart, as your father would … as a Valisar king.'

Everyone fell silent, staring between the two companions.

Leo's eyes narrowed. 'I want him dead …' He stopped, sighing silently.

'But … ?' Gavriel prompted.

Leo grimaced. 'But I can't pay attention to what my heart burns for. I will have my revenge another day.'

Gavriel looked relieved. 'Good, your majesty. So?' He glanced at Kilt, who gave an almost imperceptible nod of approval.

'We make use of him,' Leo continued.

'How?' Jewd asked.

'Bait!' Leo finished, looking at Gavriel, who smiled. 'We keep him alive for now. He's injured, so he's not going anywhere on his own. He needs us to stay alive. But now he has two enemies — me and his half-brother. I'm sure he'll be happy to comply with whomever's plans hurts either of us — and he probably doesn't care in which order.'

'You're right in that,' Gavriel admitted. 'The oddest part of this is that he trusts me. I don't really know why because I will happily queue behind Leo to plunge a blade into his heart. But there's something there and, if you'll permit it, I think I'm the best person to handle any negotiation with him. Or, better than me, Elka. He genuinely trusts Elka.'

'Do you?' Leo sniped.

'You have to ask?' Gavriel said, genuinely surprised. 'She has been my constant companion for ten anni. She not only ensured I healed properly physically but it was her idea to help me regain my memories by first visiting the Quirin at the convent, and then bringing me into Penraven. And even when she wanted to return to the mountains, she put my needs first and came with me to Francham. Even there, when we thought that might be our parting point, she agreed to accompany me into the forest.' Jewd could see that Gavriel was working to keep anger out of his voice. 'This is loyalty.'

'No, de Vis,' Kilt said softly. 'It's more. It's love.'

Gavriel glared at him. 'Don't mock me, Faris, so help me, I'll —'

Kilt struggled to his feet. 'I am not mocking you. I have discovered love; you've obviously spent so long away from your own kind that you don't know how to recognise it. Elka is not helping you out of a sense of loyalty. I'd wager everything on the fact that this woman, giant though she is, has fallen for a Penravian noble.' He grinned through obvious pain; it was a kind gesture. 'But then I suspect you've known this, de Vis, and don't need me to point it out. Come, let us talk to the usurper. I suggest you lead us, Leo. Let him see the true king, in control and not at all cowed by his presence.'

Leo nodded. 'Let's go.'

Only Jewd noticed that Kilt hung back.

Kilt had been in enough scrapes to discern the difference between the sensations of wounds, and the sensation of magic. What he was feeling now frightened him. It was deep, primeval … it was instinctive.

He needed to get away, but Jewd was leading him closer. Could he do this? Was he strong enough? He was sure his magic was. He took a deep breath and opened himself up to his own; it flooded him with warmth and a sizzling power. He had only felt like this once before — in childhood — and he had never allowed it to roam free again.

But now he felt strong and suddenly better. If he could just last the few minutes this would take, he could get away. And worse, if he didn't find the courage to face this, everything would collapse and the truth would emerge. Just *a few moments*, he reassured himself. A look of loathing, or perhaps a smug grin, and then he could dismiss the prisoner, leaving him to his minions. Let the king have all the fun.

He took another long, slow breath.

'All right, Kilt?' Jewd asked, supporting him. 'I wish I knew what this was all about.'

'Jewd, I can't stay. I'll show my face but that's all. Don't let me look weak in front of him. I can sneer from a distance if necessary.'

He sensed Jewd's anxiety and confusion. 'Whatever you want,' the big man said.

Kilt looked up and saw the Davarigon woman first. He was about to ask Gavriel whether he knew whether Elka was Vested in any way when the wave of sickness arrived again. And this time he doubled over with a giddy sense of doom, dry retching, for there was nothing else for his belly to lose. A pain bloomed through his head and he collapsed to his knees.

Jewd yelled and suddenly Gavriel and Leo flocked to his aid. Though Kilt knew they were yelling at him it was as though he was suddenly trapped in a cocoon with one other person. And the other's voice came through clearly, spoken calmly, in a soft, sinister way.

You belong to me, it said directly into his scrambled mind.

Kilt looked up from the anguished activity around him, and across the clearing to where they were headed.

And he knew the voice belonged to Loethar.

The emperor smiled in recognition.

40

Ravan finally stretched. 'It is time,' he said.

Roddy watched the last pink blaze of the sun dip below the horizon as twilight claimed the skies. 'Yes,' he said and sighed.

Ravan offered a hand and Roddy took it, allowing himself to be pulled to his feet.

'You are strong, Ravan,' he admitted.

'We will both have to be ... not just physically or in our friendship, but most of all in our minds. I suspect this ordeal is the first of many. But let us not shirk from our task now. Sergius demands this of us.'

Roddy nodded. 'What do you want me to do?'

'Go and light the torch and bring it to me. We must release Sergius's magic and hope that it will reach out to whom it must.'

Roddy ran up the beach. The torch wasn't far and he lit it from one of the pair that lit the stairway up to Sergius's humble abode. He looked up at it, wondering if they would ever return here. He liked this place. He could live here.

'Hurry, Roddy,' Ravan urged and Roddy scuttled back down the beach, careful to keep the flame steady.

'Here we are,' he said unnecessarily, feeling the weight of the moment upon him like a burden. 'Are we meant to pray?'

Ravan gave him a gentle smile. 'If you wish,' he said softly. Without hesitation he touched the flame to the kindling. 'Farewell, Sergius,' he murmured. 'You are missed.'

'Reach out, Sergius,' Roddy added, unsure whether his words could make a difference but needing to be part of the moment.

The kindling took and the flame erupted; small at first, it burned well nevertheless and within a few heartbeats, it began to spread. Roddy watched as the flames licked higher and wider, reaching out to incinerate the dry wood they had spent so many hours collecting. Hungrily the fire took hold and its voice was heard as the flames began to roar, hardly troubled by the gentle sea breeze, smoke rising into the darkening sky.

Man and boy stepped back.

'It will reach him very soon,' Ravan said, 'and we must not be sad. This is his last duty and Cyrena will reward him, taking him into her heart and letting Sergius finally rest.'

Roddy's eyes watered. He wasn't sure if it was from the smoke or the emotional impact of this moment. He wasn't sure he wanted to watch the body of Sergius burn but he sensed he and Ravan needed to bear witness. He took Ravan's cool hand and felt a reassuring squeeze in return.

Gavriel watched in confusion as Kilt screamed, clasping his hands to his head as though in pain. Across the clearing, he noticed Elka reaching for Loethar as the emperor tried to drag himself to his feet. Loethar seemed oblivious to Elka, his stare rigid on Kilt.

Glancing back, Gavriel could see that Jewd and Leo looked panicked in their inability to get through to Kilt, who now appeared to be fixated on Loethar. He looked again at the barbarian, now firmly in Elka's grip and going nowhere, back to Kilt and frowned. Amid the urgency of Jewd's and Leo's voices, Kilt's agonised groans and Loethar's sinister smiling silence, he deduced that something — impossibly — was going on between Kilt and Loethar.

'Get him away,' Kilt growled, before once again clutching his head as he tried to turn and lurch to his feet.

'What are you talking about?' Jewd begged.

'Kilt, can you hear us?' Leo yelled.

Gavriel whistled to Elka. She sharply looked towards him. 'Get him away from here.'

'What?' she yelled, confused.

'Elka, pick Loethar up and get him the hell away from here. I'll follow you in a moment.'

She shook her head in further confusion but did exactly as he asked. She dragged him away. Loethar struggled to keep Kilt in the frame of his vision, turning his neck to stare back at the man.

'Quick,' Gavriel said to his companions. 'Get Kilt back into the camp proper.' Other outlaws had arrived, perplexed and anxious to help. 'Do it!' Gavriel ordered. Jewd finally came out of his fright and turned to two of the newcomers. 'Take him,' he commanded. 'I'll be there shortly.' He swung back to Gavriel. 'What in Lo's name was that about?'

Leo looked ashen. 'Kilt's been acting strangely these last couple of days. Is there something he's not telling us?'

A glance passed between Jewd and Gavriel and Gavriel knew that Jewd was aware of something amiss.

His eyes narrowed as he thought it through, glaring at Jewd. 'Whatever it was, it was between Kilt and Loethar,' he replied.

Jewd looked taken aback. *So,* Gavriel thought, *perhaps he doesn't know any more than us.*

Jewd shook his head. 'Don't be daft, man. They've never spoken, never clapped eyes on each other before.'

'You're sure of that?'

The big man glared at him. 'In the past fifteen anni, I can count on less than one hand the number of times Kilt and I have been separated. And since Loethar came on the scene, that's only happened once and that was just a few days ago. I know he didn't see Loethar in that time and vice versa. Today was the first time they have seen each other.'

'And that was from a distance,' Leo added.

'What are you getting at, de Vis?' Jewd demanded.

Gavriel shook his head, unsure. 'Something was occurring between them. Did you not see the way Loethar was smiling at Kilt?' They shook their heads, frowning. 'It was antagonistic. He was taking satisfaction. He was all but baiting him, but without any words.'

'That doesn't make sense, Gav,' Leo said. 'They weren't even talking.'

Gavriel eyed Jewd. He took a chance. 'They didn't have to, did they, Jewd?'

Jewd baulked. 'What?'

'You know something. Whatever it is, you'd better spill it. We're not the enemy. He is.' Gavriel pointed to where Loethar had been taken. 'And I might be mistaken but going by what I was watching, it seemed he's got some hold over Kilt that we need to understand. You heard Kilt. Even he said *get him away*!'

Leo's eyes widened. 'That's right, he did. What could that mean?'

Gavriel and Leo looked at Jewd.

'Why are you both staring at me? I don't know any more than you.'

'You sound defensive, Jewd. What aren't you telling us?'

Jewd shrugged and shook his head.

'Jewd, we have to make a decision about Loethar,' Gavriel pressed. 'Whatever troubles Kilt has now happened twice and in the presence of the barbarian. You've seen it. If we're going to use Loethar, we have to know what we're dealing with here. If Faris can't be within shouting distance of Loethar, we have a very grave problem. And besides that, Kilt looked to be suffering badly.' He paused, but Jewd just glared back in silence. 'You have to tell me!' Gavriel shouted, frustrated.

Leo frowned. 'What do you mean, Gav? What am I missing?'

'Ask your friend,' Gavriel said, dismissing them both and turning to find Elka.

He got five strides before he heard Jewd's voice. 'Stop.'

'Don't waste my time!' he growled as the big outlaw approached him.

Jewd raised his palms in defeat. 'All right,' he said, soothing the anger. 'What I'm going to say remains between us. I'm only telling you this because I'm cornered and I want to help Kilt. I don't really know what's going on but I know something about Kilt that may give us a clue. This must not be discussed with anyone. Do you both understand?'

Gavriel glanced at Leo and both looked back at Jewd, nodding.

Jewd sighed, scratched his head. 'I only found this out today, so I've been oblivious to it all my life and that's no doubt what Kilt wanted. If he's going to keep a secret from me, then,' he shrugged, 'he obviously can barely admit it to himself.'

'Spit it out, Jewd,' Gavriel urged, not unkindly.

Jewd shook his head. 'He's Vested,' he said, baldly.

It took a moment for Gavriel to understand what he had just heard.

'What?'

'You heard me,' Jewd growled.

Leo approached Jewd, suddenly angry. 'What does that mean? Vested? How is Kilt Vested? I've never seen anything that remotely smacks of magic around Kilt.'

'Me either,' Jewd admitted. 'He only told me today and only because I forced him. Leo, why do you think Stracker and Vulpan were escorting him into Barronel? As far as they were concerned he was a priest looking for his sister. They had no reason to suspect him of anything else.'

'Until that blood-sucking creature tasted him,' Leo finished, understanding ghosting across his face.

Jewd nodded. 'Vulpan instantly recognised him as Vested, a secret that I now realise Kilt has kept since he was old enough to realise he possesses magic. When he was as young as you were, when we first met you, de Vis, Kilt attended the Academy at Cremond. But then I came along to tell him of his mother's death and,' he sighed, 'well, our friendship was rekindled and we stuck together, took on this new lifestyle that suited us. I now realise he was running from something. And that something was his magic.'

Gavriel was stunned. 'And he's never used it in all these anni?'

Jewd shook his head. 'Not that I'm aware of. He swears he's never even been tempted.'

'Even so, why would Kilt's magic trigger such odd behaviour in Loethar? How would he know unless ...' Leo stared at Gavriel, shocked into silence mid-sentence.

Gavriel shook his head. 'We've watched him when he's been solitary, we've watched him with people, both friend and foe. And I've travelled with him these last hours. If Loethar possesses any powers, I'm sure he would have used them.'

Leo nodded, slightly more assured. 'Yes, yes, you're right.'

'Jewd.' The three turned as Tern approached.

'He wants to see you,' Tern said. 'He demands that Loethar be kept away.' Tern looked confused. 'I don't know what that means.'

Jewd nodded. 'I'll be right there.'

Gavriel waited until Tern had departed before speaking. 'That's his own words, Jewd. Kilt knows Loethar's injuring him somehow.'

'I'll go talk to him,' the big man said.

'He doesn't have to fear us,' Leo said. 'We'll go and face Loethar.'

Loethar was quiet, suddenly feeling spent. Elka had forced him to sit. Night was closing in. The sky had only a soft suggestion of the day clinging to it. He liked this time of day. Twilight. Throughout his life, this short period betwixt day and night had always felt as though it was filled with possibility. The Wikken had always spoken of this time as a powerful one.

What had just occurred had shocked him. At first he hadn't

understood it. Now he did. And he felt an elation that was unrivalled by anything he had ever experienced before. Winning the right to rule his people, making the decision to successfully invade the Set, not even the pleasure of finally conquering Brennus could come close to what he was feeling now.

He had been silent, not answering any of Elka's questions, because he hardly dared believe it himself. He needed time to think. She'd stopped pummelling him with her angry queries and they now waited in a tense silence.

'Here they come,' she said, interrupting his thoughts. 'They'll want answers.'

'I may not have any,' he replied.

'Don't lie, Loethar. You are dependent upon us for your life right now. If you want to live, you would be wise to not treat either of these people walking towards you as simpletons. I suspect either would kill you without a moment's remorse. You'd better give them a good reason to stay their hand. There's only so much I will do to protect you.'

'I'm flattered,' he said, grimacing at the fresh burst of pain through his body.

Leo and Gavriel arrived, keeping their distance, Leo glowering at him. Loethar watched Gavriel's glance shift to Elka and sensed her shake her head.

'What happened just now, Loethar?' Gavriel asked.

Loethar forced a humourless expression of mirth. 'Ask your outlaw leader.'

'He's not my leader. My ruler, however, stands beside me. He is the only person I answer to.'

'Ah, yes, and so I finally meet the young would-be king.'

'Not would-be,' Leo said. 'I *am* king.'

'Only in your mind, boy,' Loethar dismissed.

'I have taken my regal oath at the Stone of Lackmarin. You are merely a pretender.'

Loethar smiled.

'Loethar, do you want your half-brother to be emperor?' Gavriel asked.

Loethar smirked at the suggestion. 'He's a fool and a thug. He's strong and courageous but he has no subtlety. He can rule warriors but diplomacy evades him. He would ruin the empire. Perhaps that could be your secret weapon, Leonel?'

'Don't address me as though you know me. We have nothing in common,' Leo ordered.

'Is that so?' Loethar asked, making a soft sound of disdain. 'You poor young fool.'

'What's that supposed to mean?' Gavriel demanded. 'I want to know what occurred between you and Faris. Don't deny that something was happening.'

'All right. I won't.'

Silence descended around the quartet. Loethar and Gavriel locked stares. Loethar could barely believe he was at this point. Was this the right time? Yes, it was. There would never be a better time than now.

Gavriel glanced at Leo, then returned his gaze to the wounded emperor. 'Who is Kilt Faris to you?'

Loethar took a deep breath. His expression became grave. 'Unless I'm mistaken, he is my aegis,' he replied.

'Aegis?' Gavriel and Leo repeated as one.

'Impossible!' Leo said. 'I know what an aegis is. And I'm very glad to tell you, barbarian, that you certainly are not entitled to one.'

'Only you, eh, Leo? Faris could resist you, but I'll wager he's had to work hard at it all these years he's harboured you. His mind must be as strong as an ox and his willpower too. And you were too unempowered to recognise him in your midst, you poor weak Valisar fool.'

'What are you talking about?' Gavriel demanded. He turned to Leo. 'Tell me what this is about.'

Leo briefly explained what an aegis meant.

Gavriel returned his attention to Loethar. 'What kind of nonsense is this?'

Loethar shrugged, ignoring the pain it caused him. 'You saw Faris. Go ask him.'

'I'm asking you!' Gavriel growled.

'And I've already told you, de Vis.'

'Then you lie,' Leo spat. He laughed. 'Power has certainly gone to your head, barbarian. An aegis isn't just available. He is created for a Valisar. If Faris is indeed an aegis, which I doubt … and I doubt the very existence of the role but —'

'That's because you have no power and —'

Leo ignored him. 'But other misinformed dolts like you down the centuries have tried to trammel a Vested in the vain hope it would give you power.' Leo pointed at him, his expression filled with a sneer. 'And that's maybe why you ate my father — trying to consume power where there was none.'

In an effort beyond normal strength, Loethar somehow dragged himself to his feet, hauling himself up with the help of the tree he leaned against. He pointed at Leo. 'Go fetch your outlaw. You are the fool. He is mine and that's why he fears me.'

Leo was trembling with anger. 'Only a Valisar can trammel an aegis.'

Loethar howled a laugh that turned into a sneering grimace. 'That is also my understanding. Your father was the imposter and he knew it, Leo. He always knew of my existence. He hoped it would always remain a secret. Let me share it with you now. Your grandfather sired me. *I am Valisar*, you pathetic child. I was Valisar before your father! I *am* the true King of Penraven!'

EPILOGUE

Corbel had been feeling uneasy all day. In the moments before dawn, when he had seen a shooting star and experienced a strange sensation of calling, he had begun to believe that the moment was finally upon them. And this feeling had intensified in the hours since. Now it was late afternoon and he could swear his skin was all but tingling with anticipation.

It had been so long, he couldn't be certain that he wasn't simply imagining it but he could swear magic was bristling around him. He had to trust his instincts. His father had told him that all his life. His king had given him similar advice when he had kissed his daughter farewell and handed her to Corbel. And Sergius had offered similar words of wisdom when they had walked down to the beach all those years ago. His instincts to open himself up to the magic again were not just tugging at his consciousness; they were screaming at him.

'Reg!' called a voice, startling him.

He turned and smiled as the familiar warmth rippled through him upon seeing her approaching. The spectacles she wore were plain glass and a deliberate attempt to hide her youth, lend a greater air of authority. He grinned more widely. They always amused him, especially as she'd only shared her secret of them with him.

'You've forgotten to take your stethoscope off,' he said, touching its end, careful not to touch her.

She looked down and snorted. 'I forget it's there. It feels like part of me these days. How are you?'

'Different.'

She regarded him with bemusement. 'You know, Reg, you're meant to just say something along the lines of, "I'm fine", and let the enquirer move on.'

'Why?'

'It's polite and you know it. How are you ever going to find a girl being so contrary?'

'I don't want to find a girl.'

'Whyever not? You can't live like a monk, surely?'

'Who says I do?'

That took her off guard. He smiled to ease her discomfort.

'Ooh, you make me mad sometimes.' She tugged his beard briefly and he tried not to flinch. Just feeling her simple, friendly touch could derail his thoughts, his whole night. And this evening — of all evenings — he needed to be focused.

'That needs clipping,' she said, sneering at his beard and sounding softly disgusted. 'Do you want me to do it?'

He shook his head. 'I can manage.'

'I'm glad I found you so close to the hospital,' she said.

'Why's that?'

'I wanted to apologise for missing lunch today.'

'You don't have to. I never expect anything of you.'

'Don't be so obliging,' she said, pursing her lips in mock vexation. 'Did you wait for me?'

'I always wait for you, Evie.'

She looked at him with soft exasperation. 'What am I going to do with you, Reg?'

'Make me a promise.'

She laughed. 'Oh, well, that's easy.'

'How can you be sure?'

'Because you've never asked anything of me.'

'Perhaps I will sometime.'

She gave him a sideways look. 'You can ask anything of me.'

'Thank you. If I should suddenly ask you to do something that sounds strange — even dangerous — will you do it?'

She frowned, considering.

He didn't let her respond. 'Just do as I bid, no questions asked. I would never do anything that was wrong by you, or ask you to do anything that would hurt you.'

Evie's frown deepened. 'Reg, I haven't a clue what you're talking about.'

'Then it won't hurt you to make the promise, will it?'

She shook her head, and he could see that she did trust him. 'All right, yes,' she began in a tone that suggested tedium. 'I will listen to you and do as you ask without question. Is that what you want to hear?'

'Excellent. So, how has today been?'

She brightened. 'Strangely quiet. It's rather nice to have a day like this.' She gave a small shrug. 'Tomorrow it will probably be twice as busy, though, with lots of casualties, and I'll forget there are ever quiet days like today with no blood, or weeping.'

'Tomorrow may never come,' he murmured.

'Oh, Reg, don't be depressing. What's got into you today?' He shook his head slightly and she continued, lightening the moment.

'I'm leaving a bit early tonight if there are no emergencies.'

'Out somewhere?' he asked.

'A ghastly fancy dress. I don't know whose idea it was to dress up for the Prof's twentieth anniversary bash but now we have to. It's not my cup of tea but I have to go and I'm sure you'll be pleased to know I'm actually getting out and socialising.'

He frowned. 'Where is it?'

She waved a hand. 'That new pub that's opened up near the gardens.'

'The Botanic?'

'Yes, probably. They've got a private dining room.'

'What have you chosen to go as?'

'Oh, I'm sure I'll regret it but it sounded inspired earlier to look like a peasanty barmaid. I didn't know what else to choose at the hire place. That's why I couldn't make lunch — the others forced me to go with them and find something. Anyway, this outfit looked plain and not overly colourful in the shop. Everyone else was choosing madly glittery things or very bright character costumes. I thought I'd choose something simple, not too loud or colourful. Something in which I could still appear vaguely feminine and not have to wear a wild wig.'

'And you don't think a corset is going to draw attention to your —'

'Absolutely not! Well, not if I don't draw the strings too tight. Besides, I have a cloak! I have secretly always wanted to wear one,' she admitted, mimicking flinging a cloak around her shoulders.

He grinned. 'Pay attention to your phone.'

She blinked. 'Why do you say that?'

'I don't know,' he said, shrugging. 'I've had a strange feeling since I woke up.'

She shook her head. 'That sounds ominous.'

'Then perhaps I should have said the instantly forgettable and meaningless *take care*,' he offered.

She gave him a look of tolerant indulgence. 'That's exactly what you should have said.' She pointed over her shoulder. 'I'd better get back.'

'I know. Thanks for finding me.'

'So, I'll see you on Monday, then? … usual spot?'

'Not if I see you before,' Corbel replied.

'Reg, this is the moment you say, have a nice weekend.'

He stopped his trimming of the small hedge outside the Admissions area. 'I prefer to be honest.'

She gave him a sad smile. 'Yes … and the truth is that's how I like you. Just a bit strange and always honest. All right, my friend, you have a happy weekend and I'll bring lunch for Monday.' She squeezed his arm and turned away, unaware of what that simple affection did to him.

Corbel swallowed, watching the Admissions sliding doors close behind her.

He was sure this moment was the last time she would enter the building.

There had been an emergency — a car accident on the highway with two fatalities and a number of casualties. Evie had been called in for a man in his late fifties who was experiencing heart problems. She'd already had several calls from the party and now she found herself frustrated and changing in the staff room, much to the delight of two of the young interns.

'Risk looking and I'll give you hell next week,' she warned, holding her corset on as one of the nurses laced her up. 'This was such a stupid idea!' she groaned under her breath. 'And having to get ready here. It was so quiet all day! I thought I'd have time to go home and get ready. I really don't want to go now; I hate parties at the best of times and besides, I look like I've just come from work all hot and bothered.'

'No you don't!' the elder nurse tutted. 'Of all of the women on these wards, you're the one who needs no make up. When are you going to accept that you are a naturally beautiful, young, hotshot doctor?' She smiled into the mirror. 'There, how does that feel?'

'Tight,' Evie replied. 'Thanks, Sarah. And for the confidence boost. Have I got time for some warpaint?'

'Trust me, you don't need it. Take off those glasses, plump up those breasts so they actually sit higher.' Evie groaned. 'That's how they're meant to look in this medieval maid garb,' the nurse said, exasperated but laughing. 'You chose it.'

'I thought I could just fade behind all the other loud outfits.'

'Bare skin, especially your flawless décolletage, will hardly go unnoticed,' the nurse warned.

'Well, I have a cloak!' Evie protested. 'Help me pin the brooch on, will you.'

Sarah did so. 'There, you look rather good, actually. Forest green suits you.'

Evie mocked herself in the mirror. Her phone beeped and she groaned. 'Oh no, they're saying they won't start eating until I get there. I don't need this pressure.'

'Grab a taxi and just go.'

'I'm worried about Mr Henderson's —'

'Well, don't! We're under control and you know it. Go!' Sarah left, glaring at the interns as Evie dug into her bag for the mobile phone. She didn't recognise the number the text had come from. She hit the button to read it.

Meet me on the roof of the hospital immediately. It's important and v. urgent. Reg x

She frowned. 'Reg?' she murmured with disbelief. 'I don't have time for this now.' She grabbed her bag, checking her purse was in it, and threw in the phone. She left the staff room and headed down the corridor, breaking into a jog, knowing she was holding the celebrations up, calculating whether it was more expedient to jog cross-country over the botanic gardens or queue for a taxi outside the hospital.

As she ran by one of the nurses she knew well, the woman whistled. 'Blimey, you look different,' she said. 'Have you spoken to the groundsman, that Reg bloke?'

Evie stopped, walked back. 'No, what's happened?'

The nurse shrugged. 'I don't know but he was inside the hospital just a few moments ago, asking everyone coming into the cardio unit to tell you to please take notice of the message he left for you. He said it's very important. I didn't even think you knew him. Strange man. He's so tall and imposing and scruffy. I half expect him to open his coat and pull out a pair of guns.'

Evie looked down, frowning. 'Don't be idiotic, he's a friend …
of sorts.'

'Really?' The nurse pulled a face of disbelief. 'Well, he looked
a bit freaked out. I've seen him often enough before. He's
normally very shy, very quiet, but he wasn't either this evening.
But I've always thought he was a bit crazy, you know.' She twisted
a finger near her temple.

Evie shook her head. Something must be wrong.

'I hope he isn't going to do something crazy,' the nurse added.

'Like what?' Evie said, offended.

'Well, he looks like a halfwit sometimes, doesn't he, beneath
all that beard? Maybe he *is* crazy. Maybe he's going to kill himself
or something.'

'Oh, Fran, don't be ridiculous! He's as sane as you or I. Listen,
I'd better go.'

'Enjoy the party,' Fran said, continuing on her way.

Evie bit her lip. She couldn't leave now. She had to find Reg.

She ran for the fire exit and headed upstairs.

Corbel's heart was pounding. He was sure this was the moment.
But would she come? Would she trust him? Would she do it?

He threw the mobile phone down and crushed it with his foot.
He had used it only once, to send her a text. He would never
need it again. It shattered against the concrete, which was his
intention. He dug through the ruin and found the sim card,
which he threw into one of the air conditioner funnels.

Reg heard a door bang and he turned around to see her. She
looked perfect, her outfit so suitable. Even unconsciously, she was
following her destiny.

'Reg? What the hell is going on?'

'Where's your phone, Evie?'

'My phone?' she repeated, looking perplexed. 'In my bag.'

'Can I see it?' He held out a hand.

She dug inside the bag. 'Reg, I've got a party to go to and

everyone's telling me you're acting like a loony, which they seem to think is pretty normal, but I don't. What are you doing up here and why are you texting me?'

He flicked his fingers, beckoning for the phone.

She handed it over, not seeming to notice how rude his gesture was. 'Now what is this about? I'm running la—'

Corbel flung the phone off the roof.

She stared at him dumbfounded for a blink. 'Reg!' she shrieked. 'Are you mad?'

'Apparently.'

He knew Evie was not prone to histrionics. As he watched, she calmed herself down. 'All right. You have my attention,' she said. 'Will you tell me what this is about?'

He nodded. 'Here, will you share this with me?' He held out a can of her favourite soft drink, knowing she would feel obliged to drink it.

She took it and sipped but he could see it was only to be polite. He opened another can for himself and sipped too, hoping to encourage her.

'Cheers,' he began. 'Do you know today's my birthday?' he lied.

Evie looked momentarily pained. 'No, I didn't. Oh, Reg, I — no, wait. That doesn't make sense. We've always celebrated your birthday in September.'

He smiled sadly. 'That's because you chose September when I said I didn't know when my birthday was. But that was a fib. I'm sorry about that. It's actually today.'

'So here's cheers, Evie. Wish me luck.' He clinked cans, watched her drink again, a long draught this time. Fortunately, her nervousness was making her thirsty.

'Evie, do you remember earlier today when I mentioned there might come a time when I ask something strange of you?'

'That was only a few hours ago, Reg. I could hardly forget.'

He nodded. 'I know you're angry —'

'I'm not angry. I'm perplexed, confused, perhaps even disturbed. I'm only angry about the loss of my phone. And that's fine because you can pay for —'

'Do you trust me?'

She took a breath, not showing offence at being cut off once again. 'Should I doubt you?'

'That's not what I asked.'

'It depends what you ask of me, then,' she said, glowering at him. 'I want to understand what this strange behaviour is about.'

'*This* is our past and our future.'

She regarded him gravely. 'That explains nothing. You're talking in riddles. I said I want to understand.'

'You will, if you trust me. Look up, Evie. See how the sky is darkening?'

She looked up and back again at him in silence.

'In a few minutes it will be night and too late.'

She frowned again. 'Too late for what?'

'For us.'

'For us? For us to what?'

'To return.'

'You've lost me, Reg,' she said in a stern, far more irritated voice than he'd ever heard from her previously. 'I have to go.'

'I've never lost you, Evie. I've always been here, protecting and watching over you. I would never lose you.'

She ground her jaw and he could see her thinking over everything he had said, presumably wondering whether she should call the fire department or mental services. 'Why are we up here, Reg?' she asked.

'Because it's tall enough to give the magic time to work after we jump.'

She stepped back, horror ghosting across her face. 'Jump?'

'You mustn't be frightened.'

'Why not? You're frightening me!'

'Have I ever given you cause for fright before?'

She shook her head.

'Have I ever struck you as insane?'

'You're the most sane person I know.'

'I haven't changed. Evie, we have but minutes. You need to make a decision. Take my hand and follow me. I am going to take you back to where you come from … to where we both come from. Remember our conversation about how we always feel as though we don't belong, but that somehow we belong to each other?' She nodded, blinking. 'That's because neither of us belong here. This was a haven … a place to hide. Nothing more. Your father — and I don't mean the man who adopted you, but your real blood father — sent me to be your champion, to take care of you always. Now it's time. We must return. We are needed.'

'I don't know what you're talking about.' She staggered slightly and he leapt to her, offering a steadying hand. 'Reg, I feel dizzy.'

'I can see that. Don't worry, I'm here. I've always been here.'

'I think I'm going to be sick. Did you do this? Did you drug me?' she asked, making all the right connections, injuring him with the accusation in her look.

'I had to be sure.'

'Are you going to kill me?' she said, leaning harder against him now as the drug worked.

He tried not to show how much that comment hurt him. 'No, precious one. I would never harm a hair on your head.' He lifted her into his arms. 'Hold on tight.'

She grabbed his neck. 'I'm tired and frightened. Everything feels strange. It feels like electricity in the air, as though a storm is brewing. It's crawling over my skin.' Her voice sounded wan and confused.

Reg climbed onto the ledge of the building. He had to trust it now; trust that the magic Evie could feel swirling around them, reaching for them, coaxing them, was real. 'Hold tight, Evie. I'm taking you home.'

'Home? Where's home?'

'Penraven, my princess,' he murmured into her hair. And then, holding her tightly, he stepped off the roof.

GLOSSARY

CHARACTERS
THE VALISAR REALM

Royalty

King Cormoron: The first Valisar king.

King Brennus the 8th: 8th king of the Valisars.

King Darros the 7th: 7th Valisar king. Father of Brennus.

Queen Iselda: Wife of Brennus. She is the daughter of a Romean prince from Romea in Galinsea. Comes from the line of King Falza.

Prince Leonel (Leo): First-born son of Brennus and Iselda.

Prince Piven: Adopted son of Brennus and Iselda.

The De Vis Family

Legate Regor De Vis: Right-hand of the king. Father to Gavriel and Corbel.

Eril De Vis: Deceased wife of Legate De Vis.

Gavriel (Gav) De Vis: First-born twin brother of Corbel. He is the champion of the Cohort.

Corbel (Corb) De Vis: Twin brother of Gavriel.

Other

Cook Faisal: Male cook of the castle.

Father Briar: The priest of Brighthelm.

Freath: Queen Iselda's aide and right-hand man.

Genrie: Household servant.

Greven: Lily's father. Is a leper.

Hana: Queen Iselda's maid.

Jynes: The castle librarian (steward).

Lilyan (Lily): Daughter of Greven.

Morkom: Prince Leo's manservant.

Physic Maser: The queen's physic.

Sarah Flarty: A girlfriend of Gavriel.

Sesaro: Famous sculptor in Penraven.

Tashi: Sesaro's daughter.

Tatie: Kitchen hand.

Tilly: Palace servant.

The Penraven Army

Brek: A soldier.

Commander Jobe: Penraven's army commander.

Captain Drate: Penraven's army captain.

Del Faren: An archer and traitor.

From outside Penraven, but still in the Set

Alys Kenric: A resident of Vorgaven.

Claudeo: A famous Set painter.

Corin: Daughter of Clovis.

Danre: Second son of the Vorgaven Royals.

Delly Bartel: Resident of Vorgaven.

Elka: From Davarigon — a giantess.

Jed Roxburgh: Wealthy land owner of Vorgaven.

Leah: Wife of Clovis.

Princess Arrania: A Dregon princess.

Tomas Dole: A boy from Berch.

The Vested

Clovis: A master diviner from Vorgaven.

Eyla: A female Healer.

Hedray: Talks to animals.

Jervyn of Medhaven: Vested.

Kes: A contortionist.

Kirin Felt: Can pry.

Perl: Reads the Runes.

Reuth Maegren: Has visions.

Tolt: Dreams future events.

Torren: Makes things grow.

The Supernatural/Other

Abbess: The head nun of the convent at Lo's Teeth.

Algin: Giant of Set myth.

Aludane: A Steppes god.

Cyrena: Goddess. The serpent denoted on the Penraven family crest.

Deren — a baker from Green Herbery.

Quirin (Quirin Vervine): Deaf, blind and mute seer. Also referred to as the 'Mother' of the convent in Lo's Teeth.

Ravan: Also known as Vyk, the Raven.

Roddy — a young boy, saved by and drawn to Piven.

Sergius: A minion of Cyrena.

Tod — one of Roddy's friends in Green Herbery.

Wikken Shorgan: The younger of only two wikken left alive in the Set. He can 'smell' magic.

The Highwaymen

Jewd: Friend to Kilt Faris.

Kilt Faris: Highwayman, renegade.

Tern: One of Kilt's men.

Coder

Dorv

Outside the Sets

Emperor Luc: Emperor of Galinsea.

King Falza: Past king of Galinsea.

Zar Azal: Ruler of Percheron.

Loethar and his followers

Barc: A young soldier.

Belush: A Drevin soldier.

Bleuth: A soldier.

Brimen: A soldier at Woodingdene.

Dara Negev: Loethar's mother.

Darly: A soldier.

Farn: A Mear soldier.

Fren: A page who spies for Valya.

(Captain) Ison: A soldier.

Jib: A soldier.

Loethar: Tribal warlord.

Roland: A servant in Dara Negev's retinue.

Ronder: A soldier at Woodingdene; close to Stracker.

Shev: A soldier at Woodingdene.

Steppes (Plains) People: From the Likurian Steppes. Known as Barbarians.

(Lady) Valya of Droste: Loethar's wofe.

Vulpan: A Vested working for Loethar whose talent is 'cataloguing' and tracking people by knowing the taste of their blood.

Stracker: Loethar's right-hand man and half brother.

Vash: A soldier.

Vyk: Loethar's raven.

MAGIC

Aegis: Possesses the ability to champion with magic. Is bound to a person by the power of trammelling.

Binder or Binding: The person who binds himself to an Aegis.

Blood Diviner: A reader of blood.

Diviner: Gives impressions and foretells the future.

Dribbling: A small push of prying magic.

Prying: Entering another's mind.

Reading the Runes: Ability to foretell the future using stones.

The Valisar Enchantment: Powerful magic of coercion peculiar to
   the Valisar line.
Trammelling: Awakening an Aegis' power.
Trickling: Low level magic.

HEALING PRODUCTS
Willow sap, Comfrey balm (for pain)
Clirren leaves (powerful infection fighter)
Crushed peonies (for pain)
Henbane (for pain)
White lichen (used for dressing wounds)
Dock leaves (soothes itching skin)
Bermine: A painkiller

THE DENOVA SET: the seven realms are sovereign states, self
   governed with a king as head.
Barronel
Cremond
Dregon
Gormand
Medhaven
Penraven
Vorgaven
The Hand: The continent that the Denova Set sits on.

Cities/towns within the Set
Berch: Close to Brighthelm. Home of the Dole family.
Brighthelm: The city stronghold (castle) and capital of
   Penraven.
Buckden Abbey: Religious place South of Brighthelm.
Camlet
Caralinga
Davarigon
Deloran Forest: The Great Forest.

Devden

Dragonsback Mountains: They separate Penraven from Barronel.

Droste: A realm not part of the Set.

Francham

Garun Cliffs: Where chalk is mined.

Green Herbery

Hell's Gate

Hurtle

Lo's Teeth: Mountain range in Droste.

Merrivale: Where shipbuilding is renowned.

Minton Woodlet

Overdene

Port Killen

Rhum Caves: Caves found in the hills outside of Brighthelm.

Skardlag: Where the famous Weaven timber comes from.

Tooley

Vegero Hills: In the realm of Barronel. Famed for the marble
  quarried in its hills.

Woodingdene

Places outside the Set

Briavel.

Galinsea: A neighbouring country.

Lindaran: The great southern land mass.

Likurian Steppes (or Steppes): Treeless plains. Home to Loethar
  and his tribes.

Morgravia.

Percheron: A faraway country.

Romea: Capital of Galinsea.

Tallinor.

MONEY

Throughout the Sets: Trents

Span: 1000 strides or 2000 double steps.

Half-span: 500 strides or 1000 double steps.

WORD GLOSSARY

Academy of Learning: At Cremond. It is the seat of learning for all of the Denova Set.

Anni: A year.

Aspenberry: Used to distil Kern liquor.

Asprey reeds: Used for support inside leather bladder balls.

Blossomtide/Blossom: Spring

Blow: Winter.

Branstone: A very special silver coloured stone with sparkling silver flecks.

Chest: Coffin.

Cloudberries: Forest berries.

Cohort: A group of youngsters trained to be elite sword fighters.

Crabnuts: Grow wild in the forests. They are a sweet nut, purplish in colour.

Dara: Word for 'king's mother' in Steppe language.

Darrasha Bushes: Planted around the castle of Brighthelm.

dinch: A hot beverage.

Elleputian: A Davarigon mountain horse.

Faeroe: A handcrafted sword that belonged to King Cormoron.

Fan-tailed farla hen: A bright coloured bird with a fan-tail.

ferago: A mountain herb.

flaxwood: A type of wood used for cooking.

Freeze: Late winter.

golasses vines.

Harvest: Late autumn.

Ingress: Secret passages within the Brighthelm castle.

Kellet: A spicy fragrant herb that can be chewed.

Kern: The local and notorious fiery liquor of Penraven's North.

Lackmarin: Place where the Stone of truth lies.

Leaf-fall: Early autumn.

Leaf of the Cherrel: Chewed as a breath freshener.

leem: A mountain herb

Lo: Set god.

Lo's Fury: An alcoholic beverage

Oil of Miramel: Exotic essence.

osh: Slabs of roasted meat cooked a particular way.

peregum: A mountain herb.

Roeberries: Wild berries growing in forests. They are blood red.

Rough: A very strong alcoholic beverage.

saramac fungus.

shakken: A wild Steppes animal.

Shaman: Spiritual healer.

Sheeca Shell: Found on the local beaches.

Shubo: In Steppes language it means second.

starren: A six-legged chameleon-like reptile.

Stone of Truth: This truth stone is at Lackmarin. All Valisar
   Kings must take the oath at this stone.

Strenic: A poisonous herb growing wild on the Steppes.

Summertide: Summer.

Tatua: Tattoos on the face, shoulders and arms.

Thaw: Spring.

The Masked: Magic users of the barbarian horde.

The Vested: Magics users of the Set.

Thaumaturges: Miracle weavers.

Thaumaturgy: The study of the craft of miracle weaving.

toka: A mountain herb.

Weaven Timber: From Skardlag. It is scarce.

Wikken: A tribal seer.

Wych Elder Tree: Used for woodworking.